Advanc

We

"Vivid a
woman
—Liv

"*We Shall See the Sky Sparkling* is a vivid, thoroughly absorbing account of one woman's struggle to break from the rigid roles her social class and time period impose on her. Drawing from her family's history and a series of fascinating letters, Susana Aikin crafts a marvelous tale of adventure, rebellion, and romance, taking readers on a captivating journey from the theaters of Edwardian London to tumultuous St. Petersburg and beyond. She weaves the character of actress Lily Throop Cable with a deft hand. Lily shines as a heroine of uncommon strength, determination, and passion. Her struggle to protect and foster her independence, even as she navigates through great loves and treacherous times, is one to be relished and remembered. It's a pleasure and privilege to read this sparkling debut."
—Suzanne Nelson, author of *Serendipity's Footsteps*

"Susana Aikin's directorial eye is much in evidence in this sweeping saga. Her attention to period detail transports the reader on a filmic journey that is both astonishing and tragic. *We Shall See the Sky Sparkling* is a powerful meditation on the sacrifices women have made in pursuit of their dreams—sadly, as relevant in the early 21st century as a hundred years ago."
—Helen Steadman, author of *Widdershins* and *Sunwise*

"Against the dramatic backdrops of a Russia on the brink of revolution and the colorful lives backstage of the London theatre circuit, Susana Aikin has created a feisty Edwardian protagonist whose trajectory still resonates with the predicament of women working in the arts today."
—Sara Alexander, author of
Four Hundred and Forty Steps to the Sea

SUSANA AIKIN

KENSINGTON BOOKS
www.kensingtonbooks.com

KENSINGTON BOOKS are published by

Kensington Publishing Corp.
119 West 40th Street
New York, NY 10018

ISBN-13: 978-1-4967-1766-5 (ebook)
ISBN-10: 1-4967-1766-X (ebook)
Kensington Electronic Edition: February 2019

ISBN-13: 978-1-4967-1765-8
ISBN-10: 1-4967-1765-1
First Kensington Trade Paperback Printing: February 2019

10 9 8 7 6 5 4 3 2 1

Printed in the United States of America

For Margaret

We Shall
See the Sky
Sparkling

PROLOGUE

My mother kept an old sepia photo in an oval frame of faded coral velvet on top of her writing desk in her upstairs sitting room. In it stood a beautiful, slender woman richly dressed in a long, elegant coat with a fur stole that reached below her knees, and an elaborate hat adorned with ostrich plumes, or some other exotic bird's feathers. On the back was a name and address printed in Cyrillic letters that likely belonged to a photographic studio in St. Petersburg, with the date 1902 written below.

Her name was Lily Alexandra Throop, a great-grandaunt on my father's side, an actress who fled her family in Manchester as a young girl to work in London's West End theaters, at a time when actresses were considered no better than sluts. For this, her memory had been handed down the generations clouded in a mixture of glitter and dark legend. She was beautiful and talented, but she had left home against her father's will and was disinherited. She had shamed the family. The mention of her name in family gatherings always created tension; there were those who were riveted by her story, and those who deplored it. My cousin Margaret and I formed the core of the faction who idolized Lily, with other females in the family, including my mother, who flaunted Lily's picture as a prized heirloom depicting a magnificent ancestress dame. Whenever the Throop women came together, it was only a matter of time before speculation about Lily's adventurous life would begin to bubble up.

But my father and his brothers were not thrilled with Lily's story. Having a "bad girl" in the family disquieted them. "She was no lady," they said. My father's younger brother, Uncle Tim, had been the main weaver of Lily's ominous myth. He was a passionate genealogist who'd worked for years to reconstruct our family history, and in that process had come across certain photographs, official documents, and reluctant testimonies from older family members, all of which provided key pieces to the puzzle of Lily's life.

We knew she had been born in 1880 in Stockport, Manchester, and lost her mother very young. Her father had remarried one of his cousins, a cruel woman called Betty, who mistreated Lily and her brother, Harry, but mostly Lily. At age seventeen, Lily left the family house amid disrepute and scandal. A cutting from the *The Era*'s theater-review paper listed her as playing Gretchen in a play called *Soldiers of the Queen*, produced at London's Imperial Theatre in October 1897. A note Lily sent to Harry in June 1900 requesting a birth certificate needed for a passport application was found among my grandmother's papers. Two of my great-aunts, Minnie and Bella, had talked about Lily leaving the country to travel in foreign lands, and how at some point, rumors had reached the family that she had borne an illegitimate child. A few years later she allegedly returned to England, alone, penniless and sick, and died shortly after, in disgrace.

Her death certificate, according to Uncle Tim, declared her to be a "spinster" and a "theatrical dancer," and said she died of "pulmonary phthisis" at age twenty-four. "Unfortunately, that's the sort of thing that happened to women who forgot their good breeding," he concluded as we sat around the table, while Margaret and I glared at him in fury, suspecting that part of the story had been contrived to create a perfect cautionary tale.

Lily's tragic tale and disappeared child remained sources of endless conjecture among the family's female faction, particularly the fate of her baby. Had she really had a child? And if so, what had happened to it? Would she or he still be alive? But for us, Lily's charisma outshone all else; to have an ancestress who had defied all conventions to pursue an artistic career bestowed a very particular badge on the women of our clan.

There was another photograph of Lily in our house: another sepia picture of her as a young girl, probably around the age when she left for London. She's clad in Victorian fashion, the collar of her dress closely fitted up the length of her neck and fastened with a dainty brooch of miniature pearls. Her face is a smooth oval with delicate cheekbones and a straight, elegant nose; her lips are thin and determined; her eyes stare ahead, radiant and brimming with life.

"You have those same eyes," my father would say, half in jest. "Watch that you don't follow in her steps." He wasn't the only one in the family who believed that I resembled Lily, not just in the face and eyes, but also in obstinacy and unruliness.

They say there are some children who grow in the shadow of a dead family member and unwittingly follow their fate. I think I was one of those children. There was always a secret thrill mixed with a certain dread in my affinity with Lily. I too was an artist, awkward and misunderstood, and felt the need to leave home and find a place where I could develop my creative drive. In my case, that place was New York, where I settled in 1997 to become a filmmaker and a writer. As I struggled on the path of my artistic career, I often thought about Lily and her journey all the way to Russia at the turn of the twentieth century. After all, plowing through the hardship of growing into an artist in a competitive world dominated by convention, and by men, is an eternally tough predicament for a woman, at any time in history, in any place.

But Lily's journey always felt immensely more far-fetched, braver and riskier than mine. And whenever I fell upon hard times, met insurmountable obstacles, or got close to the end of my rope, I thought of her, wondering if she had encountered similar troubles and how she might have worked her way through. Lily was always in the back of my mind as the ghostly role model of the artist I strove to become. Maybe that's why I became obsessed for years with the discovery of her real tale.

Sadly, I had to lose my father to come into possession of further clues to Lily's life. When I returned to Manchester after his death to gather his personal effects, I was surprised and overjoyed to find a few of the letters Lily wrote to Harry and his wife, Alice. They had been kept in a box in the attic of the old house in Chorlton-cum-Hardy that had belonged to my grandmother, where my father had lived the last years of his life. This was fresh material that no one of my generation, or my parents', seemed to have examined before.

There were thirteen letters in all, tied in a little stack with a string. I took them home and laid them out by tentative order of date and place across my writing desk.

Manchester, November 5th, 1897

My dearest Harry and Alice,

It's close to eight in the morning and the carriage will be here any moment. I don't have the heart to disturb you this early, so I'm writing this farewell note while I wait to have a last word with Father.

Oh, loves, if you knew how thrilled and how anxious I feel right now! My hand trembles as I write these lines. I can't wait to be sitting in the train, I can't wait to arrive in London and see the most wonderful city in the whole world. If only I could have both of you come with me, if only the three of us could be together in this adventure, I should be the happiest girl alive. But I will trust that soon you will join me, and the life we've dreamed of will come true.

So, get well, my dearest, dearest brother, and you, my sweet sister-in-law, bless you for all your love and kindness.

Much love and a thousand kisses,
Lily

CHAPTER I

Lily stood leaning against the mantelpiece folding the note into a little envelope. The room was cold. The fire had not been lit. Neither had the cinders from last night been removed or the hearth swept. Outside loomed a dreary, wet November morning with rain-darkened trees silhouetted against skies threaded in scales of gray. The grandfather clock's gloomy ticking filled the room. At the other side of the double-paneled door, she heard the muffled whimpering of her little sister, Annie, amid the swishing of dresses moving quickly along the hall and landing, followed by her father's heavy footsteps coming down the stairs. "Everyone leave the hall at once," Lily heard him say, in a loud, composed voice. "I want to talk to her alone." All stood still for a moment.

Lily held her breath as the door opened. Her father walked in and sat in his armchair by the window. He was fully dressed in his Sunday brown suit and immaculately groomed despite the early hour. Even the chain of his pocket watch was perfectly looped through its customary buttonhole. He sat upright and looked across the room, ignoring her. Then he fumbled in his waist pocket and brought out his monocle. His right eye first widened, as if surprised, and then squinted as he placed the round glass in between his cheek and upper eyelid. He picked up his cane again and leaned on it with both hands.

"Father, I will be leaving any minute now. . . ." Lily started.

"You will go nowhere. You will stay at the house and do what I tell you. If you dare disobey me . . ." her father said, straining to sound severe but ending on a deflated note. He cleared his throat and huffed. "You'll be the disgrace of us all."

Lily felt a sob cramping her throat while tears shot up into her eyes. Her father gave her a sidelong glance, while shifting his weight uncomfortably in the chair. "There's still time to call this ridiculous idea off. Should you do that, I will forgive everything." He paused for a moment. "So will Mr. Duff, I'm sure."

At the mention of Mr. Duff, Lily's cheeks flushed with anger. "I thought we already talked about Mr. Duff, Father, that I shall never marry him." The image of the clergyman's beady little eyes flashed through her mind. She shuddered, recalling the proximity of his scrawny, buttoned-up body as he had whispered, "My dear, you need to think of putting your talents in God's service at the church."

Her refusal to marry him had thrown the household into calamity only a few weeks ago. Her father had stopped talking to her, while her stepmother, Betty, had sneered to no end. "Only dishonest girls lead a man up the garden path like that. Besides, I don't know how many other offers someone like you will get." And she had hounded Lily with images of drab spinsterhood.

But all of this was now far away in the past in Lily's mind.

"Father, please, let's not quarrel anymore. You know how much I love you. And I do appreciate your thinking of my future. It's just that I am so drawn to acting, and so feel I must follow my heart."

Her father shot her a furious glance. "I will never give you permission to leave the house."

Lily rushed toward him, kneeled by his chair, took his hand, and put it to her lips. "Father, please, give me your blessing. I promise one day you'll be proud of me."

Her father pulled his hand away from hers and stiffened in the chair. She knew how hard this must be for him. He was a bland man and found it difficult to discipline his favorite daughter. But he was also bland in the presence of Betty, a strong, unwavering personality who had always sought to dominate him, and made every effort to crush Lily's spark.

As if summoned by Lily's thoughts, Betty entered the room. "I see you're already getting the best of your father with your theatrical ways," she said, closing the door. "What you're about to do is not just indecent but also ungrateful, after everything he's done for you." She was stout, with a large head and compact body. Her hands had been quick to smack Lily's head and ears in the past, but now it was her tongue she used to wound. "But you're not concerned, are you? You'll always do as you please. Well, let me just say this: I can't help but see you a fallen woman in a few years, fit only for the workhouse. Every girl I know who went in for the theater ended up in the gutter."

Lily scrambled to her feet, trembling. "You never knew anyone who went in for the theater!" She stood facing Betty with rage pounding in her ears, struggling to control herself, for she knew restraint was the only viable strategy in the presence of her old enemy.

"Oh, yes!" Betty continued. "Stupid girls who could sing and dance! They thought they would do anything they fancied, but never knew how fast they could get shot down."

Her father stood up. "That's enough! We won't say another word about this. You are only seventeen and under my tutelage. You will not leave this house! Send the carriage away and go to your room."

Lily kneeled again before her father and searched his eyes. "I only ask for your blessing, Father." The clip-clopping of horse hooves and the clatter of wheels filled the street before they came to a halt outside the house. "If you won't stand behind me," Lily added, her voice shaking, "I can only hope one day you will forgive me."

"Forgive you! I will not lay eyes on you again as long as I live. I will disinherit you properly and forget you were ever my daughter!"

Lily stood up. "All right, Father, I will just say good-bye then." She turned toward the door where Betty was barring the threshold. "Let me through," she said, but Betty was unmoved. "You shall have to step over me," she said.

A string of coughing sounds was heard approaching the hall. Then came a weak, insistent knock on the door. "Father, open up."

Betty stepped aside as her husband fumbled with the knob. "Harry! Son! Why have you left your bed?"

Harry leaned against the threshold, a gaunt figure, wrapped in a heavy gown. Behind him stood Alice, with her pretty, freckled face pulled into a frown as she struggled to place a blanket around his sloped shoulders. "Darling, please," she said. "Let's go back. It's cold out here."

Harry went into another long fit of coughing. Lily watched in agony at the red stain spreading on the handkerchief he pressed to his lips as he hawked. He looked up with thunderous eyes as soon as he could steady himself. "Father, let her go," he said, out of breath.

"Harry!" Father exclaimed in a fury. "This is not for you to interfere! Go back to bed. I will call Dr. Morton presently."

"Father, I say you give her your blessing."

"I will do no such thing!"

"She will go anyway," Harry said, locking eyes with his sister.

If Lily had one regret about leaving her father's house in this state of strife, it was Harry. In different circumstances, it would have been her brother now going to London to work in the theater. Of the two of them, Lily had always seen Harry as the real dreamer, the true actor, the director and playwright. But he had also been the eternally sick child, prostrate for months, imprisoned in bed, surrounded by medicinal droppers, bedpans, hot-water bottles, and jars of pungent ointments; though none of that had ever made him lose his spirit, for he never stopped creating theater houses inside his sickroom, building tents and stages with bedsheets, making puppets out of old socks, and writing plays and stories over his pillows. Lily had always felt the silly, inept little sister by his side, following him into imaginary worlds as a way to distance herself from the somber household, from Betty's violence, from the long, dark winter nights pelting rain over windowpanes.

Harry coughed again.

"See?" Betty said. "Upsetting your brother."

"Betty, this is not your business," Harry said, catching his breath. "It's my father's and my own." Lily rushed to embrace him, but was careful not to crush him in her arms for fear of making him cough again. "Go now, Lily," Harry said, "and write to us as soon as you get there."

"Harry, how dare you!" Betty hissed. "How dare you oppose

your own father like this!" Harry held her gaze in silence, while Lily pressed her lips one last time to her brother's cheek and dashed out into the hall. She reached the coatrack by the entrance door and glanced back while unhooking her cape and hat. She froze at the scene behind her: Harry had started coughing again, while Alice embraced him at the waist with her thin arms and burst into sobs. Everyone stood around him in a knot of sadness and concern. For a second Lily's hands felt like they would wilt and drop her cape. But Harry looked up at her again and said, "Do not think of stepping back, Lily. Just leave. Everything will be all right."

Then she heard the Cook Nelly's heavy footsteps walking up the kitchen stairs and into the hall. She held a napkin bundle in her hands. "Miss Lily, this is for your elevenses on the train," she said in her sweet manner, oblivious to the commotion in the hallway. She was an ample matron, swathed in layers of white pinafores and aprons with a pinkish, round face and kind eyes. "And, dear, do take care not to catch cold; it's miserable today."

"Cook, don't you dare give Miss Lily anything!" Betty said, coming up quickly behind them. "She'll leave the house without food or personal belongings."

Before she reached them, Lily pecked Nelly's cheek, snatched the small bundle from her hands, and fled through the door. The cold morning mist hit her face while she tingled with euphoria.

"Lily Alexandra Throop!" She turned around at the sound of her father's voice and saw his small brown figure standing in the doorway. "I shall keep my promise and disown you this very day. I shall never call you my daughter again." She watched as he removed the monocle from his eye, returned it to its pocket, and then waved his hand at Nelly, demanding she close the door. He then turned into the dark, narrow tunnel of the hall and was gone.

London, February 14th, 1898

My dearest Harry and Alice,

I just received the travel trunk you so kindly sent me from Manchester. Oh loves, you don't know how important this is, to have my clothes again with me and my books, for I have no money to buy anything, and London is very expensive. All these weeks I've been wearing Ruby's extra coat and shoes, since mine were in such a sorry state. Do you remember Ruby? She is the red-haired Irish girl with the pretty eyes who played Mary Magdalene by my side in the Passion play last year. She's here in London with me and we share a room at Mrs. Bakerloo's boardinghouse. She's such a lovely friend!

I am so happy, dear brother and sister! London is so big and beautiful with tall white buildings and elegant people coming to the play. The Imperial is just across from Westminster Abbey and the river. It's the biggest theater I've seen: It holds up to three thousand people. It's gorgeous inside, in the shape of a large horseshoe surrounded by columns and two rows of galleries. Everything is painted in red and gold, and the whole place glitters when the lights are turned on.

The play opened three weeks ago and it's been a success. I am sending the cutout of The Era's *review—can you see my name in the list of actors? I play the part of Gretchen, and Ruby is Annette. But the article doesn't mention either of us, it just says, "The minor parts are all creditably sustained." I think it means we do well.*

I feel blessed to be here, but I miss you so much, my darlings!

Your Lily

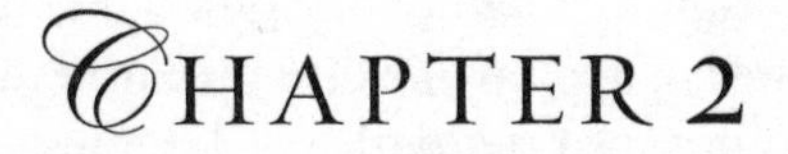

CHAPTER 2

Lily stood with her cape and bonnet, looking out the window toward the grim line of houses along Charing Cross Road. The rain fell hard over the cobbled streets. It beat against the windowpanes, sliding in rivulets along the soot-stained glass in slim, meandering paths. With the cuff of her sleeve Lily wiped clean a circle on the condensed surface and stared across the street at a woman who huddled behind her umbrella struggling against rain-threaded gusts of wind. Men walked around hunched up inside their coats with hands dug deep in their pockets, or ran holding newspapers above their heads. It was as wet and miserable as a large city can get under winter rain.

But not for Lily. No amount of rain, sleet, or snow could deter her hunger for exploring her new world. No day of the week, save Mondays, which was her day off, could ever be miserable enough for Lily not to want to be the first to arrive at the theater. That was all she thought about, getting there and rushing through its back door as soon as the janitor opened up, traversing the labyrinth of mysterious back corridors, probing dressing rooms, wardrobes, and storage rooms replete with furniture and the strangest variety of objects, or props, as Mr. Featherspoon, the property master, had taught her to call them. Ruby complained about the extra tasks that were part of their chores as players in training, but Lily relished them. What did it matter to her to have to sweep and scrub the stage before performances if that could afford her the chance of standing on that magical platform? Even empty, the stage vibrated with all the drama, laughter, and emotion that had been spilled over decades of performances. Sometimes, when no one else was around, she stood on the apron and looked out into the dark pit, imagining the day when it would be fully illuminated and swarming with patrons, roaring with applause for her.

Behind her, Ruby stood at the door spying through the keyhole. "She's still there, the old goat," she whispered. Stepping out of their room without having to face Mrs. Bakerloo was one of their most unpleasant daily tasks. No matter how softly, how carefully they closed the door, how much breath-holding and gingerly tiptoeing down the stairs, the grim matron was always waiting at the bottom, ready to scowl and threaten them with eviction. Mr. Bennett, their theatrical manager, never paid the rent on time, and now he owed more than two months. Slipping in and out of the room became harder every day the debt increased. The dining room had already been barred to them. For weeks they had been going without breakfast. But today, they were already late for the theater and just had to brave it past the old woman.

They opened the door and rushed down the stairs. "Morning, Mrs. Bakerloo," Lily and Ruby recited in unison as they hurried toward the door.

"It's already afternoon," Mrs. Bakerloo barked. "But you theater people wouldn't even know the difference."

Out on the street, Lily looped her arm through Ruby's as she opened her brolly and they walked down the street side by side. By the time they reached Stoney's Gate, the rain had petered into a drizzle. They closed the soaked umbrella and rushed toward the theater with quick little steps.

The Imperial was housed inside a large corner building with darkened façades framed by rows of long, narrow Gothic-style windows. On the sides of the main doors hung large posters announcing the play, colorful vignettes of khaki-uniformed soldiers charging at one another over green hills, carrying British flags and large sabers.

They entered through the stage door, where Mr. Featherspoon

sat perched on a stool waiting for them. He was a tall, lanky fellow with a protuberant pouch in his midriff that so contrasted with his thin torso and spindly legs, it looked like he might have eaten an animal that still lay undigested in his stomach. His face was long, etched with wrinkles and punctuated by sharp, tiny eyes that stared out of deep sockets. His nose, knobby and slightly crooked, sat above a thick imperial-style moustache that matched his gray sideburns and hair he wore parted in the middle and slicked back behind his ears. He was always dressed in the same shabby green velvet jacket and waistcoat, and a dark top hat that might have been black once. But he was a kindly fellow, Lily thought, despite his unpredictable, eccentric rants.

He jumped off the stool with surprising agility. "You are very late indeed, missies. I was expecting you ten minutes ago." Lily blushed while Ruby clicked her tongue. Surely, they couldn't tell him about the difficulties of getting past Mrs. Bakerloo. "I'm a very busy man," Mr. Featherspoon continued in a high-pitched nasal voice, "and cannot afford to be waiting on two fickle young ladies who cannot keep to their timetables." He paused to scan their unease with bemused eyes. "Anyway, let's get on with it." He took a large ring of keys out of his pocket and advanced down the corridor ahead of them. Lily and Ruby quickly removed their coats and hats and followed him.

From the day they arrived in London, Lily and Ruby had been under Mr. Featherspoon's orders, helping to move light stage props and putting them back behind locked doors before closing the theater every night. They had also been bound to Mrs. Potterlane, the wardrobe mistress, a moody woman who made them brush and iron the actors' costumes under fastidious supervision. When they joined the company, Mr. Bennett had announced he was happy to have them on board, but because they were only apprentices, he could not pay them beyond covering their food and rent. Soon, though, they might become understudies of May Withersfield, Dorothy Brown, and Mrs. Bennett, the company's professional actresses.

The weeks before the opening of the play had been very busy. Lily had never seen a cast of twenty people in action, or witnessed a battle onstage. The play, *Soldiers of the Queen*, consisted of a military plot written by Mr. Bennett himself that took place during the Boer War. It had been hard for Lily to obtain a full manuscript to read, and she struggled to understand what the whole story was about. It seemed the actors only carried the pages where they had lines, and those who didn't have lines didn't carry any pages at all. Lily only had one line in the performance, and a short one at that: "Dear soldier, let me bring you water." Her character, Gretchen, a barmaid in a gambling saloon in the middle of South Africa's forsaken lands, took pity on the protagonist, Dick Forrest, a young mounted rifleman undergoing misery in the aftermath of battle. Only one line, but each time she uttered it, her eyes filled with tears as her heart filled with emotion. A line was a line, after all. Ruby didn't have any. And this one line was spoken to the hero of the tale.

During the long, complex rehearsals, she sometimes climbed the narrow stairs up to the catwalk over the stage and stood on the wooden bridge by Harvey and Chut, the men in charge of changing backdrops by moving ropes and pulleys from above. From that high post, she admired the convoluted mechanics of coordinating action, while she thought of Harry and how he would have wondered at all this. Every time she thought of Harry something shrank inside her. It wasn't just missing him; it was the feeling of treading on the tracks that should have been her brother's destiny. It felt as if she were borrowing his life, like wearing a strange, large coat that she might never be able to fill.

Lily and Ruby followed Mr. Featherspoon down dimly illuminated corridors and arrived at the main wardrobe room. He ferreted out a short, fat latchkey from the clinking collection on the chained ring and unlocked the door. A gust of moldy dust blew out of the cave-like space as he went inside and turned on the light. Rows of costumes hung on heavy metal rods on both sides of the long, narrow room. Above them were sets of shelves escalating up to the ceiling, stuffed with crates and boxes of all sorts and sizes, some anonymous in their contents, some labeled in large, longhand writing: "helmets and swords, Roman; blood-soaked clothing and ghosts, Macbeth; wigs, beards and moustaches, French; Arlecchino masks, breeches, commedia dell'arte; crowns, tiaras, jewels and wreaths, parasols, animal furs," and so on.

The room smelled of grease and old sweat with an undertow of urine. At the far end, the space opened up into a wider alcove lit by a gas lamp, where two large mirrors stood against the walls. Here the actors were fitted, and Mrs. Potterlane and her seamstresses worked sewing and adjusting costumes. Under the room's only window sat a coal stove with a flat top, where the irons were kept hot for pressing. This was where Lily and Ruby spent hours brushing and ironing the *habillements,* or cloth accoutrements, as they were called. But today the stove had not yet been lit and the room was stone cold.

"Please step in, little ladies," Mr. Featherspoon said. "Mrs. Potterlane has instructed me to get you going with the soldiers' uniforms for today's performance." Perceiving Lily's disappointment, he added, "I know I said I'd take you into the prop room, but all in good time."

He left, while Ruby and Lily stood looking at each other. Ironing soldiers' uniforms, fifteen of them, was a most boring, thankless task. But ahead lay the promise of helping Mr. Featherspoon inside his shop of curiosities, with its rows of shelves stuffed with swords and daggers, torches, skulls and bones, banners, caskets, old string instruments Lily had never envisioned before, and chests filled with silk flowers and red petals. On her last visit there, Lily remembered seeing a full body armor and a pair of feathered wings beside a severed head of wax.

"I'll run down and bring up a tray of coals," Ruby said. "You line up the suits and the irons in the meantime." She was always quick to run to the furnace room where Mrs. Waithe, the charwoman, kept a small pot simmering with coffee and was delighted to share juicy gossip with visitors.

Lily started pulling soldiers' coats from the rack and piling them on the table, knowing that Ruby would take a while. After unhooking the last set, she noticed a floor-length red gown hanging on the opposite rack. She lifted it out of the tight line of dresses and admired it in the light. The gown was a fine cloth of smooth velvet and brocade, embroidered with artificial pearls and hand-sewn cultured beads, its edges trimmed with shimmering orange ribbons. A piece of paper was pinned to the shoulder: "Rosalind," it read.

Rosalind's palace outfit from *As You Like It*! The role Lily had always dreamed of playing. Though there was no other name on the label, Lily knew it must belong to one of the leading actresses, who were asked to provide their own costumes and brought them to the theater ahead of time to have them tailored. Did this mean that the company was planning to stage a Shakespeare play next? Lily's head reeled. Nothing would be more thrilling, even if she were only given the minutest of roles.

A woman's shrill laughter cascaded down the corridor toward the door, accompanied by a man's coarse whispering. Heavy footsteps entered and the door was hastily closed before Lily heard two bodies grinding against each other under the rustling of skirts. She hid inside the line of costumes and listened to the strange heaving and grunting sounds with a pounding heart.

"Not here, not now," the woman murmured amid the groaning.

"Why not? 'Wherever passion doth possess thee is as good a place as any. . . .'" the man quoted, his voice heavy with panting.

"Should we be found!" the woman said, but laughed again.

Lily froze. She recognized the voice. Mrs. Bennett! How unfortunate to have intruded upon a private scene between her employers. She listened to the increasing thumping sounds, startled and confused, until the woman gave out a set of little squawking cries and the man's heavy groaning peaked, and then stopped abruptly. Their breathing wound down among sounds of two bodies drawing apart and the susurration of a dress being reorganized.

Lily stood petrified with dread.

Seconds later, Mrs. Potterlane's voice was heard coming down the corridor. "Hurry up, it must be freezing in the dressing room!" Lily heard the man and the women rush toward the table area and sit down hurriedly. Ruby walked into the room with quaint little steps, followed by the older woman's heavy stride. "And where is that other girl?" Mrs. Potterlane asked as she brushed past the very garments that hid Lily. "Oh, hello, Mrs. Bennett. Afternoon, Mr. Wade. I'll be with you in a moment."

Mr. Wade! Mrs. Bennett! Lily now dared look at the scene across from her through the heavy costumes. She saw Ruby opening the stove's iron gate and shoving in the coal, while Mrs. Potterlane huffed around the pile of jackets stacked on the table. Close to the mirrors, Mr. Wade and Mrs. Bennett were smiling at each other in conspiratorial gleam.

Herbert Wade was the actor who played Dick, the mounted rifleman to whom Lily offered water in the play. Though he was probably in his late thirties or early forties, he had a boyish appearance from afar, maybe because of his trim body and clean-shaven face. But from close range, as when Lily faced him onstage, he presented a shriveled, impish countenance and penetrating, pointed eyes that made her feel uneasy. She felt afraid as she remembered his face.

The smell of charcoal embers filled the room. "Where's your silly friend?" Mrs. Potterlane asked Ruby again, irritated. "Didn't you say you left her here?"

Across from her, Lily saw Mrs. Bennett stare in her direction and fix her gaze with some alarm at her feet. Looking down, she realized the tip of her right boot protruded from the row of costumes. Reflexively, she pulled it in. Her heart was pounding so hard she thought she would be discovered on that account alone, but everyone in the room went on with their chatting, oblivious of everything. Only Mrs. Bennett started getting restless. She fussed in her chair, rearranged her hair, and smoothed out her dress, then got up suddenly. "I'll be going now."

"Can't we first fit you for the dress?" Mrs. Potterlane asked, confused.

"I just remembered an engagement. Another time," Mrs. Bennett answered coldly, and left the room, followed by Mr. Wade.

Taking advantage of the small commotion that followed their departure and of Mrs. Potterlane turning toward the irons, Lily stepped out of her hiding place. At Ruby's astonished glance, she lifted a trembling finger to her lips. Mrs. Potterlane spun around. "And where have you been?" she said with a frown.

Lily froze, but Ruby stepped in. "Please don't scold her, Mrs. Potterlane. She's been at the washroom; she's on her monthlies." Lily felt the blood rush to her face, but Mrs. Potterlane was not moved. "You ladies and your poorliness! When I was young, we were only allowed to the outhouse twice a day, monthlies or not. Now, get to work, we're behind." She held up the iron for Lily to take, but then changed her mind. "No, first you will run after Mrs. Bennett and give her her scarf. I don't want it lost in this room." Lily stood stock-still. "Go on! No more silly excuses."

Lily took the red silk scarf and hurried out of the room through the dark corridors. She knew Mrs. Bennett would most likely be at the main office with her husband by now. Her eyes smarted at the thought of facing the older actress's smug, haughty stare. She took in large drafts of air to steady the pounding behind her ribs, then approached the forbidding office door at the end of the corridor and knocked shyly.

No one responded. There seemed to be a heated discussion inside the office. She heard Mr. Wade say, "I shan't come near another military play as long as I live, Mr. Bennett. Not one of yours, in any case. By George, you'd do better to stick to directing, rather than playwriting!"

"But Mr. Wade, our agreement?" Mr. Bennett said.

"Confound our agreement!" Mr. Wade thundered. There was a moment of silence.

"Mr. Bennett," another man, whose voice Lily didn't recognize, said. "I think my nephew has made it clear that we are only willing to advance funds for the said Shakespeare plays. We'll be happy to support the production of *As You Like It* for the coming season, and *Hamlet* thereafter. Classical repertories are safe investments. Your play got reviews, but was a poor box-office affair."

Mr. Wade added, "Likewise, let's not delay injecting new sap into our insipid, stultifying troupe." Lily heard steps coming toward the door and Mr. Wade swung it open. "Ha!" he said, at seeing Lily, and then made a theatrical gesture of welcome with his arms. " 'And like a sprite called upon, she here doth now appear,' " he quoted in a grandiose manner. Then, he held the door open for her to walk in, and turning around said, "Here's our first opportunity. Why aren't we flaunting more of this little looker onstage, instead of having her hidden away, or even *hiding*, in grumpy Potterlane's room?" He held Lily by the shoulders and made her face the room. "See? A nice mare we know trots pleasingly on the scaffold, and if we can just teach her fast enough to modulate her whinnies," he said, and then interrupted his line of thought as he studied her face. "I say, let's make her understudy for Celia."

There was silence in the room.

"Mr. Wade, she's barely been with us for three months," Mr. Bennett said after a moment.

Lily stood in the middle of the room, embarrassed and bewildered. Everyone's eyes were on her. Besides Mr. and Mrs. Bennett, she recognized Mr. Harrison sitting in an old armchair, leaning on his cane. Mr. Harrison was Mr. Wade's uncle and the company's financial investor, a bony, elderly man with gold-rimmed spectacles who had been pointed out to Lily by Mr. Featherspoon the week before. On the other side of the desk sat Mrs. Bennett, who was visible to Lily only in silhouette against the gray light pouring in through the windows.

"I was asked to bring Mrs. Bennett's scarf," Lily said, holding up the red silk, hoping she might be instantly dismissed.

"You see?" Wade continued. "This is what I mean. Why do we have people scurrying around with scarves and other similar useless objects? Why aren't we training our new members of the cast professionally? Making them productive? Why aren't we challenging them instead of supporting them for years with mendicant wages, until they defect to other companies where they do finally become actors?"

"But Mr. Wade," Mr. Bennett interjected, "we don't have the means. We're not a school."

"Fiddlesticks! Main actors should be mentoring younger ones." Wade turned to Mrs. Bennett. "You should be mentoring this girl. What do you say, Mrs. Bennett?" he asked with a grin, and when she remained silent, he said, "All right, I shall undertake her, and I can promise that in three more months she will be playing at least supporting roles." He picked up his coat from a chair. "Lily, is it? Tomorrow, at my house: I shall expect you at noon. And now you will all excuse me, I have wasted enough of my afternoon." He swept past Lily and was out the door without another glance.

Lily stood, not knowing what to do.

Mr. Bennett looked up and said, "Come sit down, dear," and

pulled out a chair. Lily walked toward the ornate mahogany desk and sat down.

Mr. Bennett was very much liked among the troupe. He was older than his wife, in his fifties, while she was only in her thirties. He was a medium height stocky man, always dressed in a dark three-piece suit; in his office, though, he wore a heavy brocaded robe. It was a custom he had acquired as a young man, he related with pride, when he sat up all night writing plays in cold, dingy rooms. Despite his age, he had a sensuous, handsome face. His head was covered by a thick mass of gray curls, which everyone knew was not his real hair, but a wig he called his perruque, referring to it as "the best friend my cranium has had since it became like a billiard ball."

"Dear Miss Throop," Mr. Bennett said, sitting up straight. "As you just heard, the company will be performing *As You Like It* for the spring season, and Mr. Wade is proposing you as Mrs. Brown's understudy for the part of Celia. Mrs. Brown's health is delicate, which means you most probably will have to stand in for her a number of times. It will be a lot of hard work for you to be ready on time."

"Mr. Bennett, I will do anything to take this opportunity," Lily said.

Mr. Bennett looked at his wife, who looked back with a mask-like face and said nothing.

Mr. Harrison gave a little bow of the head in Lily's direction. "I am happy to hear it, Miss Throop. We shall start paying you eight shillings per week. I'm sure you won't disappoint."

"Now run along, dear," Mr. Bennett said. "Mr. Featherspoon will have a script for you."

Lily stood up and tried to direct her body toward the door. The mixture of fear and shock and excitement made her feel ungrounded, weightless, as if she could only float along. When her hand touched the cold metal doorknob, she came to her senses, turned around, and mumbled, "Thank you, Mr. Bennett."

Mr. Bennett nodded and turned to Mr. Harrison, while Mrs. Bennett sprang to her feet. "My scarf, girl!" Lily handed her the scarf, then Mrs. Bennett followed her into the corridor and closed the door. In the dimness of the hall she pounced, grabbing Lily's hair and digging her nails deep into her arm. "Don't let this go to your head," she hissed into Lily's ear. "Girls rise and fall every day here, and sometimes are found facedown in the river." She released Lily, shoving her against the wall. "I've seen the likes of you before, pushy little hussies sniveling at managers' feet, trying to climb fast up the ladder. You don't fool me." And she started down the corridor with a huff.

Lily stood trembling. Her arm hurt terribly. She was sure Mrs. Bennett's claws had torn the skin under her sleeve because it felt moist, as if bleeding. Tears of dread and rage streamed down her face. Her moment of triumph had been spattered with bile. She had just made a deadly enemy.

Lily heard Mr. Bennett on the other side of the door preparing to leave. She hurried away knowing she couldn't go back into the costume room in this state. She walked quickly to the stairs that led to the catwalk and mounted the thin wooden platform. It was dark and empty. She groped her way toward one of the large mounds of rope, threw herself over it, and wept.

CHAPTER 3

Mr. Wade's house was a three-story terraced, white-fronted stucco building on St. James Street, walking distance from the theater. Lily passed the wrought-iron fence, ascended the few steps to the main door, and rang the bell. After a few moments, a butler came to the door. His unsavory face fell in folds alongside his droopy eyes and long nose. His pigeon chest stuck out under his starched shirt and close-fitting livery coat. First, he looked dismissively at Lily, as if she had mistaken the front entrance for the servant's hall, but then he seemed to decide she wasn't so easy to classify and eyed her with mistrust.

"I have an appointment with Mr. Wade," Lily said.

"Mr. Wade is not at home, and I'm not aware that he's expecting any visitors today," the butler said, rolling his words affectedly. He started to close the door.

Lily stepped forward. "He asked me to come at noon."

"I repeat, he is not in. If you would like to leave word—"

"I would rather wait until he returns," Lily said, determined not to be sent away. "I work with him at the Imperial."

"I am not expecting Mr. Wade until much later," the butler insisted.

Lily stood her ground. "It's important that we start work today. We're on a deadline. I can't disappoint him by not being here at whatever time he returns." She took the script of *As You Like It* out of her bag and flashed it at the butler with a disarming smile. "I've been studying all night in order to meet with Mr. Wade."

The butler was not moved. "You may call again later when he arrives."

"Fine. I'll sit on the doorstep and wait. I just hope Mr. Wade won't be too disappointed at your turning me away."

"Very well, if you must," the butler wavered. "But the warning remains in effect: He may not come home at all."

Lily was escorted into an elegant hall with paneled walls and a sweeping staircase that led to the upper floors, and through a corridor until they reached a tall, imposing double door. "You may wait for Mr. Wade in the library," the butler said gruffly, and shut the door after her.

The library walls were covered in dark mahogany shelves filled with rows of books. Two tall windows overlooked a lush garden and filtered shafts of bright midday light into the room. A fire blazed in the marble fireplace between the windows, facing an array of leather sofas and winged armchairs. A polished wooden table stood to one side, covered with stacks of books, rolled-up manuscripts, and assorted objects such as magnifying glasses, inkwells, and other writing implements. The curtains and the few sections of wall space that were not covered by books were painted a deep crimson hue of red, matching the Oriental carpets that covered the floor.

Lily twirled, taking in the stunning beauty around her. The room was engulfed in a muffled stillness that she remembered of spaces packed with books—not that she had ever been surrounded by such an immensity of volumes. Harry's adored collection hardly filled five shelves back home, and the library at the local parish might have owned no more than a few hundred, most of them different versions of the Bible and other liturgical books. But this room was a real library, with shelves on top of shelves reaching up to the ceiling, bursting with volumes of all sizes and all types of bindings: leather, cloth, vellum. She approached the nearest row of books and followed it with her finger, reading some of the titles out loud to herself. Aristotle's *Poetics,* Milton's *Paradise Lost,* Giordano Bruno's *On the Shadows of Ideas*; and so it went on and on: theater, architecture, art; old medical treatises, history, philosophy; books in Latin and Greek, German, French, other languages she didn't even recognize.

She pulled out a fat book bound in thick green leather with miniature paintings embedded on the cover: *Arabian Nights*. The book was old and heavy. She traced the gold lettering carefully before opening the cover. The soft oniony pages slid under her touch and rustled as she thumbed through them. She stopped to look at the black-and-white illustrations, some of which were engravings of scenes in rooms with luscious drapes, where women in loose pantaloons danced for recumbent men, their heads wrapped in turbans. Toward the middle of the tome she came upon another engraving that depicted a huge open mouth with broken teeth, from which protruded a long tongue that engulfed the figure of a small man held up in a clenched fist. The caption read, "That night, the giant ate another one of our companions." The book slipped from her hands and hit the floor with a thud.

That moment, the door opened.

"What do you mean she's in here? Who's in here?" Mr. Wade asked, entering the room.

The butler scuttered in behind him. "Sir, she insisted you had summoned her for work," he explained, but Wade cut him off.

"Simmons, I thought I had made myself clear about females in the house. Under no bedeviled circumstance, pretext, or alibi," he ranted. Then he spotted Lily picking up the book from the floor and trying to stuff it back on the shelf. "Oh, you! Great hanging gadzooks! Did I really say today?" He threw himself into a leather chair. "Why does a decent fellow keep promising pearl to that swine, Mr. Bennett? Simmons, pour me some port."

Mr. Wade was disheveled, his hair greasy and tousled over his forehead; his clothes rumpled and his face unshaved, haggard, with red-rimmed eyes, as if he hadn't slept in a week. Even from Lily's distance he stank of alcohol and acrid sweat. He glared at her while he stuck out his arm for Simmons to pour him a glass of liquor. He swilled it in one gulp and reached out to Simmons for a second round. He drank that too, and licked his lips. "That's better." He waved Simmons out of the room and looked again at Lily. "The devil take me if I hadn't totally forgotten about your existence."

"Sir, I can leave," Lily said, vexed, as she scooped up her bag and script.

"Oh, we have a temper, do we?" He stared at her for a moment, amused. "I called you a little mare yesterday, didn't I? But I see you're more of a minx. Not everyone gets through the door past Hound Face; he's quite the perfect canine custodian. But a sly little fox might."

"I'm sorry to have inconvenienced you, sir," Lily said, holding back tears with contained fury. "I shall not disturb you any further." She walked quickly toward the door.

" 'Herein I see thou lov'st me not with the full weight that I love thee.' " Lily stopped short. Mr. Wade's voice had changed radically. It was now mellifluous, pleading, sweet. It was the opening line of Celia's first significant speech in the play. Lily turned and looked at him. His face, like his voice, had changed. It was relaxed, open, doting. He made a gracious gesture with one hand, inviting her to take up the lines. She relaxed and put down her bag. " 'Herein I see thou lov'st me not,' " she continued, and recited the whole speech.

They worked all afternoon. They didn't eat or drink; they took no breaks. Mr. Wade was infused with untiring energy. He paced around the room like a frenzied animal, making Lily go over Celia's lines time after time until she hated the words, until they didn't mean anything anymore, until she thought they would be etched in her mind forever. Mr. Wade knew the play by heart, every character, every line and stage direction. His voice and demeanor could instantly change to make him sound like an impassioned woman, like a tottering old man, a melancholy youth in love, or just a silly girl.

They stopped just before five, barely in time to run over to the Imperial where the curtain would go up at six on the dot. Lily could hardly stand. Mr. Wade called Simmons. "Show Miss Minx out. She's nabbed my afternoon without any reimbursement." He collapsed into an armchair, looking once more bedraggled and spent. Before Lily stepped through the door, he said, "Tomorrow you will bring all of Rosalind's lines." He pulled a mocking grin over his face at Lily's gasp, and added, "Oh, and your diction is abominable. Find a handful of pebbles. Hopefully, they can help abrade that lisp."

Lily stumbled into the street and welcomed the sweet evening air, the orange shimmer of gas lamps glowing under the mist, the quietude against which Celia's voice could begin to fade slowly away from her brain.

That evening, when, as Gretchen, she approached Mr. Wade onstage and offered him water, she looked into his eyes and saw Dick Forrest, the wounded rifleman that lay hurt and thirsty in a pool of agony and homesickness. The whole play, the entire set, every movement, gesture, action, every word that had been, and would still be, spoken on the stage, was written in those eyes.

London, April 26th, 1898

Dearest Harry and Alice,

I am sorry I haven't written all these months. Things have been so busy for me over here. But I'm so glad you are feeling much better, Harry, and that Doctor Morton's new medicine is bringing you back to health. Such good news!

You can't imagine, dear brother and sister, how my life has turned around since I last wrote. I've been signed up with the company for the next seven years. And, two weeks after we opened As You Like It, *Mrs. Brown, the actress I was standing in for, was engaged elsewhere, so now I have Celia's role all to myself. I was written up in* The Era *last week: "Miss Throop is one of the new promises of the London stage." It all feels like a dream.*

I even have my own dressing room now, and all sorts of gentlemen flock backstage bringing me flowers and invitations after the performances. Mr. Featherspoon was furious yesterday because there were so many of them obstructing the corridor. He calls them "my slobbering, worshipping sluggards" and warns me about them all the time.

He is not the only one who lectures me about this, though. Mrs. Potterlane, who has considerably softened her manner toward me since I am part of the main cast, also spends a lot of time admonishing me against the pitfalls of naïve actresses who yield to the wooing of strangers. What neither of them know is that I don't have a life away from learning my script and attending rehearsals.

There is another person who's even more upset than Mr. Featherspoon about my gentlemen admirers, and that's Mrs. Bennett. She has so many more than me, but she can't bear that I'm catching up. She hates me still, but I'll admit she's a very good actress. When we're onstage, I feel I really am her cousin and her very best friend.

But the best actor in the company by far is Mr. Wade. I told you he was giving me acting instruction, and every day my admiration for him grows. He knows all of Shakespeare's plays by heart, and many more. He makes me memorize new poems and speeches all the time. He makes me recite in front of mirrors, or with my eyes shut and my ears stuffed. He says memory is an actor's most prized treasure, a muscle that needs to be pumped all the time. Oh Harry, if you saw us when we rehearse! He makes me scream the lines, sing them, weep them, whisper them—until, he says, I make them really mine. I owe him all of my present success. He can have very a bad temper, though. Sometimes it's best to tiptoe out of the room.

Please write a long, long letter and tell me about yourselves, that I may miss you a little less while reading it over and over again.

Sending hundreds of kisses,
Your Lily

CHAPTER 4

It was impossible to fit all that was going on into the letters she wrote to Harry and Alice weekly. As time went on, she found herself writing shorter and shorter notes. Rehearsals at Mr. Wade's house and multiple performances took up most of her time. She was spellbound by everything that had to do with the theater. Stepping on the stage was an exhilarating daily venture where she learned something new about performing, about the play and about Celia, or something about herself in Celia.

But the most important thing was going to Mr. Wade's house for acting lessons. Every day she arrived at noon on the dot, beaming at Simmons whose sour face remained an unmovable feature, although he never again prevented her from walking into the house and hurrying to the library. For most of the first two weeks, Mr. Wade had also been at the library on time and devoted three or four hours to teaching. He was a hard, unforgiving instructor. He made Lily learn long speeches, or even entire acts each day, and was unsympathetic when she turned up exhausted because she had only slept a few hours. He thundered when she stumbled over lines or if she had to check her script. He wanted her to know everything about Celia, about Rosalind, about Orlando and Count Frederick, about every difficult word and expression in the play, and flew into a fury if she didn't give him the right answers.

"How come you don't own a dictionary? What decent actor doesn't? Or are you just one of those *acting ladies*, those indifferent, mediocre artistes who prowl theatrical venues looking for a good catch?" On one occasion, he walked to the table, grabbed a heavy book, and tossed it at Lily. She failed to catch it and it fell on her feet, hurting her. It was a Latin to English dictionary. "Your looks won't make you an actor. They will only help you into men's bedchambers. But that might be the right destination for you, after all."

After such an outburst, Mr. Wade would sit in one of the chairs looking shot down and dejected, as if Lily had betrayed some sacred trust by not proving herself up to his high standards. "Do you even know why you want to act? Have you given any thought to why you want to lend your body and soul to the scaffold? Why be a part of these sacramental spoofs we humans reenact over and over again to make sense of our miserable lives? Think about it. Why not just use your talent toward the more useful pretense of being devoted to a rich, old fool of a husband?" Lily often left in tears, and spent the rest of the day working fervently on the text.

Other days, Mr. Wade wouldn't show up at all. Lily sat in the library, waiting for him for hours, studying or reading books from the shelves, and had to leave before he appeared. Sometimes he would come in drunk, in a foul temper, and she would struggle to find a way to slip out of the room without getting in his way. Yet other times, he would be in strange, playful moods that she soon came to fear and detest.

"'Love me, Rosalind,'" he would say, walking up to her. Lily took it for a cue into the scene between Ganymede and Orlando, but when she replied, "'Yes, faith, will I, Fridays and Saturdays and all,'" Mr. Wade would repeat, "'Love me, Rosalind,'" multiple times, coming ever closer to Lily, even grabbing her arm or her shoulders and shaking her. Only when fear and alarm showed in her eyes, would he let go. Afterward, he'd roar with laughter. "You lost yourself there, didn't you? You stepped out of Rosalind. Would she ever doubt her Orlando? Never step out of your character."

As Lily left Mr. Wade's house and walked to the theater, she reasoned with herself that it would be best if she found a graceful way to conclude his instruction. In less than twelve weeks, she had learned more than she could have ever imagined about acting, and her performance of Celia was beyond satisfactory for everyone. Besides, Mrs. Bennett's dislike of her had reached top levels since Mr. Wade paraded her around at every possible occasion, calling her his "creation," his "Pygmalion's Galatea." Mrs. Bennett and Mr. Wade were having constant arguments in front of everyone at the theater, and he frequently scorned Mr. Bennett for not believing he was capable of producing a trained actress in three months.

Then there was the contract she had signed with Mr. Harrison. She was summoned to his office one afternoon, and Mr. Harrison introduced her to Mr. Eccles, the company's solicitor. He was a tall, heavyset individual with a hooked nose and a hanging, tawny treble chin that he strove to hide by wearing the widest of cravats available in the market. She had heard Mr. Wade laughing about him, calling him the "soliciting turkey," and denouncing him as a pompous rascal only good at requests of retainer monies from his uncle.

"Young lady," Mr. Eccles announced, "you should consider yourself lucky to be signing up with Mr. Harrison and Mr. Wade, and for such a length of seven years too. Sign here, please."

"Well, the seven-year period has to do with compensation for her training," Mr. Harrison said, apologetically. Lily signed and Mr. Eccles claimed the papers quickly and put them in his briefcase.

Wade, who was standing by the window, beamed at her across the room.

They had already started rehearsals for *Hamlet*, and Lily was to play Ophelia alongside Mr. Wade's Hamlet. Mrs. Bennett was irate because she had been cast as Queen Gertrude. Lily had heard her scream inside Mr. Bennett's office, howling with rage first, and then grief. She even smashed a thing or two. Though the queen's was a very dignified role, it was the first older-lady impersonation of Mrs. Bennett's career, and she couldn't take it. But there was nothing to be done, because it was Mr. Harrison's imposition. He was their only investor and was taking an active interest in shaping the company's productions, decisions that neither Mr. nor Mrs. Bennett could oppose. But everyone knew that behind Mr. Harrison's choices was his nephew Mr. Wade.

Lily's contract had created tension with both Bennetts. The level of stress mounted daily and left Lily feeling like a puppet dangling in the middle of a brawl. She realized that it would ease things up if she stopped being associated with Mr. Wade as his pupil and protégée, and be seen as just another good actress in the company. Also, being in Mr. Wade's presence required an increasing effort on her behalf. The more familiar he became with her, the more he swept her up into his cruel, extravagant behavior. She feared him, but she was also intoxicated by everything that he offered her. How could she leave behind the daily routine of visiting his library? How would she do without all the books he allowed her to take home so she could read them at leisure in her room at Mrs. Bakerloo's? How would she live without those jewels of knowledge, those secrets of the trade he presented her with when he was at his best, in his most concentrated mood?

"How do we take on a difficult, highly emotional scene?" Mr. Wade asked, pacing in front of the fireplace as if talking to himself. He pulled off his tie and loosened his shirt collar. This afternoon he seemed to be in a different mood, pensive and eloquent at once. "First, read your play. The Bard knew how to provide for the actor, not just images, but also sounds. Everything is in the words. Everything. The words themselves will take you into the mood. Listen to this: 'O, that this too too solid flesh would melt, thaw, and resolve itself into a dew,'" he rolled out the words slowly. "Melt, thaw, resolve, dew. Are there more pathetic, melancholy sounds in the voice of a man who desires to die?" Earlier, Lily had wavered with her lines and confessed to struggling with parts of the script. It was a leap to go from fair and happy Celia to the role of Ophelia. She was finding it hard to embody the scene of madness.

Suddenly, Mr. Wade stopped in the middle of the room. He wrapped his arms around his chest and hung his head, then started rocking himself while singing softly, "'They bore him barefaced on the bier; Hey non nonny, nonny, hey nonny; and in his grave rain'd many a tear.'" He was singing Ophelia's song of madness. He turned to Lily. "Sad, sad, *sad* words, and you still ask, what if they are not enough? What if I cannot relate to Ophelia going mad? If you do not—or cannot—go down the path the poet so beautifully lays out for you, then you have to make your own descent into hell. Spiral down and find the ground of your pain. Go to the place where you were once crushed, destroyed. Work from there. It never fails."

Lily watched Mr. Wade as he leaned against the desk, his arms still crossed over his chest, while looking out the window at the curtain of rain that fell over the garden thicket. He was an ugly man, with a receding hairline and strong eyebrow ridges over small, pointed eyes. There was a wide scar on his right upper lip that mocking theater legends attributed to a harelip, but Lily, who had had ample opportunity to look at it from close quarters, concluded it was just an old scar from a deep cut. What had happened to him? Was this related to his ground of pain?

As for her own place of defeat, Lily knew it well. On any grim day when she was feeling low, it was easy to close her eyes and see once more that last, pitiless look on her father's face before he turned and walked into the house, closing the door on her forever. He had looked away so many times before, tilting up his chin, clutching his cane with affected precision, while Betty dragged Lily out of the room and all the way downstairs to lock her in the cellar. There she would wait out her punishment, long hours of huddling in the dark; cold, hungry, and scared. And after she had exhausted herself sobbing, she would resort to singing quietly or humming, letting the song vibrate inside her throat and nose, numbing her brain. "'Hey non nonny, nonny, hey nonny.'" Then she might imagine herself walking into the drawing room where the family would be sitting, and going around offering forgiveness with gifts and kind words. "'There's fennel for you, and columbines. There's rue for you, and here's some for me. . . . There's a daisy. I would give you some violets, but they withered all when my father died.'" Many times she had asked Harry and Alice in her letters if their father ever inquired about her, or if he wanted to know if she was well and how she was faring in London, but all the letters they sent back avoided mentioning her inquiry. They hardly ever gave news of family matters at all. "'And will he not come again? And will he not come again? No, no, he is dead. Go to thy deathbed; he will never come again.'"

She opened her eyes.

"Well, that took on rather quickly," Wade said. He was looking at her with that penetrating sheen in his eyes that sparked fear in her blood. "You're a natural, as they say. I've never seen anyone learn so quickly, and yet," he said, grinning fiercely, "it still always strikes me how men toil and struggle to achieve their lot, while women just need open their legs to receive the bounty of warriors." His face was close to hers. She smelled alcohol on his breath and remembered that on her way in she had seen a bottle of green liquor on the table, a spirit called absinthe that put Mr. Wade in strange, unpredictable moods.

She attempted to compose herself. "I will study these lines some more for tomorrow," she said. "I'll need to be going now."

"You already know the lines," Mr. Wade said, not taking his eyes from her. "And you don't need to go anywhere. It's only three o'clock." He circled her, his hands clutched behind his back. "'O, what a noble mind is here o'erthrown! The courtier's, scholar's, soldier's, eye, tongue, sword, Th' expectancy and rose of the fair state, the glass of fashion and the mold of form,'" he quoted Ophelia. He then stepped toward Lily and whispered, "Is that how you see me? Am I, to you, 'the glass of fashion and the mold of form'?' Or are you here to mock me with your graces and your youth? To numb me with your loveliness, while you steal my wisdom, my hard-earned, blood-bought intelligence, that you fancy you can take away for naught?"

'Sir, I . . ." Lily stammered.

"Don't you sir me. I know you behind the scenes for what you are. A strumpet for books, a harlot for knowledge, a glutton for experiencing the world. Well, all that I can provide. And more. But we'd need to fall into a different understanding," he said, putting his hands over her throat, caressing her with coarse fingers. Lily lowered her eyes. Hot tears rolled down her cheeks. Her heart was beating so hard she felt it might burst.

"Sir, I admire you very much, but I don't love you," she managed to say.

"You don't love me? Oh, yes you do, you just don't know it yet." The hiss in Mr. Wade's voice filled her head and reverberated in her ears. "You and I are quite alike, you know? We're meant for each other. We belong to that divine race of predators molded by the gods for the sacrificial plunder of lesser worlds." His hands traveled down to her breasts. She felt she would swoon.

The door opened.

"Sir, Mr. Harrison is back from the country estate," Simmons announced.

Mr. Harrison walked in, and as Mr. Wade turned his head, Lily pushed him away and darted toward the door. She brushed hard against the old man's shoulder as she flew out of the room, through the hall, and out of the house.

Outside, it was still raining steadily under a thick, steely sky. The rain-glossed flagstones blurred before her eyes as she stepped onto the pavement from the doorstep. She scampered down the street, feeling disoriented and cold. She had left her coat, bonnet, and bag back in the house. The rain beat against her head and face, drenching her chest and shoulders, trickling down her neck and under her dress. She sobbed as she waded through the indistinct faces of people hurrying down the street.

"Miss Throop!" She heard a voice call a few times before someone caught up and stopped her from behind. "Miss Throop, are you all right?" Turning, she looked up at the face of a young man who eyed her with concern. "Lily?" he said in a softer tone, and then she recognized him as Chut, one of the theater's stagehands. "Are you lost? Are you all right?" When she did not answer, he took her gently by the elbow and pulled her under a nearby canopy out of the rain. "You're all wet." He took off his coat and placed it over her shoulders.

"Oh no, but I couldn't," Lily said, struggling to find her voice.

"But you must," Chut answered. "You're drenched. Where are you headed? Can I take you there?"

Lily looked around and realized she did not recognize the street. "I suppose I am heading back to my room in Charing Cross Road," she said, straining to wipe her tear-pooled eyes. The weight of the coat on her shoulders was soothing. Now that she had stopped running, her chest was opening again and cool, moist air streamed back into her cramped lungs.

"There is a teahouse a little ways down the street," Chut said. "Why don't we take you there for a cuppa, before you walk back home? It'll steady you, and warm you up."

She let herself be taken down the street to the teahouse. The rain was already tapering off, but she was glad when they entered the shop, preceded by the sharp tinkling of a bell. It was a small establishment with a few marble-top tables arranged across the floor. Cream-and-burgundy-striped wallpaper covered the walls, giving the simple room a cozy, warm feeling. Behind the counter, a few shelves held a collection of large urn-shaped tea tins decorated with Oriental flower designs. Smells of buttery baked goods and aromatic tea filled the air. A matronly woman dressed in a long pinafore with hair piled in a high bun walked toward them. "Come in, dears, will it be two for tea?"

"Yes. And we will need a table close to the brazier, please," Chut said. The woman showed them to a table by the hot, ornate iron stove at the right end of the shop. Chut helped Lily into her chair, taking the coat from her shoulders and hanging it on a nearby peg. He sat down across from her, took a handkerchief out of his pocket, and handed it to her. "It's clean from today's laundry," he said. Lily dabbed at her cheeks and forehead, and dried her hands while he looked on. He was young, maybe twenty, a medium-height youth with a well-built body, handsome dark eyes, and longish, black wavy hair. He wore a teal linen shirt under a plain waistcoat. His rolled-up sleeves exposed strong, sinewy arms. His face was open in an attentive stare. "Are you feeling better?"

"Yes, thank you, Chut," Lily said. She had seen him many times in the theater, working in the carpentry room, moving around large props, and setting up the stage. He once helped her up to the catwalk where she sometimes stood looking over the stage at the rehearsals of *Soldiers of the Queen*. But they had never talked. She knew he was the son of an Irish waterman and a small-time French actress, and that he had grown up between a skiff in the Thames and modest theater and circus venues in the East End. She also knew he was a protégé of Mr. Harrison, who thought Chut had enough mettle to someday become a theater manager. Chut's father had reportedly saved Mr. Harrison from drowning in the river years ago, and Mr. Harrison had sworn to repay him through helping his son. She had heard all these tales in Mrs. Potterlane's room, where the young seamstresses gossiped admiringly about Chut, who was their favorite among the young men in the company.

"Where is your coat?" Chut inquired. "Did you lose it? Did you leave it somewhere I can fetch it?"

Lily blushed and averted her eyes. A young shop attendant placed a tray on the table and served them tea from a large ceramic teapot.

Chut leaned back on his chair. "You don't need to say anything if you don't want to. Forgive my meddling. When I first saw you coming down the street, I thought you might have been robbed."

Lily shook her head.

They drank their tea. Chut stared at her from behind his steaming cup. "I'm sure you'll get it back. I mean, the coat." He mused for a moment, and then broke into a smile. He put down his teacup. "I guess I shouldn't keep on about the coat. It's brought me luck after all, in that I'm sitting here drinking tea with the rising star of the company."

"Rising star?" Lily said, taken by surprise. "Oh, not at all."

"Yes, rising star. I shall be the most envied man at the Imperial, once the lads find out," Chut chuckled. "I will become the most hated bloke in the company too. And all because of the missing coat."

At the mention of the Imperial, Lily's face darkened, and Chut's glee turned instantly into concern. "Oh no, no. I was only jesting. Of course, no one will hear about this, at least not from me. You needn't fear."

Lily looked into his guileless eyes and thought that she would always be at ease with him. She took another sip of tea. "Your mother was an actress, wasn't she?" she asked.

Chut sighed. "Yes, she was. She lived for the theater. I have few memories of her onstage, though. She died when I was seven, and my father never talks about her."

"What type of plays did she perform?" Lily asked.

"I think she worked a lot with French troupes that came to town. But most of my memories of her are in the circus. I remember her sitting on top of an elephant dressed as Cleopatra. She also rode standing on horses."

"And your father never talks about her?"

Chut's gaze wandered across the room. "Never. He was bitter for a long time after she was gone. I guess it was hard to love a woman so much and have to share her with the stage." Then he looked at Lily and smiled. "But now he's just a cranky old fellow, grumping all day long about the bad business in the river."

He talked on, and Lily found herself drifting into tales of a very different side of the London footlights, away from the posh West End theaters, away from Wade. Meanwhile the afternoon dimmed into a foggy gloom that clung behind the steamed-up windows of the shop like a starved, forlorn child looking in. Chut paid the bill and helped Lily into his coat once again, insisting she wear it until they reached Charing Cross Road.

"There's a group of us that sup together on Fridays and go to music halls in the East End," Chut said, as he took back his coat at Mrs. Bakerloo's door. "You and your friend Ruby should come sometime. It's quite the play away from the play. I think you'd like it."

"I can never repay you for your kindness," Lily said, but Chut had already nodded farewell and turned to walk down the street.

She heard his voice trailing off in the dark. "It's nothing. It was my privilege."

London, June 10th, 1898

Dear Harry and Alice,

If you could see London in the spring! How the city opens up with the longer days, how the parks burst with flowers and the songs of birds! How cheerful are the hearts of Londoners for all the season's sweet gifts.

Ruby and I have made new, lovely friends at the theater. It's a group who goes out together to music halls and supping inns in the East End on weekends. There's Harvey, who works in the carpentry room, and Freddy and Lizzie, who sell tickets at the box and double up as ushers. Also, Maisie, Penny, and Bo, who recently joined the company, but are still only walk-ons. But my sweetest, most reliable friend beside Ruby is Chut—an unusual nickname, I know, for his full name is Charles Blake, who works backstage with sets and effects, a born-and-bred Londoner who knows everything about the city. They're all such a lively lot—going out with them is most enjoyable. They're also admirable—hard workers waiting for opportunities to better themselves. Oh, and Ruby is taking music instruction with an Italian master. Boy, can that girl sing!

So, you see, dears, we're finally carving out a space in London for ourselves, and I'm beginning to feel I could live here very comfortably and call this big city my home. Although I still get very homesick at times, missing you and all our friends in Manchester very, very much.

Your Lily

CHAPTER 5

She read the letter over one more time while waiting for the ink to dry. Then she folded it into an envelope and licked the edges of the seal strip, securing the flap with her fingers. All the while she mused about the words she had written, and realized it was the happiest letter she had sent Harry and Alice since her arrival in London. Of course, it had to do with the coming of spring, with the infusion of luster and freshness that the revitalizing season always brought. Gone were the short, dark days, the cold, unending nights, nature's drab slumber in gardens and parks. But it mostly had to do with her new friends.

Arriving daily at the theater was much more pleasing than before; the anticipation of meeting Chut or Freddy backstage, of finding Bo and Lizzie in the green room; the merry joking, the sharing of stories, the quick gathering of teamwork to resolve any complication. And then, the weekend comings and goings led mostly by Chut and Freddy, who took them to the best, most economic supping inns and venues of affordable entertainment. The city was opening up before her eyes, like a spellbinding landscape sprinkled with contrasting patches of beauty and ugliness, of majesty and poverty, an immense puzzle made up of infinite pieces representing all varieties of human endeavor and dedication. She wondered at the myriad nooks and corners containing interesting little scenes of daily life along the river, inside markets, theaters, churches, avenues, and alleys. And she drank it all through her senses, with an insatiable thirst to know everything about the world.

"*I'll put myself in poor and mean attire, and with a kind of umber smirch my face, the like do you; so shall we pass along.*" Those words had been throbbing in her mind since the performance the night before, when she had realized that Celia's central hidden motives to flee into the forest of Arden with Rosalind were not just allegiance to and support of her needy cousin, but also her own love of adventure and the thrill of disguising herself in order to live undetected through extraordinary circumstances. Wasn't that what Lily did every Friday night when she and Ruby accompanied Chut and friends to the music halls and theaters of Whitechapel and Shoreditch?

Driving through Old Pye Street around the slum called the Devil's Acre to go from Westminster Abbey toward the East End, Lily would hold her breath looking out of the cab window, feeling her pulse quicken as her eyes swept over the most dismal landscape she had ever seen. Blackened muddy roads flanked by rows of toppling little houses leaning together, as if rotting against one another. Dark, silent, uneasy shadows passing and crossing, vanishing by the light of an occasional gas lamp. Women with sunken, black-rimmed eyes, carrying pallid-faced babies that looked like little ghosts. Swarms of filthy children swarming around garbage mounds like flies, fighting for orange peels and potato scraps. And the stench! Dirty smoke and putrid meat mixed with human waste rose like a noxious cloud that had been exhaled above it all. Something in Lily felt blighted as she took in the misery of these images.

Chut pulled her away from the carriage window and drew the curtain. "Don't, Lily. Life isn't worth tuppence in some of these streets. Best pass unnoticed."

Freddy leaned over. "Besides, you don't want a reputation as a slummer."

"A 'slummer'?" Ruby asked, covering her mouth with her scarf to shield herself from the terrible smells.

Freddy laughed. "Haven't heard of the latest fad? Rich people going into the East End and other poor places as tourists, clothing themselves like paupers to have a good peep, and then go back home and pray before they eat their lavish suppers?"

"It's just another one of your funny tales, isn't it?" Ruby scoffed. She found Freddy's sense of humor biting and his late-night amorous approaches annoying. He was a stubby, blondish chap with a round, flat face always pulled into an ironic grin. He worked as an usher and ticket master at the Imperial, but wanted to be an opera singer. Everyone in the company teased him for this ambition, but that did not deter him. He knew he had talent. He just needed opportunities to educate his voice. He and Ruby bickered all the time, but they glowed together when they sang, as if their voices were made to meld with each other.

"It's true," Freddy insisted, with smug confidence. "It was even written up in an American newspaper called the *New York Times* only a few weeks ago."

Lily turned to Chut for corroboration that it might all be a joke, but he only nodded in assent. "Not all are tourists," he added. "Some are good people wanting to set up missions, soup kitchens for the poor, and the like."

"And to find ways to shut down music halls and turn them into churches," Freddy said, and told them about religious groups buying the halls and saloons as a last resort in fighting the "corruption and debauchery" of the area.

Chut clicked his tongue. "Aye, they'll shut down a hall or two. But theater cannot be prevented, can it?" he asked, looking at Lily. "First comes breathin', then eatin', and after those, 'tis theater. The three main human needs, ain't it?"

"I agree, but there's other things too," Lily said.

"Like what?" Chut asked, arching his eyebrows in comical expectation. "I thought all you wanted was to have your own theater one day."

"Well, yes," Lily said, "But I also want to learn about other things, see the world . . ."

"Aye, I'd forgotten those. Oh, and maybe affection for your fellow man should be on the list too?" Chut said, leaning against the back of his seat without taking his eyes off her. Their knees touched as the cab bumped along over the cobbled streets. Lily blushed.

Taking Lily's moment of silence for confusion, Ruby said, "He's just trying to say you only think about the play."

"And not enough about him," Freddy added, snickering. He shielded his head with his arms as Chut lunged toward him and boxed his ears in jest.

Lily knew Chut to be intelligent and witty. She prized his open, honest face, so quick to break into smiles and laughter. But lately, she had noticed him drifting into pensive, self-absorbed moods when he was around her. A few days before, when they traveled together in a wherry boat toward London Bridge, they also sat across from each other, enveloped in thick river fog among the sounds of oars slicing into the cold water. Chut looked over his shoulder toward the looming gray wall of the approaching wharf. His black hair shone in the moist air as he slicked it back, away from his face. Lily glanced at his strong hands gripping the oars, and the tightening sinews on his wrists and forearms as they kept time with the rhythm of the rowing. Chut turned to her and said, "It's hard, you know, not to be distracted when I'm with you. How's a man expected to even row properly when sat in the same boat with the most beautiful woman he knows?" He said it seriously, as if delivering the most matter-of-fact piece of news, which was not his habitual way of dropping compliments. Lily looked into his keen, dark eyes and felt a rush that made her heart leap and forced her to avert her gaze. From that day on, she had found daily presents on her dressing-room table: a ginger nut, a candied fruit, a wildflower or two. And each time she went out onstage, he stood at the wing and whispered as she brushed by, "Break a leg, Lily."

Swarms of people stood before the Britannia Theatre's entrance, or the Brit, as everyone called it, at Hoxton's High Street, waiting to get in. It was such a different scene from the Imperial, where tickets were so much more expensive and audiences fancy and proper. Here, the patrons were common people, laborers with their wives and children, young women with their beaus, groups of rowdy working men who'd just put the toiling week behind them and were ready for good entertainment. Chut's sister, Emily, worked at the Brit and left tickets for them at the entrance. She had tried to get them a box so they could sit together more comfortably, but had only succeeded in acquiring seats in the pit, where it was more amusing anyway. There was the real hubbub, with people eating and drinking, smoking tobacco, cracking up in a constant chain of merry explosions and rambunctious delight.

Once in possession of their tickets, Lily and Ruby followed Chut and Freddy as they pushed through the throngs that struggled to enter the hall all at once, and gushed onto the main floor, while scouring for empty chairs, stools, or benches along the wooden tables perpendicular to the stage. Failing to secure a seat meant having to join the standing crowd in the back. The hall was enormous: It held more than two thousand people every night, and it was connected by a glass-covered corridor to a spacious tavern on one side. There were three tiers of boxes above the pit, and hanging from the middle of its oval-shaped ceiling was one of the largest chandeliers Lily had seen in a theater. The air was thick with cheap cigar smoke and smells of bacon and ale, or whatever else was being served at the tavern, all mixed with sweaty humanity.

Fanny and Maisie waved at them from a table midway to the stage where they were saving them spots. At the far end, amidst the commotion of hustling newcomers wedging themselves into the seated audience, the stage was being cleared and prepared for the next act. Judging by the many pieces of food and rotten fruit that lay about the platform and on the floor nearby, it seemed some spectators had strongly objected to one or two of the actors in the play that had just ended. Guests continued to scurry around for seats and hurried to the tavern for refreshments. Some accosted the attendants who walked along stalls and tables offering sandwiches, fried fish, or hot saveloys, and who served porter and ale from compartments with small taps along the wide zinc belts they wore around their waists. But Freddy was friendly with one of the cooks in the tavern who always provided them with the best suppers, so he and Chut took off to the kitchen after everyone gave them coins from their purses.

"Make it back quick," Fanny called after them. "Emily is soon next on the trapeze."

Lily and Ruby sat down. The orchestra at the end of the pit was reorganizing and tuning their instruments. Meanwhile, along the tables, groups of patrons sat in loud conversation, whistling and humming tunes. An assembly of Scotsmen led by a stout man in a green coat sang "My Heart's in the Highlands," while swinging their pewter cups in the air. A group of small children chased one another around tables and benches, laughing and screaming, crashing down among the sawdust on the floor before their infuriated mothers scooped them up and flung them back on the benches.

"How was the play?" Lily asked.

"They showed *Did You Ever Send Your Wife to Chingford?*—have you seen it before?" Fanny said, rolling her eyes. Lily shook her head, and Fanny added, "Everyone jus' hated the rotten husband. And they let 'im have it, they did!" she ended with a grin. She was petite, with a round, freckly face surrounded by brown curls. By contrast, Maisie was tall and thin with pale lanky hair and drooping blue eyes.

" 'Twas hilarious all the same," Maisie said, with a naughty smile. She and Fanny alternated between their day work at a match factory nearby and evening performances as vaudeville and cancan dancers in the neighboring theaters, besides weekend shifts at the Imperial. They were saucy girls who giggled all the time. Freddy called them his "soubrettes" and swore he would one day drag them into the opera with him.

Chut and Freddy returned with mugs of ale and steaming pork pies on small plates, and landed on the benches just as the curtain opened again. "And now, ladies and gentlemen," said a deep voice, so deep it was hard to believe it came from the tiny figure that walked onto the middle of the stage. To the newcomer he might look like a little old man in a neat red suit and a black top hat, but anyone who had been around knew it was the well-loved Mrs. Lane, the Queen of Hoxton, the theater manageress who was also the best cross-gender performer in town. "We will now welcome the Kaufman Sisters, who will delight us with their singing. Let us give them a hearty round."

Behind her entered a group of five girls riding bicycles, and the audience exploded into roaring applause. The girls were dressed in tight pink breeches and corset-like blouses, their hair tied up under elaborate mop caps, also rose-colored. They paraded around the stage, circling one another with their cycles. When the cheering subsided, they began to sing:

> We are the fair Ambiguity Girls,
> worshipped by bankers and brokers and earls,
> gorgeous in genuine diamonds and pearls,
> daintiest mantle and hat! Though we are
> terribly modest and coy, nice little lunches
> we rather enjoy . . .

Everyone laughed and clapped, and some started singing along with them, while others hushed them down. A man at the far end of Lily's table stood up, staggering and brandishing his mug of ale toward the stage. "I'm no banker, but I'll still worship ya!" he shouted before his mates pulled him back down to the bench. The Kaufman girls parked their bicycles to one side of the stage and engaged in a series of choreographed gymnastics with somersaults and cartwheels, while they finished their song.

> We are so beautiful, dancing in tights,
> mashers adore us for hundreds of nights,
> sending us bracelets and little invites,
> waiting outside on the mat!

This was not the first time Lily and Ruby had seen the Kaufman troupe, but it was still a shock to watch their compact bodies moving freely around the stage, their legs opening and closing in the air, while clad in flesh-cultured tights that made them look naked from afar. The first time, Lily and Ruby had stared wide-eyed at each other and joined squeezing hands under the table. Chut had then looked laughingly into Lily's eyes. "I know it's surprisin', but it's just another form of acting. Wait till you see Emily, then."

The Kaufman Sisters ended their song, took up their cycles again, and exited the stage with smiles and curtsies, blowing kisses at the audience and its frenzied cheering.

Then the man in the top hat came out again and, after waiting for the crowd to quiet down, announced, "And now, for the stars of the night, our beautiful aerial figurants, Mademoiselle Hirondelle and her partner, Swallow. I plead with you to be as quiet as possible so as to allow our trapeze artists maximum concentration in their perilous flight."

The clamor subsided and a woman with a small, agile body dressed in a short lacy tunic over a scarlet leotard walked onto the stage and stood looking at the audience. Her long black hair was tied with glittering ribbons on one side of her head and fell over her right shoulder in thick ringlets down to her waist. Even from afar, Lily could see her resemblance to Chut in the diamond-shaped face with large dark eyes and a prominent Greek nose.

Swallow, a tall, slender man with an oversize handlebar moustache, also dressed in a scarlet leotard, joined her. They held hands and bowed toward the public with the grace of dancers. Then they walked down from the stage and into the gallery where they each climbed rope ladders that led to small platforms at opposite sides of the hall.

A drum roll hushed the crowd while Emily stood on her platform for a few moments, in view of all the people, as if preparing for her moment of danger. A multitude of upturned heads watched her in silence. All of a sudden, she swung herself on the trapeze bar and leapt high into the air. The crowd held its breath, aghast. For a split second that felt endless, her small red body seemed suspended above. Then, leaving the bar behind, she flung herself across the great space, dashing through two hoops that hung from the ceiling under the chandelier, and fell into Swallow's arms. The entire hall came back to life with loud cheering as she dangled, clasping her mate's wrists and hands while he hung by his knees from his trapeze. Slowly, she gathered momentum by swinging herself back and forth while contorting her body into all sorts of acrobatic poses, until she thrust herself up once more into the open space. She grabbed a nearby fly bar, then flipped up and around, gripping the bar with her feet and letting herself hang, as she waited for Swallow to swing himself into her arms. Again and again, they repeated flying through the hoops and catching each other in the air. The crowd stared, spellbound, as Emily's and Swallow's graceful, weightless bodies glided under the glittering constellation of the chandelier's crystal prism, clasping each other in the air, clinging together as they swayed from side to side, a man and a woman seemingly naked, comingling and gripping each other in flight.

When the trapeze act ended, the intoxicated crowd turned its attention to the next play—*London Day by Day: A Farce,* read the crumpled brochure that Maisie handed Ruby and Lily over the table. Moments into the performance, Emily, now fully dressed and with her cape in hand, walked to their table and sat beside Chut. She looked at Lily with bright eyes. "I'm so glad you could come tonight," she said, taking her hands. "Now it's my turn to come see you at the Imperial." She turned to her brother and said, "Oh, Chut, she's even lovelier than you described. How will you ever deserve her?" She grimaced in jest, and after slugging down the last of her brother's ale, added, "But I've got to go now. We've another performance in an hour." She got up, kissed Lily's cheek, then her brother's, and made for the door where Swallow was waiting.

"That's Emily," Chut said. "She flies everywhere. Can't hold her down for a two-minute conversation."

Lily blurted out countless questions about her, but she was hushed by a group of women sitting nearby. "Pipe down!" one of them barked. "Want to 'ear what they's sayin', luv," she added in softer tones, before her voice was drowned in the audience's raucous laughter.

When the end of the evening arrived, the curtain rose to reveal Mrs. Lane surrounded by the members of her troupe. Each member was introduced and afterward turned to the audience to say a few words. The crowd seemed very familiar with the players and their circumstances and threw things at them, presents as it were. A group of women threw a pair of boots at a young actor; a man flung a petticoat at one of the women players; a band of rowdy, already drunk young patrons threw a joint of meat to the company leading man, who was notoriously thin. The audience roared each time, and a few women sitting in the stall closest to the stage put up their umbrellas as a defense against the possibility of an item falling short of the stage.

CHAPTER 6

It was about midnight when they rose to leave and made their way to the exit. The crowd, still drunk with laughter and entertainment, gathered sluggishly around empty mugs and dirty plates left on tables, reluctantly pouring back out into the bleak streets. Ruby, Lily, and Chut stood under the marquee outside the theater after bidding Maisie and Fanny farewell, while Freddy went to fetch a cab.

"Well, well, look who's come to the edge of town." Lily turned and saw Wade standing behind her. He wore a heavy coat over his habitual smart tweed suit, and by his side stood a handsome, fleshy woman with large green eyes and thick painted lips that were turned up in a derisive grin. She stuck out among the crowd because of her garish costume, a pink magenta dress with matching cape and bonnet. She didn't look directly at Lily but shot intense, insinuating glances at Chut. She reminded Lily of the fancy prostitutes who paraded outside the Imperial.

Wade leaned toward Lily. "Come to gawk at Mademoiselle Hirondelle's fantastic red knickers? I'll say she's the grand slam on the trapeze. Nothing like being popped out frog-like in the circus," he said, looking at Chut.

Lily knew Wade was quite drunk by the way he slurred his words and the manner in which he angled toward his lady companion. He stumbled closer to Lily and placed a heavy hand on her shoulder.

"Apprenticing in Hoxton is your best career insurance policy—much more rewarding than learning Shakespeare. Red knickers never fail, if all else does." Uncomfortable under the weight of his hand, Lily stepped back to slip away from his grasp. Wade's arm hung limp for a moment, before he flung it up again over his companion's shoulder. "Wouldn't you vouch for that, Germaine?" he asked. "Were you not also an aspiring actress in your trouble-free years?" Germaine winced, pulling her mouth into a little fake smile.

Wade leered at the group, while they all stood in silent tension. Anyone who knew Wade knew better than to contradict his rude, crazy harangues. "Look at them, Germaine, how they glow with that skin-deep grace that comes with the wrappings of youth; the beauty that results from the unwritten page, the stupidity of the blank slate. Isn't it insulting that they should be allowed to parade in front of two old warhorses like us, making us pine for the beauty we've lost?"

"Cab's here," Chut said finally, through gritted teeth. "Good night, Mr. Wade."

Wade looked at Chut and sneered. "Cab, is it? Thought you'd be taking the omni. Must be hard to escort pretty actresses on pauper stagehand wages." They stood looking fiercely at each other. Germaine tugged gently at Wade's arm.

Chut buttoned the middle button of his coat, and said, "Good night, sir," and steered Lily by the elbow toward the open door of the cab. After she and Ruby stepped in, he jumped in himself without another glance at Wade. They were silent as the carriage departed.

Freddy, who had missed the scene, looked around inquiringly. "Mr. Wade upset we didn't let 'im have the cab for his lady?"

"Lady! I know her from the promenade," Chut scoffed. Lily watched as he huddled into his coat and pressed his hands between his knees. She knew he had felt humiliated by Wade.

"Why was he going on about beauty and youth, and warhorses?" Ruby asked. "I didn't get a word of it."

"Oh, the beauty thing again, was it?" Freddy said. "That's one of his dear matters of contention. He once nearly killed a man who called him ugly."

"Nearly killed a man!" Ruby echoed, shocked.

"All London heard about it. It's a famous story," Freddy said.

"Or infamous," Chut said, and then added darkly, "That man holds a candle to the devil. Best stay away from him." Lily had never seen him so distraught. She took her hand out of her pocket and threaded it through his arm. "Don't pay any mind to anything he said. He was only doing it to offend me."

Chut flashed an angry eye at her. "Pay no mind? That's what everyone does, don't they? That's how he can keep doing all he wants." After a moment he added, "And how doesn't it affect me if he offends you?" He looked out the carriage window, furious, but didn't let go of Lily's hand.

Ruby and Freddy settled together on the opposite seat and began singing softly their new favorite Koven's song, "Oh, promise me that someday you and I will take our love together to some sky . . ." But Chut said nothing else for the rest of the journey.

Lily had told no one about the incident with Wade, and she had neither returned to his house. Of course, they saw each other at the theater all the time, but Wade had been nonchalant about it, stating that "a great burden has been lifted off my back, given the fact that some people just choose to remain within the realm of mediocrity." When Lily asked if she could have her things back, he said with a fierce grin, "No, I certainly shan't return your trappings, madam. For that you must return to the house yourself, make proper amends after stomping off so crudely, and resume your education." During rehearsals he would stand too close and touch her at any possible occasion, grab her by the arm and shake her, "'Are you honest, are you fair?'" or push her hard, making her lose her balance, "'Get thee to a nunnery! Why wouldst thou be a breeder of sinners?'" At the end, he would congratulate and flatter her exceedingly for her performance. Lily, though stiff with fear anytime he approached her, soon began to realize that most of his behavior toward her in public was just a contrivance to distress Mrs. Bennett. It was becoming plain that Wade enjoyed tormenting her. She was seen more and more flying into fits of jealousy at his affronts, while he acted as if he were bored to tears by her overemotional reactions.

"Nothing could be more tedious than a woman screeching for attention," he'd say.

A few days before the opening of *Hamlet*, Mrs. Bennett stepped into Lily's dressing room and closed the door behind her. Her eyes were pools of deep red. Lily jumped up from her stool. "You can have him if you like. Get a taste of his monstrous cruelty," Mrs. Bennett hissed, "but don't think acting as his pet will make you step over me onstage."

"No one is stepping over you," Lily said. "Everyone has their place onstage, and the public and the reviews give each their due, with no regard to personal circumstances or quarrels." She was surprised at the unexpected surge of confidence in her voice as she uttered the words. She had been interviewed by a young critic from *The Era* just two days before, a Mr. Ross Patterson, who had expressed intense admiration for her and then written an article along the lines of, "Rising young stars light up the stage, eclipsing all else as they blind the public eye."

Mrs. Bennett had evidently read the article and was incensed at the mention of reviews. She lunged at Lily, grabbed her hair, and pushed her to her knees. The hairbrush Lily held in her hand fell to the floor along with two bottles from the boudoir table that smashed into pieces at her feet.

"I shall scream for help if you don't let go of me," Lily said, out of breath, pulling at her own hair to save it from the woman's savage grip. For a split second Mrs. Bennett relented, and Lily managed to glance at her face, distorted into an ugly mask. But behind it she saw a desperate, harrowed look, the distress of someone losing hold of her life, being pulled hopelessly into a hole.

They heard voices approaching in the corridor. Mrs. Bennett released her with a forceful tug and Lily fell over the smashed glass on the floor, cutting her hands and wrist. Mrs. Bennett stood above her panting. "I'll do anything to sink you," she said, and spat at Lily's feet.

When the incident came to be known, it created a commotion in the company. Lily hadn't told, but Mr. Featherstone had seen Mrs. Bennett leaving her dressing room before he entered and discovered her injured. Everyone knew Mrs. Bennett to be a barbaric, passionate woman, and other instances of jealousy had taken place in the past with other actresses. But this violence was unprecedented. Mr. Bennett apologized for his wife, stating she had a delicate nervous condition, and promising that it wouldn't happen again.

But Wade only laughed heartily at the episode. "There's nothing more exciting than females losing their sham dignity and fighting like wenches in the marketplace."

In the following weeks, Lily observed Mrs. Bennett as she internalized her rancor, and felt that far from forgetting her grudge, she would now find more lethal ways to strike. Lily's dress for Ophelia was soon found ripped in the costume room. Mrs. Potterlane's apprentice seamstresses were blamed and fired, though nobody believed they had done it. It cost Lily thirty pounds to buy another one before the play, and she was forced to dig into the savings she was keeping for Harry and Alice's trip to London. When she was crossing the stage another day at the end of rehearsal, a heavy sandbag fell from the grid above and missed Lily by inches. Chut and Harvey later examined the lighting grid and determined someone had purposely detached the bag from the hemp rig and pushed it over. Backstage corridors and rooms became unsafe places from then on, and figuring out who might be Mrs. Bennett's accomplices in these acts of provocation was an exasperating endeavor. It took all of Lily's grit to stay afloat until the opening of the new play.

London suddenly felt like a vast, cold sea governed by unpredictable tides and dangerous undercurrents, all of which she might not have the skill to survive. She couldn't forget Wade's comment to Germaine that night outside the Britannia, "Didn't you also start out as an actress in your youth?" and the look of bitter anguish that followed on Germaine's face. For the first time, she saw how easily a girl's life like hers could be churned and sloshed in these murky waters, spit out into the streets as the next ragged tuppence harlot working in the gutter.

London, September 4th, 1898

Dearest Harry and Alice,

Something terrible happened yesterday at the theater. I wanted to write and give you the details before you become sick with worry after the stories that have been in the newspapers.

We had a fire. It was not a very big fire, but it was still very frightening. Thankfully, it didn't happen during a performance, which would have been a real disaster. It happened in the afternoon, when only a few of us were in the building. I had dropped in by chance because I'd forgotten my script in my dressing room and wanted to read my lines before rehearsal. The fire started in the furnace room when Mrs. Waithe, the charwoman, who's very old and a bit unreliable, set about hanging her coat over the burner to dry. Of course, it caught fire and so did the many stacks of old newspapers that she keeps there. By the time I heard the cries and ran out of my room, the corridors were so full of smoke that I was afraid I would choke. I was able to reach the green room—the only place with a window in that section of the theater. It was a while before the firemen could help me out of the building, since they had to first put out the fire in the carpentry room. I can't tell you how glad I was to see the street. Everyone was waiting for me there, to comfort me, swaddle me in warm blankets, and bring me hot tea.

So dears, you see, everything ended well. The damage is already being repaired, and we only have to skip three performances. Mrs. Waithe is also safe, although she has lost her job. I am so sad for her—people are saying she only has the poorhouse to go to.

But I haven't asked about you, my darlings. How are you keeping? Are you much better with your treatment, Harry?

Your little sister, who loves you more than she could ever write,

Lily

CHAPTER 7

The new room Lily occupied at Mrs. Bakerloo's lodging house was the best in the house. When she'd been cooped up with Ruby in one of the smallish, dark rooms at the top of the staircase, she'd never imagined there could exist a suite like this only two floors down. Spacious, with three windows overlooking the street, a full fireplace in the middle of a cozy sitting room, and a separate sleeping alcove at the back, it was all she could want. Ruby's room, similar but smaller, connected to hers through a side entrance. Besides, now that they paid top rent and could deliver it sharp on the first day of the month, Mrs. Bakerloo's sour disposition had transformed into stern solicitude and occasional amiability. She had agreed to bring a writing table and a bookcase into Lily's room. She had changed the curtains when it was remarked that they were mildewed on the lower edge. She was even disposed to send up trays with tea and biscuits in the afternoons, when Lily lounged in the room learning her lines or writing letters.

Then there was everything that was happening at the theater: the acclamation from the pit every night; the bouquets of flowers and notes of adoration awaiting her in the dressing room; the affection of her backstage friends; the talk of new plays ahead. The latest write-up in *The Era* described her as:

> One of the most remarkable young actresses around, with unusual talent and true stage versatility, she dares to bring spirit and character into Ophelia, instead of playing her as an obedient, vapid pawn caught up in other people's manipulations.

For a moment, Lily's life seemed to be earning fast and fantastic wings.

But all that had been disrupted now. Torn, like a beautiful canvas sliced with a knife.

She sat in the armchair by the empty fireplace, feeling the anguish that came over her in the afternoon hours when she was by herself. Her eyes roamed around the room, taking in the textures and shapes of objects that only weeks ago had given her so much comfort, but now only triggered nauseous malaise: the floral wallpaper with delicate pink flowers embedded in swirls of vegetation; the gilded oval mirror above the mantelpiece; the angel-carved chest at the foot of her bed. All these beautiful things had lost their power to soothe and delight her. The short, fat clock sitting on the mantelpiece especially distressed her, with its ticking noise reminding her of how fast her life might be slipping away from her control, and how those pitiless, sharp hands had the power to return her mind to those moments of agony—all at the stroke of four.

Four was the time she'd seen on the wall clock as she rushed into the green room, seeking refuge from the thick fumes that clouded the corridors. Four would henceforth be the time when the dreaded images would start to resurface, as if coughed up by her memory, entwined with the smell of smoke. His silhouette had come in first through the curtain of smoke, but she'd hardly seen him because the filaments of his shadow had not merged into focus until he was upon her. "Chut!" she had cried, "Thank goodness! I knew you would come."

"Waiting for Chut, are we?" he said, and she felt his hands grip her like tongs. "But Chut went to market, and sent the devil over instead." She struggled in his clasp until they both stumbled onto the floor. They wrangled in the smog while her eyes stung and teared, and she gasped desperately for air. When she let up, weak and sickened by her smoke-filled lungs, she felt the jabbing. But it was the choking smell that had never left her since, that made her gasp at the slightest whiff of anything burning, particularly when it reeked from fabric, as it had then from the thick cotton of his shirt when it was flattened against her face, smothering her.

His rough hand also reeked of smoke as he pushed it over her mouth. "Do not scream," he whispered. She listened to the firemen's footsteps in the corridor through the violent hammering of her heart. "Anyone here?" they called as they passed by.

"I will leave first, and you will give me a few minutes before you call out." His body sundered away from hers, and he lay by her side for an instant catching his breath. Then he buttoned up his breeches, and it was only when he smoothed down her skirts that the stabbing pain returned between her thighs. It throbbed, with a gushing sensation that might have been blood. Her arms were bruised and torpid from the tussle, her rib cage crushed. The rest of her body wasted and dank, like a rag.

He sat her up against the settee. He held up her face by the jawline with coarse fingers. "Open your eyes. Look at me." When she shut them tighter, he shook her face until she obliged. She flinched as she met his hard stare. He lowered his face to an inch from hers. "This did not have to be this way, you know. But you're mine now; our union has been branded by fire," he said, and pressed his brutal lips against hers. With her last strength she flung up her arms and clawed at his face and neck, and scratched him till she drew blood.

Wade stepped back, dabbing at his neck with his fingers, and laughed. "It's that little vixen inside you that I like most," he said, pinning her with his dark, hypnotic glare. She braced herself in fear that he would strike her, but he only turned and grabbed his coat. "Adieu," he said, and then opened the door and disappeared into the cloud of smoke that blew into the room.

Even four weeks later, the images were still as vivid as the first day. They swiveled in her mind like filthy swash that couldn't, wouldn't be scraped from her memory. Lily buried her face in her hands. Her eyes felt hot, strained.

There was a knock at the door. "Miss Throop, there's a Mr. Blake to see you."

"Please tell him I'm not home."

Mrs. Bakerloo sighed on the other side of the door. "He won't go away. He says it's important."

"I'll see him in the parlor then," Lily said.

"He's right here with me, Miss Throop," Mrs. Bakerloo said. "He won't be told. The only thing left to do is call the police constable."

Her heart leaped as the door opened and she saw Chut standing at the threshold beside the old woman. It hammered against her ribs, her old, young heart she thought had been lost in the fire.

"It's all right, Mrs. Bakerloo," she said, standing up.

Chut walked into the room and Mrs. Bakerloo left, closing the door. They stood facing each other, listening to the woman's heavy footsteps trailing down the corridor.

Chut took off his hat. "I apologize for the intrusion."

She had avoided Chut for the last couple of weeks and now, as she looked at him, she saw he had changed quite a bit. He had been promoted to stage-manager assistant as part of Mr. Harrison's scheme to bring young blood into the company. The position seemed to have given him a new heft, a sheen that transpired through the new gray town coat he was wearing and his matching bowler hat. She had heard all sorts of jokes about what a dandy he'd become, but how he still swaggered around like a street hooligan instead of carrying himself like a gent, as befitted the new attire.

"I know it's rude to come in like this," Chut said, "but I left three notes and not one has been answered. Every time I've stopped by, you were feeling indisposed. You don't come out to the music halls anymore. You don't even sup with any of us. What's the matter, Lily?" Unable to sustain his gaze, Lily turned and sat down in silence.

Chut paced around the room. "I'm quite worried about you." After a moment he stopped and said in a softer tone, "People are saying the part is taking too much out of you."

Lily had also heard this at the theater. People had noticed her pallor and her weight loss, her despondency. They attributed it to the amount of emotion needed to play the part of Ophelia, and how it sometimes affected young actresses. "Playing Ophelia will drive you potty" was one of the little sayings going around in the theater world. It was true that all the wailing at the screaming mad scene was difficult to shake off. Toward the end of rehearsals, and during the first week of performances, she had stumbled off the stage feeling sick and ready to retch, and arrived at her dressing room trembling, depleted. She then sobbed over her boudoir table while her attendant Tricia draped her in a shawl and called down to Mrs. Waithe to bring up lavender tea.

But that had also changed. Now, after she was done with all the howling, she walked off the stage enveloped in a tingling sensation, a feeling of exhilaration at having vented some of the shame and rage that weighed upon her chest. The euphoria then evaporated quickly, and by the time the play was over, she found herself falling into a state of mute apathy. She only wanted to go back to her room and spend the evening alone staring out of the window.

"Is it true?" Chut asked from his seat in the armchair opposite Lily's. "Is it getting to you? It does to some actors, you know. But it's surely something you can learn to handle. Others have gone through this. Even Emily knows all the breathing ways that control the fear of the trapeze. She can teach you. I'm sure they'll work for this, too."

Lily looked at his clean-shaven face, his eager eyes, and felt a pang of regret. She shook her head. "I'm quite all right. Nothing like that is happening. I'm just a bit tired," she started, but soon felt her lips quivering. She coughed a little.

"Have you taken cold?" Chut asked. "It's freezing in this room. How come the fire hasn't been lit? I'll ask that copper woman you keep downstairs to bring up coal immediately."

"I'm not cold," Lily said, but Chut had already flung the door open and run downstairs.

A few minutes later, there was a mound of coal smoldering in the grate. The evening was fast creeping outside the windows, casting purple shadows into the room. Chut switched on the amber wall lamps at both sides of the hearth. Annie, Mrs. Bakerloo's housemaid, finished sweeping up the coal around the fireplace into a dustpan. She stood up from her kneeling position. "I tell Miss Lily every day to let me get the fire going, but each time she refuses. Has nothing to do with my disposition to keep her comfortable, Mr. Blake."

Chut stood leaning on the mantelpiece. "Thank you, Annie. That'll be all." Annie picked up the empty coalscuttle and waddled out of the room. Chut sat down again, unbuttoning his coat and exposing the trim, elegant double-breasted waistcoat he wore underneath. He loosened his shirt collar and smoothed his black hair with his fingers, slicking it back behind his ears. He looked up at Lily. "What's troubling you, Lily?" He waited, watching her closely. "You have to tell me what the matter is."

"Nothing's the matter," Lily said, turning her face away.

"Why won't you let Annie light the fire? Are you still frightened after what happened?"

The mention of fire pricked her. "I suppose I am still in a bit of a panic about that." Her chest felt unbearably stifled as she uttered these words. She thought of getting up and opening a window, but she knew it was still cold in the room and resisted the impulse.

Chut shot her an anguished look. "What happened during the fire?"

"Nothing happened, I just stayed in the green room until the firemen could reach me." She felt her voice choke and realized she might burst into sobs. She hung her head in distress. "But the smoke, I can't get the smell of the smoke out of me."

Chut leapt from his chair and knelt before her. "Shhh," he cooed, " 'Tis only momentary; it will pass, and you will forget. Of course, you must've been very afraid trapped in the building all by yourself." He paused for a moment, then added, "I know how hard it must be for you to be alone in a big city like London, a beautiful young woman, with no family to take care or comfort you, no one to watch over you."

She feared he would reach out and take her hands. She hid them in her lap. There was something suffocating about Chut's proximity. Maybe it was the smell of his hair pomade, or the soft rush of his voice. She pulled her eyes away from his handsome face; in the immediacy of his tense, warm body she felt small and wizened.

Something opened up inside her, a craving she couldn't quite grasp; a need for solace or forgiveness, perhaps; to be enveloped by arms, caressed by hands; by Chut's sparing hands that lay prostrate at her feet, unaware of her tainted flesh. She stood up. "I should be all right, Chut. I've got good friends. But I must ask you to excuse me now. I need to get ready to go out."

Chut stood up too. "Go out? Where, Lily? There's no performance tonight." He held her by the shoulders and gently lowered her to her chair. "Sit down, please. There's something I have to tell you."

Lily let herself droop into the armchair. Chut sat down again across from her. He thought for a minute, looking at his hands. Then he sat up straight. "Lily, I have come to ask you to marry me."

Lily froze.

"I know I don't have the education of a gentleman, nor the means. But I have this new job, and Mr. Harrison has talked about training me as his assistant manager." He paused, as if retrieving well-rehearsed words. "And I'm a hard-working man. Besides, Emily and I just inherited a property in Ireland from our uncle, and we plan to sell it and buy a small house in London." His face was flushed, his hands clasped tightly together. "Lily, it's much easier for a married woman in the theater."

There was a silence. They stared at each other. Chut looked at her with that hungry yearning that used to amuse her so much, scanning her face for the tiniest crinkle before he would allow himself to smile openly or burst into laughter. "Chut, this is so kind of you, but you already have Emily to watch out for and—" Lily started.

"It's not about watching over you," Chut said, and then added in a sudden fit of passion, "Lily, you know I love you. I've loved you from the very first time I saw you. Spending every day of my life with you is all I can long for."

Lily looked away. She got up and walked toward the mantelpiece. "I can't marry you, Chut."

A moment passed. She stood wringing her hands and looking down at the grate, avoiding the mirror where Chut's reflection struggled to collect his confusion. "I know this must come as a surprise to you," he said, at last, "You may want to think about it and give me your answer in a few days."

Lily turned around. "Please, let's not talk about this anymore." She kept her eyes on the tips of his new lace-up boots. She dared not look in his eyes, into the pain she was inflicting. Her body felt rigid, like a shell. But inside, a scream was building, swirling toward her windpipe, and all she wanted was for him to leave as soon as possible, before it ripped out of her and blasted the whole room.

"Why, Lily? Just tell me. Nothing you could say will stop me from loving you."

"There's nothing to say. I don't feel the same, that's all. And I belong to the stage," Lily said so in the most indifferent voice she could muster. "Now I have to ask you to leave. I need to get ready."

Chut got awkwardly to his feet, walked to the rack, and collected his hat. "Is it true what they say, then?"

"What do they say?" Lily said with defiance, and wished immediately she had not asked.

Chut's fingers probed the rim of his hat. "Never mind." He shot her a last glance before he closed the door behind him. "Good-bye, Lily."

She listened to his steps walking away from the door. The room hung with his absence, his vanished voice, fading impressions of his boyish poise. Lily watched him from the window as he straggled down the street popping in and out of sight under the orange gas lamps until he was sucked into the dark. Poor Chut. How far removed from her life he seemed all of a sudden, when only weeks ago holding hands together had felt the closest thing to bliss. Now she could only look at him from behind the sullied glass surface behind which she was trapped, and watch him walk away with empty hands.

As she moved away from the window, something folded inside her, smothering all possibility of an outcry. She flung herself on the bed and buried her face in the pillow. She wanted to sob, but her body felt dry and stiff, like a porcelain doll. Dead. She closed her eyes, terribly afraid of the images that would start rushing once more into her mind.

A small, pointed knock came from the door that connected to Ruby's room. "Lily? May I come in and take the blue poplin dress for tomorrow's outing?" After a moment, Ruby opened the door and walked in, but stopped when she saw Lily lumped on the bed. "Oh, dear! Are you all right?" When Lily didn't answer, she rushed to her side. "What's the matter? Are you sick? But you are! Your head is so hot," she said, putting her hand over Lily's forehead.

Lily opened her eyes. "Chut was here."

"Chut? Did he come to take you out to supper?"

"I sent him away," Lily said in a faint drawl. Her chest burned against the bedclothes and her head felt like it would split into shards.

"Why ever did you? He's the one to cheer you up, being so sweet on you," Ruby said.

"I was terribly cruel," Lily sobbed.

Ruby climbed onto the bed and wrapped her arms around her. "Lily, Lily! You have to stop this grief. I know what happened was awful, and I don't want to sound unfeeling, but you have to get on with your life. At least it didn't get you with child, and he hasn't been at you anymore." She rocked her for a moment in her arms. "I know naught of it was your fault." Then after a moment, she added, "Let me talk to Chut. I know he'd understand."

Lily jumped up. "No, no! I'd rather die," she said, wiping her tear-stained face. "I couldn't stand his pity." Ruby sighed and gave her a little nod of the head, followed by a sad smile.

It had been very difficult to tell Ruby all that had happened during the fire. It had only been because of Ruby's unwavering, persistent questioning that she had decided to share the secret she had sworn to bury inside herself for the rest of her life. But she spared her the details of everything that came after and how in only three weeks she'd become imprisoned in a hellish dance. Wade was wrapping her fast in his spider web, controlling every glance and every step she took in the theater, isolating her from everyone through shame and fear.

During the days that the theater had been closed for repairs, she had lain in her bed shivering with fever and dreading the moment she would have to face Wade onstage again. In the evenings, she soaked her bruised body in scalding baths, furiously scrubbing her skin until it hurt. Amid the sobbing, she felt rage building inside, as she realized that no matter how much washing and rubbing she did, her body would never feel clean again.

Then there were his odious gifts. The day she returned to the theater, Tricia had presented her with a small, beautiful box wrapped in red silk. Inside was a choker of tiny white pearls and a note that read, "One for every little tooth you bit me with." The necklace had burned her fingers, and she was overcome by such fury that she flung it across the room. While the astonished Tricia stood back, the string snapped and pearls cascaded over the floor.

That same afternoon, she was called into Mr. Bennett's office and was surprised to find only Wade and Mr. Harrison waiting for her. Mr. Harrison sat behind the desk, and Wade sprawled on one of the chairs across from him.

"Dear Miss Throop," Mr. Harrison said, "we hope you are recovered from our most unfortunate accident and ready to resume performances." There was a glint in his eye Lily had not seen before, and she stiffened at the thought that Wade might have shared information with him. "As you know, the company is undergoing restructuring, and Mr. and Mrs. Bennett will be shortly moving on to other ventures. Of course, none of these changes apply to you. You are bound to us by contract for the coming years and we are delighted with your work. We'll be soon staging *Romeo and Juliet*, and of course, we would want you to play Juliet." Lily gasped. Wade snickered.

The office door opened and Chut stepped in. "Sorry to interrupt, Mr. Harrison. The chief fire officer is here and is requesting your presence for the final inspection."

Mr. Harrison stood up, adjusted his tie, and took up his cane. "You'll excuse me, Miss Throop. I must attend to this." Chut held the door open while the old man walked across the long room with quick little steps and a spastic motion of his arm, as if he were pricking the floor with his cane. Lily shot Chut a desperate glance as her skin crawled with fear. The moment the door shut behind them, she jumped up from her seat and hurried after them.

But Wade was instantly upon her. "Not so fast."

Lily stood back, trembling. The room reeled. Her ears pounded. "I will not stay. I shall leave with Mr. and Mrs. Bennett," she said, breathless.

"You might have to go with them to the jug. Haven't you heard he's up for charges of larceny and embezzlement?"

Lily looked at Wade in disbelief. "Mr. Bennett is an honest man!"

"Indeed, as honest as they come in this trade," Wade said. "But it's your own commitment that will land you in the clink. Don't you know you may not break your contract without incurring criminal charges? It helps to read documents before signing them," he added with a grin. Then he lifted his hand toward her face, but Lily slapped his arm hard and ran for the door. Wade laughed as he ran ahead and grabbed the knob. "Oh, the sweetness of the hellcat! I swear I shall make it my holy task to tame you." Then he added, theatrically, "After all, we have been espoused by fire, madam. There's no turning back on that."

"Let me out," Lily said, radiating hatred. Her fury emboldened her to look him directly in the eye, past the leering mask of his stare into the foul mass that lay behind it, a cesspool of lust. It pulled at her with the force of a whorl, eager to devour her again. She took another step back, horrified, while Wade's face clicked back into his usual gloating expression. Then he opened the door, but before Lily rushed through, he caught her by the wrist. "Another thing: If I ever I catch that pigeon-plucker looking at you that way again, be sure he'll be out on the street in a heartbeat. Him and his singing, bacon-faced mate, and everyone else." Then he released her and bowed pompously. "Good day, madam!"

For the next days there was an air of strained industriousness in the theater. There were those who were leaving and too distressed to make commentaries, and there were those who were staying and just relieved they had saved their skins. Mrs. Potterlane, who was being kept on, avoided all familiar conversation and was busy reorganizing her department under the new management. Chut, Harvey, Freddy, and some of the other young members of the company not only stayed on, but got promotions and raises, so they were initially too glad to complain. Ruby had also been asked to stay. But Mr. Featherspoon was to leave with the Bennetts, and everybody was distraught about that.

Weeks had passed since all this had happened, but in Lily's mind it felt like years. She had officially become the company's leading actress, and certain obligations came attached to this privilege. Presently, she was bound to dine with Mr. Harrison, who wanted to introduce her to a group of theatrical investors he was wooing. Wade, of course, was also sure to be there.

Lily glanced at the clock on the mantelpiece across the room and started gathering herself anxiously. She looked at Ruby. "I'm so late! Please help me dress for this evening. The cab will be here to pick me up anytime."

Ruby opened the wardrobe and gasped. "Is this the dress you'll be wearing? Blimey, Lily! It exceeds anything I've ever seen. Where on earth did you get it?"

Caviar.
Potage Tortue.
Mousseline d'éperlans aux truffes.
Filets de poulet au beurre noisette.
Artichauts aux fines herbes.
Agneau de lait à la broche.
Petits pois frais.
Nymphes glacées au champagne.
Salade Mignonne.
Pêches de Vénus voilées de l'Orientale.
Mignardises.

London, November 15th, 1899

Dearest Harry and Alice,

Last night I dined at the Princes' Hall, and before I left I asked M. Fourault, the lovely French maître d'hôtel, to allow me to take one of the menus to send to my dear brother and sister. Of course, he promptly agreed and asked me a lot of questions about you. It's one of the fine London restaurants where fashionable people dine before going to a play, or after they leave the theater. Such a gorgeous place!

The food is heavenly as you can see. All French, of course. The first time I dined here, I was puzzled with the menu, I didn't understand a thing, and my fellow diners had to painstakingly explain every detail of the dishes. But then, it all started coming back to me, the lessons of Mademoiselle Doudou. Do you remember our French governess? That petite woman with a pince-nez and the most terrrrrible accent in English, who you used to call—very cruelly—Mademoiselle Frog? Don't laugh! Well, I have found out that she did teach me a lot of French after all. The realization came when the words started jumping off the menu and making sense on their own: tortue, poulet, agneau, even mignardises.

Oh, my darlings, what a long list of places I have waiting for you in London! Don't lose faith, Harry. I know you will get better and better and, before you know it, you'll be escorting Alice and me into the Princes' Hall or the Hotel Savoy or, even better, into the Cecil's.

Good-bye, my sweets! Tomorrow I shall write to you about Romeo and Juliet, *which is already being staged.*

Your Lily

CHAPTER 8

Lily watched the people coming in and going out of the great room, a dazzling salon with big panels, long mirrors, and clusters of electric candles on the tables. The ceiling of the Princes' Hall was lined in heavy moldings of white with gold detailing that contrasted handsomely with the brick-red panels and golden fleur-de-lis on the walls. Pots of spiked palms stood in every corner of the room while daffodil bouquets enlivened the center of every table. Across the floor was the white railed-in musicians' gallery, where a band played cheerful music that mingled with the elegant crowd's chatter. A host of waiters clad in black with silver numbers in their buttonholes hovered, serving guests, or stood at tables carving roasts and preparing flambéed platters. To Lily's right sat a family party entertained by a circumspect bald-headed fellow with a gray moustache and black silk cravat tied in a great bow. Beyond them, two smooth-faced young men flirted with two young women. At another table, a fat gentleman, who looked like a banker or financier, smiled at a girl who wore many rows of pearls round her throat.

Lily sat between Wade and Mr. Harrison, like an escorted prisoner. Wade sat to her right, impeccable in a black evening coat with satin lapels and silk bow tie. Large gold cufflinks in the shape of lion heads stared at her from his starched wrists.

Colonel Hamilton observed her from across the table with small, eager eyes. His ruddy face, reportedly tanned from his India campaign days, contrasted with the sizeable white Imperial moustache that all but hid his smile. "But my dear Miss Throop, I'm afraid you are not impressed with the *potâge tortue*."

Lily looked down at her soup where a jade-cultured semisolid blob floated in a dark liquid, and then smiled faintly at him. "On the contrary, Colonel Hamilton, I'm finding it delicious," she said, but made no attempt to pick up her spoon. It was a boring ritual she had to go through at many of these dinners where rich old men pretended to be extremely concerned about her lack of appetite.

"Maybe the lady would prefer a solid English dinner," Lord Godfrey Malory said, staring solemnly at her. He was a stuffy, bony gentleman, with a red bulbous nose. "I myself am not a devotee of French hokum."

"I think Miss Throop might be happier with a bowl of borscht than with the *tortue*," said another gentleman, Benjamin Gerard.

"Borscht, Mr. Gerard?" Lily asked.

"The queen of soups, Miss Throop—a rich magenta cream made of beets, known to brighten ladies' cheeks and color their lips."

Gerard appeared to be the youngest member of the present company, excepting her, and maybe Wade. He could have been in his early forties, an elegant man with chestnut hair sprinkled with gray and long sideburns that reached to his downturned, melancholy mouth. His light-blue gaze was, by contrast, lively and engaging. Lily had learned earlier that Gerard traveled all the time within the Continent, and to Russia, where he promoted English theater in St. Petersburg. He was currently putting together a troupe for a summer season at St. Petersburg's Mariinsky Theatre.

"Miss Throop is colorful enough, Mr. Gerard," Wade snapped, putting his hand over Lily's on the table. "Too colorful, in fact, for her own good," he added with a twisted smile. Lily shrank, afraid he would launch into one of his tirades. Slowly, she slipped her hand away from his and pretended to readjust the white kid gloves over her fingers.

"Just make sure you keep the lady fed, my dear sir. We don't want our bird of paradise to lose her sheen," Sir Godfrey said gravely.

Wade shot him a furious look and, clucking his tongue, signaled to M. Fourault, who was instantly by his side. The maître d' was a little man with a moustache and rather long silver hair, though bald on top of his head.

"Monsieur Fourault, would you bring Miss Throop an order of *bécassines rôties* and *crème glacé a la vanille?*" M. Fourault took note with his usual solicitude. Lily swallowed at the thought of snipe. She disliked eating birds, and Wade knew it. The *crème* would be all right. "And another bottle of Clicquot for the company, if you please," Wade added.

The conversation resumed among the men on the topic of theater financing: *Othello* as the chosen bill for the autumn season and *Troilus and Cressida* for the spring.

"Are you only interested in staging Shakespeare, gentlemen?" Mr. Gerard asked. "Would you ever think of venturing into a Russian bill?"

"A Russian bill, Mr. Gerard?" Mr. Harrison asked, packing in large chunks of the *agneau rôti* with a teetering hand.

"I have the rights to a new play which I'm having translated, and that I believe would be a total smash in London. The playwright is called Chekhov, and he brings a very original chart to the table. The said play is called *The Seagull.*"

"A Russian play? Never heard of such a thing," Lord Godfrey said. "They do have caviar and bearskins, but theater?" The other men laughed and Gerard joined in, good-humoredly.

"Actually, it's a very interesting moment for the arts in Russia, especially theater," Gerard continued. "Two men are especially compelling: an actor called Stanislavsky and a playwright, Nemirovich-Danchenko, besides Chekhov, of course. They've recently established the Moscow Art Theatre, an impressive effort of a new ensemble for an open theater."

"You mean *popular theater?*" Wade said, derisively. "Well, there's little new in that. It's been rampant in the Continent for a while. And how would *popular theater* ever beat the classics?"

"I don't think it would be a question of beating anything, Mr. Wade," Gerard replied. "It's more the idea of inclusion of larger audiences and the use of realistic elements on stage. Its aim is to do away with clichés and outmoded traditions—"

"My dear sir," Wade interrupted. "There is a category of plays destined to never be outmoded."

"Tell me more about this actor Stanislavsky, Mr. Gerard," Lily said, stepping over Wade's words and ignoring his murderous side-glance.

"He's an amazing man, Miss Throop," Gerard said. "His rehearsals are something to be seen. He deals with a totally new method of acting."

"A new method of acting?" Lily echoed.

"Dear Lord," Wade snapped, "not another actor with a new theory on how to skin the cat!"

Mr. Gerard shot him a look, and turning back to Lily said, "I'd be happy to lunch another day with you and Mr. Wade to talk about this, so as not to bore the present company."

"Oh, yes! I would like that so very much!" Lily said.

"Unfortunately, Miss Throop has had to give up her lunch excursions," Wade said. "She is too busy becoming one of the best Shakespearean actresses in London."

"And so she is," Colonel Hamilton agreed, eyeing her with a besotted grin from across the table. Lily flashed him briefly with a sweet smile, an expression she had learned to pull on demand for this sort of occasion, but waited for an opportunity to ask Gerard further questions regarding Russian theater.

A handsome, slender waiter removed her untouched plate of *bécassins,* and placed another, small and golden, with a swirl of bisque-color *crème glacé* topped by a mound of caramel and pierced by three vanilla sticks. She recognized the waiter from other dinners at the Princes' Hall. She seemed to remember that he spoke with an accent that might be Italian or Greek. He smiled at her with quiet, twinkling eyes as he slid a shining silver dessert fork and spoon alongside her golden bowl. Thick, dark lashes shaded his eyes, and he wore his black hair slicked back, like Chut.

"Bring cognac and cigars, boy. And hurry," Wade barked. The waiter left and Wade glowered at Lily. The men around the table fell into an embarrassed silence. But soon after the cigars and liqueurs were brought and served, they resumed their business talk, ignoring her as they always did toward the end of long dinners.

The table next to hers, where the young men with orchids in

their coat buttonholes had sat with their sweethearts, was empty and being cleared. The girl wearing rows of pearls was pleading with the fat banker who looked away in disdain. The large family was getting ready to leave, their faces flushed with good food and contentment.

"My dear sirs," Lily heard Harrison say, "I'd be delighted to have you come to Boodie's Club after this, where we will meet with Lord Hamstring, who is also interested in our venture." A flash of alarm flared in Lily's brain. This change of plans meant that Harrison might not be escorting her home tonight, that she would have to ride alone with Wade.

Lily stabbed the *crème* a few times with her spoon before deciding she was not in the mood for dessert. The little silver fork sparkled under the candelabra lights beside her on the white damask tablecloth, and she fingered its cold, glistening body for a moment. Then, after checking that no one was looking, she opened her purse on her lap and slipped it inside.

It was past eleven when they rose from the dinner table, and she stood in the foyer waiting for her cloak to be brought up, avoiding her reflection on the beautiful mirrors decorated with painted flowers that surrounded the entrance hall.

Mr. Harrison tottered toward her. "My dear Lily, you look so spent. But as you see, investors do need a little gratification when about to empty their pockets." His crinkled nose and cheeks were tinged with deep pink as they always were after dinners in which wine and liquor ran freely, and there was that look of satisfied anticipation in his eyes that Lily had learned to associate with lucrative business transactions. Making money was what made Mr. Harrison tick. "I must go on with our guests tonight, dear," he explained. "Duty calls, but I have asked Herbert to get you home safely."

Lily clenched her jaw.

The coat-check girl arrived with her cloak, and Mr. Fourault helped place it over her shoulders. "*Ah, mademoiselle, quelle grande cape magnifique!* I hope you have the loveliest of evenings. It's always an honor to have you as our guest," he said, with gallant affection. Lily wrapped herself in the folds of the thick green velvet cape, amid the admiration of everyone around.

Wade walked quickly toward them adjusting the collar of his coat, took Lily by the arm, and hurried her out through the door. "Good night, Mr. Fourault. I hope the *bécassines* are more palatable next time, so your honored guest doesn't have to starve."

Outside a brougham cab waited and the cabbie stepped forward to open the door. It was a beautiful night with a clear indigo sky illumined by a pale sickle moon. The air felt cool, soothing, and Lily's frayed nerves felt momentarily relaxed in the quiet that enveloped her.

But the night was not over yet.

They settled inside the cab and Wade said, "I hope you're finished distributing your graces among manservants. Of course, Benjamin Gerard cannot be counted exactly a servant, but you were ready to rush over to Russia with him."

Lily closed her eyes and sighed.

A whole year had passed since the fire, and here she was, still wrestling with Wade. True that in that time she had gained much by way of professional success. She had acted in more than six plays and was now considered a seasoned actress who attracted audiences and could count on dazzling reviews in *The Era* and other papers. Most of it, if not all, was acting with Wade as male lead. Everyone who saw them perform together—public, critics, fellow actors—raved about their performances. It was said that they were graced with the divine chemistry that only certain actor pairs possess. Lily knew it too. There was just a way in which they meshed their energies that rendered the stage electric.

But how could that be when she hated him so much? When she felt so injured, so strangulated by him? When he had forced his brutality upon her, leaving her broken, spoiled forever? Could it be related to his training her? To his having molded her into the actress she was? He repulsed her physically; she detested his conversation; his constant tirades and ramblings; his stench of liquor and other signs of nightly debauchery. Most of all, she feared him horribly. And yet when they were on the scaffold all that changed. His mere utterance of words, the cadence of his voice as he recited texts, took her out of herself and made her rise into a different sphere, a place where her whole being quivered with meaning and reached a strange understanding of things.

Wade had remained the same desperate man, tenacious, driven by obsession to the point of destruction. But his overbearance had lately turned to a single goal: to obtain her ultimate surrender. Many times he had said to Lily, "I was not quite myself when I took you. But now it's done. We belong to each other and it is only a matter of time before you yield." He would insist she accept him as a lover, or even as a husband. Lily rejected him again and again, but he never ceased to persist. It grieved her to no end that most people who saw them together so often at public events believed she was his mistress. And how he gloated at these speculations.

Wade leaned over and looked out the cab window. "Oh, my! There goes our old pigeon-plucker. What a coincidence now that we are talking about manservants. I wonder what he's doing, daring to come into a fine neighborhood like this, and with a fine girl, too. And if it isn't little Lizzie Matchet, the daughter of old Matchet at the Alhambra! Always worming his way up, the scum."

Lily looked out her portion of the window and saw Chut, dressed in dark evening clothes, walking arm in arm with a pretty, well-dressed girl whose wavy red hair cascaded from under her bonnet past her shoulders to her waist. Chut strode by her side, engaged in attentive conversation. As the carriage glided by, Lily caught a closer glimpse of his profile, the corners of his eyes pulled into a laughing gaze, his lips stretched into a wide smile reaching close to his sideburns on his otherwise clean-shaven face. His handsome face, honest and untroubled; his jovial company, his graceful poise; all these things smacked Lily instantly, making her sit back while her chest contracted with a pang of misery.

Wade watched her intently. "I did hear rumors about her father offering him a job at the Alhambra Palace, and that he was planning to quit the Imperial soon."

"That can't be," Lily snapped, forgetting herself and beginning to tremble.

"And why not? It's extremely plausible for someone as ambitious and ungrateful as he," Wade said. By the tone of his voice she knew he would begin to tease her horribly. “Anyway, what’s it to you if he stays or goes? If he ever had any aspirations, I’m sure he’s found out by now that I made you mine. He wouldn’t want you after that, would he? I mean he might pretend at first in order to enjoy you, but later he would despise you. I know the darkness of men’s hearts when it comes to fallen women.”

A sob shook Lily so hard, that for a moment she felt the whole carriage shudder with her. She covered her face and wept.

Wade sighed. “Oh, that I would live to hear you weep like this for me,” he said mournfully. Then he added, sniggering, “But tonight, I’d be content to be your dog and lick your little hands and feet to console you from your woes.” He moved toward her and hugged her forcefully. Lily pushed him away, but he insisted, saying, “Not just your dog. I’m your beast, your Caliban, and only you can transfigure me into my angelic form. Don’t you see the power you hold over me?” He held her face and tried to kiss her while Lily fumbled with her purse and pulled out the silver fork. She wielded it above his face and strove to plunge it in, before Wade grabbed her hand. For a second he stood in shock at the gleaming weapon looming above him, but after recognizing it as a dessert fork, he exploded into roaring laughter. “My sweet Amazon! Stealing dainty forks to add to her armory collection,” he said, choking with mirth.

Lily pulled her wrist away from his grip. She was blind with rage. In a quick stabbing movement she jabbed him in his right arm. Wade howled and Lily dropped the fork. The carriage was brought to a halt. The alarmed cabbie said, “Sir, are you all right?” Lily opened the door and jumped into the street, turning her head one last time to see the cabbie descend from his box seat, crying, “Sir, sir! What’s amiss?”

She ran down dark labyrinthine streets, around the Inns of Court, pursued by the cabbie’s whistles for the police, until she came upon the open avenue that faced the river. Few carriages were in sight and even fewer pedestrians walked along the bank. She crossed the street toward the embankment and walked quickly along the riverside walkway, staying close to the retaining wall, until she was fully sure she was not being followed. Then she loosened up her pace, striving to calm her heart that still hammered in her throat and ears, deafening her. Unbearable thoughts rushed to her mind, shock and self-hatred at how she had conducted herself in the carriage; her wild, murderous rage against Wade, the smell of his hands as he came over her, images of the stuffed *béccassines* drowned in butter sauce over her plate. She stopped and leaned against the wall panting, and then bent over, sure that she would retch, but there was nothing to bring up. Neither could she cry. Her chest felt hollow; her gut bruised in the aftermath of her frenzy. The thought entered her head that she was beginning to resemble Wade, as if he were infecting her with his depravity. She was becoming desperate and insatiate, murderous, like him. Fits of violence seized her like demons and took her in the direction of actions she otherwise would never have chosen for herself. She had never hit or assaulted anyone in her life, not even in self-defense against Betty when she beat her hard. The thought of wielding a knife had never crossed her mind, or a fork for that matter. What was happening to her?

The old feeling of being sullied descended on her again, and a raw lucidity shone through her, filling her with self-deprecation. She was like a slave shackled to the stage by virtue of the contract she herself had signed. She had signed it distractedly, blinded by ambition to soar in the theater world, above the hordes of actresses roaming the West End. She had thought she was cutting through the mass of beautiful, talented girls hungry enough to do anything for a role, but her own arrogance had sold her into the hands of the likes of Harrison and Wade. They would own her to the very end, and hunt her down to the last set of boards in town if she dared to defect.

She carried on, dragging her feet, until she came to the opening of Lambeth Bridge, where she turned and walked along its barrier. It was an old, narrow suspension bridge, with two sets of tall towers from which stemmed long, twisted cables that curved down between the masts. The bridge had been closed to horse-drawn carriages a while ago, and was now only transited by pedestrians. But it seemed deserted at this hour, and with few lamps to illuminate its length, the long overpass was mostly steeped in shadows. She glided along the dark iron balustrade and stopped where the railing was at its lowest height. She leaned over it, resting her hot face on her folded arms. Toward the south bank, the thick cylindrical piers that supported the bridge stood like the legs of a colossus emerging from the water, as if holding up the ghostly structure and drudging it to the shore. The great city loomed dark across the riverside, with tall stone buildings heavy and brooding in the dim light. In the distance, carriages clattered over cobbled streets and remote voices of men shouted over a brawl. Farther away, the sleeping city pulsated with a low, barely perceptible hum.

But in her midst all was uncannily quiet, with not even the sound of a dripping oar to be heard. Looking down she faced the deep, silent body of the river. The mist had lifted from its surface and the water was thick and still, like fluid hematite. She thought of Chut's eyes, how much they resembled the flowing mass that lay below, so vast and fathomless, yet indulgent and kind. If she could only fold herself away from her frantic, crazed life, slip into this liquid bosom and be lost in the immensity of its depths, how soothing that would feel, what an easy and beautiful death it would be. Did she have the courage to remove her cloak, take off her shoes, climb over the balustrade, and jump into the river? And why would the river take her? It might not care to enfold her into its expanse. It might just spit her out toward the drab margins where she would be found in the morning by mud larks, a torn, breathing piece of flesh washed over the shingles, still blistering with shame.

"Halt there!" She jumped at the sound of a man's voice behind her, and turning around she saw a bobby standing a few feet away. His right hand was strapped over the truncheon hanging from his belt. The badge on his helmet shimmered in the dull light as he stepped toward her. She watched him study her rich dress under the open velvet cloak, trying to size her up. His face was young under the heavy helmet. "Miss, you shouldn't be here. This is not a safe place for a lady," he said softly. His eyes darkened as they shot toward the river and back to Lily. "Can I offer any help?"

"Yes, constable," Lily managed to say. "I think I'm lost."

CHAPTER 9

The next day Lily awoke curled up in Ruby's bed. She was completely dressed, hadn't even taken off her shoes. She vaguely remembered climbing onto her friend's bed and snuggling up to her, desperate to feel her body's warmth, to listen to the pace of her rhythmic breathing.

"Lily!" Ruby was in shock when she found her by her side. "When did you come in? You don't look well. What's the matter?"

"You never told me Chut was courting another girl," Lily said, conscious of her sunken face.

"I didn't tell you? And when do you and I talk anymore?" Ruby said. Her face was split between a yawn and a frown. "I haven't seen you for weeks. You live in a different world. Why are you surprised to find out that life goes on for everybody else?"

It was good to hear Ruby chide her in her brass sisterly way, and it brought the ghost of a smile to Lily's lips. Ruby with her strawberry-blond fuzzy hair in the morning, plump, red cheeks, and brazen blue stare, lying by her side in her thick flannel nightgown.

"I'm back, Ruby," Lily said, with a sigh. "Last night I fell short of dropping the ball."

"Aye, you look like you're back from the dead, bless your soul." Ruby sat up on the bed and gathered her woolly mane, combing it with her fingers and tying it with a ribbon behind her head.

"What about Chut?" Lily insisted.

"Nothing about Chut," Ruby said, feigning a bad mood. "You take your time off your high horse and find out by yourself," she added, turning to the window, still preening her unruly tresses.

Something on Ruby's finger shimmered as it caught the light streaming in through the glass. Lily reached out and seized her hand. "Ruby! Did Freddy give you this?" she asked, poring over the thin gold band engraved with flowers and leaves on Ruby's ring finger. "Are you engaged to him?"

"Not yet, not formally, but there's some talk of getting married." Ruby's face shone with a contentment Lily had never seen in her before. Lily sat up and hugged her friend. "Oh, Ruby, this is such splendid news!" she said, but behind the tight embrace she felt her chest shrink with a pang of solitude. Yes, life was going on, away from her, in spite of her.

"And we're nearly ready for our show at the Camel Hall. Oh, Lily, do come to the rehearsal today!" Ruby and Freddy had been working for weeks on a repertoire of Gilbert and Sullivan songs, but Lily had two performances that day, afternoon and evening, and had to decline the invitation.

"Pity! You'll miss it then," Ruby said, disappointed. "Later, everyone will convene at Madame Wattine's if you want to come," she added, giving Lily a sly look.

Mme. Wattine! Lily suppressed a cry of joy. Mme. Wattine was an old French woman who hosted a home-cooking establishment in her apartments, and had the best and most real French recipes in the whole of London: hearty, home-cooked food from Bretagne, her original homeland. Mme. Wattine had been a friend of Chut's mother, and it had been Chut who had introduced them all to her dining room. If everyone was going to Mme. Wattine's tonight, Chut would most probably also be there.

Lily went about her day filled with hope. She ignored Wade at the theater, where he walked around with his arm wrapped heavily in a bandage, telling everyone garish tales about his misfortune. "Deep in the thicket of London's night, I was accosted by a most fearful female brigand armed with machetes and poisoned arrows," he was saying to a group of young newcomer actors who groveled around him. "She jumped my carriage and stabbed me as I strived to save my lady's neck." He brandished the bandage-swathed arm at Lily as she passed. "Behold, madam, I shall bear this wound as the misused lover's badge of pride." His young audience laughed, while Lily swished by thinking him grotesque.

She walked around the theater looking for Chut, but didn't find him. She even went to Harrison's office, where she knew he now spent most of his working days, assisting the old man with the books when he was not accompanying him to meetings, but the office was empty. He might be working out of Harrison's apartments on Marylebone, where the old man would set up shop on frequent days when his gout acted up. She suddenly realized that she never saw Chut anymore. Gone were the days when he was always busy around the theater, when she often saw him standing above her on the catwalk, as he leaned over the rail. Or when she walked past him as she exited the stage, and he stood silhouetted against large footlights, arms akimbo, a black star against the moon, eyes swimming with side-glances.

Was it true that he was planning to leave the Imperial? Was his presence already seeping out of this drab old building toward the new glittering façade of the Alhambra Palace Music Hall? A sort of fever overtook her as she became restless in her search for him, scouring every backstage nook to no avail. Her anxious frenzy became hard to rein in when the time came to enter the stage, where she also struggled to concentrate on her lines. Even Wade shot her a few reproachful glances, furious at her scattered presence. Something felt amiss in the absence of Chut, something was being carved out of her, sliced out of the tissue of her abdomen, that made her want to cave in and cry.

After the balcony scene, when she exited the stage to wait on Friar Lawrence's speech, Wade clutched her by the wrist. "Where are you today? You're pulling out of the scene. Stay focused!" he hissed.

She shook him off and rubbed her wrist. "Touch me again and I shall scream of your monstrosity to the whole pit."

Wade shot her a burning look. "And I shall unbandage and expose your abuse, madam, so that your audience might begin to see the harpy that abides behind your cherubic face." He had started on one of his favorite harangues, but couldn't finish because it was his turn to walk back onstage.

Lily sat on a little stool by the wing, feeling spiritless. For the first time in her life she thought she might not be able to go back on the scaffold and finish the play. It wasn't even Wade. It was a feeling of being washed out, drained of the desire to stand upright, to open her throat and have her spirit flow out with the words she loved and lived for every day. Something inside her was closing down, enfolding her in a dark, shroud-like veil. She felt herself standing again on last night's bridge, looking out into the cold water. *Why didn't I jump*, she thought.

"Miss Lily," she heard a small voice say, "you must hurry, they're calling you in." She opened her eyes and saw Genevieve, her new assistant, kneeling in front of her. The girl placed a tiny, cold hand over hers and whispered, "Miss Ruby just stopped by and wanted me to remind you that she will see you at Madame's tonight. That *he* will also be there."

Lily had no time to acknowledge the message. An electrified shock sent a tingling streak through her, rousing her back into motion. She jumped up and strode toward the stage. The word *tonight* sang in her brain; it battered against the tight mesh of her being like the rapping of drumsticks. "Come, night; come, Romeo; come, thou day in night; For thou wilt lie upon the wings of night, whiter than new snow on a raven's back." She walked with ease into the stuffy setting of Capulet's grove and dove right into the teasing scene with the nurse: "Sweet, sweet, sweet nurse, tell me, what says my love?" But the word *tonight* would not leave her; it pounded inside her chest, it pulsed in her veins, opening a second track of lines that began to run silently in her throat. "Come, gentle night, come, loving, black-brow'd night, give me my Romeo; and, when he shall die, take him and cut him out in little stars. . . ."

If nothing else, she kept thinking, *I will live through until tonight.*

After multiple bows for the exhilarated, applauding audience, she rushed toward her dressing room amid exclamations of admiration and compliments from members of the cast and crew. "Oh, Miss Lily, that must've been one of your best performances," Genevieve said, as she helped her out of her costume. "You had us all crying at the wings. You should have seen Mrs. Potterlane! She was sobbin' her 'eart out, she was." The girl rattled on, while Lily became increasingly impatient to finish dressing up and flee the theater.

A din of voices and movement was quickly gathering in the corridor outside the door, and Lily heard the new stage manager, Randy, say, "Please gentlemen, line up nicely, no pushing."

"Genevieve, give me your cloak. I'll take it for tonight and you can have mine instead."

"Oh, Miss Lily, but I couldn't," Genevieve said, blushing.

"Yes, you could. Help me get out of here without being noticed. I've urgent business to attend to."

Genevieve gave her a knowing nod. She opened the door and said in a shrill voice, "Gentlemen, Miss Throop is making her way to the entrance hall to meet you all." The girl, despite her tiny, lithe figure, had a voice that could command crowds. A wave of protests and disappointed clucking of tongues followed as the horde of admirers trotted down the corridor toward the hall.

Lily wrapped herself in Genevieve's cloak, a plain, tawny piece of cloth, perfect for stealing out into the night undetected. Outside the theater she got into an old horse-drawn hansom and gave directions for the drive, careful to keep her face hidden inside the large hood. Wade was popular among many cabbies because they knew how generously he tipped after long nights of dissipation, when he was drunk and lonely enough to fraternize with anyone. He had, this way, acquired numerous confidants who watched for anything juicy to report to him for a good shilling.

The cab clattered over the streets while Lily sat back in the seat, a small squirm of disquiet uncoiling inside her belly. All of a sudden, her confidence was diddling away. What would she do if she were to find Chut with this new girl? How come she hadn't taken more time to groom herself? She'd hardly wiped off the stage makeup from her face and hadn't even given a last look in the mirror before she flew out of the room. And her hair—she was still wearing Juliet's tressed hairdo.

The cab stopped and Lily paid the fare before stepping down onto a deserted, somber little street. She walked up to the crusty façade of a small wine shop and rapped at the door. A woman dressed in black opened immediately. It was Mme. Wattine. In her hand she held a bottle of wine that she seemed to have just picked from among the piles of bottles that could be seen in half-light reaching up to the ceiling. The shop's interior was heavy with dusty wooden surfaces and thick mahogany floor planks. It smelled of wine-soaked wood.

Lily pulled back her hood and Mme. Wattine looked twice at her before saying, "Ah, Mademoiselle Lily, *ça fait si long temps*, we haven't seen you for so long. *Entrez*, come in." She was a tall, stately woman with a handsome face that featured one large, beautiful green eye while the other was covered by a black silk patch. There was a long, tragic legend about the loss of her eye, which Lily never seemed to remember. She and Mme. Wattine had always had a strained relationship, possibly due to the fact that she had never liked Lily for Chut, toward whom she felt an auntlike affection.

"Madame, what a pleasure to see you again! Ruby told me she was coming and I—" Lily started.

Mme. Wattine cut her off. "Oh no, Ruby and Freddy are held back at the Alhambra, something about their debut tomorrow."

Lily stood feeling uncomfortable, reluctant about turning back, until the old woman said with a sigh, "Come up, mademoiselle, since you are already here. Have a little coffee with us."

Lily followed Mme. Wattine up a narrow staircase and along a short corridor that opened into the dining room, where a group of about ten people sat around a large rectangular table engaged in lively conversation. The room was dimly lit by a few sconces placed along the walls, and a small round chandelier with artificial candles that threw a pool of dark yellow light into the middle of the table. There were two windows with muslin curtains overlooking the dingy street, and between them stood a cottage piano. Photographs of famous actors and musicians who frequented the house hung by the fireplace, along with a disparate collection of paintings, some of which were gifts from poor artists as gratitude for Mme. Wattine's culinary generosity.

The conversation was momentarily interrupted when Mme. Wattine and Lily walked in. Chut, who was sitting on the left, looked at her with surprise and stood up, saying, "Lily, what an unexpected pleasure!" He stepped toward her, politely shook her hand, and introduced her to the group. There were five men and two women, and a blond boy of about sixteen who sat next to his grandmother, an elegant older lady with wavy white hair. The boy, Amos, was introduced as a genius violin virtuoso who would be playing the following day at Covent Garden. He sat holding his musical instrument and smiled brightly at Lily. The two younger women were comediennes working out of some of the East End theaters that Lily had frequented in the past. They nodded at her.

One of the men, a young Italian restaurateur with round bulging eyes, a waxed moustache, and an ample red cravat, drew out a chair for Lily and sat by her side, eyeing her admiringly. 'Signorina Throop, what a privilege to meet you in person!"

Lily sat across from Chut and they stared shyly at each other. The table's coarse tablecloth was strewn with remnants of what looked like a thoroughly enjoyed supper. An array of empty wine bottles and siphons stood over knives and forks, pieces of bread and saltcellars. In the middle stood a glass cheese dome and a large platter with a few pieces of a Breton butter cake, a favorite among the guests. Through an open door at the far end of the space a bedroom could be seen, with a large bed on top of which the guests left their coats and wraps before they sat at the table, and where Mme. Wattine had just deposited Lily's cape. A bare-armed servant in a print dress walked in from the bedroom carrying a great tray laden with coffee utensils and served the guests.

The conversation resumed at the table. "Please, Mr. Quinn, do tell about this infamous play," said a heavy-accented middle-aged gentleman with short gray hair and a grizzly beard sitting at the head. He had been introduced as a Polish publisher of poetry and rare translations of philosophical works.

"All right," Mr. Quinn replied. "As I was saying, this happened in Paris four years ago, at the Théâtre L'Oeuvre. The play was *Ubu Roi,* by an Alfred Jarry. Imagine the shock of the audience when the first word spoken in the play was none but *merdre,* a most truculent French word for excrement. Forgive, *mesdames et mademoiselles,* the obscenity. Many spectators left immediately, while the remainder jeered and shook their fists until they broke into a riot at the end. Needless to say, the play was removed right away."

"But sir, Parisians are certainly not naïve when it comes to theater," said Beatrix, one of the comediennes. "Why did it shock them so?"

"It wasn't just scandalous language, dear lady," a gentleman called Mr. Coby said. "Its satirical content disrespected all authority, secular and religious, in the most vulgar ways." He slurped his coffee from the tiny cup he held daintily with two fingers. "The whole thing was sheer intention to provoke."

"But I heard that was the interesting point about it," Chut said. "A most insolent and comical banter on tyrants, a sort of caricature of *Macbeth*."

"A parody of *Macbeth* and *Punch and Judy* bundled up together," Mr. Coby said. "The actors pretended to be puppets, sir. It was most insulting."

"And what does our lovely tragedienne think of all this?" the Italian restaurateur asked Lily.

The question took her by surprise. She had been scrutinizing Chut with as much discretion as she could muster, recognizing the changes that had come over him since she last saw him, how he looked so much more mature and self-assured, and how at ease he felt among the company of intellectuals and artists that gathered at Mme. Wattine's little supping salon. "I welcome new ideas, sir," Lily said, without taking her eyes off Chut. "Actors are, after all, empty shells through which stories might be told in many different ways."

"Bravo, signorina!" the Italian restaurateur said, gawking over her. "It seems you don't just have a pretty head, but also a sharp brain inside."

"Yes, actors as empty shells," echoed the heavy-accented gentleman who had started the conversation. "And this idea of actors as puppets is a theory also propounded among us by young Gordon Craig—you know, Dame Ellen Terry's son. It tries to strip our stiff, actor-centered plays and return theater to more primitive and symbolic elements," he added as the conversation flowed into other topics.

There was a small commotion at the table as some of the guests got up, thanked and paid the hostess, and left after taking their leave of everyone. Beatrix and the other comedienne, Marina, the young musician, and his grandmother stayed behind. Amos sat at the piano and started playing the notes of a sonata. Mme. Wattine came to the table with a big pot of tisane and offered everyone a cup. Lily accepted. Her stomach was empty and the coffee had set her pulse racing.

The comediennes took chairs at either side of Chut. "I hear congratulations might be in order," Beatrix said, rubbing Chut's arm with familiar affection.

"Oh, nothing's official yet," Chut said, returning her smile.

"Is this about the Alhambra Theatre, or about its manager's dainty, gorgeous daughter?" Marina asked, combing his hair with her fingers in a taunting fashion.

Chut blushed and laughed uneasily. "Oh, I was just saying about the Alhambra."

"But they sort of go hand in hand, don't they?" Beatrix said teasingly.

Chut pushed her affectionately. "Of course not! And stop being so nosy."

"We already put down our bets on it, and we don't intend to lose our shillings," Marina said, ruffling his hair.

Chut slicked it back into place, and smiled at them. "Good night, ladies." The women got up laughing and went to the bedroom to get their coats.

Lily stared at Chut from across the table. "Is it true that you're leaving then?"

Chut looked up and said, "I'm thinking about it. It's a very good offer."

"I thought you were content with Harrison at the Imperial," Lily said.

"I have learned much with him these two years," Chut said, "but now it feels like a dead end." Lily hung her head. After a moment, Chut added, "But it doesn't mean I won't come back to see your plays."

"With your sweetheart?" Lily said, instantly regretting her bitter tone. Chut looked a little taken aback but said nothing. He only held her gaze, until she lowered her eyes. She felt exhausted, on the verge of collapse.

A new group came into the room, three young men and a woman, and settled noisily around the table. Amos got up from the piano, took up his violin, and started playing a few tuning notes in a corner of the room.

"He's still a bit nervous about tomorrow," said his grandmother, as everyone quieted down and turned to the young boy. "You know, Beethoven's violin concerto is a most challenging score."

Amos readjusted his chin on the instrument's rest-piece and after holding the bow over the strings for an instant, he began to play in bright, clear sounds that electrified the room. His left hand moved back and forth rapidly over the fingerboard while the bow rubbed the strings with a sort of fury. The music that poured out of the violin was the most beautiful Lily had ever heard: a pure, uninterrupted flow of soft, lyrical notes. At first they filled her with a thrilling tension that brought tears to her eyes. But as the notes escalated into more piercing sounds, she felt her nerves becoming taut, stretching through her whole body, like raw, almost painful tendrils reaching into the space around her. She became aware of every detail and texture in the room: the brown paper with tiny floral patterns that covered the walls, the china figures of cats sitting on the mantelpiece, the guests' faces that looked carved in wax under the dark yellow light that hung above the table. She was conscious of how estranged she felt from the whole scene; and yet how vulnerable she was to everything surrounding her.

She searched for Chut's eyes but he was looking away, plugged into the music. A quiet joy reflected on his whole being as he sat back in his chair, his shirt collar unbuttoned and loose above his trim waistcoat, his lips upturned in a sweet, sensual smile. *I've loved him all this time,* Lily thought, *but now it's too late—I've let him pass me by.* The violin notes became so shrill they felt like razors slicing the strings of her heart. She felt she would die if she didn't leave the room at once. She looked around for a way to escape, but realized it couldn't be done without being terribly disruptive. She held her breath and waited out the excruciating moments before the music abated.

The music stopped with a dramatic down-bow and everyone clapped heartily. As soon as the enthusiasm started dying down, Lily stood up and said, "I must be going now. Thank you, madame, for your kindness—" but she didn't finish her sentence because as she took a step, the room became a swirl of darkness that swallowed her up.

When she came to herself, she found Mme. Wattine over her unlacing her bodice and loosening her corset. "Mademoiselle, you are so tightly laced; it's no surprise you can't breathe properly," she said in her thick accent, working quickly with skilled fingers. Lily realized she was lying on the bed with the pile of coats, which had been neatly heaped on top of one another to make space for her.

The bedroom had no windows; the walls were covered with bottle-green wallpaper that made it look small and dark. It had two doors, one connected to the kitchen on one side, and a second that opened into the dining room and was slightly ajar. Through the opening she could hear the other guests getting ready to leave.

There was a slight knock at the door and Chut came in with a cup in his hand. "Here, Lily. It's warm wine, it'll do you good." Mme. Wattine lifted her up by the shoulders while Chut arranged a pillow behind her. She closed her eyes as they put the cup to her lips. She felt the sweet wine entering her body, pumping up the blood through her chest.

Mme. Wattine stepped back. "We shall let her rest awhile, and then you will need to take her home. She cannot stay here."

"No, of course not," Chut said. "I'll ask Amos to help me fetch a cab and have it wait downstairs until she's ready."

Behind her closed eyes, Lily felt them bustling around the bed as they picked her cape out of the coat pile and covered her body with it. Lily heard Mme. Wattine's dress rustling toward the door and leaving the room. She opened her eyes and saw Chut half-closing the door. He stopped for a moment. "Are you better? I sent for a cab to take you home."

"Don't abandon me, Chut," Lily pleaded, hardly aware of what she was saying.

"I'm only going to check on the cab," Chut said. "I'll be back up in no time."

"Don't leave me," she insisted, pulling her arms from the cape and reaching out to him.

He walked toward the bed. "Abandon you, Lily? I'd never do that. You know I'm always your friend." He sat down beside her and held her hands. "Oh, you are so cold! Don't talk now, just rest."

But Lily couldn't control her agitation. "Chut, I've thought so much about the time you came to see me. I was so savagely unkind."

"No, Lily, you were just honest. You belong to the stage and you need your freedom to follow your career."

Her eyes pooled with tears. "And so I thought then, but now I find that my career has all but usurped my freedom."

A frown came over Chut's face as he considered her words. "You can still make changes, Lily," he said. "Don't think that anyone can ever take away your greatness. It will follow you wherever you go." He gave a reassuring smile and then made a gesture to stand up, pulling his hands gently away from hers. But Lily held on tight.

"Can you ever forgive me?" she asked.

"Why, Lily, there's nothing to forgive. Life is like that." Chut shook his head smilingly, as if talking to a worried, silly child. "Love is like that."

But Lily saw a sting in his eyes. She clung tighter to his hands. "I don't deserve you, Chut."

"What are you talking about?" He was no longer smiling.

"It's my luck that when I finally realize I can't stop loving you, you've already made headway beyond my scope."

"But you never said—" Chut started.

"No, I didn't. That's why I don't deserve you."

They locked eyes. A moment passed. Slowly he bent down and touched her lips with his. Then he disengaged his hands from hers, held her face, and kissed her.

Mme. Wattine knocked on the door. "The cab, *cheri, c'est içi*, downstairs."

London, March 1st, 1900

Dear Harry and Alice,

For some time you have been asking me to write to you about the river Thames, for it has mesmerized you since you were a boy, Harry, when you read in history books how it provided a defense barrier against invading armies, and how it bore for centuries the riches of the world. So, today I shall write about the river.

But I won't write about it as a place to recall the greatness of the past, or about the engineering works that have cleaned up the waters that were once filthy. I will do as you ask and give you a personal view on this gentle body of water that glides along banks peopled by merchants, harbormasters, and all sorts of good city folk.

No matter the weather or my mood, I love walking toward the openness of its embankments—its brightness and bustle always make me forget the squalid overcrowding of the city. From here, the Thames is a landscape of contrasts. In a single gaze, one sees gasometers as well as the dome of Saint Paul, lime-heaped wharfs as well as the grassy gardens of the Temple, gloomy warehouses as well as handsome mansions with sweeps of white stairs lapped by the river water.

My friends who grew up along its banks tell me of the fisheries that used to be here, where perch and salmon were caught in great quantities. Of course, those don't exist anymore, and many of the fishermen's cottages have been turned into inns and eateries. These are the places we go on weekends to eat jellied eels and whitebait suppers, and sit outside on warm days watching wherries sculling up and down, and steamers bursting with happy holidaymakers.

But the river is most beautiful at dusk, when the

darkness gathers round its silver stream—and if the departing day turned ablaze in the twilight, the water carries pink and crimson reflections over its waves and eddies until night plunges everything into black.

Oh dear, how silly and poetic I feel today. . . .
Your Lily

CHAPTER 10

They met in a room over the river in the afternoons when Lily had a free day or just one performance in the evening. They both traveled separately so not to be seen together, and they exchanged notes for their rendezvous through Genevieve, who lived on a road close to Chut and Emily's, and could drop the little envelopes into their mail slot. Chut arrived mostly through the water, and Lily in a cab she had secured for her personal comings and goings through Annie, the maid at Mrs. Bakerloo's house.

It was also Annie who helped her find the room. She took her to her sister Mary, a young widow with two small children who lived in a fisherman's cottage in Putney by the river, and had a large private room on the second floor that she needed to rent.

Lily and Annie sat on a wooden bench by the hearth inside the crummy little cottage, while Mary, a plump, rosy-faced girl with lank yellow hair, sat on a stool facing them, and stared wide-eyed at Lily.

"Mary, the lady wants a room to meet with her betrothed, whom she will be marrying soon," Annie said to her younger sister. Mary didn't reply, she just gaped at Lily's hat, dress, and the colored beaded purse between her gloved hands. "She will pay you good money and will be very discreet," Annie added with some impatience.

"Mary," Lily started, "if you feel the arrangement is inconvenient—"

But Mary quickly said, "Oh no, it suits me very well." After looking Lily over again she said, breaking into a smile, "Oh, you theater ladies are so beautiful, and so free! God bless you, miss!"

Lily then paid her three months in advance and gave her an extra amount to have the walls painted, the floorboards well scrubbed and polished, and the woolen mattress beaten thoroughly. The next day she gave Annie money to buy the best, thickest Flemish linens available in London, together with a goose-down quilt, and shopped herself for embroidered hand cloths and a porcelain pitcher and bowl decorated with flowers. When the room was ready, she stared at it, pleased. It was a sunny afternoon in April and the glittering reflections of the water dappled the walls in little dances of light and shadow. The wrought-iron bed stood beautiful against the wall, and across from it the window opened like a large, unblinking eye over the river. She threw herself on the bed and buried her face in the soft pillow scented with lavender. *Tomorrow*, she thought, *I shall lie here with him*.

Seducing Chut had taken some persistence. She had surprised herself with how bold, how unrelenting she had been in seeking him out after the evening at Mme. Wattine's. Chut's initial reaction had been to back off with kind words, reassuring her of his friendship and offering all kinds of support, implying that he was engaged elsewhere. But she could feel his tension every time she approached, his in-breaths of self-control. And every time she searched his eyes, she pushed further against the membrane of his ambivalence, knowing how frail his defenses stood.

One day she asked him to walk with her along the embankment. They strolled for a while in silence, breathing in the cold air thick with smells of mud and water, listening to the sloshy lapping along the shingles of the river. "I realize this might be the last time we walk together like this," Lily said. "If your affections are engaged with your other girl, you need to tell me straightaway."

"There is no other girl anymore," Chut said in a matter-of-fact tone, looking ahead.

"And the Alhambra?" she asked.

"I turned down the offer."

"But is that wise? I mean, it's such a good opportunity," Lily said with suppressed joy.

"Nothing's wise about following one's heart," Chut said with a frown. "But sometimes it's just what one must do." Lily sensed a sadness in his voice. They walked on for a while without speaking; then he turned and stood gazing into her eyes. He lifted a hand to her face and pushed aside a strand of hair that had fallen over her cheek. "I'm a man who needs to keep things simple." His face was close to hers, their breath, like clouds of steam, intermingled in wreaths.

"But you doubted."

"I never doubted who I loved best."

"But you doubted me."

Chut said nothing, only took her hand and led her away.

Later, they sat across from each other in an old, dark tavern drinking ale, riveted upon each other's eyes. There still remained a discussion about the logistics of their togetherness, an explanation about the delicacy of her position in the Imperial. "Chut, if I were to love you openly," Lily said, "my position at the theater would become very complicated."

Chut knit his brows while he considered this for a moment. "Are you worried about Wade's feelings?"

"He's nothing to me. But I'm bound to him by an awful contract that gives him much power over me."

"A contract? Have you consulted a lawyer about it?"

Lily faltered. She took a sip of her ale and averted her glance. She didn't want to discuss the contract with Chut now. She had consulted lawyers and they had all come to the same conclusion. As unscrupulous as it was, it was legal, and she had signed it freely. It would just have to run its course for five more long years.

Her silence weighed on the table.

Finally, Chut said, "Come, it's late. I'll walk you back home."

Days later she brought Chut to the cottage in Putney for the first time. She asked him to close his eyes after they stepped off the skiff onto the dock, took him by the hand, and led him along the towpath into the house and up the small, rickety stairs. Once inside the room, he opened his eyes and marveled at the pretty space, walking around and observing everything with pleasure. Then he sat on the bed, took her hands, and looking up into her eyes he asked, "Are you sure this is what you want, Lily? I can wait, you know."

"Is that what you want?" she asked.

"You know I'd still marry you."

She kneeled before him. "Chut, I just want to love you. Will you think any less of me for it? Tell me if I'm being too brazen, too bold . . ."

"Why do you even ask such things?"

They lay on the bed fully dressed holding each other for a long while, with shy kissing and stroking, glancing at each other as if they were seeing each other for the first time. Little was said. A cool, pearly light filled the room. Distant sounds were heard out on the river: a steamer crossing and sending ripples washing against the banks, two women walking and laughing on the path below. Lily felt her body flutter all over, yearning for Chut's warm hands, and yet, she was gripped by fear. How would her scarred body react to Chut's lovemaking? How would she begin to confess her brutal deflowering? And if she didn't, would he notice her wound and shrink away? Unease crept into her as she considered these things and realized how much she was putting herself at risk.

She opened her lips to speak, but Chut said, "Oh, Lily, you're trembling," and pulled her closer. Then he looked into her face and broke into a chuckle. "I hope my suffragette is not getting cold feet, for there's no turning back here. And I intend to make every second of this very worthwhile." Then he kissed her passionately.

So, she let everything go. How did she ever think she'd be able to resist Chut's caresses after having come this far? The tenderness of his lips as they kissed, his smiling eyes watching hers while deft hands conquered the impossibly tiny buttons of her bodice. Her body ached to be engulfed in his, as if it knew that his warmth had the power to soothe her painful scars, to overturn the ugly memories that were etched in the tissues of her skin. How could the same scenario unfold either into paradise or into the most vicious hell? Was it love that made the difference, or was it the quality of the soul, the inner substance of the man she held in her arms? Why was she afraid? Whatever she had experienced in the past had nothing to do with this. Her flesh rippling with exquisite thrills, her whole being craving for a union that would rewrite the poetics of love all over again. Chut was undoing what Wade had mangled, restoring the innocence of her flesh, melting away her unease until her body could soften, open of its own will and sprout into flames. Then all thoughts and memories blurred, and she was swept into the swirl of their embrace.

Since then, the room had become their secret meeting place. Lily nearly always arrived first, rushed up the creaky little staircase, and after a quick smoothing of a pillow or two, she stood by the window looking out for Chut, hoping to catch sight of his wherry approaching the wharf; see it bob gently in the water while he stacked the oars inside; watch his agile body leap up onto the dock and pull the bow toward the post, where with quick, skilled flips of the rope he would tug her tight. Then Chut would straighten his jacket and comb back his hair with his fingers before looking up to the window. But she would have already retreated toward the chair by the bed, trying to steady her pounding heart as she heard his limber steps climbing the stairs to the room. The moment he entered, closed the door, and turned to her, Lily jumped up from her chair and ran to him, clasping him tight in her arms, breathing in the smell of water he always brought with him. "Oh, Chut, why did you take so long? I thought I'd die if I had to wait a moment longer."

"Shhhh," he would say in an extended whisper, lifting her a few inches from the floor and walking her to the bed. "There might be little children sleeping in the house."

The hours flew by as they lay together. Time was always a short commodity between them, every moment precious. Glances, caresses, every word competed for a slot in these cramped, passionate encounters. Time slipped by so quickly it felt cruel, a swift knife carving away at their slotted term. For something in Lily knew they had only been allotted a certain quantity of moments, and this consciousness made her anxious, desperate to enjoy every drop of the present, so that she sometimes drowned in her own agitation. Then only Chut could bring her around, holding her until she relented, mooring her slowly until she could lie low, like his wherry down by the dock, rocking placidly in the water, oblivious of everything.

So the spring weeks sailed by.

Back at the theater, the run of *Romeo and Juliet* was coming to an end, and rehearsals for *Othello* were starting. A new actress had been engaged as understudy for Ophelia, a young, pretty Cornish girl called Angharad Bates, whom Wade had taken under his wing, much to Lily's hopes. Besides that, a small controversy had emerged around keeping Sam Drake, the actor who had played Mercutio in *Romeo and Juliet*, to play the role of Iago in *Othello*. Part of the problem was that Drake's reviews had somewhat overshadowed Wade's. He was a brilliant actor, a wiry individual with knifelike features and stinging eyes, whose gesturing and mobility onstage were spellbinding. But he was also personally awkward, a loner who slunk away from society the moment he stepped off the stage, and many in the company found him disquieting and distrusted him.

"He's a dark horse holding back on some secret," Mrs. Potterlane said one day in front of Lily. She was annoyed because Drake's slim body required extensive taking in of the former Iago's costume and it was needed in a hurry for the next day's dress rehearsal. One of her seamstresses agreed, "Yes, miss, no wonder they call 'im Sam the Snake, that is, behind 'is back they do."

Nonetheless, he was hard to dispense with, and all efforts to find someone equal in level of performance proved futile. So Sam stayed and played Iago, and Lily was glad for it because she found him intriguing, although she didn't dare befriend him for fear of provoking Wade any further.

Although *Romeo and Juliet* had not been a great commercial success for the Imperial, it had brought Lily very good reviews and many notes of adoration from admiring audiences. The day after the last performance, Wade walked into Lily's dressing room with a bottle of champagne and closed the door after having rudely dismissed everyone lined up in the corridor. He poured two glasses and after offering her one raised his and said, "To the woman who is ruining me, but still gives me the most pleasure on the stage."

"Ruining you!"

"Yes, ruining me. If I could bed you, madam, like any ordinary mortal, I wouldn't have to put up costly productions just to enjoy you briefly in my arms."

Lily laughed, spilling her champagne. "What a pompous old geezer you are!" She felt at ease, happy, her body still throbbing with memories of Chut's lovemaking hours before. She had even pronounced "old geezer" with some affection, and was looking at Wade with an open smile, the type one offers to an old friend. But she saw his face cloud over, as if he read into her, darkly. She checked herself. "Is it true that there have been losses with this run?"

"More than we can handle at the moment," Wade said. She could see him sliding into one of his black moods. They sipped champagne in silence. Wade looked around the room with a scornful eye. Bouquets of flowers sent by patrons and fans were arranged on the floor. "We might soon have to leave this old ship with its exorbitant rent and find a new stage. Hopefully, your flowers and corny notes will follow you." He picked up a couple of cards from the roses nearest to him. " 'My dear Miss Throop, please receive these flowers as a sign of my adoration,' " he read aloud. "Dear Lord, how humdrum and pathetic people can be." He took up another note. " 'Miss Throop, you are my angel, someone who makes me weep with uncontrolled joy . . .' " He put the card down and said, "Well, this one is downright revolting." His eyes fell on a small bunch of violets on Lily's boudoir and he picked them up. They were tied together with a simple string and looked as if they had been purchased at the market or from one of the little ragged girls out on the promenade. "Look at this," he said, "a true token from a simple heart." He tossed them back over the boudoir. "There is one thing you won't deny: I've made you grand. Your fame extends from the patrician to the plebeian; from mansions to shanties they sing your praise. And you, madam, still ungrateful, still snubbing."

Lily knew that a chain of pleading would follow and thought of possible excuses to have him leave the room. But Wade stopped short, turned to the boudoir, picked up the violets again, and sat looking at them with intent.

Lily stood up nervously. "I need to ask you to leave now. I must dress and get ready to go." But Wade didn't even raise his eyes. He was fingering the flowers, deep in thought. She tried to stay composed through her mounting anxiety. She couldn't bear the image of Chut's flowers wilting under Wade's touch. She wanted to rush over and snatch the violets from his hands, as if it were a small child in danger of being hurt. She took a step toward him and tried to seize the flowers, but he tugged at them, hard. The string unfastened and the violets scattered over the floor. Wade crushed them with his foot.

"You're a monster!" Lily cried, bursting into tears.

"And you, the monster's very own whore. And his whore only." He stood facing her, pounding with rage. Then he turned and began scooping up the bouquets and floral wreaths around him and tearing them apart. When the floor was covered with the carnage of multicolored petals and twisted stems, he stopped and stood panting. His hands were bleeding, his face glistening with sweat. Lily sobbed quietly, pressed up against the wall at the back of the room.

"Call your maid to clean up this mess," he said. His eyes had stopped radiating hatred, and now looked bruised with infinite grief. "It's you who turns me into a monster, with your unlove and your disdain." He left the room, slamming the door behind him.

A few days later, when Lily arrived at the cottage, Mary opened the door with an expression of concern on her face. "They've been 'ere miss, two blokes, asking questions. Didn't like the look of 'em. Very cheeky they were, wanting to come in the house and look around." She stood at the threshold swathed in a long yellowed apron sprinkled with baking flour, with her youngest perched on her hip, a pallid toddler with corn-silk hair and a snotty nose. "I told 'em to beat it, I did, or I'd call my brother-in-law."

Lily went up to the room and sat by the window. Chut wouldn't arrive until later in the evening and she had a few hours to kill. He'd been away for over a week in Bristol where Harrison was negotiating a lease in a theater for a summer run. It was a bright early summer afternoon. She'd come in with the intention of taking a walk along the water and maybe sitting in the sun outside the cottage for a little while, but now she felt afraid. Her hiding place was no longer a safe haven. In truth, it had become harder for her and Chut to disentangle from each other and they had started spending nights together, every day more neglectful of their secrecy.

Now the hunt had begun. Wade had hired a couple of sleuth rogues. She might, of course, have anticipated something like this after the recent scene with him. Things were again very strained between them, Wade having taken on a dark, silent, deeply injured bearing on the matter. He walked up and down the theater in the company of Angharad, pretending to ignore Lily, but reeking of rancor and violent yearning.

The tension between them was at its height during rehearsals. It was just so ridiculous, Lily thought, that they would be performing *Othello* at this particular time—a stupid, cruel joke of fate. The bill had been decided nearly a year ago, but that it had merged with this particular moment felt grotesque. And the way the production was being shaped seemed to bring her predicament full circle. Following the financial crash of *Romeo and Juliet,* there had been a discussion about how to stage *Othello* to draw audiences back into the Imperial, and Wade and Harrison had hired a new director with an innovative approach, William Swift, who had just returned from working in Paris at *La Comédie-Française.* Swift, an energetic man with shrewd eyes and a pointed goatee he pulled at constantly when in thought, proposed a looser delivery of the text paired with closer physical relationships between characters and more movement on stage. The murder scene between Othello and Desdemona was to be blocked in a very dynamic way, to effectively create a real struggle between them. Desdemona would put up a fight against her jealous husband, first trying to seduce her way out of the situation, and then attempting a desperate escape, while Othello encroached upon her with violence and finally smothered her under a long, brutal kiss. The result was quite fearful. Cast and crew members observing the final dress rehearsals from the wings stood frozen with consternation.

Even Mr. Harrison was sort of shocked, and Lily heard him say to Wade, "Isn't this a bit overboard, Herbert? We need to consider our audience." And she was incredulous to hear Wade reply, "Come on, Uncle, this is perfect. Let those prigs sitting comfortably in the pit be reminded of their own cruelties toward their wives and daughters."

The night of the opening, the audience was indeed very disturbed, with a lady or two swooning in their seats and a few uptight, indignant couples leaving the theater at the most inconvenient moments. But the press had raved. An article in the *Daily Telegraph* the next morning read:

> "We've had plenty of stuffy, straight-laced desdemonic smotherings along the last decades; enough of limp, whimpering murders committed over brocaded settees where not even a drop of spittle might fall. We need to take back our Elizabethan and Jacobean stages where vials of real blood were lavishly dispensed alongside sheep's lungs, gall-bladders and livers to furnish carnage scenes. Not to speak of those dead bodies actually hanging on the stage. We can only applaud this new valiant approach to our classics."

Despite high controversy and hot discussions all over London's drawing rooms, gentlemen's clubs and tea houses, audiences fought for tickets and the house was full at all times.

Lily's reviews were also outstanding. It was the height of her career so far. And yet, since the beginning of rehearsals and peaking in the first few nights, acting out the murder tore her apart each time, brought her back to the experience of being assaulted by Wade in the green room during the fire. As much as she tried to use the scene to resurface and expiate her memory of pain, shame and the core of her fear would not leave her. Every time Wade as Othello hissed, "Down, strumpet," as he threw her to the floor and she beseeched, "Kill me to-morrow: let me live tonight!" she felt as if she were reliving every excruciating snippet of the rape. She started to think that a part of her soul would be forever more trapped in those moments with Wade.

Otherwise, her most pressing concern was the need to confess everything to Chut, but her fear of the outcome overrode her daily intentions of straightening it all out. She knew this piece of knowledge would open a can of worms. Chut would be horrified, furious; he might want to take it further with Wade, with Harrison, even with the police.

"Well, don't you want to be avenged?" Ruby asked her one afternoon, when they were washing each other's hair with vinegar in Mrs. Bakerloo's washroom. "I mean, wouldn't you want your man to restore some justice? I'd want Freddy to go out there and have his mug smashed for my sake. You think of Chut as a boy who needs protecting, as if he would never man up to Wade. I see him differently. I know him as a tough lad who can handle things."

Lily shook her head. She saw Chut as too clean-handed to contend with a beast like Wade, but she realized how her silence slighted him. One night she woke up shaken by these thoughts. He lay beside her, his body heavy with sleep and splayed across the bed. She lit a candle and hovered above him. His lips were slightly parted, his black curls disheveled on the pillow. The thick linen sheet was thrown over his hips, and his chest, covered in fine dark hair, rose gently with each breath. His strong arms lay stretched out and upturned, revealing a thick network of blue veins descending toward the relaxed, sturdy hands.

He opened his eyes and smiled. "What time is it? Why didn't you wake me?"

"I wanted to watch you sleep," Lily said.

"You tumble me to no end and then let me sleep so I miss my turn looking at you? That ain't fair."

"Who said love was fair?"

"You're right, it ain't," he replied. "But you are. Fair. The fairest lass I've ever laid eyes on along these banks," and sliding his hand through her tresses, pulled her face to his and kissed her. They lay in each other's arms watching the pale dawn spill into the room and efface the shadows around them. "I've been thinking that if we go on like this, we might be in danger of calling in a little one," Chut whispered. "What shall we do then? Me, I wouldn't mind a babbie girl that looks like you."

Lily turned her face away. "I cannot have a baby now."

"But if it comes."

"It cannot come."

"But if it does."

Lily's eyes filled with tears. Of course, she understood there could be a complication. She was taking certain precautions that she and Ruby had learned about from one of the older actresses who also lodged at Mrs. Bakerloo's, but she knew that they could fail any day given their frequent, ravenous lovemaking.

But she wasn't crying about the baby question. She was crying about Chut; about her deceit, her betrayal of him; about the fact that, even right now, she felt incapable of opening her mouth and confessing the tale of her despoiling. She was crying about his dark eyes, the way they would contract with pain when he learned of the rape, and how those tender, laughing irises would be ripped open, stripped of the veil of goodness through which they saw the world.

Chut held her face and said, "What is it, Lily? You can't be so upset about what I just said. Something else troubles you. Why can't you talk about it?" But she denied it as usual and surrendered in silence to his soothing embraces.

Now it was all just a matter of time. The rape lay between them in the very bed like the corpse of a child murdered in the woods waiting to be discovered.

CHAPTER 11

A distant rumbling shook Lily from her slumber. Wind rattled the window frame, and as she looked through the glass she saw a mauve sky darkening with thunderheads. They sailed in angry, flowering masses over the river, with outbursts of weak, far-off lightning blinking around their charcoal fringes. It was seven o'clock in the evening. It would soon start raining. She hoped Chut wouldn't be caught in the water.

As soon as she had formulated this thought, she heard the main door open downstairs, and Mary's voice greeting him. She stood at the top of the stairs, impatient to embrace him, but Chut followed Mary into the kitchen. She listened to their conversation, and to Chut promising to help her reinforce the door against the upcoming autumn floodings, something Mary had been fretting about. Lily grew impatient at their extended talk and decided to go down to meet him, but he finally started up the stairs.

She put her arms around him and felt his jacket and hair moist from the rain. "You're wet. Let's hang your jacket."

But he pushed her aside gently. "It's nothing." He walked into the room and took a seat by the window. "I won't be staying long, Lily. I have to get back," he said avoiding her eyes.

"But I haven't seen you in over a week. What could be so pressing?"

He didn't answer, only looked out the window, his face pulled into a frown.

"Why?"

He turned to her dark, muddy eyes. "I saw you yesterday in the play."

"I didn't know you had returned early from Bristol—and why didn't you come backstage?"

Chut attempted a grin. "I left after the strangling scene."

"Oh," Lily said, and froze when she saw him drop his eyes to the floor. "Many people are distressed by it. Did it upset you?"

"I might begin by saying it ain't easy watchin' one's woman being thrashed around the stage."

"You can't look at it that way," Lily retorted. "It's a performance and I'm an actress."

"True. And I ain't never said anything before." He turned to the window again.

"What's the matter, Chut?" Rain fell over the windowpanes like gusts of shot.

He looked down at his hands. "When we talked about other people in our lives, you said you had never been his lover." He pronounced each word slowly, as if measuring every sound. *And so I haven't,* Lily wanted to reply instantly, but she felt her lips trembling. Chut then added, "When I saw you with him last night, I understood differently."

Lily's heartbeat quickened. She sat down on the bed and said in a choked voice, "Chut, I swear to you before God I've never been his lover." She wrung her hands, fighting back tears. He glared at her. His eyes smoldered in a way she had never seen before. The darkened light stealing in through the window gave his face a swarthy hue, a wolfish quality that reflected along the jawline sharpened by the room's shadows. It made her shrink with fear.

"I swear I never gave him anything," she added in a smaller voice, and then took a deep breath. "During the fire he . . ."

Chut stared at her with wide eyes.

"He forced me. I tried to fight him off, but couldn't escape." She paused. "There's been nothing else."

"During the fire!" Chut echoed. He sat for a moment gazing at her without seeing her, as if he were processing every fragment of information contained in those three words. Then he stood up abruptly, took a few heavy steps toward the window, rushed to the opposite wall, and punched it hard. The room shuddered. A picture hanging by the bed fell to the floor, its glass scattering in shards. Chut's fist hit the wall again and again, and then he leaned his forehead against it, panting. "Blasted deuce!" he murmured. "Bloody, fucking fiend." Then he turned around with furious reddened eyes and said in a hoarse voice, "And you never thought of telling me this before?"

"I know I should have. It was just so difficult, I was full of shame."

"Shame! You lay in bed with me all these times and you didn't think of telling me this? And you talk of shame?" Chut paced up and down the room. "You let me walk by that devil for months without knowing anything!"

"I was afraid. The man is mad. I wanted to protect you."

Chut's expression turned into an ironic smirk. "You wanted to protect me?"

The question hung in the air.

There was a long silence. Outside, the wind blew in gusts and the water lapped wildly over the docks. The room was filled with yellowed, charcoal light. Lily sat holding back her sobs. She ached for Chut to comfort her, but he didn't move. After a moment, he returned to the chair and sat with his elbows on his knees and his head in his hands. The dull patter of rain filled the room as the thick of the storm drifted away.

"What am I to you, Lily? Just a plaything? You know how much I've given up for you, but in return you can't even deign to give back a little bit of truth."

"A little bit of truth! Chut, if you knew how hard this has been . . ."

"How am I to know anything if I'm not told!" he thundered. They heard one of Mary's little boys crying downstairs, as if he had woken up, startled. They were silent until the child stopped whimpering.

"Can you forgive me?"

Chut didn't answer. After a moment he said, "I was never enough for you, Lily. I should've listened to others when they said that a lady befriending a workingman never squares up. And why I ever agreed to this game . . ."

"This game!" Lily cried out. "How's that fair?" She wiped the tears from her face and rushed over to him, kneeling at his feet. "This is how you see me, a lady befriending a workingman? I'm just a woman loving a man." She put her hands on his knees and looked up at him. "What I feel for you is beyond what others may say or understand, that part of my heart is open to you alone. . . ."

Chut stood up. "You're full of pretty words, Lily. But you don't love me, or anyone else." He made toward the door and shot her a last hard look before he left the room. "You only love the stage."

It was past one o'clock in the morning when she returned to Mrs. Bakerloo's boardinghouse. Her eyes were swollen and she had the most horrific headache. Moreover, the trip back had been grueling, with the horse-drawn cab getting stuck in the mud several times along unpaved roads, and she having to step down while the cabbie pushed the carriage along with the old draft horse. She was thoroughly drenched and the fringes of her dress and petticoat were soiled and splattered with mud.

Annie opened the door, surprised to see her come in so late and in such a state. "One of the girls from the theater's been 'ere for hours, miss. She says it's urgent."

Up in her room, she found Genevieve huddled up in a ball in one of the armchairs facing the empty fireplace, asleep. Lily tiptoed around her trying not to wake her, but Genevieve opened her eyes and sat up as if she had been stung. "Genevieve, what are you doing here?"

"Oh, Miss Lily, I had to come. I had to tell you. 'Tis so terrible," and she started crying.

Lily sat by her side. "What is it? I'm sure something can be done about it."

"Mr. Chut has been arrested, miss. They took him from the theater after he beat up Mr. Wade. He burst into the evening rehearsal with Miss Angharad, took off his jacket, ran toward Mr. Wade and started hitting him without a word. It took five men to get him off of him. And you should 'ave seen how Mr. Wade was bleedin' all over the floor—they say he has a broken nose; his eye was shut and his face all banged up. Someone called the constables and they took Mr. Chut away. Mr. Wade was calling him names and sayin' he'd make sure he goes to prison. Oh, Miss Lily, everyone's so upset."

Lily stood up. Her head was reeling. "Genevieve, where did they take him, do you know?"

"I don't, miss. I figure you can't do anything until morning." Genevieve dried her tears with the back of her hand and stood up. "I'll be going now."

"No, Genevieve. Stay the night. Please." After Lily settled them both in the bed, she bid her to narrate every detail of the event again, until she could no longer keep her eyes open.

The next morning she rushed to the theater. The charwoman, who was on her knees still scrubbing the stains off the wooden boards, gave her more or less the same version of the story. "Never knew our young Chut was so hot-blooded, but then, I've 'eard Mr. Wade puttin' him down so many times. He's a mean master, he is." She wiped the sweat off her forehead and threw the washing rag down on the floor. "Even his blood is as hard as the devil to clean off."

A group of stagehands and other crew members confirmed the story, and added pieces of information about Chut that distressed Lily, such as how his knuckles were swollen to nearly double their size as he finally offered his wrists to be handcuffed, and how his nose and lip were badly cut and bleeding all over his shirt. There were also discussions about where they might have held him during the night and if he had seen the justice of the peace in the morning, and whether they had already transferred him to a prison.

As to the origin of this altercation, rumors were quickly rising and people were giving Lily looks. Around a corner, Lily overheard Mrs. Potterlane murmuring to a small group outside the costume room, "She's been playing them both, she has, one for the money and the other one for the fun."

Inside the green room a group sat in tight, whispered conversation. Michael Falloway, Othello's understudy and one of Wade's adversaries, was discussing the situation from a legal point of view.

"It would be assault, only that Wade's recent history of brawls and brothel arrests weakens his position as plaintiff. He'd do well to withdraw charges if he doesn't want scandal leaking into the press."

Lily marched into Mr. Harrison's office and found him sitting with his lawyer, Mr. Eccles.

"Dear Lily, what an unfortunate incident," Mr. Harrison said, his hand teetering more than ever as he tried to clean his eyeglasses with a little cloth. "And the worst part is that Herbert is certain that Chut has misappropriated funds, and is intent on incriminating him. I myself would have never thought . . . I know him since he's a boy."

"Mr. Harrison," Lily said, "you don't believe for an instant that Chut has misappropriated anything. This is all ludicrous."

"I'll say, it would explain many things in terms of your books, Mr. Harrison," Mr. Eccles cut in bluntly, ignoring Lily. "Someone's been keeping a double ledger that has masked the situation of insolvency and led to the present state of ruin."

"But I don't remember Chut having the key to—" Mr. Harrison started, but seemed to forget what he was going to say, and then added, on the verge of tears, "Who's going to help me now with all the paperwork and the running around?" Suddenly, he looked a very old, shriveled little man.

It was two o'clock in the afternoon when Lily arrived at Wade's house and rang the bell. Simmons opened the door and began reciting a well-rehearsed script: "Mr. Wade is indisposed and cannot receive . . ." But Lily pushed past him leaving him in mid-sentence.

She tore down the corridor toward the library, and stormed in. "Release him immediately!" she cried.

Wade lay recumbent on a large chaise longue next to the window that seemed to have been improvised as a bed for the occasion. He turned toward her, unfazed. "You finally condescend to come take stock of the injuries I've endured for you, and the first thing you do is give me orders?" His face was a mass of purple turning black at the edges. A large piece of white gauze had been placed over his nose and secured with bandages; one swollen eye was shut and appeared elevated in a greenish mound, tortoise-like, and the other eye seemed to have been injected with blood around the iris. Wade's right arm was in a cast.

But Lily was not moved. "Release him or I'm capable of killing you," she screamed.

Wade laughed. "Oh dear, always the tragedienne! And what better thing could you do for me than seal my fate with a passion crime? I should be honored."

"I'm serious, Herbert. You don't know how far I can go."

"Herbert! Do I hear you call me by my name? If so, even the butchery of my countenance has been worthwhile."

"Withdraw charges and publish an acknowledgment of error in the papers."

Wade opened his functional eye in fake surprise. "I see Miss Minx has had a splash at the Inns of Court."

"You know very well this is all a farce. He's innocent. Everyone will vouch for him."

"He's not innocent of assaulting a gentleman."

"A gentleman! Knowing your reputation he'll get off with a fine that I'll be happy to pay myself."

Wade sat up. "He won't get off with a fine on embezzlement charges." His tone was no longer humorous. "The courts couldn't give a hoot about who vouches for him at this point. You see, bankruptcy tends to be a process where ferocious creditors will stop at nothing to bludgeon possible culprits to death. He'll not get out of this in one piece. A charge of embezzlement within insolvency procedures is quite sticky, I'm afraid."

Lily gasped. She felt crushed, as if Wade had administered her a blow and taken the wind out of her. She was back in his power, a small bird in the hands of a depraved hunter. What was it that made her feel so impotent in his presence? She only knew it had something to do with the change of tone in his voice, that dark, sordid sibilance he had just employed. Its sound engulfed her, spreading harsh, dissonant vibrations into her deepest fibers, making her undulate with fear.

"Charges of theft have always had severe consequences," Wade continued, "particularly for the dispossessed. In our Middle Ages, a poor man charged with theft might have his hands cut off. But of course, in today's civilized England, we don't subject our convicts to such barbarities. We let them rot in dark, dank prison pits, until their flesh and bones dissolve of their own, until their souls snap by themselves."

He paused and Lily stood dejected, her eyes lowered to the floor. For the first time she understood that the same voice that made her soar over the stage feeling invincible could also mash her into a soft, pulpy mass of powerlessness. Wade's dominance of her—and maybe of everyone else—lay in his masterful manipulation of speech. She realized with terror that she might never be able to overcome this weakness.

"Mind you," Wade carried on, "still to this day a man can hang in London for robbery. Not publicly anymore, but behind the gates of grimy penitentiary yards."

Lily felt the life drain out of her body. She looked around for a chair to lean on, but she was in the middle of the room, away from all furniture. She stood, pushing away the horrifying images that threatened to invade her mind. She ached to embrace Chut, to wrap him up tight in her arms and, in a desperate, swooping dive, pull him out of his sordid jail, but realized she herself was about to be put to the rack by her tormentor.

Wade gave a melancholy sigh. "I suppose it is more humane. At least for the viewer. It's quite fearful to watch the drop, to hear the grind of the rope as it sways with its grappling load."

The room felt hollow, unreal. Lily's fingers tugged at the trimmings of her sleeves. She swallowed hard. "Release him and I'll do anything you want."

Wade perked up. "Anything?"

She didn't answer, only stood looking directly at him, stinging with shame. They stared at each other for a moment, while every instance of her disgrace at his hands burned in her eyes. He stood up, with more suppleness than she would have thought him capable of given his injuries, and took a few steps toward her. Her whole body flinched with fear. Her heart thumped painfully against her ribs. She parted her lips to take in a fast few breaths.

Wade stopped in his tracks. Lily thought she saw a wince behind the smug mask of victory, but he covered it over, saying, "No, none of that. Offering me a mere blood sacrifice to save a lover would only humiliate me further." He paced, while Lily hung her head, mortified. "This is what I propose and nothing less: You shall marry me, and we will travel in the Continent for at least two years, before we return to London and take back the stage. Of course, you will never see him again."

Lily gasped. "Marry you!"

"Yes, madam, it's the least I will accept in this bargain. This way I shall set right what was done in the past. And you will bury the hatchet and grow to appreciate me with time."

Lily staggered toward the empty fireplace and lowered herself trembling into an armchair. She held her head in her hands. "Why would you want to marry someone who hates you?"

"Hate me? I thought you would know by now that love and hate sit back to back in hell with not even a split hair in between. The same goes for beautiful and ugly, master and slave, war and peace. None of them mean anything without the other. You don't hate me any more than you love me."

Wade walked back to the chaise and lowered himself onto it. "In that way, we're a perfect match for each other." Then he leaned back and placed his hands behind his head, adding, "I'll give you until tomorrow morning to think about it."

Silence hung in the room. Lily closed her eyes. She thought of Chut, of what he might be enduring. Images of the Old Bailey's grisly façade, where he might be escorted any moment now, filled her mind. That his fate depended on her acceptance of this monstrous proposal made her sick to her stomach. That she was being saddled with the decision to save or condemn her lover crushed her. But she knew Wade well. If she refused his offer he would keep charging at Chut like a blind bull. So many times she had thought she would die for Chut's love; now she realized what a childish fantasy this had been. Never mind dying, could she *live* an excruciatingly abominable life just to save him? The sole proximity of Wade made her shudder with disgust; she knew the power he had to twist her soul and transform her into a beast. She thought of Mrs. Bennett, the way her once-beautiful face had contorted during her violent tirades, and Lily understood that she herself would easily fall into the same abyss.

The door opened. Simmons stood at the threshold taken aback by the tension in the room. "Sir, should I serve tea?" he asked in a hoarse whisper. Wade took a moment to consider. "Why, Simmons, what a brilliant idea! High tea at that. And, tout de suite, prepare the red bedroom for Miss Throop. She will be staying with us for tonight, possibly longer."

Lily clenched her jaw and stood up. "Don't bother, Simmons. I shall not be staying, tonight or any other night. I shall be leaving instantly." When the confused butler stepped out of the room, she turned to Wade. "We shall never marry, sir, no matter what power you wield over me. Take away from me whatever you choose. I'd rather die than live in the shadow of your iniquity."

Lily took off down the street on foot after refusing the cab Simmons had scrambled to bring over for her. A fine, silent rain fell from the leadened sky and she was glad to have it douse her face. It superseded tears. She walked in the direction of Charing Cross Road hoping she would never get there. She walked, hoping she would just keep on going until she might be outside the city gates, onto roads and country lanes, a vagabond, a tramp lady, someone who would roam the land, ragged and derelict, and eventually dissolve into the mud or putrefy inside thickets by the roadside. There was nothing to live for anymore. She had refused Wade's offer and in doing so had condemned Chut. She had never been anything more than Wade's strumpet, acted as his mistress all this time just by virtue of having stayed in the theater and putting up with his roguery and abuse. Yet when it came to saving the life of the man she loved, she had been unable to make the ultimate sacrifice. She had betrayed Chut doubly, first by dragging him into Wade's circle of corruption, and then by abandoning him to his fate.

Mrs. Bakerloo opened the door and pulled a sour face as soon as she saw Lily.

"Miss Throop, I cannot afford scandal. My house is a decent, proper dwelling."

"What are you talking about, Mrs. Bakerloo?" Lily said, indignant.

The haughty old woman turned to pick up a newspaper from the console cabinet by the wall and presented Lily with a copy of the *Daily Telegraph* where the front page headline read, "A Twisted Tale of *Othello*: The Bludgeoning of the Noble Moor by Desdemona's True, Sore Lover."

"If you're going to be in the paper for the wrong reasons," Mrs. Bakerloo continued, but Lily just snatched the newspaper from her hands and ran upstairs to her room. Once inside, she locked the door and sat down to read the whole article. It was a ridiculous piece, giving details of a story that only Wade could have fed to tabloid journalists. In it, Wade had enamored the beautiful Miss Throop, and Mr. Blake, the jealous contestant of the young lady's favors, had lost his temper and walloped the interloper.

Ruby walked in an hour later with two evening papers that followed up on the same theme: "Beautiful West End actress turned bone of gory dispute between real life Cassio and Othello," read *The Star;* and the *Daily Mail* printed: "The rewriting of *Othello:* Cassio's long-awaited, grisly revenge satisfies audiences after centuries of rage at Othello's misuse of lovely Desdemona."

And on and on they went, as scandal sheets always do when they find a good, juicy story with which to stanch the world's hunger for infamy.

Chapter 12

The next days were a whirlwind of slander, gossip, and harassment. The theater was reopened to the public on the third day after the fight, and Michael Falloway acted the part of Othello instead of Wade. He was a fine actor, so the play went smoothly and Lily was comforted to find that she had commanded the stage at all times, even though it was the first time she had worked with a male lead different from Wade.

But the public that now flooded the theater wasn't looking for high-end performances, but to satisfy the morbid curiosity incited by the tabloid press that kept blowing the backstage drama out of proportion. All sorts of creepy social columnists roamed the theater at all times, bribing porters, janitors, night watchmen, and any street vendor, prostitute, or petty thief hanging around the area. But their main target was Lily. They would have killed to receive a handful of words from the horse's mouth. They waited for her all morning outside Mrs. Bakerloo's place and followed her to the Imperial, where they lurked around during shows, posing as fans to get backstage, slipping in through the back door at any possible opportunity. Mr. Harrison was forced to ask for bobbies to be posted at the theater doors. Then they would still meander outside on the street, waiting to spot Lily leaving so they could follow her back to her lodgings, where they also looked to scrap any piece of information that could feed their yellow monster.

Mrs. Bakerloo was initially furious and pressured Lily to leave the house, until an article appeared that was dedicated to her lodging house, putting her in the limelight as a patron and protector of young actors, and assuaged her. She stopped her badgering, but Lily lived as a prisoner, taking meals in her room and thinking daily of new ways of disguising herself to make it back and forth from the theater.

Meanwhile, nobody knew for certain where Chut was, though it was believed he had been transferred to either Newgate or Fleet, two of the most feared prisons in London, to await his trial at the Old Bailey. All sorts of stories were whispered in the theater about the horrid, crowded conditions of prisoners, the cruelty of wards, the violence of inmates. Falloway was the worst of them. Having dabbled in the law in his youth, he had a consuming passion for morbid details concerning anything related to crime and punishment, and spent his days describing possible outcomes for the case. He told Lily that Chut most probably faced transportation to Australia, even if he were to be deemed clear of fraud and misappropriation charges. He'd also told her that inmates were as good as what money could buy them in penitentiaries; from the size of their irons and their cells, to the amount of obtainable bedding and food, everything depended on the ready to be had for bribery.

"How can I help him?" Lily asked him one afternoon as they waited for the performance to begin. "Can I go directly to the prison? Should I retain a legal counselor?"

"Oh, my dear, that would be such a costly procedure. Very few can afford such luxury."

"But would no barrister be interested in the case, seeing how much the press is making of it?" she asked.

He sighed. "Barristers are too hoity-toity to consider mere scandal cases, unless they involve royalty. Common people are left to deal on their own." Lily felt her face sink under the cake of rice powder she had layered on to hide from the audience her hollowed cheeks and the dark rings around her eyes. There was a certain sadistic way in which Falloway enjoyed describing the horrors of the situation and then assuring her there was no way out. It filled her with fear and hopelessness.

"Of course," Falloway continued with a twisted smile, "a good guinea or two never hurts a case. And it's always needed inside the clink." But he wouldn't give any practical information about how to accomplish it. However, an idea that hadn't occurred to Lily before flashed in her mind: Someone out there had to be helping Chut.

After the afternoon performance she rushed back to her room and fished out the tin box where she kept her money from the back of her press. She emptied it into a handkerchief, tied it, and put it in her purse. There were two hundred and sixty pounds in all—the money she had been saving to bring Harry and Alice to London. But now there was no question where it should all go. She called in Annie and asked her to arrange for a cabbie to pick her up from the alley that led out of the scullery. She also asked to borrow her cape and bonnet. After she was all dressed up, she stole down the stairs to the kitchen and left the house unseen.

The cabbie dropped her off at 145 Fournier Street where she stood facing a run-down three-story terraced house with wide windows and a weathered front. She hurried to the door and knocked. A curtain shifted momentarily behind the window and after a few moments Emily opened the door.

They stood facing each other. Lily recognized with a pang the features that so resembled Chut's, the large dark eyes, the chiseled cheekbones and jawline, the sweet lips. She was overtaken by emotion and wanted to step closer and embrace her. But Emily stood unsmiling at the threshold, as if she weren't going to let her inside.

"Emily, forgive this unannounced visit, I need to talk to you. Please."

Emily didn't move. Lily knew that she had been displeased when Chut broke up with Lizzie Matchet, because she had become fond of her as a possible sister-in-law. The breakup had also affected relations with Lizzie's father, Mr. Matchet, who managed the Alhambra Music Hall, an important venue for Emily's performances. Ever since, she had been hostile to Lily and had asked Chut not to bring her to the house. "She'll come around, you'll see,"

Chut had said, "when she gets to know how lovely you really are." Those words now rang in Lily's ears, as Chut had whispered them again and again to soothe her distress.

"Emily, please," she beseeched. The door in the next house opened and a drab-looking woman with a grayish face and hungry eyes stood looking at them. Emily sighed and stepped aside to allow Lily to enter the house. They walked into a bare drawing room with faded sage-green walls and dark wood panels. Emily stood facing her without inviting her to sit down.

Lily fumbled in her purse and brought out the handkerchief. "These are my savings. Please take them, use them to retain a lawyer, for his expenses inside the prison, for anything you deem—"

"Mademoiselle, you think everything can be bought," said a voice with a thick accent coming from the far corner of the room. Lily recognized Mme. Wattine hunched over a table in the shadows. "You come here to throw your banknotes around after bringing misery into our family." She stood up and walked toward Lily. She looked old and shabby in her brown dress, frail beyond what Lily remembered from a few months ago when she had gone to her supping salon looking for Chut. Mme. Wattine examined Lily with her good eye, which seemed thickly veiled, perhaps by cataracts. "We don't need your charity."

Emily stepped in and said, "*Tante, ne vous enervez pas,* I'll talk to her," and taking Mme. Wattine by the arm, led her out of the room.

Lily stood trying to rein in her embarrassment and agitation. She looked around the room, now empty and silent. It was sparsely furnished with a hard sofa of burgundy color, a few chairs to one side, a round oak table at the far end, and a small wood cabinet with a glass door behind which sat a collection of books. A faint smell of nutmeg hung about the space. She knew Chut and Emily had ended up buying an old house that had once been a master silk weaver's abode and mill, but long since fallen into disrepair with the rest of the Spitalfields district. She noticed remnants of fine wood panels and carved details on door cases and the fireplace that attested to better days.

Lily walked toward one of the corners where an array of trapeze equipment, balance beams, hoops, and ropes lay bundled together and leaning against the wall. On the opposite corner stood a cello upright on a stand, its voluptuous body glistening with dark varnish. She remembered Chut telling her that his mother had played the cello and he sometimes fiddled with it, having inherited her instrument. *This would have been my home had I accepted Chut two years ago,* Lily thought, *had I come clean, had I trusted his open, fair face and listened to my heart.* The thought felt strange as she looked over the room. The whole space throbbed with his absence, walls still ringing with the echo of his voice, aching with rubbed-out traces of his poise.

Emily appeared at the door. "You must leave now. We can't take your money. But thank you," she said coldly.

The bundle inside the kerchief at once felt heavy and foul. Dirty money. Lily's hand trembled and the pouch fell to the floor. She stooped to pick it up, but faltered as she strove to straighten up again. "Oh Emily, I'm in such agony," she sobbed, and crouching over she began to weep. Emily stood above her for a moment, then took a few steps away and halted for another bit, before Lily heard her gown swish around as she returned. Then she bent down and put her hands around Lily's elbows. She pulled her up gently. "You must leave now," she repeated in a kinder tone.

Lily looked up at Emily and saw her face conflicted between annoyance and pity. "How can I get into the prison to see him? Please help me," she pleaded, and then added, "Can't we put aside our differences and stand by him together?"

Emily averted her eyes. "You cannot see him. You should stay clear of all this."

"How can I do that? We parted in such a terrible way," Lily said, drying her tears and putting back the bundle into her purse. "And now to think he is jailed, undergoing all kinds of misery. . . ." she added, covering her face for fear she would burst out sobbing again.

Emily took her by the arm and drove her toward the sofa. "Sit a minute. I am going to tell you something you may not repeat under any circumstances, and then you must promise you will leave and never come again." They sat facing each other. "Chut was released today from the Old Bailey, after the grand jury found insufficient evidence for the case. Mr. Matchet has been helping him and has taken him into his house."

"Mr. Matchet?"

"Yes, Chut is now under his protection. But procedures are not over yet; he needs to lie low."

"This is the best news! Please, please let me write him a note!"

Emily's expression hardened. She stood up. "I'm only telling you this for your peace of mind. You may not contact him in any form. It's enough that you've put him in this danger and brought him ruin, that this affair has disgraced us all. Stay away from him." Emily walked out of the room and down the hall to the entrance. She opened the door for Lily. "If you really have affection for him, let him go. You're no good for him. He's still got a future ahead."

The evening papers already reflected the piece of news that had been delivered to Lily with so much bitterness. Ruby, Genevieve, and Harvey were waiting in her room with copies of *The Star*, the *Daily Mail*, and some of the penny papers that working people bought before jumping on the omnibus on the way home from work. The headlines read: "Blake released for lack of evidence"; "Public enraged at theatrical employer's spiteful incrimination of honest, working lad"; "Mobs ready to go rough musicking outside Old Bailey against shady gent prosecutor." Some of the articles attacked Wade, exposing him as a known carouser and gambler, a man of questionable morals and violent temper. One of them pointed at the state of bankruptcy inside the Imperial, and talked about Chut Blake's incrimination as "a squirt of ink from a dying octopus, a strategy to create confusion and facilitate escape." The whole affair seemed to be backfiring into Wade and Harrison's quarters, and the little company of friends gathered in Lily's room was giddy with relief at the outcome of the situation, happy to know that Chut's neck had been saved.

"So good of Mr. Matchet to bail him out," Harvey said. "Always had a soft spot for 'im."

"Really wants Chut at his side in the Alhambra, I s'pose," Genevieve said.

"And Chut might now go back to his Lizzie," Ruby added, with an uncomfortable chuckle. Everyone gave her a look, while across the room Lily flinched, as if she had been stabbed.

The days passed with no news from Chut. Lily didn't dare go

back to Emily, so she sent Genevieve one afternoon instead. But even she was turned away and came back with nothing to report. Lily had also sent letters to the Matchet residence, but those had been returned, unopened.

The press had tired of covering legal details of the case and dug deeper into hearsay and dirty linen. The room at Mary's house in Putney had been discovered, and Mary had been lured into revealing what she knew about "the theater lady and her sweetheart." "They was like two lovebirds," she was quoted literally, "so 'andsome together, spent all theys time locked up in their room, very discreet they was in all." Mary had also spilled the story of the detectives coming to hunt Lily and Chut down, and how threatened she had felt when they stood at her door demanding to inspect the house. This part was added to Wade's legend as a rapacious pursuer of his employees, alongside the context of his debauched nightlife and gambling sprees that now flooded the papers and grew by the copy.

But the press had also started targeting Lily. An article in a women's weekly paper, *Hearth and Home*, mentioned "the laxity of our present moral standards, when public opinion winks an eye on ladies choosing to openly woo lovers below their social station." Another in the *Ladies' Treasury* admonished sternly against "corrupting our young women and daughters by making celebrities out of dissolute actresses no better than ladies of the evening."

At the theater, the dynamics were approaching pandemonium levels. Everyone was jubilant over Chut's release and enraged at Wade, but they were also aware of the dark cloud that hung over their own heads. The company was obviously sliding into insolvency, and the staff and performers would be out of work in no time. Harrison was already behind in paying wages, and there was talk of rioting and boycotting the performances. There were also rumors of the theater being leased to Mrs. Lillie Langtry, the renowned actress and producer who was a media celebrity, and how she had plans for a whole refit of the building.

The Imperial as everyone knew it was about to disappear.

One night after the evening show, Lily lingered in her dressing room after sending Genevieve away, reluctant to return to her room at Mrs. Bakerloo's. She had postponed the arrival of her carriage with hope of getting back after everyone was asleep. She heard the janitor walking down the corridor, stopping every so often to turn off the gas lamps. She went out to meet him, anxious not to be caught alone in the dark. "Mr. Vinge, I'm still here waiting for my hackney to pick me up. How long before you lock the building?"

"I'll wait for you, miss," he told her. "It's a rotten night out there. Just stay near the entrance or sit in the stalls by the door. I'll be watchin' out."

She gathered her things and walked to the entrance hall, but turned instead to the theater, separated the thick velvet curtains that draped the doors, and made her way down the main aisle along the stalls. Around her, the auditorium was dark, save for a few dim wall sconces glimmering at the sides. She stumbled into a middle row and sat in one of the frayed red velour chairs. A thick silence filled the space. The rancid smell of sweat and mold floated through the air. She couldn't recall the last time she had been in the middle of the pit like this, surely never in an empty, unlit house. On the stage shimmered a small light placed downstage center, the so-called ghost light, emitting a faint glow for anyone who had to plod through the dark in search of some prop. It shone shyly, as if forlorn, inside the cave-like gloom of the stage.

Lily remembered how Mr. Featherspoon had told her and Ruby of the old tradition of placing a light on the scaffold at night to keep theater spirits appeased and away from mischief. "It's true," he had said, watching them with a seemingly earnest, straight face. "Ask anyone. Even the Palace Theatre keeps two seats in their balcony permanently lit and bolted open to provide seating for their ghosts." She remembered Ruby's round eyes at hearing this, and her own wonder at the fact that theaters might have living ghosts that needed tending to. How Mr. Featherspoon must have laughed at their naïveté, the dear old man!

To think how young and silly she and Ruby must have been then, only seventeen and just out of sheltered, provincial homes. Unbelievable that it was only three years ago. How many things had happened since then, how much she had grown, changed, learned, aged. And here she was now, an established, mettled actress, both laureated and hounded by the press, about to lose her work, her place at this beloved theater, and rattling around with a crushed heart inside her chest.

"Look at those boards, they seem nothing," she heard a loud voice say behind her, and jumped in her seat. "Just a few, sad planks forgotten and wasting away in the dark." She turned and saw Sam Drake, the actor who played Iago, walking down the aisle toward her. "But behold their magic unfold as they light up and the players step to the stand."

"Oh, Sam! You gave me a fright," Lily said.

"The stage, our Holy Whore!" he continued. "How she seduces us with her devilish graces. What will she not have us do, or give up, for her sake?"

Lily laughed. "You sound quite fired by your muse tonight, my friend."

"I have no muse but her. She's my heart's only love, the great harlot of my dreams." Sam slid into the seat by her side. "Vinge told me you were still here and I came to say farewell. I'm leaving tomorrow for Paris."

"You are? I had no idea. Everything is dismantling so quickly," Lily said with a sigh. Then she added, "Sam, I've so enjoyed working with you. I wish we could have had more opportunities to talk and exchange impressions." His gaze was shrewd, fervent, hard to sustain. His presence onstage was magnetic, and here, as she looked at him, she also realized how strangely hypnotic he was in real life. There was something very attractive and mysterious about his angular face and his dark amber eyes.

"I do too, but I saw how the Noble Moor kept you under lock and key," Sam said with a grin. Lily's face dropped at the mention of Wade and she turned to the stage.

A moment passed.

Sam leaned against the back of his chair and lowered his voice to say, "Lily, I'd like to take the liberty of offering some advice. Leave London as soon as you're able and don't come back until the storm has passed. Scandal has a way of dying out when unfed; no one will remember anything in a few months. Meanwhile, you'll be saving your life."

Lily froze. She sat unnerved, as if someone had discovered her atrocious captivity and was muttering a dangerous plan of escape. "But, how could I do that?" she whispered. "What about Chut? How could I leave him in this uncertain situation?"

"Don't worry about Chut," Sam said. "He's already emerging as the little hero of the tale, and Wade is the villain—but what audience doesn't enjoy a good villain? It's you who they'll pick apart. You've already seen how the story degrades by the day. The same audience who acclaims you now will devour you tomorrow. The more they loved you in the past, the more viciously they'll ravage you." Then he added, without taking his eyes off Lily's incredulous face, "I speak from personal experience. I've been involved in situations far more dangerous than this. Let it suffice to say that Sam Drake is not my real name."

"Not your real name?" Lily echoed.

His eyes glistened in a way that transmitted some piece of knowledge better left unspoken. Images of Sam gratuitously helping the stagehands as they moved props flashed through her mind, as did some burning glances she had seen him exchange with Randy, the handsome stage manager. She recalled, too, how many in the company disliked him, though no one had ever dared criticize his brilliant acting.

"Forbidden love leads to treacherous places," Sam continued. "The world makes sure that grief comes to those who follow their hearts freely, or even their loins. And then, some loves are more unspeakable than others."

"But to have to change your name!" Lily said.

"You're not old enough to remember, but there was a story in the papers years ago—'Young lord shoots himself after leaving bitter letter to father'—before it was hushed up and turned into a murder case by a perverted actor who sought to force the innocent youth. I was tried for murder and gross indecency and condemned to hanging. I was lucky to escape from one of the hulks, and fled to Germany. Roland, who shot himself, was my lover. It's all in the remote past now, but I've never stopped running."

He paused while Lily looked at him with wild eyes. "You poor man," she said.

"Never mind," Sam said. "Consoling words do nothing for me. I just ask that you think of yourself now. Disemboweling a beautiful young actress is a feast the mob won't resist."

"Where could I go? I have nowhere. I have no one to go to."

"I know someone, a Benjamin Gerard, who's still putting together the second part of a troupe that will travel to Saint Petersburg next week. He's quite reliable and would be thrilled to include a female lead of your skill."

"Gerard!" Lily cried. "I met him once. But Saint Petersburg—it feels so far-fetched."

"It will only be for the summer season," Sam said, "maybe a few weeks into the autumn. He always returns to London for the winter."

"But to tear myself from London at a moment like this?"

"Once away, you'll be glad."

The thought of freeing herself from Wade and the stifling twister of gossip and tabloid stories flashed before her, together with the pang of leaving Chut behind. The image from a story told to her long ago of a small animal chewing off its leg to escape a trap flickered in her mind. She shuddered.

"Would you connect me with Gerard before you go?" she asked.

"I'll send him word tonight."

He stood up and taking both of Lily's hands, kissed them. "Good-bye then, Lily—may you soon be far away and safe from all this. And may we meet on the scaffold again."

All was dark and quiet at Mrs. Bakerloo's, but as Lily stepped into her room she heard a small noise that sounded like muffled weeping. It was coming from Ruby's room. She listened behind the door for a moment and then knocked softly. There was no response, but Lily turned the knob and entered anyway. Ruby lay on the bed with her back to the door. A small lamp on the bedside table shone around her curled-up shape.

"Ruby?" Lily called. Ruby didn't answer. She lay with her face flat against the pillow. Lily sat on the bed beside her. "What's the matter? Are you upset about the closing down of the theater? You'll find other work very soon. What, with the success at the Camel Hall, and the new repertoire . . ."

Ruby turned red, swollen eyes to her. "I'm sorry about what I said of Chut and Lizzie Matchet the other night," she said.

"Oh, don't worry about that," Lily said, with a pang of misery. "It's probably true, anyway."

"No, it ain't," Ruby said, sitting up on the bed with a sudden surge of energy. "Chut ain't like that. He's true and honest. Not like that dog, Freddy."

"What's with Freddy? I haven't seen him in a long while."

Ruby burst into sobs again. "He's gone and got Maisie with child, that's what."

"Are you sure about this? Did he tell you?"

"No, the bugger's in hiding, and Maisie's father's looking all over London for him with a butcher's cleaver." She sobbed for a moment more, then stopped abruptly and looked up at Lily. "I'm done with him. This is not the first time I caught him with another. Don't want to see 'is mug again. Putting miles between us this time."

Lily rubbed her arm affectionately. "I'm so sorry about your heartbreak." She took Ruby's hand and they both lay back on the bed in silence. "I came to tell you that I'm also thinking about putting miles between London and myself," Lily said. "Going away for the summer with a traveling troupe. Leaving this mess behind me, and just wait until it all settles down."

"You're leaving?" Ruby asked eagerly.

"There's a man getting a group together to go to Saint Petersburg in Russia. Sam Drake knows him. He's looking for actors."

"Oh, Lily, that would suit me very well too."

"Let's go meet him together in the morning then."

Ruby thought for a moment. "Where did you say Russia was?"

London, June 20th, 1900

Dear Harry and Alice,

Just a quick note to tell you I have accepted Mr. Gerard's engagement to travel to St. Petersburg for the summer season to perform at the Mariinsky Theatre with his troupe. He is a very fine gentleman and has promised to introduce me to theater and artists' circles in that city. I am especially interested in a certain Mr. Stanislavsky, an actor who is developing new methods in acting and stage performance. So you see, my dears, it will just be a few short months abroad, but they will be filled with wonderful adventures and interesting encounters.

Meanwhile, Ruby and I are busy packing and running to the passport office to get our papers ready for the journey.

I promise to write at every stage of the way.

Much, much love,
Lily

P.N. Thank you, Alice, for keeping newspapers away from Father's desk. I wouldn't want him further upset by libelous stories.

CHAPTER 13

From the open, velvet-lined jewelry box, Lily chose an emerald pendant set in gold that had been gifted to her the year before by a Polish count who'd been smitten with her performance of Ophelia. She placed it into Genevieve's little hand. "I want you to have this. No, no fussing. You need to do something for me in exchange, though. Something very, very important," Lily said, looking into the girl's astonished eyes. "I need to leave a letter with you. And you must promise me on your life that you will deliver it personally."

"But of course I will, Miss Lily, even if you give me naught."

"No, I want you to have it. For your loyalty, too."

Genevieve had stood up for her in front of detractors at the theater, she had even struck a journalist with her umbrella once, because he was harassing Lily on the street, and now she went with her everywhere and stayed nights at the boarding house to keep her company. Lily didn't know what she'd do without her; losing Genevieve was another source of grief she tried not to think about by keeping herself in a frenzy preparing for her departure.

Her room was strewn with boxes and crates half full with books, scripts, and multiple objects that had been gifted by her admirers, from the china figures that sat on the mantel and windowsills to the collection of personal ornaments locked up in the small box on her bedside table. Dresses, hats, gloves, and other clothing had been emptied out of her wardrobe and lined up across chairs and tables. There was more to pack than she would have imagined. Three and a half years in London had proved ample time to accumulate all sorts of trinkets. But all these pretty things that had once given her so much pleasure now repulsed her. They felt like icons of an age of innocence she had been torn away from. She became possessed by a fever to rid herself of everything and started giving things away to people at the theater and lodgers at the boardinghouse. Mostly, she gave to Genevieve and Annie.

"But Miss Lily, I can't take this," Genevieve would say, a thwarted look on her pale face. "You're going to need it when you come back." She had pleaded with Lily to take her on the trip, but Gerard's terms were strict on attendants. Actors were to travel alone and be self-sustaining around their performances. "Because you are coming back, ain't you?" she'd ask, her voice fraught with anxiety.

After a lot of coaxing, Lily agreed to have a trunk of her belongings stored at Genevieve's mother's house, together with her collection of books and scrapbooks of cuttings of her newspaper reviews. Her last days in London had become a turmoil of unaccomplished chores, last-minute details, and farewell visits. People came up to her room all day long to say good-bye and hear about the fantastic journey to St. Petersburg, offering all kinds of advice for the trip and warnings about graceless foreign lands. It was heartening to see how many friends and sweet acquaintances she had made in these years. But the more people paraded through her lodgings wishing her well and expressing affection, the more she ached with the absence of Chut.

No word had come from him, but somewhere deep inside, Lily still felt their bond unbroken. At night she dreamed she lay in his arms, nuzzled against his warm skin, her nose engorged with his musky smell as they tossed and turned in the sway of sleep, tightly clasped between thick, slippery sheets. Her every thought was locked inside the depths of his eyes. Time ceased to exist.

But as soon as dawn's bleak light edged around the bed and crept over her, she awoke to find herself cold, alone, thrown back into that awkward, unreal world where Chut had been taken from her.

Then time would start ticking again and she would be filled with pain. It throbbed inside and around her as if her body had just been sundered and all she could do was hanker after the missing part. Nothing could give her comfort. Only a fury of activity could pull her mind for hours at a time away from her wretchedness.

There were only two days left in London. Everything was ready for the journey. The only errand left was to pick up two traveling suits she had ordered the week before from the dressmaker, but they needed final alterations done on the spot, so she couldn't just send someone else to fetch them.

She took Genevieve with her to Mrs. Bell's shop. It was a fashionable establishment, a large ivory-colored room with ceiling-to-floor windows overlooking Dover Street, a quiet little venue in the Mayfair district. Long counters ran along the walls, and behind them, fabric bolts of all colors filled tall shelves next to multiple sets of drawers full of lace, braiding, ribbons, buttons, and beads, the sort of dainty trimmings that only a few weeks ago she had so relished fingering in the company of Ruby when they shopped for trappings. Behind the counters stood assistants attending lady customers who examined fabrics and looked through booklets that lay open over display cases.

One of the attendants marched briskly toward them. "Good afternoon, Miss Throop. Please come with me. Mrs. Bell is expecting you." A significant silence gripped the room as heads turned in her direction. Genevieve stepped to Lily's side and took her elbow. Keen eyes followed her as they swept through the elegant space to the fitting room in the back. A trail of susurration ensued behind them. Genevieve's small hand tightened around her arm.

But Lily was oblivious to it all.

Her mind was fraught with the thoughts that had been obsessing her since the morning. The letter she had torn up so many times had to be finished; its envelope sealed and put into Genevieve's hands. It all must be done as soon as possible.

And yet, she was still unsure of every word.

My only love. She had struggled with this address. It defeated the purpose of a parting letter. It called out desperately to him. *My love, my heart, my dearest one.* And wouldn't it fill him with disdain, now that he thought she loved nothing but the stage?

They entered a smaller room in the back with walls draped in salmon-colored silk. Headless mannequins with torsos of thick, coarse cloth stood on poled stands, unclothed and marked with tailor's chalk or pinned with half dresses along their curves. By one of the windows three young girls sat in low chairs, busy with a piece of sewing, possibly Lily's suits. As soon as they saw her come in, they pulled their heads close and started whispering.

Mrs. Bell turned to Lily. "Miss Throop, how lovely to see you. We're mostly done, we just need to fit you for the waist and sleeve length."

I know I have disappointed you; I know that for this reason you might not feel the same as I do about you. How many times Lily had rewritten this, how she had feared to materialize those two words, *might not,* with the tracing of her pen.

Mrs. Bell led her to the small round platform where she fitted customers. Lily stepped up while Genevieve sat on a stool by the door. Mrs. Bell's assistant helped her out of her dress.

That I have hurt you with my silence and dragged you through the mud into this ugly affair is the agony and torment of my days.

"It would seem you have lost weight since our last fitting," the assistant said, holding the measuring tape in a circle between her fingers for Mrs. Bell to see. "We shall have to further take in the suit." One of the seamstresses sitting by the window tittered. Mrs. Bell gave her a look, and she returned to her work. But all three kept stealing glances at Lily, faces rippling with suppressed giggles.

I don't expect you to forgive me. I'm used to losing everything I ever love. It's just that this time, I've broken my heart beyond what I can bear. A fat tear rolled over the rim of her eye and tumbled down her cheek and bosom onto the hand working at her waist.

Mrs. Bell looked up, alarmed. "Oh, I must have pricked you with my pin. I am terribly, terribly sorry!" Lily shook her head to dismiss her worry, but found that the movement toppled even more tears out of her eyes.

"Oh, dear lady, you must be exhausted. Step down and sit over here. I already have all the measurements we need." Mrs. Bell led her to a chair on the side. Genevieve sprung up and came to Lily, with eyes urging her to becalm herself. The seamstresses by the window perked up and watched her in a suspended state of alert. One of them emitted a long sigh. Mrs. Bell whisked around and quietly ordered them to leave the room. They scurried out in a huddle.

Lily gazed out the window where the girls had been sitting. Golden shafts of light quivered through shrubs of blue delphiniums in the little garden beyond.

Before leaving London I had to write and say this. That I never felt there was any good in the world until I lay in your arms. That my thirst for that happiness, for floating adrift on the tide of our bliss, made me forget all that is desirable and proper in the crude reality without. "You're full of pretty words, Lily." Chut's voice reverberated in her head as he had uttered the last of his mind before walking out, leaving her kneeling in mid-sentence.

Mrs. Bell looked into her face with kind eyes. "Miss Throop, everything will be ready by evening and sent to your apartments. I wish you very happy travels and hope you come back soon." Lily nodded and offered her a hand.

Now throw these lines away and forget me. And I will wish you a long, happy, blessed life. "If you have true affection for him," Emily had said, "let him go." Her eyes had shone hard as she uttered the words.

Let him go.

Lily gathered her things and hurried out of the shop.

Outside, the street was quiet. The horse-drawn carriage stood by the curb, waiting. The afternoon light was bright over the row of handsome houses across from her. It sparked on the windowpanes in scintillating reflections.

She turned to the cabbie. "Please drive Miss Genevieve home. I shall walk to Charing Cross Road."

Genevieve raised her eyebrows in protest, but when Lily whispered, "Please," she got into the hansom without another word. Lily watched the carriage clatter down the street. Something inside her tightened. It clinched down on her, sending waves of shock through her body. Defiance began to ripple over the surface of her grief.

She would let everything go. London, Genevieve, the Imperial, even Chut. She would clench her jaw and move on, toward Russia, the Mariinsky Theatre, Stanislavsky, and wherever else life took her in pursuit of the full width and breadth of what was written for her. And no heartbreak, no regret, no pain would hold her back.

Now, burn these words.

And forget me.

She headed toward the theater. Her velvet cloak was still in her dressing room, and although she had decided days ago to abandon it there, she now thought of fetching it as an excuse to revisit the Imperial for the last time. She advanced in quick, long strides, eyes focused solely on the pavement ahead, while the street became a swirl of broken, fleeting images in the periphery of her gaze. The city she had come to love had turned and was squeezing her out, a hot plate sizzling a mere drop of water into nothingness. The illusion of belonging, of having carved herself a little space in this mass of stone and brick speckled with myriad beings in hectic, ant-like activity, was dissolving in her mind. How the roaring applause from enthused audiences had fooled her. It had picked her up and carried her on a cloud of false dreams of glory and self-aggrandizement. And now, after the final settling of all dust and glitter, the big city was revealing its true countenance: a chimera feeding on human energy to uphold its brutal construct. She choked on these thoughts. That she had defied the measly gods of convention by making her own choices against family and society had placed her on the front line of expendable entities. She was on her own now. Tiny. Fragile.

She arrived at the Imperial and knocked on the front door. Vinge would be inside, keeping an eye on things, making sure only the appropriate people walked in while the company was being dismantled. She waited a few moments before he came to the door, and as she turned to the side where the old posters still hung announcing the play, she saw that underneath the picture of Othello approaching the four-posted bed with the sleeping Desdemona, her name had been scratched out and Angharad's had been written over it.

Vinge opened the door. "Ah, Miss Throop, I wasn't expectin' yer."

"What is this about Miss Bates's name on the play poster?" Lily asked.

"The run 'as been extended for three weeks, miss, while the theater's turned over. Miss Angharad will be leadin'," Vinge said with an embarrassed smirk, blocking the door with his large, drab-clad body.

"I need to get something out of my dressing room, Mr. Vinge, if you'll be kind enough to let me in," Lily said, annoyed.

"I'm so sorry, Miss Throop, but I has orders from Mr. Wade."

"Let me in this instant or I shall call the constables," Lily said, losing her temper.

"Miss, I wouldn't want to lose me job," Vinge started.

That moment a hansom pulled up behind them and came to a stop with a jangle, the horse snorting and puffing, shaking its clinking traces. The door opened and Wade descended. He grinned in mock surprise at seeing her. His face was still darkened with shades of bruising, but his nose seemed back in place with no major distortion. He appeared youthful and energized. He turned to help Angharad, who stepped out after him looking radiant in a green silk dress.

They walked toward Lily arm in arm, and Wade said, turning to Vinge, "Any trouble at the trenches?"

"Miss Throop wanted to come in get somethin' she left behin'," the old man explained.

"I need my green cloak," Lily said icily.

"Oh dear, I'm afraid that has been assigned to your successor," Wade said, pointing to Angharad with a histrionic gesture. "Along with everything else. See how well the green cape will go over the green gown," he snickered. Angharad blushed and gave Lily a shy, apologetic look. How young and innocent she was, the stupid girl, Lily thought with a shudder, how soon she would be trampled.

"The cloak is my personal property," Lily said, as fury began to boil inside her. But she knew she was plunging into a lost battle.

"Nothing is personal inside these doors, madam," Wade said,

stepping closer to her. "While you play, you appertain; once you stop playing, you vanish. As so many have vanished before you, and so many after you will." His eyes were hard, hateful. "Did you think there was something special about you?"

A wave of bitterness swept through Lily, but she resisted the impulse to walk off. Wade stood close enough that she could feel his body heat, the tightened tension of his muscles, his acrid breath. She was determined to hold his gaze. For the first time she felt no fear in his presence. She stared into his turbid eyes, sticking fast before the shield of ferocity with which he always challenged the world. She stood as if naked in the face of a surrounding army. He flashed at her angrily, but all his metal felt trivial against her frailty. Pliable, tender bareness had become her powerful weapon. Three years of fear and loathing were melting away from her, and she felt her flesh tingling with renewed life force. The thawing washed down all memory of rancor, leaving just the original feeling of pain. It throbbed, unflinching, raw. Unsullied. She ventured further into Wade's glare, through his crumpling armor, behind the scenes where his voice was stripped of all power to charm and terrorize, into the deep source of his quickening. And there she saw a small, ugly boy, beaten and forlorn, transfiguring his craving for love into an elaborate, hellish artifact that could inflict suffering. He stared back at her, pale and terrified.

Wade dropped his eyes.

He turned, grabbed Angharad by the arm, and pulled her into the building, while shoving Vinge to the side. Then he stepped in himself, and without another word, slammed the door and bolted the latch from the inside.

Lily heard his pointed steps walk away.

July 2nd, 1899

Dear Harry and Alice,

Forgive my wobbly handwriting, but I am trying to write on one of the little tables in the train's restaurant coach as we ride through Belgium toward the German frontier, where we're bound to change trains, and I will have a chance to post this letter.

It has been less than a week since we left London, but as I'm lulled under the choo-choo sound of wheels and the lush landscapes rushing past the windows, it already feels like months. I'm exaggerating, of course, but you can imagine how I feel after having emerged from a roaring cyclone into a placid, silent pathway rolling me away from the eye of the storm.

Let me tell you how that very storm pursued me to the end. Crossing the English Channel from Dover to Calais we came into very rough weather and got stranded off the coast of northern France, unable to dock. The captain was forced to ride out the gale for hours, while passengers huddled together and chairs slid from one side of the boat to the other. I feared the paddle-steam would drown—how it struggled to stay afloat in the ferocious sea! Outside, rain fell like pellets over the massive waves and the skies bore down like sheets of lead. Many of us felt terribly seasick, but couldn't step out on deck because of the high winds.

I confess that at one point I thought it might be the end for me, and I held Ruby's hand so hard she shrieked. Now, thinking back on it all, I find it silly. But believe me, I nearly went down on my knees and kissed the ground when we finally stepped onto the port of Calais. I hope you'll also have a good laugh at your naïve sister's traveling adventures when you read this letter.

I'll say I miss you much more as my journey takes me farther away from you into unknown lands. It would've been a dream to visit you in Manchester before leaving, but these days my life seems to fly out on its own without much consultation of my opinion or any attention to my wishes.

Of course, my heart is always at your side, and that will never change no matter how far away the rest of me strays.

Your Lily

CHAPTER 14

Lily and Ruby looked around the section of the harbor where they had disembarked. Everything around them seemed wrapped in haze, making it look fuzzy, unreal. It was only four in the morning, but the sky was luminous with a strange opalescent light, as if the previous day's dusk had not ended. They were exhausted and in desperate need of refreshing themselves. Ahead of them stood a few imposing customs officers, dressed in dark uniforms with sentry hats over long hair and beards, pointing to a large, gloomy stone building. Lily and Ruby followed the other passengers into the customhouse, where they were made to line up before a tall counter behind which three officers stamped passports. The officers scrutinized all travel documents and shouted questions in a sibilant language full of harsh consonants.

With their paperwork in hand, Lily and Ruby stepped up toward a beefy officer with green, greedy eyes and a nose like a dog's, with which he seemed to sniff out their documents before reading them. Lily looked around, hoping to find Gerard waiting for them somewhere inside the large, dismal hall, as he had promised, but he was nowhere to be seen.

Ruby fumed at her side. "I need to get to a ladies' room. Soon." She had already approached one of the guards about this, spelling every word for powder room she knew—*toilette*, *badezimmer*, *toalett*—and when no sign of understanding appeared in the indifferent gaze above her, she engaged in additional gesturing, combing her hair and washing out her eyes. But the officer only uncrossed his arms to point her back to the queue. After this, Ruby was in no mood for smiling, so Lily simpered for both of them while repeating the only word she knew in Russian, *spacibo,* "thank you." "*Spacibo!*" the passport officer barked back as he brought down the stamp on their papers with a thud.

They were directed into another hall where the luggage was examined. In one section, travel trunks and portmanteaus were opened on long, wide benches, and at the opposite end of the hall large crates of merchandise stood subject to examination. Ahead of them in the passenger queue was Eunice Chamber, a young governess who was traveling to Moscow to work for a rich family, and whom Lily and Ruby had befriended on the boat. She stood by her luggage while two bear-like officers searched the contents of one of her valises, pawing through her belongings and scattering them all over the bench. One of the officers pulled out a white, lacy chemise, holding it up for closer scrutiny as if it were the strangest object he'd ever seen. Eunice burst into tears. But the guards kept up their display of her undergarments, lifting corsets and petticoats from the suitcase.

At the sight of a pair of drawers being held apart by the legs, Ruby stomped up to the guards, pulled the garment from their hands, and cried, "That's more than enough, you brutes!" Annoyed surprise flickered across their faces while another officer stepped up with a whistle in his mouth, which he proceeded to blow forcefully. The whole hall froze. Ruby was quickly surrounded by guards, who took her to the side and, hoisting up her luggage, began tearing through its contents with even more savagery than they had employed with Eunice's. Out flew her crinolines and colorful corsets, her glittering silk stockings and other beautiful unmentionables, all examples of Ruby's supreme taste in delicates. One of the guards found a small bottle of perfume at the bottom of the trunk and showed it to the others as if it were a dangerous artifact. Ruby looked like she was about to explode.

Meanwhile, Lily's indignation at the whole scene had shaken off her fatigue. She was itching to intervene, but wasn't sure it would be useful. As she looked on, bleeding sympathy for her friend, she heard whispering and nervous cackling behind her. She turned to find two young officers in Russian military uniforms seemingly sniggering at the scene.

"Sirs," she said in English, "I can't imagine what sort of gentleman would look on a scene like this without helping out a lady. Much less laugh."

The two officers blushed, and after a moment one of them replied in French, "Mademoiselle, we too deplore the situation, but any Russian who interferes at this point will get arrested. We live in a police state, and customs officers take their work very seriously."

His companion stepped in, saying, "But please, do not think for a moment we laugh at the lady's misfortune, but at our own friend who's also undergoing misery." He gestured toward another corner of the room where guards were ravaging a beautiful writing desk, while a man dressed in civilian clothes, very much in the European fashion, stood by them with arms folded over his chest, riding out the plundering scene. One of the guards was intent on breaking the lock of the private drawer, while two others ransacked the rest of the drawers. A host of papers, letters, and cards of address scattered toward every corner of the room. A fourth guard groped the blotting book, spilling the ink and mixing up the wax, wavers, and a set of watercolors as he shook down the desk.

"May I ask, sir, what on earth do they expect to find?" Lily asked.

"Anything in the long list of things that are interdicted to introduce into the country," the young officer replied somberly. He then added, "Our Russia is still a recalcitrant nation."

Lily felt puzzled at these words. As she returned her gaze to the spectacle, she saw that two of the guards had surrounded the gentleman and were questioning him in a menacing manner. One of them brandished a book he must have found in the desk. The gentleman remained undaunted in the midst of their hollering. He was tall and slender, somewhere in his late twenties, and wore his elegant travel suit and overcoat casually, as if he were used to affluence. His face was pale and handsome, punctuated by fine bones and thin lips; his gray hooded eyes stared impassively at the bullying officers. The officers presently flanked him and marched him to a door in the back. The man shot a mock look of contrition at his friends, as if apologizing for the situation and how it might inconvenience them. Then he saw Lily, and they locked eyes for an instant. A strange thrill invaded her as she took in his cool, fearless gaze. A second later, the guards hurried him along out of the hall.

"Where are they taking him?" Lily asked.

"They will now interrogate him," said the first young officer, his eyebrows knitted with concern. "But don't worry, mademoiselle, he's been through this before. He knows how to handle it," he added, with an uneasy smile.

Before she could ask any further questions, she saw that the guards nearby had hoisted her luggage onto the bench and that it was her turn to be inspected. They opened up the lid of her trunk, but before they could dive into the contents, a loud whistle pierced the air again. The guards looked at a monumental clock than hung above the hall's entrance. It marked seven o'clock. They immediately gathered their effects and darted toward a small side door. The whistle blower waved at Lily and indicated in gruff tones that she was free to take her valise and go. A ragged porter came to her aid and they hurried away to look for Ruby.

Lily found her standing outside the customhouse with Eunice, by the curb of a wide avenue. Around them stood a swarm of men, apparently the drivers of the bizarre-looking carriages lined up along the street, shouting in turns. Lily froze for an instant, fearing for her friends' safety. But the men seemed to be discussing among themselves, oblivious of Eunice and Ruby. They were tall, bulky men, and though it was quite hot, they were all dressed in big padded blue coats bound about the waist by thick belts, above which hung the largest beards Lily had ever seen. Soon, their howling contest abated, and one of the drivers rushed toward them, picked up the luggage at their feet, and carried it away.

They walked behind him to the strangest carriage imaginable: a cushioned bench on four wheels, with no doors, lifted only inches off the ground, and all of it painted in bright greens with gold filets. They would soon learn that this was a droshky, one of the traditional Russian hack carriages in which everyone jangled around the city. The driver took off right away, not bothering to listen to the address Lily gave, as if he knew where to take them. Maybe Gerard had sent for them after all. But the daring of sending them this sort of transport! The seat was so small that the three of them could hardly fit. They rode with their feet up on their trunks and clung fast to one another while clattering along, afraid they'd fall off the sides.

Lily's annoyance dissolved as the cab turned onto the Dvortsovy Bridge that connected Vasilyevsky Island with the mainland, where the skyline of St. Petersburg emerged above the waters of the Neva, its tall domes and golden spires glinting in the morning sun. They sat breathless taking in the rows of palaces and canal bridges that formed a magnificent waterfront over imposing granite quays.

"Look!" Eunice said. "That must be the czars' Winter Palace!" and she pointed left to a huge rectangular structure set in red stucco with a sweeping extension of white columns segmenting hundreds of windows. Eunice rattled on about the history of the city. She was evidently a little bookworm who had read everything there was to read about Russia, a humbling reminder that Lily hadn't even thought about gathering information on the country she had just landed in, but that she had rushed to it in blind desperation, like a refugee.

The droshky surrounded the palace square and entered the Nevsky Prospect, a long, wide avenue lined with majestic buildings as she had never seen before. Everything seemed immense: all architectural structures, houses, mansions, squares, and avenues. So large indeed, it made her and her companions feel miniscule in comparison, three tiny dots on a toy carriage cruising the massive avenues. To add to the sense of colossal proportions, the city appeared virtually empty of inhabitants, and the few groups of citizens they did see presented a motley mixture of individuals attired in all sorts of strange and fantastic ways.

Crossing one of the squares, Lily caught sight of a man trotting on a horse, wearing a round fleece hat and a long, open-fronted crimson coat, and carrying a lance in rest, as if he were pursuing an enemy. "Look, a Cossack," Eunice said.

"Where is he going?" Lily asked.

"I don't know," Eunice said. "They're perennial warriors, always busy with their drills."

They turned into narrower streets running alongside a grid of intersecting waterways until they arrived at Frau Krüger's lodging house at the far end of the Catherine Canal. The man delivered their luggage across a grim courtyard and through the heavy wooden door of the inn, taking off his hat and grunting lavish terms of appreciation as Lily put money in his hand. She and Ruby waved farewell to Eunice as the droshky whisked her away to the train station.

An older, fleshy woman, with large droopy eyes underscored by heavy bags of skin, welcomed them from behind a counter and checked them into one of the rooms. "Mr. Gerard has had to leave for Moscow and will be back in the next few days," she informed them. "He asked that you join Mr. Lambeth tomorrow at noon to start rehearsals." Frau Krüger spoke in a thick German accent and seemed very chatty, soon telling them all about how she had also been an actress in her youth, until she married a Russian hussar and settled in St. Petersburg.

She showed them into a room with two small beds and arched windows that overlooked a plain servants' courtyard. "Dear fräuleins, this is the only room I have left at this late time in the season. But it's cozy, and quieter than those in the front overlooking the street."

"Blimey," Ruby said, after the burly frau had closed the door behind her, "we're back to old Bakerloo's original pigeonhole. And worse."

The next day they met with Mr. Lambeth and the other players, and were shocked to find out that they were not performing at the Mariinsky or any other important theater in St. Petersburg, but at the Chamber Opera House, which, in spite of its pompous name, was only a small theatrical venue of sixty seats located near the river. The building had been the mansion of a baron exiled to Paris that had been reconverted into a tiny opera house. It was beautiful inside, a swirl of baroque and classical style with white gilded voluptuous stucco ceilings and walls surrounding dainty rows of red velvet seats. But only sixty seats!

"What did you expect?" Lambeth said in disdain after perceiving Lily's disappointment. "The audience for these performances belongs to a class marginally interested in English theater. If Gerard only had listened to me when I suggested we stage musical comedy!"

Lily was also surprised to learn that most of the actors came from a theater company in Leeds and had mostly performed in melodramatic and musical theater, but had little experience in Shakespeare or drama. Why would Gerard hire such a group to perform six dramatic plays in ten weeks, already a very ambitious program for a seasoned actor? As soon as they started rehearsals she realized how mediocre and careless Lambeth was, and how uneven and chaotic the work of the rest of the troupe. The male lead, Robert Moss, had an untrained voice and frequently tripped over his words onstage. He refused to do any extra rehearsals when Lily proposed they polish their lines together. This suggestion alone earned Lily an instant reputation of haughtiness, and when people started pointing to her and Ruby as the best players, the rest of the company retaliated by ostracizing them.

They now sat every evening alone at their own separate table in Frau Krüger's dining room. Ruby poked at a round, fat little pie sitting on her plate. "I don't even like the food. Why can't they just cook their potatoes like everyone else, instead of tuckin' 'em into the pastry?" She hadn't recovered from her disgruntled mood since the episode at the customhouse. She found everything distasteful from the room at the inn to the people they met to the sweltering summer heat.

"Mademoiselle, you don't like our *vareniki?*" asked Boris, Frau Krüger's son, as he hovered over them with a pastry loaf on a dish. When Ruby didn't respond, he said, "I'll bring more kvass then." He'd taken a fancy to Ruby and insisted on playing maître d' around them on the evenings he oversaw the dining room. He was a thin man in his thirties with sunken cheeks and clear-blue eyes that stared out hungrily.

Ruby glared after him as he walked away. "More kvass! What wouldn't I give for a pint of good ol' English ale!"

"Come on, Ruby," Lily said, "we're only here for a short time, let's just enjoy the adventure. We'll have so many stories to laugh about when we get back."

"I wish I'd never left. I wish I could go back right now. I'm not cut for adventure."

Lily sighed. True, the circumstances were far below what they had expected when taking on the tour. The boardinghouse was uncomfortable, with its ever creaking, wood-paneled rooms and rationed hot water; work was complicated, unsatisfying; and everything about St. Petersburg was strange and difficult to navigate. Ruby was as homesick as a beat-up dog. She lay in bed when she was not at work, waiting out her days, as she said, to get back home.

But Lily was rather glad to be far away from London and all the troubles she had been through. Even her heartbreak was a little more tolerable because of the distance, without the daily reminders of known streets where she might spot Chut, or constant exposure to textures, smells, and sounds that could trigger painful memories of their togetherness. All of this made her eager to plunge head-on into her new environment.

The first day she set out to walk around by herself, Frau Krüger stood behind the counter in the foyer looking at her with a critical eye. "Miss Throop, you do know this is not London and a lady does not go out alone. Not just that you don't speak a word of Russian, but that it's not proper. You would get immediately approached by all the officers coasting the streets."

"But Frau Krüger, how would I do?" Lily asked. "I very much want to visit the city."

"Well, dear, the custom here is to hire a *lackey-de-place.* They interpret for you and get you tickets to the palaces and other sights. They charge about two silver rubles a day, but, believe me, they're very worth it. I have a Mr. Shuttleworth to offer for the job. He's the clerk at the English church, but takes on extra jobs to pay for his wife's medical bills. She's very ill, you see, and doesn't seem to ever recover."

Two silver rubles was quite a bit for Lily, considering the modest salary she had agreed to, but she asked Frau Krüger to arrange for him to come in the morning.

Next morning, Mr. Shuttleworth stood waiting for her in the foyer. He was a small individual with shy, furtive eyes and a sanctimonious smile. He was dressed modestly, and the little round eyeglasses he wore low on the bridge of his nose gave him a bookish air. He reminded her instantly of Mr. Duff, the clergyman who had wanted to marry her back home. This amused Lily. How she'd made a mountain out of a molehill at the time, how she'd feared that a man such as this would engulf her and smother her freedom.

"We shall start by visiting the Winter Palace," Mr. Shuttleworth said.

"Oh no, Mr. Shuttleworth, I first want to see the streets. Please take me along the Nevsky Prospect," Lily said. "From beginning to end." Mr. Shuttleworth complained, saying it was an extremely long avenue and that the heat wouldn't do for a lady. But Lily insisted, offering to pay an additional ruble for the effort, after which he agreed.

They set out on foot along the Nevsky Prospect. Lily's first impression of this street on her arrival to St. Petersburg was correct, as it intersected with all the rings of the city, from the suburbs of the poor to the showy areas of commerce and the sumptuous quarters of the aristocracy. They walked through an area of low wooden houses that led to a cattle market, where groups of peasants, or muzhiks, as Mr. Shuttleworth called them, swarmed around spirit shops. They were dressed in filthy tunics belted at the waist and wore long, shaggy hair and beards. They stood in groups, drinking and singing. Their song was heavy with low, heart-wrenching tones. "The moment they get hold of a kopeck they spend it on liquor and get savagely drunk," Mr. Shuttleworth said. "Then they mope for days, or pick up fights with one another. Sad to say, but it's the only possible distraction from their harsh lives."

Further along, they came upon groups of stone houses with small shops, and a large bazaar under an arcade called the Gostiny Dvor. Its booths held all sorts of wares, samovars, furs, military goods, books written in Cyrillic, sacred images, and icons that Lily was seeing for the first time. There were also food shops, bakeries, and eating establishments. Many of the houses were painted in yellow and red, and grocery shop façades were decorated with luscious, bright colored folk art. When she peeked through their doors, Lily saw huge heaps of summer fruits—strawberries, peaches, cherries, plums—piled high on counters and gleaming irresistibly at customers.

The variety of costumes of the populace was remarkable, and Mr. Shuttleworth pointed out all the different inhabitants by dress: Russians in dark kaftans and long beards; Armenians in silken gowns; Chinese with dangling ponytails; Muslims, Jews, Italians, Germans, Estonians, Yankee sailors, Mongolians, Arabians. St. Petersburg seemed to hold a sampling of all peoples of the world.

They stopped at a tavern to drink *sbiten*, a honey-based drink Lily had learned to like at the inn. Mr. Shuttleworth ordered *medovukha*, an alcoholic version of *sbiten*. He was visibly collapsed from the walking and the heat. He sat slumped on the bench, drying off his face with his handkerchief. At the far end, a muzhik played a fiddle for a group that drank and sang together.

After a couple of *medovukhas*, the tavern landlord served Shuttleworth a small glass of vodka. "It's the custom to serve complimentary vodka," Mr. Shuttleworth said. "I hope you don't mind." When Lily answered that she didn't in the least, he added, "I'll say, Miss Throop, I'm enjoying our little outing after all. You're very different from the English ladies I meet here. Of course, being an actress might explain your gaiety, your easy ways." He faltered as he looked at her with a glint in his eye that quickly dissolved into general burning across his cheeks, and then his face darkened. "But I fear you have come to the wrong place for your profession. You would have done better for yourself to go to Paris or New York. This is no place for a young English actress."

"How would you know that, Mr. Shuttleworth?" Lily asked, piqued by his comment.

"Believe me, I've seen many of our countrymen and women come and go. This is a strange country. Fascinating. But also brutal and cunning, like its proverbial mascot, the bear."

"So what brought you here, Mr. Shuttleworth?" Lily asked.

"I set out to experience the world, but the world closed in on me before I knew it. Or rather, I thought I could escape myself by running away, but didn't realize that the same troubles would be waiting for me wherever I arrived. It seems we carry them with us, our predicaments."

Lily felt unease at his words, but then remembered Frau Krüger's gossip about his valetudinarian Russian wife, and the fact that he had to keep her parents in addition to his own household. Mr. Shuttleworth said no more, but sat looking down at his empty glass. The landlord waddled over to them and refilled his glass making boisterous comments Lily didn't understand. The vodka flushed Mr. Shuttleworth's cheeks and sparkled up his shy gaze. They talked for a while about many things, and Lily found out that he was from Stretford, a town south of Manchester, and that he had considered taking the robe before a failed romantic engagement sent him traveling. The similarities with Mr. Duff, her old suitor, were uncanny.

Finally, they emerged from the tavern back into the street. At this point even Lily understood that a droshky was in order, so she let her companion deal with the throng of *izvozchiks*, or drivers, who barked out prices around them. Once on the droshky, they turned to look ahead as the carriage crossed a bridge over the Fontanka Canal, from which the gilded spire of the Admiralty was already in view, a sign they were entering the aristocratic sector of the city. Here, mansions rose to three and four stories high, and a host of private carriages replaced the large horse-drawn trams they had encountered along the way. Elegant passersby, the majority of them in splendid-looking uniforms, walked among the sumptuous shops, along façades of imperial palaces, beautiful cathedrals, and churches in different styles. Everything looked scintillating under the hazy sun of the early afternoon. *It's so beautiful, it looks nearly unreal,* Lily thought, *as if it were the illustration of some fairy tale come alive.* Even the faces she was seeing above the uniforms looked uncommonly handsome, with piercing ice-blue eyes, high cheekbones, and strong, square jaws. They eyed her with interest as she clattered by in her unlikely carriage. Frau Krüger was not being facetious when she had assured her of the shortage of women in the city. At least in the open city, females seemed to be markedly outnumbered by men.

When they returned to Frau Krüger's establishment, Lily paid Mr. Shuttleworth and thanked him, promising to put his name down for free tickets at the theater. "Miss Throop, if you ever need a friend in St. Petersburg, think of me," he said, and took his leave. She watched him walk away, crestfallen, his shoulders bowed, as if weighed down by a hefty burden, or just already hung over from the vodka and the mead.

Lily ran up to her room. She found Ruby sitting by the window looking out into the yard, and proceeded to tell her about her outing. Ruby only perked up when she described the hordes of handsome men milling around in sparkling uniforms. "They look at you in the most yearning manner and whisper *krasivaya,* which means 'beautiful' in Russian, when you pass by," Lily said. None of the men she had encountered had done such a thing, but she had asked Mr. Shuttleworth to teach her the word *krasivaya* so she could tease Ruby with tales about the city men.

But after that first flicker of interest, Ruby shut down again. "They'll all be like Freddy, murmuring sweet words to cover up their dirty dealings," she said, without taking her eyes off the servant hanging long, white sheets in the yard. "And I'm sure they'll be much harder to resist if they're stunners. At least that ol' dog of mine had an ugly kisser."

After a few more efforts in shaking her friend out of her dejection, Lily sat back against the bed pillows and closed her eyes. The fantastic images she'd just guzzled floated for a while more in her mind, and then faded as memories of London crept back into her consciousness: her dressing room at the Imperial after a good performance, stuffed with flowers, crowded with smiling faces complimenting her; Chut's mischievous smile as he bent over her whispering sweet nothings; dusk over the Thames from the window of Mary's cottage. It had been like this for her on the boat every night, as she lay in the dark on the upper berth of the cabin lulled by the movement of the sea. Images of her immediate past would resurface in her mind, like schools of fish gliding through water, stroking her with their slippery bodies as they darted by her. But after a while the sweet, glittering visions would sink and memories edged with unease would begin to rise from the inky ravines of her mind. Chut's bruised eyes doubting her innocence; Wade closing the theater doors on her; malicious faces leering at every detail of the newspaper scandal. Then she churned with anguish as she realized how hard returning to London was going to be, how difficult to take up her acting life again, and plough ahead day after day until she could leave Chut behind. If ever that came to be.

She sat up, deciding none of this would do. She was in St. Petersburg, miles away from her old life, determined to push onto a new stage. All these thoughts had to be brushed aside, locked away in the past, so she could move on. While she was in Russia, it was imperative she acquire some new kind of tool or key that would allow her to leap into the future. She decided to pressure Gerard once again about introducing her to Stanislavsky.

CHAPTER 15

Gerard was staying at the Grand Hotel Europe at Mikhailovskaya Street, off the Nevsky Prospect, and had agreed to meet with Lily at four o'clock. She had begged Ruby to come along with her, to no avail. In the end, she decided to set off by herself.

As she was leaving the inn, Frau Krüger called her over to the counter and said in a hushed voice, "I've known Gerard for over ten years and this is the first time I'm worried about him." Lily understood immediately the piece of gossip she was about to bring up; she'd also heard from leering members of the troupe how Gerard was consumed by a love affair with a certain Countess Natalia Mayevskaya from Moscow, which was keeping him away from his St. Petersburg responsibilities and making him neglect the company. "Such a fine man in the clutches of that jezebel!" Frau Krüger sighed. "She's notorious for bringing men to ruin." But Lily was in no mood for hearsay. She was ready to take Gerard to task without any thoughts about his possible excuses.

Gerard received her in his rooms on the second floor of the elegant hotel. They sat in plush chairs around an elaborate hand-carved table while a manservant poured tea in round porcelain cups from a silver samovar. Lily couldn't help gasping at the lavish furnishings around her, and comparing them to the middling atmosphere of Frau Krüger's establishment. Across from her, large windows opened onto a stone balcony overlooking the richly decorated domes of the Church of the Savior on Spilled Blood sparkling in the distance.

"I apologize for this season's poor organization, and for my sustained absence from the city," Gerard started, while dabbing his neck with a white silk kerchief. "My other business enterprises keep me away in Moscow." He seemed exhausted. His face looked ashen, clammy, and he was perspiring far beyond what could be expected in the present weather. His pallid blue eyes roamed the room, as if restless and unable to find a comfortable point to affix themselves to.

Recollections of a recent conversation among the troupe members rushed to Lily's mind while she sipped her raspberry tea. "She's eating him alive," she had heard Moss, her companion lead-actor, say. "Soon enough we won't have any more Gerard."

"They say she's infected him with phthisis, and who knows what else," Mirabelle Gray, another actress said.

"It boils down to a matter of national incompatibility," Lambeth, the director, added with peremptory flair. "Russians are domineering, over-passionate lovers, and tend to override the more delicate, romantic English constitution. One may find oneself reduced to a mouse in the face of an anaconda." Everyone had laughed at this, save Lily, who found the comment rude and ridiculous. But now, looking at Gerard, she agreed that a great change had come over him since she had seen him in London. He had lost weight and seemed distracted.

She put down her cup. "Mr. Gerard."

"Oh please, call me Benjamin. And I hope I may call you Lily," he said.

"All right, Benjamin, I've come to discuss the situation at the theater," she said, and she rattled on, following the script she'd prepared for this conversation in the past days. "I'd also like to remind you of your promise to introduce me to Mr. Stanislavsky."

Gerard looked embarrassed. "I'm afraid little can be done about the company at this point. As for Stanislavsky, I promise to contact him when I return to Moscow." He got up and walked to the window where he went into a fit of coughing over his handkerchief. Then he returned to his seat. "Excuse me, this humid climate seems to congest me." He proffered Lily a weak smile and continued, "Meanwhile, I have a proposition which I think you might like." He went on to say that a friend of his, Countess Elena Volkova, wanted a recital of English poetry for her grandmother's ninetieth birthday celebration, which was to take place at their summer residence in the outskirts of St. Petersburg, and that it would be interesting for Lily to get acquainted with Elena and her family, in addition to obtaining a handsome fee for the performance.

"I will be happy to accept," Lily said. "But Ruby has to come along with me, with a performance of her own."

"Can she sing Mendelssohn? The old princess is very fond of his songs."

The date for the performance was set for the next Saturday. Gerard sent the texts and music for the performance to Frau Krüger's. The old princess, Anna Alexandrovna, having heard that *Romeo and Juliet* was being performed and not being able to attend the theater because of her fragile health, desired to listen to Juliet's monologues. As for Ruby, she got her sheets of music and practiced on the Krüger parlor's old piano.

A carriage came to pick them up Saturday early afternoon and drove them to the family *dacha*, or summerhouse, on Kamenny Island. They arrived at a yellow brick mansion with turrets surrounded by a lush garden shaded by old linden trees. A ceremonious servant in livery welcomed them in English with a German accent and showed them into a parlor with tall, latticed windows that overlooked one of the island canals. They gaped at the dome-like ceiling painted in pink and gray with gilded moldings, and at the silk wall coverings featuring delicate flowers on spidery branches. A tall, stately woman walked in and introduced herself as Elena Volkova. Her dress of white muslin gauze created a luminous halo around her as she offered a long, cold hand in greeting. Her face was narrow and unsmiling, although her gray eyes were kind. She thanked them for coming and inquired about their trip. She then led the way to the back garden, through plush, pastel-colored rooms furnished with rare, beautiful furniture. In the garden, a large group of people sat in the shade of tall trees enjoying a luxurious picnic served on exquisite china arranged across small tables. Everyone seemed to be dressed in white or ivory; the women, like Elena Volkova, wore muslin dresses, and the men, elegant linen suits. Even the children running around the lawn were clad in impeccable white costumes. They wore straw hats with long ribbons and darted about in play with screams and happy laughter. The adult crowd chatted while seated in stylish wicker chairs, or recumbent on rugs and blankets spread over the grass.

Elena Volkova brought them to the main group, gathered around an elderly lady who held court with the majesty of an empress. Elena introduced her as Princess Anna Alexandrovna, who gave a small nod in greeting. Lily stared wide-eyed at her delicate beauty. It was otherworldly, like a china doll aged by an artist. Her white hair was arranged in a simple coiffure held by two silver combs studded with diamonds. Her serene gray eyes under heavy lids and the contented smile over her lips suggested a life that had been an extended, blissful dream. She looked at Lily with unexpected sharpness while uttering a few words of welcome in German, which Elena Volkova translated into English.

Lily curtsied, feeling annoyed with Gerard for not having instructed her more about the protocol of addressing Russian nobility, and about how to dress for an occasion like this. Both she and Ruby stood out with their brightly colored silk dresses. But she relaxed some when she was introduced to other members of the family, who were all graceful and welcoming. Elena Volkova had them sit by one of the small tables while one of the many hovering servants offered them tea and sandwiches.

A lithe young woman with dark hair and sparkling eyes walked up to them. "I'm so pleased to meet you. I'm Lena's sister, Katerina Volkova. But they call me Kitty. I'm so glad you're here to instill some fun into our tedious afternoon."

"Tedious afternoon?" Ruby cried. "I've never been to a lovelier picnic in my life."

"Of course it's lovely," Kitty replied, "but you know what I mean. I want excitement, not just perfect loveliness around the clock." There was something skittish about her quick movements and in her laughing gaze. She was very pretty, with a smooth oval face and large round eyes that peered hypnotically like a cat's. Kitty was, in fact, thought Lily, the perfect nickname for her.

Kitty pulled up a chair and sat next to them. "What's it like to be an actress and travel the world? Have all sorts of men dying for you after every performance, drowning you in flowers and diamonds? Women weeping and swooning in boxes at climactic moments in the third act?"

"Oh, it's nothing like that," Ruby said, scooping up an extra helping of raspberry tart. "It's just a lot of hard work, and struggling to keep one's head above the water. As for the men . . ."

That moment a rustle went through the group as a man entered the garden from the house and hurried toward the princess. He was dressed differently from everyone else, in a traditional Russian skewed-collared shirt, or *kosovorotka,* that Lily had seen peasants and certain townsmen wearing. It reached down to his mid-thigh and was belted at the waist, under which he wore dark trousers tucked into tan leather boots. His face was framed by a short, neat beard, and his flaxen hair, long and tousled in the front, covered his eyes and forehead so that Lily couldn't get a sense of his full features. Everyone started up in surprise at seeing him. When he reached the princess, he took both of her hands and kissed them, uttering what sounded like heartfelt apologies. But the old princess just smiled and pulled him into an embrace, kissing his forehead and holding him to her for a while. When she released him, he sat at her feet still holding her hand, while a servant brought him a drink. Some members of the company approached to talk to him.

"Who's he?" Ruby asked.

"Oh, that's just my cousin Sergei Nikolayevich," Kitty said. "He's the enfant terrible of the family. Always late for family gathering—when he deigns to appear. But he's *Grandmaman's* favorite, so how could he not come today? Look at him, always trying hard to shock the Philistines." She pulled a face, a jesting grimace of disgust, and quickly broke into laughter. "He's one of those, though—impossible not to adore."

"How come you people speak French all the time," Ruby asked.

"I thought Russians would speak Russian and look Russian, but all of you look so, so . . ." She stared at Kitty, embarrassed, afraid she had overstepped her boundaries. But Kitty was unfazed. "So European? Yes, we do. We relish in it, and we're also much criticized for it. But I love my French, and my German, and my English. What am I to do?" she replied, and batted her eyelids coquettishly at Ruby.

A gust of warm breeze blew through the garden, rustling the treetops and casting a sprinkle of sweet-smelling yellow specks that descended lazily around them. Looking up, Lily saw the swishing branches laden heavy with leaves and dried-up linden flowers. She returned her gaze to the group sitting around the princess. Sergei Nikolayevich sat reclined on one elbow at his grandmother's feet, while a little girl kneeled before him and offered something in her open palm, a stone, a flower, she could not see. He took it, smiling, and the girl pecked him on the cheek before she sprung up and ran away. Sergei then lifted his eyes, not in the direction of the girl, but toward Lily, as if he knew she had been watching him for a while. Their gazes met and Lily recognized the man she had seen at the customhouse with the ransacked desk. The same thrill she had felt then swept through her again. There was something reckless in his eyes that made them magnetic. She struggled to pull away from his stare.

Elena Volkova walked toward them. "Let me take you into the drawing room where we will have the recital, so you can become acquainted with the space and meet the pianist, who's just arrived."

Lily and Ruby got up and followed her into the house where they waited in a room decorated in tones of green, adjacent to the drawing room where the family gathered and the servants had created a little auditorium with sofas and chairs facing a grand piano. Lily and Ruby stood looking at each other. They knew their pieces well, but they had never performed in a private, intimate setting like this. Lily couldn't quite put her finger on why it was unsettling. This small, beautiful world they had just entered felt dreamy and unreal, intoxicating with its genteel luxury and graceful manners, but also exclusive, closed. For the first time she felt an object of entertainment, instead of an entertainer in command of the show.

She brushed away these thoughts reminding herself that it would soon be over, and kissed Ruby on the cheek. "I can't wait to hear you sing along that grand piano."

"Aye, it'll be very different from the Krügers' sad upright," Ruby said.

Lily performed first, reciting Tennyson's "The Lady of Shallot," which was the princess's favorite English poem, and then Juliet's main monologues from the play. In the middle of her performance, she saw the door open and a servant tiptoe to the back row where Sergei was sitting. He whispered something in his ear, after which Sergei and another man who had been introduced earlier as Elena's older brother, Andrey Volkov, stood up and left the room. A few annoyed heads turned in their direction, but instantly returned to the performance. Everyone hung on Lily's words with utmost attention. The old princess, who sat a few feet away from her, listened to every syllable as if in a trance, and Lily sensed that these pieces had had a special significance in her past life, maybe related to her dead husband or a lover she had adored. When the last monologue ended, everyone applauded, save the princess, who seemed overtaken by emotion. Elena, who sat by her side, offered her a lace handkerchief to dab her eyes.

Then the pianist, a small man dressed in a black frock coat, wearing round eyeglasses and long whiskers, sat at the piano while Ruby took a few steps to the middle of the room and, after waiting for him to give her a musical cue, began to sing. Her voice was a rich, melodious soprano that filled the room. Lily, who was standing to one side behind the piano, looked at the faces of the family audience, riveted by her singing, and thought how talented her friend was, and how little recognition she had gotten in London for it. How unfair Freddy had been to her, not just in their romantic dealings, but also in their professional relationship where he kept her to himself, instead of helping her network into wider circles. Lily felt an old pang grip her as her mind drifted toward her own fiasco and the thought that her burning passion to soar onstage was a dream hard to match with reality. Why was her desire to be an actress so hard to manifest in the world? Her life might be so much easier if she were to collect herself and wait for opportunities to unfold. But instead, her craving to act tormented her to no end and lugged her into strange, difficult paths. What was she hoping to achieve at the end of it all?

She was so lost in these musings that she was hardly aware Ruby had finished her repertoire and everyone had begun to applaud. Kitty jumped up from her seat and rushed to take Ruby's hands, exclaiming, "Oh, but you sing like an angel, you need to give me lessons, I need to learn everything from you."

Elena Volkova also walked up to Lily and said, in her more decorous manner, "Mademoiselle Throop, you were wonderful. Won't you come to my grandmother? She wishes to compliment you personally." Lily followed her to the princess, who took her hand and squeezed it. "You have warmed my heart tonight," Elena translated. "You're a true jewel. Never let anyone kill your sparkle." Lily smiled and gave a little nod, confused at this singular piece of advice.

As the family gathered and moved out of the room, Elena Volkova took her aside and said, "Mademoiselle, I'm wondering if you wouldn't want to stay with us for a while more, if you're not too tired. We have another reunion after this one, a more unorthodox one, and I was hoping you would read from the text of a play my cousin has just brought from Paris."

"I'd be delighted to, but I'm afraid my French is not strong enough," Lily said.

"The play is in English," Elena replied. "It's a controversial work banned in your country that can only be obtained in the Continent." Her expression had changed from an impassive, diplomatic face to open eagerness. "Do you know Oscar Wilde? We're very interested in his work." Lily did know Wilde and had read a number of his plays.

Lily and Ruby followed Elena and Kitty out again into the garden and walked down a path that followed the river on the other side of the house. At the far end they came upon a cottage, its façade overgrown with creepers twisted around latticed woodwork. Inside, they found themselves in a large room covered in wood paneling. It was so dark in comparison to the garden and the pastel interiors of the main house that it took Lily a few moments to discern the space, and the very different crowd that sat around an immense but empty stone fireplace. They whispered in small groups, smoking and drinking from tiny glasses. A considerable portion of the walls was covered with bookcases lined with books, and the garden they had just traversed looked somber and remote through the small, narrow windows. There were animal rugs on the floor and stuffed deer heads with long antlers hanging on the walls. The head of a massive brown bear was mounted over the fireplace mantel.

"Now we're stepping into the real Russia," Ruby exclaimed, looking at the dark, fierce head. Kitty had been telling them how the cottage started out as a hunting lodge, and then became the gamekeeper's abode until their late father decided to accommodate it as a playroom for the family children away from the house. "But now we're all grown up and still hang on to it, and all sorts of silly, highbrow nonsense exchange takes place when we get together. Everyone's become such a bore!"

Elena Volkova introduced Lily and Ruby to the group. There were six men and two women. The men stood up and bowed their heads in greeting, but the women only nodded briefly and remained seated. One of the women had short, cropped hair and was dressed in a very plain, almost drab, dress. She smoked a long cigarette and sat with her legs crossed, like a man. She hardly deigned to look at Lily. She was introduced as Sophia Alexandrovna, a teacher and a women's rights activist. Her face was flat, punctuated by dark eyebrows and large eyes. She would have been pretty, but for the stern look about her. The other woman, Anna Shanyavskaya, was also dressed in an austere tawny dress, and wore her hair in a neat bun at the back of her head, but her face was kind, her eyes earnest. "Our cousin is one of the first women to graduate in medicine in Russia," Elena Volkova said. "We're very proud of her." Lily realized she had never met a woman doctor in her life.

Sergei Nicolayevich was among the men. He stood leaning against the mantelpiece, while next to him sat Andrey Volkov, Elena and Kitty's older brother. Andrey resembled his sister, tall and thin, with a clean-cut, handsome, grave face. He was the only man still dressed in his elegant ivory suit from the garden, which was now unbuttoned with the cravat loose around his neck.

"And this is Anatoly Marchenko, the family painter," Elena said, as a slim young man with bright eyes stood, took Lily's hand, and kissed it, saying, "What a lovely performance you delivered in the house."

But there was a tension in the group. Lily sensed they had been discussing something of a secluded nature, before their conversation was interrupted. It struck her that the group seemed to hold two very distinct types of people: the Volkov family and their cousins, and Sophia and the other four men, who sat in the background dressed in dark clothes, composed in a thoughtful demeanor. One of these men, whose name she didn't catch, sat close behind Andrey Volkov like a shadow. His face was ashen and his small eyes penetrating. He was the only one who wasn't drinking anything.

"I have asked Mademoiselle Throop to read to us from Wilde's play," Elena Volkova said. "But if the meeting is not over, we might leave it for another evening." She spoke in French to include Lily and Ruby in the understanding, since the group had been speaking Russian when they came in. There was a moment of hesitation, then she added, "They are friends of Benjamin Gerard."

This revelation seemed to have some conciliatory effect on the group. Andrey Volkov, lifting sly, humorous eyes towards Sergei Nicholayevich, said, "Since the book in question landed our Seryozha at Peter and Paul's Fortress for one whole night, I think we should honor this request."

Everyone laughed, and many raised their small glasses to Sergei Nicholayevich who, taking a bottle from the mantelpiece, refilled them all. But before he took his own to his lips, he halted. "In fact, if we drink to anyone it should be Sasha. He was instrumental in the whole operation." And he called to one of the servants who had entered the lodge with fresh hot water for the samovars and was lighting candles around the room. Sasha stepped forward, a short boy about fourteen or fifteen years old, with straw blond hair and luminous eyes. He approached Sergei with a glowing smile and let himself be enfolded in a gruff embrace. Sergei then served him a shot of vodka and offered him a toast, "*Za Sashinu khrabrost!* To Sasha's courage!" Everyone gulped down the shots, including Sasha, who coughed and gagged a bit, but stood grinning at the company surrounding him, as some slapped him on the back while they all laughed. Then he resumed his chores as everyone else sat down again, looking contented and relaxed.

Elena Volkova led Lily to the side and took a small book from a shelf. The play, which Lily had heard about but never read, was called *Salomé* and it was based on the biblical story of the beheading of Saint John the Baptist. Elena was planning on staging this play after translating it into Russian, but she was burning to hear it read aloud in its original language. She marked the passage she wanted Lily to recite and gave her a few moments with the text.

It was a monologue by Salomé, as she spoke to Saint John's decapitated head, which she had obtained on a silver platter after dancing for Herod. The prose was exquisite, the content sensual and profane. Lily read aloud while Elena and Sasha held candelabra at her sides, since the room had grown very dark and the candles did not provide enough light. After the reading, everyone clapped and then a discussion ensued about the text.

"It might be daring in that it challenges the scriptures," Sophia Alexandrovna said, blowing out clouds of smoke from her cigarette, "but it is far from being a play for the people."

"It does talk about the inherent power of women, though," Anna Shanyavskaya said. "I think any audience would recognize that. The story could happen in any peasant community, factory setting or slum, not just in a king's court."

"The power of women to obtain horrid feats through sexual teasing of a powerful man, you mean," Sophia Alexandrovna retorted.

Sergei Nicholayevich stepped in. "True, but it mainly talks about the power of desire, and how we tend to destroy that which we desire but fail to possess. I agree with Annushka that this is universal language."

"Still, I don't think this sort of topic can be a priority for a people's theater at the moment," Sophia Alexandrovna went on. She turned to a man called Ivan Kolotov, who was sitting in a corner observing the scene with shrewd, deep-set eyes. "You're a writer, Kolotov, what do you think?"

Kolotov pulled at his goatee for a moment. "Well, I'm not a playwright, but I would agree that, for the moment, we need plays that talk directly about political power, exploitation, and how to overcome it through revolution."

Sophia Alexandrovna looked satisfied. "Precisely. Our peasants and workers are hungry and trampled over, they don't need to be looking at a horny woman dancing the dance of the seven veils."

"And who says they don't? Why wouldn't peasants and workers be also entitled to beautiful art?" Sergei's voice was suave but firm. It was hard to know whether he was serious or just teasing Sophia Alexandrovna.

"Seryozha, if you hadn't recently spent a night in the company of dear old Trubetskoy, we would begin to think you're a hedonistic bourgeois instead of a soldier to the cause," Andrey said jestingly, in an attempt to break up the argument. There was some good-humored sniggering and the conversation drifted elsewhere. People split up into small groups while they drank tea or vodka, or both.

Kitty and Ruby, who had been playing some notes on the piano at the far end of the room, came over to Lily. "See how stuffy they all are?" Kitty whispered. "Talking about nonsense instead of asking you to dance the dance of the seven veils." Lily laughed. She saw they too had been drinking vodka and were feeling very merry.

"But who is this Trubetskoy everyone jokes about?" Lily asked.

"Oh, that's just the name of the prison at the Peter and Paul fortress," Kitty said, with a bored look. "They take you there if they think you're plotting against the czar, and it's become some sort of a badge of honor to pay an occasional visit. A short visit, mind you." Her gaze drifted across the room where Anatoly sat working at a charcoal sketch of the scene of the reading. She took Ruby's hand, saying, "Let me introduce you better to Tolik. Undoubtedly, he'll want to paint your picture," and they moved away.

As she turned around, Lily saw Sergei walking over to her. "Mademoiselle, you have a beautiful voice. What a pleasure it must be to see you performing fully onstage."

"That pleasure is very accessible, if you condescend to attend the Chamber Opera House at the Galernaya Ulitsa and sit through the pathetic production I'm in."

"I'm sure it can't be pathetic if you are in it," he said.

They stood silent for a moment, looking at each other, and Lily felt surprised at how easily they could lock eyes without feeling shy or embarrassed, as if they had known each other for a long time. A tingling warmth enveloped her as she searched his gaze, and images from the customhouse and the picnic replayed themselves in her mind.

Then she asked, lowering her voice, "Is it true that you endured a night's arrest to bring in this book?"

"I did. For this book, and others," he said with a smile, and drew closer to her. "But it wasn't as meritorious as it seems. I knew that given my family circumstances, I would be quickly discharged. At least one last time."

Lily was intrigued. "One *last* time?" she asked, and then added, smirking, "Have you been a regular smuggler?"

"You could say that. A smuggler of words," he said, laughing, "but not always of poetical words."

"Not always of poetical words," Lily echoed, and remembered that when she had related the customhouse incident to Mr. Shuttleworth, he said that Russian authorities were on the constant lookout for anything that could feed political unrest in the country, so that they were probably searching for political literature inside the desk.

That moment, Anna Shanyavskaya joined them. "Mademoiselle, you must think we're a wild bunch, tearing to pieces a beautiful play while we argue about people's politics."

"Not at all," Lily said. "I found the discussion very interesting."

"I wish we would do more and talk less."

"My dear Annushka, who does more than you?" Sergei said, putting an affectionate arm around her shoulder. He turned to Lily and added, "Do you know she works all week in a slum taking care of women and children? *Ona nasha malen'kaya svyataya*, she's our little saint."

Annushka pushed him playfully. "What nonsense! I'm just practicing my profession." She looked back at Lily. "They've allowed us a Women's Medical Institute, but after we graduate they only offer us work in the dumas. Some see it as punishment, but I love my practice, and am happy to serve all sorts of people."

"I've never met a woman doctor. I have so many questions to ask you," Lily said.

"You may visit me in my clinic at any time, but now I must leave, for tomorrow I shall be up at dawn, dealing with snotty, squealing children." She took her leave gracefully and left.

The entire group was preparing to leave, and Sergei was called to a small hub collected around Andrey. "I should ask my cousin Andrey to introduce you to his playwright friend Anton Chekhov," he told Lily. "You would have much to discuss with him, but I also want to come see your plays." After being called again, he excused himself and walked away.

Elena came over to Lily and said, "I have a carriage ready to take you back. I hope we meet again soon. How I wish you would speak Russian so you could act in the play when we stage it."

Polite farewells were exchanged and Lily and Ruby left the cottage, followed by Kitty, who insisted on seeing them to the carriage. She chatted all the way to the driveway where a handsome coach awaited them, and made them promise they would return within the week before she let them go.

They drove back in silence, gazing out of the carriage window at the mauve light that enveloped the island's thick foliage, as they swept by driven by powerful horses. Violet clouds streaked the horizon over St. Petersburg as they crossed the Troitsky Bridge over the Neva. It was already the end of July and the so-called white nights, in which the sky remained bright from dusk to dawn, were mostly over. But tonight the magical opalescent light seemed to linger above, bathing the city in a pearly glow.

Lily held in her lap the envelope stuffed with ruble notes that the German butler had given them before leaving. The payment had exceeded their expectations. She looked at Ruby's rosy cheeks and bright eyes gleaming in the night air and remembered that such had been her face when they first met, full of hope and genuine joy, before the complications started at the Imperial, before she met Freddy. It was the original Ruby, but she was now immersed in such remote reverie that Lily was pricked with a sense of estrangement.

In the days that followed the visit to the Volkov family, everything about their stay in St. Petersburg began to change. Kitty appeared at the Krüger house the next day and ran up the stairs to Lily and Ruby's room. "I have tickets for tonight's ballet at the Mariinsky," she said, "and I want the two of you to come with me."

"But our show only finishes at six," Ruby said, flustered. "We'll never make it on time. Besides, I've nothing to wear."

"I wouldn't worry about that, I have plenty of gowns, and I think we're more or less the same size," Kitty said. "Anyway, I like the red dress you wore yesterday. As for getting there on time, we can do it, as long as you run out of the theater the instant the curtain drops."

"That's hardly ever possible," Ruby said. "Part of our duties have to do with putting away props and closing down the actors' dressing rooms, and—"

Kitty held her by the shoulders and said, "Do you want to come or not? I can think of a thousand ways of getting you out of there in a rush." She walked over to one of the beds, and flopped on top of it with dramatic affectation, saying, "For instance, you can swoon as the curtain's dropping and I'll rush in with my driver, Ilya, and between us we'll put you on a stretcher and take you away, saying we're driving you to the hospital. Meanwhile, I'll procure costumes to disguise us as doctor and nurse." They all laughed, and Kitty kept on spilling out all sorts of outrageous plans to get them to the Mariinsky on time. Behind the jesting, though, Lily understood Kitty was determined to carry out her intention. She also noticed how Ruby was working herself into a frenzy of excitement.

When Kitty left their room they had made no definite plans, and Lily had doubts about it having all just been charming banter. But that evening, as soon as the curtain went down, they saw Kitty marching toward Lambeth. She was dressed in a stunning pink gown and wore a matching, sparkling tiara on her head. Behind her trailed Ilya, carrying an enormous bouquet of chrysanthemums the same color as her dress. At his mistress's indication, he placed the flowers in Lambeth's incredulous arms. "Mr. Lambeth," Kitty exclaimed, "thank you for the most wonderful production of *As You Like It* that Saint Petersburg has ever seen! You made me weep throughout. You're a true genius." And then, taking advantage of Lambeth's astonishment, she added, "And now, I need to borrow your two actresses for a few hours, if you will allow me." Lambeth could only nod with a gaping mouth, dazzled by her gorgeous presence and the sweet, sibilant sounds flowing out of her red mouth.

Lily and Ruby changed hastily in the dressing room and ran out of the theater through the back door, past the suspicious glances of the other actors, with Kitty leading them to an elegant carriage which, no sooner had them all safely tucked inside, bolted through the streets toward the Mariinsky. Ruby laughed all the way, recalling the whole incident, while Kitty sat back, watching her with satisfied, mischievous eyes.

The lights at the theater were already dimming as they reached a plush box overlooking the orchestra pit, and they settled into their seats with beating hearts when the first musical notes arose at the conductor's baton downbeat. A huge stage was revealed behind a grand proscenium arch as the curtain pulled up, where groups of dancers swept gracefully, twirling around one another, with slender ballerinas prancing on pointe like delicate, weightless birds, and male dancers jumping across the stage with long strides of powerful white-clad legs. They were watching *Swan Lake,* and Kitty soon whispered the whole story of Odette and the prince into their ears. They sat mesmerized at the grace and beauty of the show, hearts wrenched, as Odette's tragic fate unfolded before their eyes. When the lights went up during intermission the magnificence of the theater was revealed, and they stood on the balcony of the box admiring the scintillating three-tiered chandelier hanging from the high ceiling, and the elegant crowd meandering below through the rows of blue velvet chairs that lined the auditorium. Kitty introduced them to innumerable people as they took refreshments in the lounge. Everyone was civil and seemed earnestly interested in the fact that they were actresses who had traveled all the way from London to Russia.

When they returned to their seats, Lily saw a number of ladies in opposite boxes spying at them through their dainty opera glasses, and even a gentleman or two. But she soon forgot about everything as Princess Odette returned to the stage, where, mortally wounded by her own unsuspecting lover, she struggled to fight death in lithe, ethereal movements, only to collapse finally in a gracious fold of limbs and reclining head. The whole audience rose and applauded for a long time, and then they poured out of the theater, where the cloud of emotion instilled by Odette's sad beauty dissolved into the bright St. Petersburg night.

They arrived late at Mrs. Krüger's, and Boris had to come down to unbolt the door for them since it was past midnight. When they reached their room, Lily was so fatigued and drunk with the excitement of the evening that she could only lie down on her bed fully dressed. Ruby lay next by her side and embraced her. "How come I have never been to the ballet before?" she muttered. "How come I've always lived like a pauper? It just doesn't make any sense in view of all the wealth that's out there, all the riches we've seen today."

Lily closed her eyes and smiled. "Watch out, Ruby, you're losing your sense of self. *They* are rich, we're not."

"But we can become, or at least better ourselves in this respect," Ruby said, sitting up and looming over her. "Listen, Kitty has asked me to give her singing lessons, and she suggested we both move into her house so we can be closer and—"

"Kitty must be teasing you. How can she ask us to move in when she only met us yesterday?"

Ruby stood up and began to undress. "She's not teasing. She's serious. Don't you see? These people can have anything they want. Each child in the family has their own nanny. Kitty herself has her own chambermaid," she said, pulling out the pins of her hairdo so that her golden red mane tumbled in ringlets down to her waist. "Now she will have her own singing teacher."

"Oh, and what will I be? Her little lap dog?" Lily said with a laugh. "*Your* lady companion? The singing teacher's chambermaid? Oh darling, you just drank too much champagne tonight." She too got up and prepared for bed.

Ruby sulked in front of the mirror and combed her tresses. "I don't see why you laugh. This is serious, Lily."

CHAPTER 16

In the weeks that followed, Kitty came to fetch them frequently with tickets to the opera and the ballet, with invitations to balls and private parties, to fashionable coffee and tea establishments where she treated them to delicious meals and introduced them to her myriad friends and acquaintances. They rode in her carriage along the elegant parts of St. Petersburg and strode with her in the Summer Gardens, or the Peterhof grounds, and navigated the city canals in large, ornate skiff boats pulled by robust oarsmen. Kitty was always sprightly and merry, ready to concoct any scheme that would procure her excitement and fun. There seemed to be no end to her desire for entertainment.

Soon Lily realized that Kitty's most favorite pastime was to pay social calls and attend parties swarming with young officers, with whom she would dance quadrilles and mazurkas, flirt, and later gossip about for days. Following her around felt like riding on the surface of a whirlpool, where no meaningful acquaintance was ever made, where there was never any time to discuss the interest of a performance or to dwell on the beauty of a visited garden. Lily was also disappointed that they had not again met with Elena Volkova or any of the cousins from that first night at the dacha, or even gone back once to Kamenny Island. Instead, Kitty often took them to the family's main residence, a large palace by the Kryukov Canal, inhabited only by servants during the summer months. There, she entertained them in her rooms and encouraged them to change into her clothes for their outings, since Lily and Ruby had such a limited amount of fancy apparel, and so below the level of the society they were now frequenting. Lily reluctantly agreed to this a couple of times, but soon decided she'd rather wear her own garb. Ruby, however, relished in it, as if wearing different costumes were a constant exercise in carnival. This difference quickly set them apart, and created discussions between the two friends that, though conducted with good humor and grace, became an increasing source of disassociation. It was becoming clear that Ruby flourished day by day as if she had been waiting for this all her life, while Lily was fast growing weary of it.

She started looking for excuses not to join Kitty's outings, and strove to come to terms with the city on her own, exploring the long avenues and canals by herself, still against Mrs. Krüger's advice. She visited the interiors of churches, admired the artistry of the palace façades with their colossal caryatids upholding huge portals and long protruding eaves. Sometimes she called upon Mr. Shuttleworth at the Anglican Church and asked to borrow books about Russian history and its theater. If she could only make contact with some of the actors and theaters that were staging the new work she had heard about! But how could she do this without speaking Russian?

She began spending more time with the theater troupe and realized that behind their hostility there was just great insecurity. Now that they could all blame Ruby for being disdainful, they were ready to embrace Lily fully into their company. Lambeth, she found out, was not a great director, but could be a generous teacher. She stood by him during the shows, assisting him, observing every detail of his work, wondering what it would be like to direct plays.

"There are plenty of women managing theaters," Lambeth said to her one day. "Did you never meet Mrs. Lane, the Hoxton Queen, in London? She's one. And Lillie Langtry is another. There's also Emma Cons at the Royal Victoria Hall. Here in St. Petersburg I've heard of a woman called Vera Komissarzhevskaya who owns her own theater."

At these words Lily remembered with a pang that she and Chut had always dreamed of managing a theater together one day. It was rare she thought of him these days, but when she did, his memory invaded her like the aftertaste of a strong, bittersweet draft, the lees of which she was sure would never leave her.

One afternoon, as Lily was returning from the opera house, Mrs. Krüger gave her a small envelope with her name written on it. It was a note from Elena Volkova in which she invited her to a dinner party. *Dear Mademoiselle, I would be delighted if you could join us on the occasion of our cousin Anatoly Marchenko's name day celebration. Many of the guests will be artists and writers, the acquaintance of whom I am sure you will enjoy very much. Truly yours, EV.* Lily was touched by the personal tone of the invitation, and as she sat in her room writing a note of acceptance, Ruby and Kitty burst through the door.

"Did Lena invite you to the dinner party?" Kitty asked.

"And will you accept?" Ruby added.

"Of course," Lily said.

"Don't say that as if it is a given," Ruby said in the reproachful tone that she now employed daily with Lily. "You've become a hermit these days, refusing to go anywhere with us."

"Oh, but this is different," Kitty said, and taking a chair, sat facing Lily, "because all these artistes will be there, with their high talk about art and form and meaning." A taunting smile spread across her lips. "It's also different because Sergei Nicolayevich will be there." Lily blushed, and Kitty laughed. "You see? I knew it! I saw you looking at him during the picnic." There was malice in her words, and she laughed with abandonment. Then she took Lily's hand. "I know how you feel. As a little girl, I was utterly crazy about him. My handsome cousin, always original and daring."

"But you grew out of him. . . ." Ruby said, sitting by her side.

"Oh, but never totally," Kitty said, her eyes flashing at Lily. "It's hard to share love, and just about *everyone* loves him." Kitty held Lily's gaze for a moment longer, and added, "But he's a powder keg. I recommend you stay away from him. Unless you want to explode up in the air with him."

Lily pulled her hand away from Kitty's and reclined in her chair.

"I thank you for your advice. But I wasn't thinking about him in that manner," she said, annoyed.

Kitty stood up. "Good!" She looked around the room with a bored expression on her face, and then said, matter-of-factly, "Anyway, he's married."

"Is he?" Ruby asked. "He carries himself as if he were as free as a lark."

"Well, he isn't. He's technically married. Of course, the silly thing lasted less than a month. And it was many years ago, but still . . ." She waited, knowing her revelation might bring about many more questions, but Lily made it a point not to give her any satisfaction.

After a few moments, Kitty prepared to leave, and when she was at the door, she turned to Lily and Ruby, her face sweet and merry once again. "Shall I come pick you up tomorrow evening?"

Small lamps covered by delicate shades cast an intimate glow across the dining table and its diners, away from the cool, cobalt light shining outside the bay windows at the end of the room. The long table was laden with masses of flowers and silver stands with hanging arms that held baskets spilling over with fruit and sweets. Red and white wineglasses sparkled among the crowded surface, alongside silver jugs and crystal decanters. Lily looked at the exquisite gold-rimmed plate that lay before her and the complicated constellation of all sizes of knives, forks, and spoons surrounding it. She reflected on the modest table etiquette she had learned in the London restaurants she once thought so elegant. Across the table, Ruby's brow was also knitted in bewilderment while Kitty amusedly instructed her in the use of the multiple accoutrements.

But Lily soon realized that rigid etiquette was not a Volkov family preoccupation, at least not for an occasion like this. As the servants started serving dishes, she observed that some of the guests were making indistinct use of the different pieces of cutlery, paying no attention to manners or convention. To her right, Smolokov, a heavyset, dark-bearded individual dressed in a threadbare coat, who had been introduced as a brilliant painter, was piercing his fish filet with the fruit knife, and another guest, a poet by the name of Ivan Tavarovich, had insisted that the butler pour his white wine into the champagne glass, which he felt was superior in capacity. By contrast, Sergei Nikolayevich, who sat between them, handled all his tableware with extreme grace, while conversing casually with both men. Occasionally, he shot glances at Lily, and she wished he had been seated next to her.

Elena Volkova sat at the head of the table, presiding over a lively conversation that took place in several languages at once. Some of the artists only spoke Russian, while others could also communicate in German, or in a little French. Only the Volkovs and their cousins spoke English, and Anatoly, who sat at Lily's side, did his best to translate the animated exchange.

A man with a long face and fiery eyes, by the name of Belkin, said, "Why does Russia have to always mope around in deep pessimism? We are living in a time bursting with creativity and new ideas, we are reinventing our art forms, and yet, we're always feeling doomed, full of dread for the future. It's like trying to walk with feet shackled to cannonballs." He got up from his chair and trailed around the table with heavy, shuffling feet. Everyone laughed.

"Why, Belkin," Smolokov said, "There's nothing we can do about our country's melancholy soul. But not everyone is morose. Tavarovich's poems can be very humorous, and Anatoly's portraits are full of cheerful colors. As for your own dark and stormy landscapes . . ."

Belkin waved a hand at him, as if to dismiss his argument. "Don't provoke, Smolokov, you know very well what I mean." Everyone pealed with laughter as if this was an ongoing joke between them. Belkin, flustered, sat down again and drained the wine from his glass in one gulp.

Andrey Volkov, who sat opposite his sister Elena, spoke next. "I think Russia will always feel doomed until we are able to change our political structure." Everyone regarded him with a sort of reverence, as he put down his silverware on his plate and looked gravely around. "Our obsolete government and archaic class system condemn us to stagnation. In all areas of life, including art."

"Andrey Ivanovich, don't you believe in the revolutionary power of art?" a small bald man with long, twirling whiskers, asked. "Art is always at the vanguard when it comes to social and political change."

"It will take much more than art to propel the revolution we need, Pavel Vasilievich," Andrey replied. There was a moment of silence, after which the conversation broke up into smaller groups around the table.

Anatoly turned to Lily. "Sorry, mademoiselle, my poor translation is not giving you the best of our discussion."

"Oh, I think you're doing very well," Lily said, smiling at his pale, candid face. She felt she was abusing Anatoly's kindness on his celebration day.

Toward the end of the dinner the toasts started. Servants poured shots of vodka between courses, with everyone at the table standing up each time and raising their glasses at speakers while they pledged their drinks. Most of the toasts were offered to Anatoly, and everyone clinked their glass with a neighbor before gulping down the shot, amid laughter and rejoicing.

It was the first time Lily drank vodka. It burned her throat and stomach as if she had swallowed fire, and then spiked up to her head, making it blaze with enhanced perception, while the rest of her body tingled. After the second toast she began to feel dizzy and started thinking of ways to decline the long string that was yet to come. But the servants bypassed her from thereon, as if this might be some sort of convention with young, inexperienced ladies.

She was still feeling a bit unsteady when the company moved into the smoking room, where more spirits and Turkish coffee were served, as well as cigars and cigarettes passed around. Ahead of her was a group of women sitting around an actress called Maria Ivanovna. She was a small woman with dark hair and deep, melancholy eyes, who had been sitting to her far left at the table and knew quite a bit about experimental theater in St. Petersburg, as Anatoly had said. Lily was heading toward the group, hoping to find another translator, when Sergei intercepted her.

"How are you enjoying the evening?"

"Very much, thank you," she said. "I'm just frustrated at not being able to follow conversations or talk freely. There are so many things I missed at the table."

"There's a simple solution to that," Sergei said. "Stay in Russia and learn Russian. Then you'll be able to speak with whomever you like, and give us the benefit of your performances in our own language." She looked at him expecting his face to open into a smirk, as if it was all in jest, but he remained earnest. "I'm not joking, I do mean it."

Lily laughed. "Are you suggesting I turn my whole life around and come to live in your country?"

"Why not? This is going to be a new nation in no time. And you will be one of the first new women in it. You're talented, independent, inquisitive, daring. You are a mirror image of the new century, a torch of change, and we need women like you among us."

She felt her cheeks burning, as if the vodka were bolting once more inside her. "How can you venture all these judgments about me? We've only met twice, and hardly exchanged a few words," she said, sliding into the same mesmeric feeling that had trapped her during their first conversation.

"Thrice, if you remember well," Sergei said. "At any rate, the number of times one meets someone has no bearing on the level of connection to that person. Why, one knows people for years and deep feelings never develop; they might elicit one's affection, but never bring forth any heartfelt emotion. Then one day you lock eyes with a stranger, and there it is, the divine spark of recognition. And you know you cannot escape that bond."

Lily watched him, feeling the thrill of his proximity and wondering at the meaning of his words. "So you believe in predestination? That people meet and interact because it is their fate to do so?"

"Maybe. I haven't thought much about it. I only know I'm sometimes irresistibly attracted to certain persons, or to certain situations."

She forgot all about Maria Ivanovna and her experimental theater and wandered out of the smoking room, following Sergei through dim-lit corridors and rooms, until they reached a large glass door that opened into the garden. The lush, darkened meadow sprinkled with long-branched linden trees opened before them as they crossed a stone path shimmering with moonlight under their feet. They reached a stretch of marble veranda along the river and leaned over it. Small, silken sounds of buzzing dragonflies and croaking frogs echoed in their midst above the silvery surface of the water.

Sergei bent down with boyish limberness, picked up a pebble, and flung it toward the water. It skimmed the skin of the river until it disappeared under twinkling eddies. The small, sharp noise it made as it dropped froze all other sounds around them for a moment, and Lily thought of all the times he might have performed this same action before, playing in the garden as a child, with his cousins, in the timeless beauty of their summer mansion.

"Your family is fortunate to have such a beautiful house," she said.

"It's been in the family since the seventeen hundreds. Peter the Great gifted the land to our great-great-great grandfather, who was the first to start building the house. But he died before his time and never finished it."

"He died before his time?"

"He was out in the woods, lost from his hunting party, and he was attacked by a massive brown bear. They fought fiercely until he killed the bear, but he was already mortally wounded. He dragged himself back to this cottage, which then was just a hunting lodge, but had lost so much blood that he died in a few hours. Do you know what his last words were? 'Find the bastard, cut off his head, and hang it here on the wall. He fought like a lion.'"

"What a story!" Lily said.

"It's become a family legend now." Sergei looked out over the water smiling. "I could tell you many stories and show you many places, if you would allow me." His voice had descended to a near whisper. Lily felt it rushing past her cheeks, like a caress.

"I'd be happy, during my leisure time after work," she said, leaning back, trying to sound cheery. She felt dazed. She was riveted to the ground and yet her feet felt restless, as if they must run away as quickly as possible. Something was moving too fast, bypassing her sense of control and capsizing the tight-disciplined little ship she tried so hard to make out of her life.

"Maybe that way I'll persuade you to stay in Russia," Sergei said. "Don't think I'm rambling. The moment I lay eyes on you in the customhouse I felt I knew you, that maybe I'd just been waiting for you." She felt his cool, smooth hands as they took hers. They gripped her tenderly, yet with tenacity. "Maybe that's why I'm sad at the idea that you will leave."

The moonlight accentuated his fine features and shadowed his heavy-lidded eyes. His pale stare held her as if under a spell, while his words bounced around in her mind, words that sounded like lovers' hot air, similar to much she had dismissed in the past from other men wanting to seduce a young actress like her. But the way he delivered his speech was different; it reached her like the susurration of a promise she'd been seeking all along.

Sergei brought her fingertips to his lips. "There I go with thoughts of doom. Belkin was right, we always emphasize the dark side of things in Russia."

A sudden call of voices from the house distracted them, and they saw that Ruby and Kitty had entered the garden and were crying out their names. Lily's and Sergei's eyes met in a flash, and without a word he clasped her hand and they slipped away from the veranda, running noiselessly into the shadows of the foliage, away from the domesticated garden, past the cottage, where the grounds grew wild with tall grass and led to a grove of dark trees looming against the phosphorescent sky. They slowed down, catching their breath, and walked with fast-beating hearts through the clusters of birch and aspen trees, brushing against the thicket of dark ferns at their feet. Smells of damp, musky soil replaced the sweet scents of lilac bushes and honeysuckle that had engulfed them in the garden. They turned to each other full of childish glee and listened. From this vantage point Kitty's voice sounded remote, a thin wail muffled by the distance. For an instant, Lily was gripped by the sensation that this scene had taken place many times before, flighty shapes of teetering children darting through a fragrant garden and disappearing into the shadows, crouching as they hid, panting and listening for the youngest, most annoying one left behind.

"Poor Kitty, I don't think we're being fair," she said, and her memory flickered back to her friend's tiresome warnings about Sergei.

But he only laughed. "When it comes to Kitty, any avoidance is not just fair but necessary." He was leaning against a tree. His face was half in shadow, but she could see his eyes shining with amusement. His mood seemed to have lightened after their little fugue and he sank back against the bark, smiling. An owl hooted and the canopy of leaves above their heads rustled as it took flight. It caught Lily by surprise, startling her.

"And beware, for she's known to bribe forest owls as her informers," Sergei said, looking up to the treetops. "There, you've just gotten a good glimpse into the Volkovs—women preoccupied with owls and men obsessed with bears."

A sudden burst of mirth rippled through Lily's body making her giggle, as if this moment was the most absurd and yet the most charming of her whole life. Sergei stepped up and took her into his arms, hushing her against his chest. "Shush, you'll get us found out." Slowly her laughter yielded, and they stood kissing under the trees.

CHAPTER 17

The next day Lily woke up feeling tired and sick. She remembered having strange dreams all night, full of anguish and heart-thumping flight. But she pinned it all on the vodka and decided it was not a drink for her. She recollected the scenes with Sergei in the garden and the darkened grove, and how passionate he had become before she persuaded him to drive her home, with the promise of seeing him again the next day. Smushing her face into the pillow, she thought of the way he had held her head with both hands as he kissed her; the distinct sweet taste of his lips; his pale, handsome face, dreamy under the moonlight filtering through the trees.

But would this do? Not only was the man married—although never really lived with his wife, as Kitty told it—but, wasn't she rushing into an affection that would be truncated in a few weeks when she returned to England? Would it be worth it? And, what would happen if she got attached? This last question hung in her mind. She was still hurting from her breakup with Chut. Would a new friendship ease her heart? The memory of Sergei sweeping her across darkened woodlands returned to her mind. No, this would not be a friendship. Judging by the exhilaration she felt when he was close, the ease with which he seemed to carry her off her feet, this would quickly mount to much more.

A knock on the door shook her out of her musings. Mrs. Krüger entered the room to announce that Mr. Gerard had returned from Moscow the night before, and had sent word for Lily to come see him regarding an important matter as soon as possible. The first thought that darted through her mind was that Gerard might have arranged a meeting for her with Stanislavsky or one of his associates so, shaking off her sluggish mood, she rushed to meet him even before she took her breakfast.

When she arrived, Gerard sat on a brocaded chair by the window and eyed her wearily. He lifted a hand to indicate that she should take a seat facing him. "Benjamin, I hope this is not too early, and that you will have had enough time to rest from your journey," Lily said, out of breath.

Gerard shot her a somber look and sighed. "I am fine, thank you, Miss Throop."

She was momentarily puzzled as to why he had returned to addressing her formally. "It's important we talk about a certain matter concerning our professional contractual relationship," he said, and without taking any notice of her visible disappointment, he continued, "I have received a letter from Mr. Herbert Wade stating that you are under contract with him and Mr. Harrison to perform exclusively for their company, and that this legal instrument precludes you from working with anyone else without their stipulated written consent." He paused and scanned Lily's face. "Is this true, Miss Throop? Are you presently under contract with them?"

Lily's heart skipped a beat. "I did sign a contract some years ago. But they released me from the theater and didn't pay my salary for weeks after they filed for bankruptcy. I thought the commitment was over," she stammered. Her head was reeling, her lungs narrowing in spasms, as if all air would be squeezed out of her chest.

Gerard looked at her for a long moment while she withstood his gaze with burning eyes. "Legal contracts are not terminated through bankruptcy until a court of law stipulates so," he said icily. Then he got up slowly and stood by the window, looking out with hands folded behind his back underneath his frock coat. "You have placed me in a difficult position, Miss Throop. He could demand compensation; he could take me to task in front of the London theater community. He's not an easy adversary to have." He started coughing and had to sit down again, while he took a handkerchief from his pocket and wiped his mouth. "You are to return to London right away. He's offering to pay for your journey expenses."

Lily began to shiver. "But Mr. Gerard, the plays at the opera house! We just started on *The Cenci*—how can I leave now?" Her body felt cold while her head was scorching. To return to London now, and be delivered back into the hands of Wade!

"We'll need Miss Kirkpatrick to take over your work," Gerard said. A moment passed and Lily buried her face in her hands. She heard Gerard pacing up and down the room. She was afraid she would dissolve into tears. She felt him sit down across from her again. "Forgive me if I sound short-tempered. I'm sure you misunderstood the situation. I just cannot afford a squabble of this sort and must oblige him."

There was a knock at the door, and Gerard excused himself briefly to answer the door, where he exchanged a few words with a messenger. Lily stood up, smoothing her face and hair. Her mind darted around like a monkey inside a cage, wild with terror. A taste of metal flooded her mouth as Wade's hypnotic pinpoint stare flashed into recollection. She took in large drafts of air and turned to the window, struggling to control herself. Was there to be no healing with the passing of time? No soothing, even through the 1,700 miles that separated London from St. Petersburg?

She fixed her gaze across the Griboyedov Canal, where the Church of the Savior on Spilled Blood was being built. It was a shrine destined to stand over the exact spot where the Czar Alexander II had been assassinated years before. Its onion domes and swirling multicolored turrets gleamed in the sun, imprisoned behind dark grilles of scaffolding. She thought of the time she had seen the torn military jacket of the dead czar displayed in the Hermitage when she visited with Mr. Shuttleworth, and how much pity she had felt at the sight of the ripped, ragged sleeves that would have been blood-soaked at the time of his agony. It was touching that his son had spent years building a whole church over the location of his onslaught. Something settled inside her chest at these thoughts, as if she had been reminded that human suffering must pass after all, and may even be recorded in the timeless works of artists and poets. But who would record and embellish her troubles? Wouldn't they just be buried, like those of most people, in anonymous graves?

Gerard returned to the window. "No one is more grieved to lose you than I, Lily. Your performances have saved my reputation at this challenging point in my life, and I shall be ever grateful to you for it." When Lily remained silent, he added, "I will write to Mr. Wade immediately and request he allows you to end the present program, which will give you a few more weeks."

She prepared to leave. Gerard walked her to the door. "They're back on their feet at the Adelphi Theatre, and he undoubtedly has work for you at their new venue. It won't be all bad." She turned away and left the room.

Lily arrived dejected at the Krüger house and went up to her room to give Ruby the terrible news, but she found her friend weeping disconsolately on her bed. When she ran to her, asking what the matter was, Ruby turned a blotchy face with swollen eyes. "The baby has been born, Lily. And Freddy has acknowledged him."

She burst once more into sobs. "How did you find out?" Lily asked.

"Fanny sent a letter through Mr. Gerard that was delivered here this morning."

"Are there any letters for me?" Lily asked.

Ruby got up rubbing her eyes, and walked toward the window. "Not that I know of." She leaned her forehead on the pane. "Fanny also wrote," she started, and faltered for a moment before adding, "that Chut is engaged and they're to be married by Christmas."

Lily first sat up, and then instantly sank back against the bedstead as if Ruby's words had punctured her. She closed her eyes and reflected that she had anticipated all of this; that she had long ago given up all hope and every claim to Chut as her lover. Why, even the night before she had kissed Sergei feeling that the past was behind her and she was now free to engage her affections elsewhere. But the wave of pain that pumped into her had no consideration for any of these ruminations; it rammed into every nerve, making her throb with misery.

Lily and Ruby sat in silence, each immersed in their own wretchedness. At least one hour passed this way until Ruby got up, picked up her shawl and bonnet, and, turning to Lily as she reached the door, said, "There's one thing I know. I'm not going back to London."

Ruby left the inn in the next few days, taking all her luggage, after having accepted in firm the invitation to move into Kitty's apartments. She urged Lily to do the same, but Lily stalled. She needed to be alone to think about her new situation and how she would confront it, and joining Kitty's carousing raids was the least useful circumstance for the purpose. She knew Ruby would be drowning her grief in merrymaking and long evenings of dancing and drinking. But then she only had to take care of her broken heart, whereas Lily had that and the trepidation of being forced to return to her indentured servitude with Wade and Harrison. She considered writing to Harry and asking him to plead her case before her father, so she might return to Manchester and stay at his house while she procured other arrangements, but she knew it would be in vain. Even if her father took her back and she went to Manchester, or to Leeds with Lambeth and the troupe, Wade would still seek her out and force her to return to him. He had the law on his side, and he would make sure to hound her to the end of the world. She shuddered at the thought.

Day after day passed and Lily steeped deeper into uneasiness. She walked up and down her chamber for hours, wringing her hands. She lay sleepless at night, wrestling with anguish. She could not touch food. She could hardly sustain a serious conversation with anyone. She felt restless and lonely. Besides Ruby, she could only think of two other people who could give her any comfort at this time. One was Shuttleworth, but his wife was going through one of her sick spells and he was unavailable.

The other was Sergei. But he had disappeared.

It had been over two weeks since they met at Anatoly's celebration and wandered into the garden, but despite his promise to meet her the following day, Sergei hadn't yet made one appearance. Through Ruby she found out he had been called to Moscow on urgent business, but it was still very disappointing that he hadn't thought to send a note of excuse. Maybe it was for the better. Her life was now too sad and complicated to attend to seduction and banter.

It was already September. The days were much shorter and the sky was frequently overcast, with a dull gray film of gloom hanging over the city. "Just wait," Boris would say, "come the first of October, everything goes dark as if a black curtain has been dropped. Then all we do for seven long months is dream about spring." But Lily would stare at him indifferently. She wouldn't be there to experience any of it.

One evening, as she was walking into the actors' dressing room at the end of her performance at the opera house, she spotted a massive bouquet of red roses sitting on the table by the mirror where she sat to put on her makeup. Mirabelle, a fellow actress, said, "A gentleman sent these in and is asking to see you."

"Please, Mirabelle, I'm not in the mood for anyone. Would you go out to him?"

"But they're saying he's the late Count Latvin's son. How're you not to see him?"

Lily walked toward the little pink parlor by the refreshment lounge wondering who this count's son could be. The audience attending the opera house usually consisted of middle-class families or impoverished lower nobility; mostly mothers with daughters, modest anglophiles, and students of English. Aside from Kitty's cameo appearance, she'd never encountered any other grand figure among the crowd. So she was surprised to find Sergei sitting on one of the salmon-colored sofas in the lounge. She throbbed with joy at the sight of him, but then her mind began to puzzle. It shocked her that she hadn't spotted him in such a small auditorium, and she reflected bitterly how her distraught state was disturbing her perception.

Sergei sprung up from his chair, took her hands, and kissed them. "I have no words. Your presence onstage—it's irresistible; it's electric."

She might have laughed in other circumstances. The play was quite controversial. She played the role of Beatrice Cenci, a patricidal murderess of a tyrannical father, and many people were at a loss when they tried to comment on the production. But tonight she was feeling numb and drained. She thought of all the days she had expected a visit or a note from him, only to end up disappointed. She offered him a small, curt smile.

"I have reserved a room in a restaurant nearby," he said, watching her with pale, intense eyes. "Please come with me."

"I thank you, but I must decline. I'm expected at my rooms immediately."

"Oh, but I must insist." He raised a hand to caress her face, but she stepped back.

"I truly cannot accompany you today, Sergei Nikolayevich. I'm otherwise engaged."

"Would you allow me to inquire about the nature of your engagement?" he asked.

Lily wavered at this audacity, but then realized she had little energy to keep up pretenses. "My engagement consists of my own preoccupations, monsieur. And as much as I appreciate your invitation, I'm afraid we must leave it for another day."

As she turned to leave, Sergei seized her hand and whispered, "There might not be another day."

From the corner of her eye Lily could see Mirabelle and another actress who had taken seats at one of the other tables in the refreshment lounge just to watch them. Lily pulled her hand away from Sergei's and walked to an armchair in the corner, away from her colleagues' view. Sergei followed, and they sat facing each other.

"I am leaving Saint Petersburg tomorrow," he said, "and I need the blessing of your company before I undertake this journey. It's my most challenging trip yet."

Lily sighed, trying to figure out ways of freeing herself from him. She sensed agitation in Sergei, but it seemed to come more from some sort of thrill rather than anguish.

"I know you're upset with me for not coming earlier, or writing to you," he continued. "All I can say for myself is that the nature of my present work is such that I cannot give account of my whereabouts. I must protect anyone I care for."

Lily studied his face for wile, but only detected earnestness on his countenance. His last words hung in the air between them. Her guard began to dissolve as her hunger for affection crept to the surface.

"Do you think I haven't thought about you every day?" he said.

"Sergei Nicolayevich, I shall also be leaving Saint Petersburg, for London, soon. There might be no point. . . ."

"On the contrary, all the point in the world," Sergei said with sudden zeal. "Let's drink like Cossacks the night before the battle." And at Lily's smiling but doubtful face, he added, "Let's then revel in each other's company over some excellent caviar and champagne."

She peered into his cool, gray eyes, feeling helpless. The sequence of upcoming events played itself out in her mind. They would go to a fashionable restaurant and fall into a dreamy cloud over caviar and champagne, and then Sergei would take her hand and lead her into a plush carriage that would whisk them away to his apartments, where he would sweep her up magnificent stairs into his bedroom to a large, elegant bed surrounded by books and beautiful artifacts, and there he would ravish her while she sought oblivion and mental blankness from her misery.

Let it happen then, she thought. *There might not be another day.*

Outside the night was cold and moonless. A carriage with four fine black horses waited on the curb by the theater and, sitting beside the coachman on the box, Lily recognized Sergei's servant boy, Sasha. He turned a smiling face to her as she stepped inside. She shivered as she sat on the cold leather seat, thinking that her summer coat was too thin for the increasingly chilly evenings of St. Petersburg. But before following her in, Sergei turned to Sasha and the driver and said something in Russian, after which Sasha stepped down from the box and brought a blanket to her door. Lily watched his rosy, glowing face as he placed the cover in her hands. He winked at her with a slight bow of the head, a small, charming gesture she had noticed when she first saw him at the cottage. She unfolded the woolly fabric and threw it over her legs, luxuriating in its instant warmth. "Isn't this a bit late for a young boy like him?"

she asked, as Sergei settled by her side and the carriage took off. "Shouldn't he be in bed by now?"

Sergei smiled. "He'll be fifteen in a week or so. In Russia, that already counts him among the ranks of men."

"I bet you were in bed by this hour at his age," Lily said, "and being tucked in lovingly by your mother."

Sergei laughed his joyful, deep laugh. "That might be true. But it would have been done totally against my will. So in retaliation for over-nurturing, despotic mothers, I let Sasha do whatever he likes."

"Whatever he likes at your service?" Lily taunted. She was amazed at how quickly she had swung from morose ennui to shameless flirting, and how in the presence of Sergei she felt lighthearted and oblivious of everything else. She was only conscious of his slim, compact body beside her, his long, muscled legs stretched out before him and his arms folded casually over his chest. He stared out of the carriage window considering her words, with lips curled into a tickling smile. She watched the dappling of shadows play across his face, as if it were a screen reflecting nebulous events unfolding in the remote outside world.

"Sasha loves me as a little brother," Sergei said. "He doesn't mind following me to places. In fact, I have a hard time persuading him to step down from any chore."

"I can see he's crazy about you. I sort of understand why, with all this liberalism. . . ."

"I'm sure he'd love me the same if I put him in a straitjacket," Sergei said with a chuckle. "He's one of those one-sided souls who if they love you, they do so till the death, and if they don't, they couldn't be bothered with you."

"Is that the way you're used to being loved?" she asked.

"It's not the way I'm used to, it's just the way I prefer," he said. "What about you? How do you like to be loved?"

The question took her by surprise, and she knit her brow for a moment. "I want to be loved for everything I am, and everything I want to be. Half measures won't do."

"Hmm. It sounds dangerously close to my own preference."

"Why dangerously?"

"Because, how would two people who demand the same quality of love from each other survive together?"

"I don't see why not."

"It's a game where you're mostly a giver or a taker. Wouldn't you agree?"

"Not necessarily," she said, but was instantly smitten by the thought that, if anything, she might be classified as a taker: Chut, Harry, and Alice, her adoring audiences—hadn't they all been plentiful givers? "And why couldn't two people just take love from each other, as opposed to struggling in a relationship of opposites?"

"Why?" Sergei echoed, amused. He gazed out the window again, taking a moment. "The problem is that true love is not just rare; it's also our strongest tool of survival, the ultimate thing that might keep us afloat. All of which makes for an irresistible possession that everyone wants to hoard."

"Well, if ever I heard a worthy quote," Lily said with a little whistle.

Sergei laughed. "It's not mine. It's from some old, forgotten Russian poet I must have had to read in school."

"Forgotten or not, it seems you've assimilated it quite well into your own cache."

That moment the carriage stopped abruptly. Sergei looked outside and extended his arm to slide the window open, but the driver had already jumped down from the box and was standing close to the pane, whispering hoarsely in alarm. A quick conversation in Russian between the driver and Sergei followed. Lily only caught the mention of the name Ivanka, which she thought might be the driver's name. Seconds later, she heard Ivanka swing back up onto the box, and the carriage started off again. The wheels swerved onto a dark, narrow humped street.

"What's happening?" Lily asked.

"We're being followed," Sergei said. "It seems the czar's police got whiff of my plans."

"The police! But why would they follow you?" she asked, bewildered.

"Don't be afraid. No one better than Ivanka to lose them in no time," he said. "I'm truly sorry I didn't anticipate this, but everything will be all right."

"Where are we going?" Lily asked.

"We'll have to drive all the way out to Kamenny Island. They won't dare trespass onto the dacha grounds." Sergei looked to the sides and through the back window as he spoke, glittering with an excitement Lily hadn't seen in him before.

Ivanka cracked the whip over the horses, making them brake into a canter as the narrow street opened up to a wider avenue. The sound of hooves and wild rattling over cobbled streets echoed inside the carriage. Lily looked around for the safety strap to hold. She was afraid she would be hurled out of her seat at any moment. Through her window she could see they were now rushing along the Nevsky Prospect and heading toward the Troitsky Bridge. She looked back and saw two police droshkies galloping behind them in the distance. She heard Ivanka's hoarse, whinny-like cries charging the steeds forward as their carriage raced onto the Troitsky. Once on the bridge, he swerved the horses around the slower coaches in front of them. They lurched from one side to another with shocked and indignant cries from other coachmen. Lily saw a phaeton with two passengers careen out of control as the horses panicked. Loud neighing reverberated in her ears as the terrified beasts ducked their heads and kicked up their heels, while their driver stood to rein them back in. Another carriage was driven sideways, and Lily saw the police droshkies stall and lose ground in the chaos that ensued on the roadway.

Their carriage rushed on. Sergei stuck his head out the window and cried out something in Russian that Lily thought sounded like praise of Ivanka and Sasha for their skillful maneuvering. Her heart thumped wildly in her chest, even as they left the bridge behind and relented into a slower pace over the Kamennoostrovsky Prospect toward the dacha.

"Are you all right?" Sergei asked. "We'll soon arrive, now that we've lost them." His eyes shone with gleeful triumph as he took her hands. "You're cold. As soon as we get there, I'll ask Sasha to build a fire," he said.

Lily was in too much shock to articulate her distress or even ask questions. She turned away from him and gazed out the window at the still, black waters of the Krestovka Canal as they crossed it, hoping to restore some tranquility of mind. But a small, roaring sound growing quickly behind her made her look back, and there she saw a group of horsemen galloping behind them. They hovered at a distance, a sinister cluster of glistening motion rising in their wake. Her chest contracted with more fear than she had felt so far.

"They think this is serious enough to send out the Okranka guards, the idiots!" Sergei grumbled.

Outside, Ivanka's cries were joined by Sasha's shrill yells. The whip cracked again over the horses as the coach lurched forward. Tree branches whipped against the sides of the carriage as they flew over the pitch-black roads with the horsemen gaining ground behind them. Just when Lily thought everything was lost and that the riders would overcome them, the carriage veered to the left and she saw the lanterns burning over the iron gates of the dacha. Ivanka shouted and whistled as he pulled the horses to a stop. A lanky, ghostlike, bareheaded shape stepped up and began pushing the heavy gates open with maddening slowness, while the horses snorted and puffed, kicking their hooves nervously. Sasha jumped down, dashed to the gate, and lunged against it, and the carriage crossed its threshold just as the horsemen came into view and pulled to a stop.

Sergei sat back with a sigh. "That was close!"

Lily's foot trembled as she stepped off the carriage. Ahead of her, the black mass of the unlit house with its ghostly turrets loomed against a dark indigo sky with pin-like stars shining far above. Frost wrapped around her with tiny, icy claws, making her shiver. The horses stood glistening with sweat, steam billowing from their pounding bodies into the cold night. She could hear their labored breathing. Nearby, Sergei, Sasha, and Ivanka held an excited exchange, none of which Lily could understand. Sergei slapped them both heartily on the back and then walked toward her.

"The house is already closed down for the season," he said, "but we can stay at the cottage tonight." There was a frenzied look in his eyes, as if he were a different person.

"I'm not staying anywhere tonight," Lily said. "I want to return to the city immediately."

"That's not possible. They'll be watching the gate until morning. You'll have to stay here until it's safe for you to drive back."

"Safe for me to drive back!" she echoed, indignant.

"I'm sorry you had to be brought into this," he said. "There's real danger out there. I cannot let you leave now." Lily stood shaking with cold and exhaustion. "You're cold. Let's get inside." Sergei said, and gripping her hand he led her around the house to the cottage.

The cottage was dark but for the huge fire already blazing at the far end of the cavernous space. Silhouetted against the flames, Sasha's slender shape moved quietly, unloading pieces of wood and sweeping around the hearth. A large leather sofa had been placed in front of the fireplace, and a thick animal rug lay at its feet.

"Sasha, bring vodka," Sergei cried out, and even Lily understood the words in Russian. Then he turned to her and said, "It will do you good. It'll take off the edge."

But Lily resisted following him to the hearth. She stood staring at the flames. The smell of smoke lingering in the room wafted into her nose and lungs, filling her with unease. Terror of fire flooded her mind, threatening to regurgitate loathsome memories. Everything around felt unfamiliar, disjointed. A suffocating sensation of being lured into a trap seized her, and she was overcome by an irresistible desire to flee the room and rush out into the dark cool night of the forest.

"*Malen'kaya khozyajka*," a whispering voice said, and she saw Sasha standing by her side with a tiny metal tray on which he bore a shot glass of vodka. "*Malen'kaya khozyajka*," he repeated, twinkling his eyes toward the glass. "Little mistress," she knew that to mean; she had heard Boris refer to a young girl the same way at the inn. Little mistress! The thought that Sasha would address her in these terms filled her with tenderness. She took the glass and sipped the vodka. It spread quickly along her veins, like gunpowder. She strode toward the hearth feeling steadier.

Sergei stood lighting a kerosene lantern over the mantelpiece. As soon as she walked up he turned around and swooped her into his arms. She felt his pounding body clinching hers, his avid lips delving into her throat. The shot glass fell from her hand and smashed to pieces over the floor. She struggled out of his embrace and stood back. He took a step toward her, saying, "No need to be nervous. We're safe now." And grabbing her again, he tried to kiss her.

Her hand was fast to smack his face. "Don't you dare!"

A shadow spread over Sergei's face, even as his cheeks reddened. "Forgive me . . ."

"I'll have you know I don't belong to you in any way," she said, fuming. "And that I don't trust you anymore." She was panting. She heard Sasha scooping up the glass shards at her feet, and regretted her harshness. But she still trembled with fury at the thought that she was being kept in the dark about why a simple invitation to merrymaking at a restaurant had spiraled into such tribulation.

She settled into a corner of the large sofa, the dimensions of which were closer to a bed's, over the lush blanket of dark fur that covered its seat. Sasha brought her another glass of vodka on the same little metal tray, but she refused it. She sat in silence watching the boy as he started making tea from a samovar by the hearth, while Sergei took another shot of vodka and sat on a stool by the fire. Long minutes passed and Sasha finally brought her the tea.

"*Malen'kaya khozyajka,*" he whispered again, and then added with beseeching eyes, "*prostite ego*, forgive him." She was surprised at these words, and even more surprised at understanding them. But then Boris was always apologizing for everything and everyone at the inn. Lily sipped her tea in silence as the boy resumed his chores by the hearth. Was it part of a local custom that servants pleaded for their masters? This idea amused her, and she found herself suppressing a smile.

"Now tell me what's going on," she said, putting down her cup and looking up at Sergei.

Sergei took a moment to consider his answer. "I understand I owe you some sort of an explanation," he said, "but it's not mine to give. There is a very important mission to be accomplished in this upcoming trip, that much I can say, and that you'll be safe here until morning. The czar's police would never dare enter my grandmother's property without a search warrant from her cousin, the czar himself. Now you see the advantages of coming here. I'll make sure you get back safely tomorrow, even if I'll already be gone."

"You'll be gone?"

"Yes, we'll have to leave well before sunrise. In fact, in just about four hours."

"We?" Lily said. "You're taking Sasha?"

"Yes, I'm taking Sasha." It was clear that he didn't wish to speak about any of this anymore. Across from her, by the hearth, the boy lay on the floor, sleeping.

"Poor thing, how quickly he fell asleep," Lily said. "Shouldn't we bring him over here onto the sofa?"

Sergei's smile lingered across Sasha's recumbent figure. "That's how he always sleeps. Even in my room, he always ends up on the floor at the foot of my bed. That's how poor peasants sleep. They don't know any of our comforts."

"We also have our share of street urchins in London," Lily said.

"How could you compare? Our peasants are still slaves, living in the most miserable conditions, used as war fodder and hard-labor chattel. This is why we need to turn Russia around." He got up, walked over to Sasha, and stirred him with gentle nudges. When the boy roused, Sergei helped him up and spoke to him softly, after which Sasha left the cottage.

"Where is he going?" Lily asked.

"There's a room above the carriage house with a proper bed. He'll rest there until we leave."

Sergei returned to his stool and gazed into the fire. Lily watched his face, illumined by the flickering flames, as if reflecting fiery thoughts of political and social change that might be raging across his mind. How unusual it was for a man who had everything imaginable in life—youth, handsome looks, education, wealth, social class—to be so concerned about the fate of others below his station, to feel the pain and hardship of their wretched lives. She realized that she had not thought much about these things, that she was only focused on her own good and her ambition and, at most, partial to the interests of those she loved. Yet, here was someone who felt that happiness was tied to the need of lifting others to higher levels of well-being.

Exhaustion descended upon her, making her eyelids feel like lead. The excitement of the chase, the spiking flare of the vodka, her fury at Sergei, everything was dissolving, slumping into overpowering lassitude. But the thought that she might not see Sergei ever again kept her eyes open. "Come sit beside me," she said.

He got up slowly and moved toward her. She put up her feet so as to lie fully stretched out on the sofa, and patted her hand beside her to indicate where he should lie. His body glided into place next to hers and she put her arms around him.

"I'm cold," she whispered. "Hold me."

He got up and threw two big logs onto the fire. Then, from a corner of the room, he produced another fur blanket that he spread over her.

"But I still want you to hold me," she insisted.

He lay down again, and with cautious, deliberate arms pulled her to him and pressed her against his body, but she felt him strained all over with tension. She wondered if he might be feeling wary after her slap, the imprint of which was still fading from his cheek.

Stifling a yawn, she said, trying to sound humorous, "I had a very different vision of what tonight was going to be like—a grand seduction in high Russian style. Instead, I find myself clutching a fugitive stinking of vodka and . . ." But as she looked up, she saw that Sergei was again distracted, staring back at the hearth, lost in thought, oblivious of her and everything around him.

After a few moments he seemed to mark her pause, and turned to her. "I promise to pick up all arrears when I return," he said, kissing her forehead. "Sleep now."

She perked up. "Are you ordering me to go to sleep? Here, lying in your arms, after everything you've put me through, with those sinister men looming out there, and an empty belly still smoldering with that atrocious firewater? You have a nerve, Count Latvin," she said, propping herself up, glaring at him in mock anger.

He stared back in confused amusement. "Just moments ago you led me to believe—"

"You're full of beliefs, Seryozha. Indeed, bursting at the seams.

With that, and your archive of unspeakable secrets, you appear quite the mystery man to a simple girl like me. But you shall not order me about."

Sergei laughed. "Fair enough," he said, and then added in a whisper, "Call me Seryozha again and I shall be the one at your command."

"Very well, Seryozha. Love me then until you leave."

Saint Petersburg, November 1st, 1900

Dearest Brother and Sister,

I haven't written you for a very long time and here's why: I have been very sick for over a month and only recently allowed to leave my bed. It's just as well that I couldn't write, for I wouldn't have wanted to alarm you. I'm now well on the road of recovery, so you needn't worry at all.

It all started as a bad cold that later was diagnosed as pneumonia. For the first time in my life, I thought my body would not respond and I would never heal. I struggled with fever and weakness to no end, and only recovered very, very gradually over weeks. Luckily for me, I was taken under the care of some friends who transported me to their home and tended to me with the utmost kindness, sparing no number of measures to make me comfortable. Their cousin Anna Shanyavskaya, or Annushka as she's called, is a woman doctor and came to see me every day until I was out of danger. She's such an accomplished scientist, with a quick intelligence and the most loving touch—and so young, too! I don't think she's more than twenty-five. I'm very inspired by her.

So here I am, still at our friends' beautiful palace by the Kryukov Canal, where I shall stay until Christmas when my lovely physician thinks I will be fit to travel back to England. I just don't know how to repay them for their generosity. I have offered to catalog their collection of English books, which are just a tiny portion of their huge library. They have agreed, of course, mostly out of an exquisite graciousness to make me feel useful, since they already have a full-time librarian in their employment.

It's now suppertime and I must go to dress up before sitting at the table. This is one of the family's charming traditions. Everyone attends evening meals dressed as elegantly as they would if attending the ballet or the opera. So I will say good-bye for now, and promise to write again soon.

Much love, my darlings, from your sister,
Lily

CHAPTER 18

Lily had been out of bed for less than a fortnight and, although still weak, she insisted on sitting afternoons in the library and helping with the books that had just been brought to the house from Princess Anna Alexandrovna's Moscow country estate. It was extremely cold outside. From the library window she watched the slabs of ice floating along the canal under amber street lamps, its bridge glittering with sheaths of frost that grew thicker every hour.

Herr Straff, the German librarian who had been in the Volkovs' employment for twenty years, sat across from her at the long oak table writing library tickets on each book, while Lily copied them onto ivory cards that were then placed in alphabetical order inside index boxes. Every now and then, Herr Straff lifted his shrewd, metallic gaze above his gold-rimmed pince-nez and looked at her, and she would offer a reassuring smile to indicate that everything was going smoothly at her end. He then lowered his head of thinning gray hair and continued his work. He was a spindly man of about forty, a wizened sort of fellow who was feared and detested because he had obtained total authority over the library and its contents. He was known to resist book loans even inside the household, and to send servants searching for overdue materials in personal rooms and apartments.

Kitty spared no opportunity to criticize him. "He's all groveling with *Grandmaman*, but with the rest of us he's a pitiless tyrant. "'Katerrrina Alexandrrrovich,'" she said, imitating his German accent. "'Have you borrowed *La Nouvelle Heloïse* without filling out the library card? It won't do. You must bring it back *jetzt gerade*, right away!'"

But Herr Straff had taken an instant liking to Lily, and everyone in the family had been shocked by how quickly he had accepted her into his bastion and unlocked the Volkovs' magnificent book repository before her eyes. From the first day, Lily sat at the table facing the carved ceiling-to-floor bookshelves containing collection after collection and volume after volume of every book imaginable, while Herr Straff clambered up and down the ladder bringing her all sorts of treasures to peruse. Like a miser, he fingered them greedily as he passed them to her, sometimes even voluptuously, as if they were fetching little bodies filled with irresistible charms. He expounded endlessly not just on their contents, but also on their physical graces, remarking on the fine leather bindings, the gleaming, gilded edges, and spines embossed with seals and heraldic symbols pertaining to different royal collections.

The vast majority of books, of course, were in Russian, and Lily quickly fell in love with the clear, bold letters of the Cyrillic alphabet and decided she must learn the language. She proposed an exchange of basic Russian for advanced English lessons, which Herr Straff readily accepted. So, after hours of tedious classification, they sat in the library gibbering in three languages, and Lily was surprised at how soon she mastered the new alphabet, and began to read and speak a little Russian.

She was glad to have this distraction. Her illness had wiped her out, not just her physical body, where she had lost considerable weight and still looked gaunt and sallow-faced, but also in her mental faculties. She felt abstracted, as if in a daze. She had vague recollections of how the illness had started; how snow fell into the open carriage as she was driven back from the dacha the day after her night with Sergei, the soft white flakes falling and thawing over the exposed skin of her face and throat, while she anguished over the strange events of the day before. Later that evening, she felt the first sharp pain behind her ribs as she cried out her most dramatic lines onstage. The night that followed had been a whirlpool of anxious dreams mixed with feverish, hurtful coughing. She woke up drenched in sweat and exhausted, with hardly enough strength to send word to Ruby to cover for her at the theater. The coming days were a descent into delirious turmoil, alternating between spells of unbearable body heat and chills with bouts of coughing and suffocation. One day she opened her eyes to see Ruby, Kitty, and Annushka gathered around her bed, with two women servants who were swathing her in blankets. "We're taking you home," Kitty said, "until you get better."

Lily's condition improved immensely at the Volkov residence, where she found herself in a large, beautiful room with a clean, warm bed and all sorts of attendants. Kitty and Lena had been extremely doting, making sure she had everything she could need or desire, and bringing Annushka by daily to oversee her progress. They had made sure Gerard was informed of her situation, and when Lena found out about Lily's critical state of affairs with Wade, she wrote him a personal letter explaining that Lily would return to London as soon as her health permitted.

But it had still taken Lily another three weeks to get well enough to leave the bed, even just to sit for a few hours by the window, or to go down to the family room where tea was served in the afternoon. Annushka had warned Lily that her lungs were not strong and that she needed to remain indoors and stress-free until her complete recovery. "You say your mother died of consumption and that your brother also suffers from it. If you want to live a long life," she cautioned, "you will have to take extreme care of your health. And make sure you don't let your emotions carry you away." She smiled as she added this last bit, but Lily knew she meant every word.

For the moment, her vitality was so low that she couldn't even think about her previous fears and anxieties, they just felt a blurred mass that she could easily postpone. Instead, she felt extremely homesick. Every detail around her bounced her mind back to England, to her father's home in Manchester, to her previous life in London. A smile from one of the family's young children, Ruby playing a Russian song on the piano, the spectral morning sun reflecting over the canal, any of these impressions could remind her of how far she was from home and bring tears to her eyes. She yearned to be back where things were familiar, where she belonged, even if it meant confronting a sea of troubles. And yet, she knew something had been torn inside her and that homecoming would never be simple.

A month into her stay at the Volkov residence, a great calamity shook the house. Sergei Nicolayevich was arrested on his way back to St. Petersburg, and Andrey Volkov and another cousin, Pyotr Nevinski, had to flee the country overnight. The situation was serious, and Sergei was not released quickly, as in previous times. There were rumors that he was facing exile in Siberia.

"I always knew something like this would happen one day," Kitty said, wiping her tearful, swollen eyes. "How could they put the family through this? Poor *Grandmaman*'s been crying for days, and now she'll have to go on her knees before the czar and beg him to mitigate Seryozha's sentence." She blew her nose, adding with a sort of fury, "Did they never stop to think about the consequences of their stupid political activities?"

Lily burned to ask a thousand questions about the arrest and the actual conditions of Sergei's imprisonment, and about the nature of the political activities he was entangled in. But she bit her tongue. She was very aware by now of Kitty's jealousy and possessive feelings toward her cousin. She hadn't even told Ruby about her last evening with Sergei.

She lay sleepless, recalling the events of that night, how she had awoken in the dark with her warm, naked body still tingling with his imprint under the fur blanket. She watched him, already fully fitted in his travel coat, as he raked the fire. It blazed anew and his silhouette stood cut out against the flames, while the wall above him flickered with shadows from the legendary stuffed bear head looming over the mantel. Then Sergei walked toward her against the backdrop of the hearth's luminescence, a mouth of fearful flames that might suck him back into its incandescent gut at any moment, and she felt a pang of anguish over his departure. "Ivanka will return for you in a few hours and drive you back," he said, embracing her one last time. "Meanwhile, I'll leave you under his wife's care." When Lily kissed him passionately and clung to him, he pulled away from her with gentle but firm arms, saying, "It's time to go. But I promise we shall soon meet again." As she searched his eyes, she saw that estranged, distracted look drifting back into his gaze, the determination of a warrior manning up before a battle, and she knew he was already far-gone.

She hadn't thought much about him in the last weeks, she now reflected, as if she had put a safe lid on everything that had happened, so stunned had she emerged from her sickbed. Now every memory was coming back with full force. Snippets of impressions flooded her senses, the smell of vodka and sweet-sour sweat, his hard body pressed against hers, soft kissing and tender glances in the aftermath of their love. Then the thought of his confinement became unbearable. To think that he was undergoing misery, even downright torture, filled her with pain. But then again, the rumination that she might never see him again, that he might soon be banished to some remote hell, sobered her into realizing she might have to put all of those emotions and recollections away. She had enough troubles of her own. She had allowed herself to be pulled into a wild, riveting dream, and it was time to land back in reality.

In the meantime the whole Volkov household pulsated day and night around Sergei's situation, and the general anguish relented only somewhat when he was finally released from the Trubetskoy prison and sent to his apartments under home arrest. He would have to remain there under strict supervision, until a final decision was reached about him; that much had been granted to Princess Anna by her cousin the czar. Though there was apparently little evidence against him, Sergei's case still hung in the gallows, for there was outrage in the government and the royal palace about revolutionary and nihilist movements shaking the country, particularly about the involvement of nobility and intelligentsia in such activities.

The next day, Countess Tatyana Mikhailovna, Sergei's mother, arrived back in St. Petersburg after a yearlong stay in the German spa of Baden-Baden, and visited the Volkovs. She was statuesque and striking, her beautiful features dampened by an air of supreme arrogance. Her eyes, an icy version of Sergei's, looked around the table. When they met Lily's they lingered on her, giving her a chill.

Later in the drawing room, as they all drank coffee and Lily played board games with the children, she overheard a conversation among the older women about the possible motives of the culprits.

"In the case of Sergei Nicolayevich," she heard Tatyana Mikhailovna say, "I'm certain it's all coming from hidden rebellion against his father's boorishness."

"Oh dear, I'm not sure that would account for it alone," Princess Anna said. "Andrey is the driving force of the whole operation, and his father was a saint." After a moment of sad musing, she added, "I have many times regretted some of the tutors that the prince selected for them. Brilliant men, but so radical in their views."

That evening in Kitty's apartments, Lily learned a few things about Sergei's childhood, how he grew up neglected in the Ural country estate of his father, Count Nicolai Latvin. The count, now dead for three years, had been much older than Tatyana, and a sample of ancient, uncouth Russian rural nobility, immensely rich but beastly in his ways. When the marriage became unbearable for the young Tatyana, she left him and returned to St. Petersburg, but the count refused to let her take the child. Sergei had stayed back with his father, a wild boy relegated to servants and gamekeepers in a vast, mountainous estate. It had taken years for his grandmother, Princess Anna, to convince the grisly count that the boy should be brought up in St. Petersburg under her auspices. Finally, he agreed to send the nine-year-old Sergei to her. But the estrangement with his mother had not since been bridged. She never fully warmed to him, for he always reminded her of his feral father.

"I remember the first day Sergei Nicolayevich arrived in this house," Kitty said. "How we laughed at him; he was dressed in such silly, old-fashioned country clothes. He was so shy, too; you couldn't pull a word out of him. I walked up to him, took his hand, and said, 'Come, you're one of us now.'" Kitty faltered for a moment, overcome by emotion. "Oh, what fun it was to grow up all together. And how terrible that everything has to change, that nothing in life can remain the same."

One evening in early December, Lily was in the library with Herr Straff, sitting at the long table overlooking the canal. It was snowing heavily outside, and drifts had piled outside the windows, curving around the panes. Lily marveled at how warm the palace was always kept, despite the fact that there were hardly any rooms with fireplaces. Herr Straff proudly explained the central heating systems of St. Petersburg's buildings as the work of his engineering countrymen. He was penciling out a sketch of the pipe framework that diffused heat throughout the palace when the door opened.

A figure in a large, snow-covered coat entered the room and walked toward them, leaving a trail of white flakes and ice on the carpet. He stopped at the sofa, took off his coat, and shook his head to dispel the snow from his hair.

"Sergei Nicholayevich!" Herr Straff exclaimed. "I thought you were—"

"Yes, Herr Straff, I am. Under strict house arrest," Sergei said. "But presently on most urgent and private business with mademoiselle, so you will excuse us. *Jetzt gerade*, right away!" he added, mimicking the librarian's classic expression. Herr Straff grumbled some term of compliance, snapped his ledger closed, and slunk out of the room.

Sergei slumped into the sofa, and then looked down at his overshoes sitting in a puddle of muddy water on the carpet. With a gesture of annoyance, he took them off and threw them across the room near the door where Straff had exited. Then he looked up at Lily, who sat frozen in her chair at the table, watching him with a pounding heart. Dripping locks of hair hung over his red-rimmed, swollen eyes. He looked disheveled and exhausted, as if he hadn't slept for days. A thin scar still crusted over streaked down his pale cheek as if he had been cut with a blade.

"Forgive me," Sergei said, "I'm not quite myself." He got up and tramped across the room, where he picked up the overshoes and set them by the door. "I had to come see you," he said sitting down again. "I was told you were very sick, but I trust you're better now."

"How did you manage to make it over?" Lily finally mumbled. "I'm sure they're watching every inch around your apartments. Aren't you putting yourself at inordinate risk?"

Sergei shook his head as if to dispel the importance of any peril. "I'm more worried about the danger I put you through that last evening. That you might have fallen into the hands of the police," he said, and his eyes flashed at her with dark pain.

Lily took a chair across from him. "The police never came to me. But what happened to you?" she asked, leaning over and lifting her hand to the scar on his cheek.

He sat back, avoiding her touch, and gazed at her with crushed eyes. "I was feckless, a perfect bastard. I didn't consider anyone's safety, only my own selfish, immature, stupid castles in the air." He lowered his tone and continued, "After what happened to Sasha, I've thought a lot about the risk I put you in, and how blessed I am that you're still alive and well. If anything had harmed you, I don't think I could go on living."

"Sasha? And what happened to him?" Lily asked.

Sergei peered into her face disbelievingly. "You don't know?" He got up and paced around the room. "Kitty, Lena, even this moron Straff—they've told you nothing?"

Lily shook her head. A dark hunch began to creep inside her. "Where is Sasha?"

Sergei sat down again. "Sasha is dead. He was killed in the prison."

"Killed in the prison!" Lily echoed. "But he was only a boy. Boys don't go to prison. And how could anyone . . . ?"

Sergei buried his head in his hands. "I'm telling you they killed him. They arrested us together, and they interrogated him, and when he wouldn't give me or any of us away, they bludgeoned him to death."

Lily's eyes filled with tears. Words choked in her throat as Sasha's smiling face floated in her mind. She saw his luminous eyes shooting adoring glances at Sergei, his young, lithe body sleeping in a heap by the hearth in the cottage. She was overcome by sobbing. After a moment, she took hold of herself and wiped the tears from her eyes.

"Forgive me. Ever since the pneumonia, I cry at everything."

"Forgive you! This is the first decent reaction I've seen. Everyone else, including my friends and family, regard me with either pity or disdain. But Sasha—no one gives him a thought."

"But, Seryozha, they also hurt you. I was told—"

"They hurt me! Yes, they belted me in the beginning, before they knew who I was. When they found out, I was kept in one of the fancier cells. But the peasants, the workers, the scum, as they call them, their lives are worthless, like the vermin you crush under your boot." He staggered to the window. "But who's talking? As if they were the monsters and I, an innocent bystander. Didn't I put him into the danger without even thinking of what he really wanted?"

"I'm sure you couldn't have anticipated this awful consequence. You were just giving him an opportunity to better himself in your service," Lily said.

"Don't take any of my blame away!" Sergei thundered. "I'm responsible for every bit of his death." He stood frozen in the middle of the room, arms clutching his chest, head hanging. The whole space throbbed with his agony.

A sudden fatigue came over Lily and she sat back in her armchair feeling short of breath. "What good does it do to torture yourself like this? You will just be helping them kill two birds with the same stone: Sasha, and your still unbroken soul." Sergei shot her a look as if someone had splashed him with cold water. Even she was surprised at the words that had come out of her mouth.

He took a deep breath as his body loosened up. Slowly, he walked toward Lily and sat back on the sofa. He gazed at her for a long moment. "How I missed you during the long days in the prison, how I thought about every single instance of our time together."

"Even about the whack I gave you?" she asked, forcing a little laugh.

"Oh, I so deserved it," Sergei said with a sad smile.

"No, you didn't." As she lifted her hand to his face again, she realized that the cheek she had slapped back then was the same that now sported the ugly scar. "And who else dared bust your handsome face? If I ever find them, I'll . . ."—she faltered as fury blazed through her teasing—"I'll be the next one to commit a crime," and pulling his face to hers, she put her lips to the scar.

The door opened and they pulled apart, startled, as Lena and Kitty rushed into the room. "Sergei Nicolayevich, are you totally mad?" Kitty cried, furiously. "What are you thinking coming here? Do you have no respect for anything anymore?"

"You must leave immediately!" Lena said. "If *Grandmaman* heard about this, after all she's been put through!"

"Isn't it enough that you've broken all of our hearts already?" Kitty added, looking as though she was about to burst into sobs.

Sergei stood up. "You're right. I shall leave instantly." But no sooner had he taken a step than they both dashed toward him and embraced him, crying and covering him with kisses. They engaged in all sorts of lamentations and wouldn't let go of him. Only after Anton Alexandrovich, one of the elder uncles who also lived in the palace, walked in and said, "Enough of this! You must go now. None of us want to see you more punished than you already are," did Kitty and Lena step back.

Sergei then put on his coat, embraced his uncle and cousins again, and walked out of the library giving Lily one last burning glance. "Good-bye, Lily."

Everyone followed and the door shut behind them. Lily was left alone in the room listening to the trail of footsteps and moaning. She sat back, shaking with the range of emotions that had bolted through her during this unexpected encounter.

A moment later, as she was preparing to leave the library herself the door opened again and Kitty stepped in. She walked toward her, her usual light, girlish step now turned into a heavy glide, her face drawn. "Have you been sending him letters?"

"Me? No, not at all." Lily sat up. "I was as surprised to see him as everyone else. And how would I even know where to send him a letter?"

"How?" Kitty echoed, flashing dark eyes at her. "I've learned to appreciate how resourceful you can be under that innocent, pretty face. Why would he come directly to the library instead of any of the other family rooms?"

"I have no idea. I assure you—"

"You were kissing him!"

Lily blushed and said nothing.

"You were kissing him in this room without a thought about the danger he was putting himself and the rest of us in by coming here," Kitty hissed, glaring at Lily with ferocious eyes. "But what can be expected of someone like you? I know all about your loose ways and the trail of scandal you left behind in London, and now you're bringing the same sort of trouble into our household. A fine way to repay hospitality!"

Lily stood up, trembling. "I'm sorry you feel like this. I'm sure nothing I say can convince you otherwise. I owe you more that I can ever repay and I do not want to inconvenience you any longer. I shall leave the house immediately." She walked quickly out of the room with her heart hammering against her rib cage, realizing, to her mortification, that she would have to wait until the morning to leave the palace for it was already too late for traveling tonight.

Back in her room, she threw herself over the bed and wept with equal measures of fury and angst raging inside her. How could she make sense of everything that had just happened?

"I promise she didn't get any of that from me," she heard a voice whispering behind her, and she turned to find Ruby standing by the bed. "Wade wrote back to Lena and told her about the newspaper scandal. Kitty just told me. I knew nothing about it till now." Ruby sat down and put her arms around her. "Don't mind her, Lily. Kitty's hysterical. You know how she loves him. Please don't leave."

"I cannot stay one more day in this house, Ruby. I shall return to the Krügers' tomorrow." Her rib cage was sore with sobbing and her head hurt terribly.

"You can't do that. You're still so fragile."

"I'm quite recovered. I shall not stay in a place where I've been insulted. As for Sergei—"

"I know this is not your fault," Ruby hastened to reassure her. "I saw the way he looked at you from the first day. He's made every effort to seduce you. Kitty will understand that. She'll come around." Then she added with a little sigh, "But you've also let yourself be carried away by him, you've—"

"I've what?" Lily snapped, feeling fury rise to her throat.

Ruby sighed. "Listen, everyone knows everything here. Walls have eyes and ears. Do you think these armies of servants are here just to carry trays around?"

Lily stiffened. "Well, if this isn't the final argument! Why stay in a place where I'm being spied on?" She got up and walked to the armoire, took out her old canvas bag, and put it on the bed. "Whatever I do is my own business, isn't it?"

"Lily, be careful. I see how infatuated you are. It's hard to resist people like these. I should be the first one to know. Even I can sense he's real trouble."

Lily walked back and forth from the wardrobe piling her possessions into the bag. She decided not to engage in further conversation with her friend. After a while, she slowed down, feeling fatigue overcoming her. She sat down and looked up at Ruby. "There is one last favor I will need from you. I have to borrow your coat to get to the Krüger house. I shall send it back as soon as I arrive."

"You'll need much more than a coat to step out there," Ruby said.

Later, Lena came into her room and pleaded with her to stay. "Please, forgive Kitty. She is overwrought with all that's happened. I don't think she meant half of what she said. We would wish you not to go until you're ready to travel back to England. Your health is at stake. And our peace of mind." She admitted to Wade's slanderous letter, but assured her that it had had no bearing on her opinion of her, since Gerard had already advised on Wade's dubious character. But Lily would not be moved from her decision to leave.

As she watched Lena's concerned, frowning face finally assenting to her adamant decision, Lily understood the reasons for her recovery from the Krüger house and the weeks of careful nursing. It all flashed through her mind with blinding clarity. The Volkovs had known everything about her last night with Sergei, and how she had been stranded at the dacha until the morning and smuggled into the city through back roads in the middle of a snowstorm. Maybe they felt some family responsibility to clean up after their prodigal cousin, the way that rich fathers pay their sons' gambling debts or extravagant tailor bills. But most of all, they were making sure that Lily was far away from the reach of the czar's police and the possibility of providing any incriminating evidence against him and his accomplices. Even Sergei had just expressed to her his fear that she might have fallen into the hands of the police. It all made perfect sense from this powerful family's point of view and, to be fair, they had indulged her in exchange with every possible grace within their gorgeous palatial rooms. The delusion of their selfless kindness would have lived on until her departure if this incident with Sergei had not happened. But now that the tapestry of deceit had been revealed, Lily felt used, betrayed, a tiny pawn in a large, complex game that she would never gain complete oversight of. She was glad she would now leave it all behind.

She lay sleepless all night, tossing and turning in a whirlpool of images and sensations from the day. At one point she decided it wouldn't do, that it would be best to put it all behind her and just look ahead. Sitting up in the bed, she lit a lamp and then brought over the little velvet pouch where she kept the remainder of her savings. She spread the bills and coins over the quilt and divided them into three equal mounds. One would go to pay Frau Krüger for room and board; the second to buy her own winter coat and boots; and the third she would keep for her trip back home. She lay back on the bed going over all sorts of plans for her return journey. There were only two weeks to go. She had a passage for the eighteenth of December, and it would take her five days thereafter to reach London. She would resist all trepidation and disquieting thoughts about what might happen after her homecoming. She would arrive at Genevieve's mother's house and start clean from there. She would bide her time and work quietly for the remainder of her contract, avoiding all confrontation with Wade and Harrison, and lie low until an opportunity arose to start a new chapter of her own. As for Chut, he would already be out of her reach, safely, though painfully, packed away in his new marriage.

The whole plan was simple enough. It would work.

She would make sure of it.

Early the next afternoon, Lily rode along the Kryukov Canal toward the Nevsky Prospect in the open sled pulled by three horses that Lena had put at her disposal to get to the Krüger house. Lena and Ruby had wrapped her in furs and blankets to keep her warm during the ride. But Lily was glad to be out in the open after so many weeks of confinement, and relished the purifying cold that flooded her lungs.

The city felt unreal with its icy beauty. A winter sun blazed above in the clear blue sky as the troika dashed along with its tinkling horse bells chiming all around. Along the frozen waterways, happy, laughing echoes of children's voices could be heard, and as she looked to the side, she saw groups of youngsters skating and pulling sleds over the ice, with heads and throats wrapped in colored hats and scarves and large clouds of breath billowing out of their smiling mouths. Everything around her was covered in snow and glistened like a magical landscape from an old fairy-tale book. Thick blankets of white covered the streets and avenues, and everywhere above frosted roofs and domes of churches and palaces sparkled in the sun, while spidery, snow-laden trees swayed over gates and front lawns below. She had admired St. Petersburg all these months as the handsomest city she had ever seen, but this was the icing on the cake. A sudden pang of regret at the idea of losing all this beauty shot through her chest, and she sat back, stunned, realizing that for all her plans of the night before she was still not ready to leave Russia.

She was immersed in these thoughts when she heard a different set of jingling bells drawing near behind, and turned to see another troika fast approaching. It caught up and swerved ahead, with the driver shouting unintelligible words. Her own *izvozchik* pulled the horses to a stop and a conversation ensued between the two drivers, which Lily could not understand. She became alarmed when the two men got down from their seats and proceeded to unload her luggage, indicating that she should step down from the carriage and cross over to the other. Her mind reeled in bewilderment as she groped for Russian words. "*Net, net,* I shall not move from this troika," she stammered in Russian at the new *izvozchik,* who was wrapped in his long blue coat, girdled at the waist, and wore a fitted sentry cap that all but hid his eyes. He spoke back to her with a firm softness, but she was too frazzled to even catch one word, and held fast to her seat and refused to budge. After a while, both drivers got back on their seats and proceeded to turn around their horses and drive alongside each other in silence. As she sat frozen with dread and filled with wild thoughts about what all this might be about, the troikas rushed past the Nevsky and crossed the Fontanka Canal and endless other avenues until they reached a silent, empty street at the end of which a group of soldiers guarded a tall gate in front of a bleak old mansion.

The guards encroached upon the troikas and engaged in what seemed a convoluted conversation with the drivers. One of them, who looked of a higher rank, approached Lily, took her purse, and extracted her travel documents, which he reviewed. Others took her bags and groped through their contents. Lily glared at them, while struggling to coin a Russian sentence to the effect of, "I am a British subject, *Ya britanskiy poddannyj,*" but the guards ignored her. Finally, two of them stepped toward the gate and dragged it open. As the troika pulled into the grim courtyard, she heard the howling of dogs and then the great door of the house opened, and she saw Sergei emerge from it flanked by two large wolfhounds. He walked down the stone steps toward her while the dogs woofed and whined wildly as a servant restrained them back into the house.

Sergei stood before her, smiling with pale, earnest eyes. "Forgive this unexplained abduction. I had no time to write you a letter."

It must have been close to four o'clock when the last moments of the afternoon started trickling into premature dusk, and Lily still found herself stuck fast to the seat of the troika, demanding to be allowed to drive away to the Krüger house. Sergei paced up and down before her, giving all sorts of arguments about why she should stay with him, while she fumed at the audacity with which the members of this arrogant aristocratic family were interfering in her life.

"I am not a toy," she had said a number of times, "that you and your family can toss around from troika to troika, and decide where to house."

"I only want to offer you my home, instead of you having to return to that ghastly inn. You will be more comfortable here."

"And I'll be kept safe and quiet, away from the police?" Lily said. "That's been the main motivation for protecting me all along, hasn't it?"

"The main motivation for your protection is my love for you."

"Your love for me!" Lily laughed. "You're not even free to offer your love, Sergei Nikolayevich! You're a married man."

"Married, yes, I am. If you count a decade-long annulment case standing in church courts, after an act of adolescent folly."

They glared at each other. Then Sergei added in a softer tone, "But it will eventually get resolved. And if it doesn't, all that will soon change anyway with the new Russia. Divorces and all sorts of free marriages and relationships will come about."

"It's always about the gilded future with you, Sergei Nikolayevich. You're living in a dream."

"I might be living in a dream, but my heart isn't. My heart knows what it wants and why."

Lily turned her face away with a sigh. "Please let me go."

Twilight deepened around them and the temperature was falling fast. She hid under her furs and blankets, but even those were failing to keep her warm. Already after the first ten minutes or so of their deadlock about staying or leaving, the servants had started milling back and forth from the house bringing Lily blankets, and hot stones to put under her feet. A shaggy young boy with dark round eyes brought her a ceramic hot-water bottle that he placed respectfully on her lap. Then, together with an older servant, he rolled four big metal barrels and set them around the troika. They filled them with timber and lit fires inside. The *izvozchiks* threw thick stable blankets over the horses and gathered around the fire barrels. The two servants stood holding lanterns and, together with the drivers, shot concerned, puzzled glances at their master. Even the sentinels at the gate seemed to confer now and then on the bizarre scene that was taking place inside the courtyard.

But Sergei continued to pace in a short town jacket as if he didn't feel the cold. He approached the troika once again. "Will you consider just having supper with me? Just that. Then you might leave if you still desire."

"Sergei Nikolayevich, I've learned not to trust you. I'd rather leave now," Lily said.

A moment passed in which Sergei again started walking back

and forth. It was clear that he wasn't going to give up, but neither was Lily. She was beginning to feel the cold chill her to the bone and didn't even dare consider how it might affect her health. Worst of all, she was beginning to realize that her anger toward Sergei was melting into desire. A part of her couldn't help watching his remorseless strategy with fascination.

She stiffened in her seat.

From the corner of her eye she saw the group of sentinel guards whispering in a huddle at the gate, shooting concerned looks at the scene ahead. One of them walked toward them and when he reached Sergei's side, took a pistol out of his holster and offered it to him. They talked quietly and gravely for a few minutes. Then Sergei took the pistol.

Lily became alarmed. "What are you doing?" she asked.

"He's telling me that this might be my last recourse," Sergei said, with a somber face. "He says that his brother shot himself in the leg as a last resort to convince his disgruntled fiancée to marry him, and that even to this day he swears that a good wife is worth an amputated leg."

"This is preposterous," Lily said, annoyed but unsure if Sergei was joking or not. Recollections of Kitty's and Lena's accounts of Sergei having been provoked into past daredevil stunts flashed through her mind.

"It might sound preposterous to you, but stories like these are not unheard of in this country," Sergei said. "You have no idea what the Russian male is capable of when he decides he's desperate enough."

The guard and Sergei spoke a few more words, and then Sergei pointed the pistol to his right thigh and looked up at Lily. The guard stepped back and everyone else around, the *izvozchiks,* the servants, and even the sentinels by the gate, all froze in silent tension. Lily looked around, incredulous at the astonishing scene, and reflected that anything could happen in the midst of this remote reality. The courtyard now blazed with a strange blue light punctuated by the reddish glow of lanterns and torches. From the fire inside the barrels streamed waves of haze that distorted the faces around her. Even Sergei standing before her appeared blurred and unreal.

He cocked the pistol and Lily's heart began to race. A moment passed. When she could stand it no more she jumped up from her seat and cried, "Stop! Stop this nonsense!"

But Sergei only repointed the pistol, saying, "Will you come into the house with me or not?"

"Yes!" she screamed. "But point that gun away. Right now!"

He arched his brow as if he needed stronger reassurance.

"I said I will come into the house," Lily insisted through gritted teeth.

Sergei lowered the pistol and the guard stepped forward and took it from his hand. Then he took two steps toward the troika and lifted her into his arms.

"You wouldn't have done it," she whispered with fury as he put her down.

Sergei stiffened. "You want to try me again?"

"No, no," she said quickly, and clung to him, breaking into a shudder of exhilaration.

He picked her up again, saying, "You're frozen stiff," and carried her in his arms up the stairs into the house while the guards cheered and the *izvozchiks* rushed to lead the troikas and the horses away.

CHAPTER 19

Four months had passed since she had stepped across the threshold of Sergei's house, and every day she was still being sucked deeper and deeper into an affection that threatened to dissolve all her boundaries. Sometimes, when she was by herself in one of the vast empty rooms of the old mansion, she might consider the folly of having agreed to join Sergei in his home arrest instead of reverting to the old Krüger Inn and following her original plans. But almost immediately she would reject any sense of regret. Ever since she had seen Sergei that first day at the customhouse, she had been tugged into a magnetic place where all she could do was surrender to the stream of events.

Their first weeks together had been enthralling, to the point that Lily lost all sense of time. Imprisoned with Sergei, there was nothing to do but fold into his extraordinary world. She remembered the uncanny sensation when first entering the dark mansion, rushing past a maze of stark corridors toward the main hall, where a long heavy table stood by a smoldering fireplace; sitting in a tall chair while she was served warm *medovukha* and a steaming bowl of borscht. She sat sipping the mead opposite Sergei, feeling her flesh and senses thaw under his laughing gaze, and watching the euphoria glow across his face. *Like the exultation of a hunter*, she thought with amused pique, *when he's won a rare, precious trophy*. And although she saw straight through his swagger, she still found the train of his seduction irresistible. Later in the night, when she quivered under Sergei's hands undressing her in the dark four-columned bed of his vast bedroom, the voices of the sentinels and soldiers echoed outside like a chorus. And as they made love till the first hours of dawn, she still heard them through her reverie, carousing and laughing, and imagined them standing, warming themselves around the fire barrels, drinking the vodka that Sergei would have sent out to them, and telling tales of conquest and seduction of women. It made her feel once more like a prized treasure in a warrior's bounty from some barbaric land, and she wondered about the strange world she had penetrated.

Getting used to the bizarre house that would become her whole universe for the coming months had also been a peculiar experience. The Latvin mansion was outlandish enough to satisfy all the tropes of Gothic romantic novels back home. The house was a limestone building hundreds of years old with a blocklike façade surrounded by an unkempt garden filled with overgrown bushes and trees. At either side of it stood two recumbent stone lions with heads turned toward each other. The property had been Count Latvin's Petersburg residence; after his death, Sergei moved in, leaving behind his own splendid apartments at the Volkov palace. The difference between the two was extreme.

The Volkov residence was a lavish feast for the eyes and the senses. Every room had large windows and colored walls covered with brightly decorated silk draperies. Costly mirrors reflected the array of extravagant furniture and ornaments of extreme beauty, and all around were pastel corridors with mosaic floors overlooking neat, manicured gardens.

In contrast, the Latvin mansion was smaller and decorated in austere Old Russian style. Its halls and rooms were mostly stripped of furnishings, and many featured wooden interiors with elaborate carvings covering whole walls and vaulted ceilings. Portraits of sallow-faced women and men in ancient military garb hung in corridors alongside hunting trophies of deer antlers and stuffed animal heads. The main hall was large, with bare columns and long narrow windows. A stone-carved fireplace stood at the far end flanked by two stone statues of patriarchal figures, saints probably, since they held books engraved with Coptic crosses to their chests. Many rooms had somber tapestries on the walls; others, religious icons similar to those she had seen in old Orthodox churches. Wood-mounted figures of madonnas haloed by engravings of silver and gold surrounded by altars where candles burned throughout the night.

The house was kept in immaculate order and running condition, though only four servants attended it. There was Maria Petrovna, the housekeeper, a surly matron of some fifty years old, who ran the household with quiet, flawless efficiency; Fedor Ivanovich, a butler of sorts, also older, but still strong-bodied and shrewd-eyed; Grisha, the youth who had brought hot water bottles to the troika, and Masha Ivanova, a round, blond girl of about seventeen years old with shy, laughing eyes, who did most of the cleaning and kitchen work. They were very different from the servants at the Volkovs', for all of them were Russian and only spoke their native language, and were clad modestly, but suitably in styles that Lily had seen on plain, independent townsfolk. They moved around the house freely and seemed contented and carefree around Sergei. Lily observed how they all venerated him, how they approached him with an affection bordering on devotion. She saw, too, how Sergei looked back at them with the same love, and that there was a deep bond between them that would never be broken.

Sometimes, Sergei would spontaneously join them in chores, such as chopping wood or shoveling snow. Other times, one or two of them would wander into the room where he was reading or writing and sit in a corner for a while just watching him; no words would be exchanged, no need for any explanation would arise. There seemed to be a silent understanding when they were together, as if they belonged to the same family of wild dogs or wolves, ever acutely aware of one another, always akin.

Sergei had told Lily how he had brought them over from Taganay, his father's Southern Ural estate, where he had grown up with them and their elders, and that they were as good as his blood. "I would have brought others with me too," Sergei said, "but most of them refused to leave the land. When I take you there and you see it with your own eyes, you will understand."

He had told her all sorts of stories about Taganay, the vast country estate in the vicinity of the city of Zlatoust, or Golden Mouth, so called for its rich deposits of gold along the river Ai. Taganay itself meant "the moon's stand" in the language of the Bashkir, ancient inhabitants of the region. Sharp, ridged mountains stood like fangs overlooking blue-hazed valleys and dense woodlands where Sergei had been taught to ensnare and track wild animals as a boy. They would follow the streams of stone rivers for days, and camp nights on rock plateaus under the stars. Sometimes, while the youngsters listened wide-eyed and huddled around the fire, hunters and trappers shared stories of the peasant rebellion led by Pugachev over a hundred years before, and how their Bashkir ancestors had joined in.

Taganay became the backdrop of their play, and Lily found herself becoming enamored of this remote country. At night, Sergei would weave its gilded tales into their embraces, until the blazing images burned into her mind. Then her flesh became the land, with its caves and peaks and deep forests, where running wolves and huntsmen clashed and thrashed and fought, and then rippled away into luscious waves; where rushing torrents of cold rivers ran into their breaths, as they climaxed together, and tumbled down over each other, bodies dank and slick with sweat. In the morning, she would wake up having dreamed about the estate so vividly that she thought she could describe all its wild paths.

But other times, Sergei would talk bitterly about his homeland. "I grew up in a household where servants might still be flogged as punishment. I've seen whole families famish in the long, frozen winters, and men hang on iced branches for poaching."

The more she knew about his past, the more she understood the contrasting layers that overlapped in Sergei. On the one hand, there was the sophisticated, charming man educated in St. Petersburg in the midst of a rich family; on the other, a soul embedded deeply in rural Russia, entwined with wild, untamed landscapes and fostered in ancient customs of peasant life. His capacity for crossing back and forth between these worlds was striking. He could wear an elegant three-piece suit with the same ease as he could a peasant *kosovorotka* shirt, and he could switch from perfect English or French to Russian in less than a syllable. But in between these two opposite realms was some sort of gash from which sprung his political fervor, his anguish to save Russia from iniquity and deliver it into a world of progress, where justice and peace could prevail.

Here also lay the source of his unrest. He oscillated between fabricating feverish plans of action and feeling crushed under the colossal, ungraspable task. When he was at this lowest tier, he slumped into dark, melancholy moods. Lily watched him languish thus for days. It was then that she resorted to luring him into writing articles as a form of advocacy, and had succeeded in engaging his attention from despair.

They spent long days in the study reading and working on the articles. Sergei paced back and forth in front of the large vaulted windows, looking down at a bunch of papers in his hand. "The casements in the Trubetskoy Bastion," he read, "are the only cells in that vast state prison, the entire map of which might be unknown to any one single person of this day. Between the cells and the dungeons, and the underground torture chambers of the fortress's various mainstays, there are an unknown number of men and women languishing in detention. Some are serving sentences while others await trial for years under conditions that threaten to deprive them of health, sanity, or life."

A drab morning light filled the room. Outside, the heavy overcast sky promised another snowfall. Across the room, Lily sat listening from her armchair by the fire. Lying at her feet were Maksim and Mavra, Sergei's two Irish wolfhounds, their shaggy gray heads resting on burly outstretched paws.

"As a political detainee," Sergei continued, "I was kept in solitary confinement in one of the bomb-proof casement cells, a gloomy, damp space with high-grated windows looking at a blank wall, and a Judas pierced door through which I was constantly watched. Day after day, I lay there in solitude, with only the sound of the melancholy bells of the fortress cathedral breaking the silence. Sometimes during the night, I'd be roused by the piercing screams or hysterical weeping of other prisoners along my corridor, and shuddered for hours thinking about what they might be undergoing. Insanity is the most terrible of fears inside those walls. Living in total solitude and all lack of occupation requires the utmost fortitude to survive."

Sergei faltered. The article had been originally written in German, but he was reading it aloud in English for Lily's benefit. He sat down at his desk and penciled out a few corrections on the text.

"Go on," Lily said.

"Only the hope of communicating with other prisoners can mitigate desperation inside the Trubetskoy Bastion. I had expected that there would be a chance of exchanging information with neighboring prisoners through the system of tapping on walls or pipes which I knew well, but even that had been thought out by the architects of this living grave. The floors of the cells are covered with a painted felt, and their walls are double; they are also covered with felt, and, at a distance of five inches from the wall, there is an iron-wire net, coated with rough linen and yellow painted paper. This has been designed to prevent the prisoners from communicating with one another by means of taps on the wall. Moreover, an unprecedented exception is made in the fortress of the rule that all convicts wear leg-fetters for the same reason. The clanking of chains would become the means of communication between cells, and would throw the whole system out of control."

"What is this tapping system you talk about?" Lily interrupted. "And how did you already know about it?"

"It's a sort of Morse code used by prisoners," Sergei explained. "They tap or clink on any surface that might resonate through the walls. Every letter is tapped out with two sounds. It's very easy once you understand it. We used it all the time as children in our games, and to scheme against our nannies and elders. It was taught to us by one of our tutors, a man called Nikita Sholomov, whose grandfather had been a Decembrist. My grandmother fired him shortly after, of course." He shook his head with a chuckle. "I don't know how many tutors have come and gone in the family." He gazed at Lily with a lingering smile, but his amusement faded quickly and he looked at the text again, holding his head in his hands.

Lily got up and walked to him. She stood behind his chair looking over his shoulder at the manuscript written in agile, elongated script. "This is brilliant. As I listen, I feel I'm inside one of the cells, lying on the narrow cot at night, shivering with cold, listening out for messages."

Sergei's face broke into a dubious smile. "I don't know that the editorial world will be as enthusiastic as you."

She walked around his chair, threw her arms around him, and kissed him on the lips. "Will you write about Sasha?" she asked peering into his eyes.

He looked away. "I'm considering another piece on the different treatment of prisoners according to their class."

"That sounds appropriate," Lily said.

In terms of publishing, Lily had proposed they contact Gerard, who was now in Paris, and probably had a good network in England and France. She also wrote to Harry for leads as to what existing political papers existed in Manchester. One definite venue for these articles was *Iskra,* the newspaper published by the Russian Democratic Labor Party in exile. *Iskra* was presently being published in London, where Vladimir Lenin and Julius Martov, the party founders who had fled Russia, had taken refuge. This was the party that Andrey Volkov and another cousin, Pyotr Nevinski, belonged to, and that Sergei had collaborated with, traveling back and forth with envoys of money and smuggling political literature into Russia for dissemination in factories and peasant communities. Lily knew quite a bit by now about the party and the Volkovs' involvement in it, though never as much as would satisfy her, for Sergei still insisted that her ignorance would protect her if anything happened. But after reading about czarist police proceedings and prisons, she quite doubted that anything could shield her at this point. If Sergei went down again, only her British citizenship might save her from the horrors she now knew existed.

However, Sergei's case had been settled for the time being. He had been spared a trial and instead had been "administratively banned" from St. Petersburg, and was to be sent to Vladivostok, a remote city on the Asian border of the Russian empire. There he was to abide for the next five years holding an obscure, petty clerical position within the Department of Customs, under the strict supervision of General Rudakov, a despotic military colleague of his father who had agreed to help the family. Sergei was to report to Rudakov by the end of May. It was a slap on the hand for a member of the nobility whose influential family had used all possible connections to save him from a Siberian labor camp.

After Sergei's banishment had been officially established, the conditions of his home arrest relaxed. At that point, some of his family members came to pay their respects and wish him an uneventful stay in Vladivostok. Sergei insisted that Lily be with him when visitors came, and that she acted as his consort. Lena and Kitty came and behaved as if they were just stepping in for casual afternoon tea. They put on their most charming social manners and at no point referred to Lily's presence as anything out of the ordinary. But they didn't bring Ruby along, and Lily understood this as a meditated punishment toward her.

Other people came to see Sergei: his uncle Anton Alexandrovich; a couple of old military friends from his Corps of Pages days; and an extravagant and distracted aunt, Vera Federovna. All of them treated Lily with respect, as if she was in fact a sanctified companion. But she knew that in their eyes she was just an adventuress, and that behind their social graces they held her in contempt.

The visitor Lily and Sergei most enjoyed was Annushka. From the moment authorities gave clearance for family calls, she had been coming to supper every evening her work ended at a respectable hour. She arrived hurriedly, her lovely face glowing from the cold air, always happy to see them and famished for "good and hearty peasant food," those recipes from the Southern Urals exquisitely cooked by Maria Petrovna and Masha.

After supper they would all sit in Sergei's study while he read aloud his latest piece, and afterward engage in the most stimulating discussions. By now Lily had read a few books about political thought and the situation of peasants and factory workers in Russia, and could follow some of the conversations between Sergei and his cousin. She was astonished at their vast knowledge on many subjects, at the sophistication of their arguments and the boldness of their political thought. Sergei and Annushka always paused to explain unusual terms to her, and briefed her on authors and ideas, such as Marx, Stuart Mill, nihilism, Tolstoy, Proudhonism, and so on. The next day, Lily would scour Sergei's library for books in English related to last night's talk and devour them.

It was during one of these sessions that she came across Engels's *The Condition of the Working Class in England in 1844,* and read about slums in Manchester. She was shocked to realize that she knew nothing of the poverty and suffering in her own city. Her heart ached as she read about the filthy, soot-covered slum cottages surrounded by tall, smoking factories, where whole families lived in dark, wet cellars amidst heaps of garbage and pools of human waste. She was also shocked to learn about the employment conditions and long working days in poisonous tanneries and cotton mills. Her eyes were being hacked open to a terrible reality she hadn't given any thought to before. It wasn't just a Russian problem then, it was widespread, everywhere around. She began to understand how some people were moved to act against the injustices of implacable systems that trampled whole masses of human beings for the benefit of a few.

One afternoon, Tatyana Mikhailovna came to visit. She swept into the main hall like an icy gale, not even deigning a side-glance toward Maria Petrovna, who fussed around her as she received her winter trappings and showed her into the drawing room. Tatyana sat by the great ceramic stove in perfect composure and nodded slightly in Lily's direction, murmuring "Mademoiselle," before turning to stare inscrutably at Sergei. They talked about administrative family matters in a mixture of French and German, and Lily struggled not to yawn through the long conversation of which she understood nothing. She excused herself, saying she would see why tea was taking so long to be served, and as she was leaving the room, she heard Tatyana ask Sergei, "Will your little friend be following you to Vladivostok?"

Lily stopped short behind the door and listened.

"Lily is my fiancée, Mother, and we shall marry as soon as I'm able," Sergei replied. "I would appreciate it if you addressed her with respect."

"I've heard you express this intention before with other girls," Tatyana said, "but so far you've done nothing to further your case in the Ecclesiastical court. You don't seem to pay attention to anything other than your political tomfoolery. I heard you rejected the position at the Geographical Society that your uncle so wanted you to take. The whole family is waiting for you to grow up, Sergei Nicolayevich."

That moment Maria Petrovna and Masha arrived with trays and a steaming samovar, and Lily reentered the room in their company to find Sergei and Tatyana glaring at each other across the room like two stone basilisks. Then Sergei stepped toward his mother, took her hand, and kissed it. "Dear Mother, I am truly happy to have seen you after all these months," he said, "and sorry that you have to leave and cannot take tea with us. Let me accompany you down to your carriage," and he led the petulant Tatyana out of the room, leaving Maria and Masha baffled with their tea service. They had brought out the most refined china in the household just for Tatyana, a beautiful, hand-painted set from the Imperial Porcelain factory. For the rest of the evening Sergei fell into one of his dark, silent moods. Lily decided not to tell him about her eavesdropping, but she brooded about Sergei and Tatyana's conversation all night long.

Although Sergei always talked about fantastic plans for their future together, he never mentioned any realistic plan of action that would free him from his former marriage. As for Vladivostok, they had both avoided the topic till now as if it were a bomb planted in the room that had to be tiptoed around. For her part, Lily refused to think outside her present bubble that felt so blissfully sealed off from the world. *When the moment comes I shall deal with it,* she thought. For the past months, she had lived to spend every moment of the day with Sergei; that, together with reading the books stacked in his library to keep up with his articles, had been her only pursuits. But time was flowing very quickly now. Their droplet of bliss was evaporating in the face of the outer world.

And Sergei was drifting again into dangerous paths.

Only the night before, he had left the property through a hidden passage connected through a trapdoor in the stables, dodging the soldiers and sentries posted around the house, to go to a secret meeting. Lily pleaded with him not to take such a risk, but he was unmoved by her arguments. Now that he was going to be stationed in Vladivostok, the party was planning political work for him at his new post. Lily spent the long hours he was away in utter anguish. He returned very late, looking pale, his eyes flashing with the same frenzy she had seen in him the evening they ended up stranded at the cottage.

He lay beside her in the night, his back turned to her, his whole being sunk in heavy, unshakable slumber. She ran soft fingers over the scars still embossed in his skin, remaining welts from his beatings that had never fully faded, and knew that if he got caught again and imprisoned, she would die every minute of the day to think that any part of this body she so loved would writhe, or bleed, or just wince under any form of torment or violation. She awoke determined to confront him with the gravity of his actions, but he refused to talk about it. When Lily pressed him, he only said, "This is my life commitment. Don't ask me to give up my duty."

One evening when Annushka had come to see them, and after a feast of beef stroganoff cooked especially for her, Sergei left the room to look for a book. Then Annushka turned to Lily. "What will you do when Seryozha leaves for Vladivostok?" she asked. Lily looked into her candid brown eyes at a loss for words, while a hundred conflicting replies crossed her mind.

Only a few weeks ago she had been toying with the possibility of following Sergei to Vladivostok. But things had become increasingly strained between them after he started attending underground meetings and refusing to listen to arguments urging him to think of his safety and that of those around him. And although their moments of love were as tender as ever, they were also having real quarrels about his dangerous ventures, and Lily was starting to foresee how excruciating a life with Sergei might be.

She had received a letter from Gerard informing her that he was staging a set of plays in Paris and that he would be delighted to take her on, if she still refused to return to London. He had also written that Wade was involved in another scandal, was once more on the brink of bankruptcy, and that this would be a good time to try to legally invalidate her contract.

She showed the letter to Sergei, and pleaded that he come with her to Paris, where he might continue his political work through writing, now that his articles had been accepted by a few publications. "It doesn't have to be Paris, it can be London or even Berlin, where you would be close to your cousins Andrey and Pyotr, and collaborate with them too," she said. "Applying pressure from abroad and educating international opinion might have even more of an impact than trying to stir things from inside the country. Annushka said so the other night, and you agreed."

Sergei only stared into her face, unblinking. "I will never leave Russia. Not until things have really changed."

"But why can't you temper your zeal with practical measures to protect your safety? After all, a dead man, or even an imprisoned one, can do little toward changing anything."

Sergei paced, flustered; then turned to her with blazing eyes and said, "What kind of a man would I be if, after everything I know, after everything I've seen, I ran off to a cozy place instead of staying put and taking on the task right here where the struggle is? Just tell me. And would you even respect such a man?"

A tense moment passed while Lily tried to steady herself before asking the question that had been burning inside her for the last weeks. "And you're assuming I will follow you in all this," she said at last, "that I shall leave everything behind and accompany you across the earth to some remote place where you will stop at nothing to pursue this struggle?"

Sergei sat down and sighed. He looked exhausted, sad. "I assume nothing. You know I love you. But I can only offer you the man I am."

They argued no more, but Lily already knew she had no more power to change Sergei's mind than she had in capping the winter blizzards of Petersburg.

That night, after Annushka was gone, Sergei prepared to leave again. He had a shabby, ragged coat and cap he wore for his escapades, perfectly fitted to pass undetected among the crowds in the night. Lily rushed to him as he finished putting them on, and clung to him. "I am so afraid," she said.

"Don't be," he said. "I shall be perfectly all right. Everything is well planned. But I won't return tonight, I'll have to wait until tomorrow evening when it's dark again." And he kissed her sweetly before he stole out of the room.

Lily wiped her tears and walked to the window. It was a black, moonless night. At the front gate, lanterns flickered above the iron doorway patrolled by two guards. For the first time in all these months, she could see herself stepping through that threshold and leaving all of this behind.

CHAPTER 20

She woke up when Maria Petrovna and Masha entered the room and drew the heavy curtains from the windows. She had slept badly, tossed by anxious dreams, waking at intervals to feel small and lost inside the cold bed. As soon as the first gleam of light reflected on her pillow she opened her eyes and glanced around hoping to find Sergei. But he wasn't there, and she remembered he had told her that he would only return on the evening of the next day. Anguish washed over her and she struggled to hold it back while she waited for Maria and Masha to leave the room.

They didn't, however, withdraw immediately, but fussed around the room and bed, straightening covers and piling pillows behind her so she could sit up. She wondered about this new extended morning procedure. Usually, they only entered the chamber to draw the windows and bring tea, after which they left hurriedly. But this was the first time Sergei was away, and protocol might be different.

She still found the world of Sergei's servants impenetrable. They treated her with deference, attended instantly to all her requests, all surely in honor of their master. But behind their masks of affability she felt their suspicion and estrangement. Maria Petrovna, in particular, was constantly watchful. The reserved, grim matron was jealously vigilant, and could be trusted to stride day and night around the house silently, like a keen custodian. Lily had learned to ignore her and wasn't bothered anymore by her prowling.

As she sat up in the bed, she felt her stomach lurch, and bent forward feeling nauseous and light-headed. Then she felt Maria's cool hands smoothing her temples and forehead, gently propping her back against the pillows, while cooing soft words that Lily failed to understand. Masha brought in a cup of tea, and Maria helped put it to her lips. At the first sip she realized it was not tea, but some herbal infusion, its bitter taste dampened with honey. She turned to question the women, and was astounded to find them watching her closely with beaming smiles.

"Drink, *matushka*," Maria said a number of times, "it will be good for you," and Lily finally understood her words. She drank and felt immediate relief to her stomach, while she mulled over this new address, *matushka*, that she knew to mean "little mother." Of course, the terms *matushka* and *batyushka*, "little mother" and "little father," were common among Russians, particularly when servants or people of lower rank referred to masters, but they had never called her so. She thought that Maria and Masha might be commiserating with her in terms of Sergei's absence, since they had seen her crying and begging him not to leave the night before.

But the meaning of this label didn't clarify in Lily's mind until later, when Masha, while rearranging the bedsheets around her once again, patted Lily's belly softly and murmured a word that pierced her like a bolt of lightning.

Rebyonok. Baby.

Baby! Lily's breath froze, and a dizzying whirlpool of impressions swirled in her brain, consolidating the significance contained in those two syllables. Her late teary moods, the swelling tenderness in her breasts, the peculiar warmth inside her belly, the excessive emotion she had displayed the night before with Sergei, it all pointed to the obvious. She was with child. Her mind reeled with panic, and then turned in despair toward arguments of denial. She might just be late; it was not uncommon with her. And her heightened feelings might be just a product of all that had been happening with Sergei. Nothing out of the ordinary was taking place inside her body. The drama was all coming from without.

She tried to hold fast to this last thought while Maria and Masha brought her dainty morsels for breakfast, which she left untouched. She lay collapsed in the bed, overpowered by her thoughts. Time passed, and then Maria, seeing she was not going to move by herself, helped her out of the bed. With Masha's assistance she disrobed her, and sponged her body with hot wet towels before combing her tresses and dressing her in the clean, ironed clothes they had brought in for her. Lily was so distraught she could only muse distractedly about the unprecedented amount of attention she was receiving. Of course, Masha had helped her before into her bath, but never groomed her like this, and certainly not Maria Petrovna. She felt like a precious child, or a selected bride being prepared for ritual or sacrifice. These women were certain of something.

These women knew.

By the time she settled downstairs in the drawing room she was in a flood of tears. The two Irish wolfhounds sat uneasily around her, whining and licking her hands. Being with child! This changed everything. Why hadn't she anticipated this outcome? Had she been lost in a world of delirium all these months, not even tending to essential precautions? Why hadn't she consulted with Annushka about more efficient ways of prevention? The thought of Annushka made her perk up. Yes, she would go immediately to see Annushka and confirm this agonizing doubt.

She looked around feverishly for her dictionary. Before calling in Maria Petrovna, she needed to carefully compose on paper everything she would say to her. She would request the carriage to go visit Annushka, and she would want to go alone; once there, she would send back car and driver, and return later on her own.

Maria Petrovna was surprised and displeased at Lily's request. She tried to dissuade her from leaving the house, saying she would call in the family doctor if she desired. She also objected to her being driven into the neighborhood where Annushka had her clinic. "*Plokhie ulitsy*, bad streets," she kept saying. But Lily stuck to her script, and Maria ended up giving in and organizing everything she requested.

Lily finally sat inside the closed carriage driven by Pavel, the household *izvozchik*, and the soldiers nodded in salute as she passed through the gate. It was the first time she was crossing this boundary in all these months. Although Sergei had told her that she was free to do so after his arrest was restructured, and that it would be good for her to go out, visit sights, and do shopping, she had chosen to remain inside by his side. She now understood that her refusal to resume the outer world had been the only way of preserving the ecstatic bubble she had been locked inside with Sergei. Its singularity would never have resisted being contaminated by the mundane. But their small, unique world was about to be pierced and dissolved. She had been living in a dream, and now the bleak moment of reckoning had come and was rapping at her window.

It was the end of April. The day was gray and windy. Façades of tall buildings still wet from yesterday's rain loomed around her. Sheets of ice covered pavements and clumped around the streets. They drove along the Fontanka River Embankment away from opulent quarters into the crowded streets around the Sennaya Ploshchad, the chaotic Haymarket Square, bustling with farmers and peasants trading wares in frantic activity. Then, turning behind the square, they entered the dark, sordid alleys of the *trushchobas*, or slums, that Annushka had talked so much about. Huge, run-down apartment buildings with crumbling façades and broken windows covered with oilskins came into view as they crossed narrow, grimy streets. The stench from courtyard latrines was so thick it filled the air inside the carriage. Across the entryway of one of the yards she saw group of scrawny boys fighting savagely, while two squalid young women stood indifferent and flimsy-clad with their backs to them. The girls' hungry faces were fixed across the street where a filthy tavern door spit out a staggering drunkard who stumbled away in a daze.

At the far end of one of the passageways, a smaller, neater building stood in striking, dignified contrast to its neighbors. There the carriage stopped and Pavel indicated to Lily that they had reached their destination.

She entered the courtyard and climbed up a dark stairwell of pitted stone steps. A rumor of voices and wailing children grew in volume as she approached the third floor. There, lined up along a narrow entryway through an open door stood a crowd of about twenty, some sitting, most standing, and others slumped in corners. She walked into the tight group, asking "*Vrach?* Doctor?" and people assented shyly as they let her through. Most of them were women and little children, but there were also elders and a few men. Their extreme poverty was apparent in their ragged attire and drawn, sickly countenances. The overcrowded space was filled with stuffiness and foul body smells. After a few moments of silent surprise at her appearance, the sounds of the chattering women mixed with heavy coughing, and children's howling swelled up again into a cacophony that sent Lily's head spinning. She looked around for a place to sit or lean to no avail, and wondered how long it would take for her to alert Annushka of her presence. A shriveled old woman with deep grooves around her cheeks sitting at the end of a bench got up and offered Lily her place. Lily at first refused, but the woman insisted in an unceasing murmuring litany and wouldn't take her seat back, so in the end Lily thanked her and took her place, embarrassed. Everyone stared at her, but all averted their eyes when she looked back.

Across from her sat two young women alongside a boy of about ten or twelve on crutches. One of the women was pale and wasted, with an enormous belly swelling out of her emaciated frame. She sat collapsed, leaning back against the wall, misery written all over her gray features. She must have been no older that seventeen. The woman sitting next to her held a skinny infant who was sucking fiercely at one of her breasts, and at intervals pulling away from it screaming, while the mother hurriedly changed him over to the other side. Lily watched the woman's long, withered breast as the child sputtered away from its purplish, pointed nipple, and felt her own breasts pressing painfully against her tight dress.

She closed her eyes and thought of the secret conduits that might be connecting her bosom's tenderness to the tight spot she could already feel inside her belly. All the happiness and pleasure that had shaken her to the root while lying with Sergei had culminated into this instance, into this tiny blob weaving itself around the tissues of her gut and already beating with an unstoppable will of its own. And this pulsing speck shackled her not just to Sergei and his circumstances but to all the heartache of this world.

She would never be free again.

She raised her eyes and glanced around. The misery of the human race paraded before her in all its absurdity and monstrous gloating: the horror of poverty, the futility of suffering, the waste and senselessness of it all. And still, life kept renewing itself in blind, unceasing turmoil; things were born, prolonged themselves mechanically, and then died as ludicrously as they had lived. All of a sudden, all phenomena, all things, seemed to be collected into the same indistinct, meaningless mass. Squalor and misery weren't that different from beautiful forms; a dying old drunkard was tantamount to a pink, glowing baby, a beautiful night sky to a dark, cadaverous hole. All were just variations of form floating from one end of the spectrum to another. There was no substantial difference between the stupid rich and these miserable beings. The Volkov sisters were made of the same rotting flesh as these wretches, only puffed up with excess food and dressed in filigree and lace. After all, these pained beings sitting around her had also once lodged inside a warm belly, had also looked with love into a mother's eyes.

And now she herself would be pouring another being into the corrupting tide of time, where all things moved along uncertain paths until they stumbled into death. This realization turned her heart upside down. It filled her with fury and fear. The world was being emptied out of meaning, slipping through her fingers. She sat back stupefied, stunned. A huge wave of nausea gushed into her. She bent over her knees gasping, and uttered a shrill sob before burying her face in her hands.

From the end of the room came a loud rapping with alarmed cries, and as she lifted her head she saw a young girl knocking insistently on a door. A moment later, Annushka swung it open, her face angry and knitted at the brow, and started scolding the girl. The girl pointed at Lily. Annushka's face first opened into a wide smile and then creased into a wrinkle of concern. "Lily, you're here! Why on earth didn't you let me know ahead of time? What's wrong? Is everything all right?" She took her by the hand and pulled her into her office. "Come in here. You can watch me treating the last patients for the morning slot, and then we'll eat together during my break. Oh, I'm so glad you finally decided to visit my clinic." She helped Lily out of her coat and had her sit by the window.

The room was bare but clean, with the smell of some mild antiseptic pervading its space. A simple desk with two chairs, an examining table, and a small metal cabinet completed the sober furnishings. There was but one picture upon its whitewashed walls, a small painting of the veranda overlooking the Neva from the dacha on Kamenny Island, that Lily instantly recognized as one of Anatoly's works. It made her wince with melancholy recollection, and reminded that she was still within Volkov territory.

On one of the chairs sat a woman with a baby who wouldn't stop screaming. As soon as she settled Lily, Annushka asked the woman to lay the baby on the table and unswaddle him. Lily watched the mother unwrap the child. Underneath the heap of rags she pulled away from the little body there appeared a filthy shirt and diaper covering patches of red, angry skin. Annushka started telling the woman off, yelling above the escalating wails of the baby, and rebuking her for keeping the child so soiled, while the mother sulked in shame. Finally, she examined the rashes and gave the woman some medicine from the cabinet and a small bar of soap, before screaming at her again. Lily had never seen her so angry. The woman left after long expressions of gratitude and proffering all sorts of blessings. Annushka closed the door and turned to Lily with a sigh. "How's that poor baby going to survive under all that filth? And the things they feed them! No one has taught them anything. I have to scream, terrorize them. It seems the only way to make them understand," she said.

Next came in an older woman with both legs bandaged. She sat down and started removing her bandages while Annushka took her information behind the desk. An unbearable stench arose from the woman's legs as she finished taking off the dressings and large green and crimson sores were revealed on her shins and ankles. The putrid smell overtook the room, and Lily thought she would be sick. But Annushka noticed her pallor and sent her out through a side door into a small kitchen, where she asked her to make tea.

When Lily came back with the tea, the woman was gone and Annushka was writing notes at her desk. Then she went to the door and sent the rest of the patients away, asking them to come back in the morning. She returned to the room and took off the long white apron that covered her dress and the linen kerchief wrapped around her head. "Well, you're getting a sense of what my day is like," she said, smiling at Lily. "I've been seeing patients since eight o'clock, and now in the afternoon after my break I must rush out to do house calls. It never ends."

She walked toward Lily and took her hands. "What's wrong, Lily? You don't look well," she said. Then she added in affectionate jest, "Is that rascal Seryozha giving you grief?" When Lily's eyes filled with tears, she folded her in her arms saying, "Come, come, you're going to have to get used to his comings and goings. But things will be better in Vladivostok. Surveillance will slacken, and he'll settle down to boring organizing work."

Lily pulled away from her embrace. "Annushka, I shan't be going to Vladivostok. I have to get back to my life."

"I see," Annushka said after a moment with a sobering wince. "And I also see how difficult this will be for him. I've never seen him so much attached." She sighed, and wandered around the room for a while before returning to her. "But I understand; you must follow your heart. And of course, Seryozha, for all we love him—"

"Annushka, you have to help me," Lily interrupted in a sudden, whispered frenzy. "I think I am with child."

Annushka wasted no time in stripping the table of its former sheet and spreading out a clean one. She had Lily take off her dress and lie over its surface. She sounded out her abdomen with short, knuckle thuds before examining her breasts with strong, knowing hands. Then she placed a small horn-shaped instrument on her belly and put her ear to the other end. After moving it around over a few different points, she straightened up and said, "Beating like a drum. You must be ten weeks in." She shook her head with a smile. "Maria Petrovna would be the one to spot it from miles away. After thirteen children, I suppose it becomes second nature. And then, in those Ural provinces, matrons have no choice but to become midwives. They fill in for the absence of doctors. And in truth they know more than them; they hold the ancient keys to the female body. But even among them, she is exceptional. I've consulted with her many times about my patients."

She helped Lily down from the table and handed her back her dress. "Your health has really toned up of late, Lily. I am very pleased. And I anticipate a good pregnancy and a robust child," she said. Then she burst into a joyful giggle. "Oh, how happy Seryozha will be! I'd give anything to see his face when he learns of this."

Lily leaned against the table, pale, trembling. "Annushka, I cannot have this child. And Seryozha must not know." She watched Annushka's smile drop. "Please," she implored, "understand my situation."

Annushka turned and walked away toward the desk. She stood rummaging through her papers. A moment later, she looked up at Lily. "And you need to understand the position you're putting me in," she said.

Hours passed, an indistinct amount of time Lily couldn't quantify after the daylight first dimmed outside and then plunged into pitch-dark. She went back and forth with Annushka inside the little room, from the table to the desk to the chair and back to the table again. She begged, pleaded, vindicated every reason why a woman in her position could not have a child; listed every dramatic angle of Sergei's present circumstances; went into every argument she had heard at their table about women's rights, every contention of women's need for freedom and independence from family. She whined, broke down, even wept openly. All the while, Annushka paced up and down, wringing out her conscience behind a stern, impenetrable face.

"I know I have no right to ask, that it's not fair on you," Lily said one more time, "but at least tell me where else to go." Annushka shook her head. "There's nobody I trust. It's heavily criminalized, as you know. People who take chances are not reliable."

Finally, Lily collapsed into a chair feeling drained, too weak to utter another syllable. Her lips were dry and she was faint with hunger. Annushka sulked in silence behind the desk. Outside the window, Lily saw Pavel sitting atop the carriage by the curb, still waiting for her, although she had asked him hours ago to return to the house. She stood up, gathered her coat and trappings, and began toward the door.

"All right, Lily," she heard Annushka say from across the room. "You will come here tomorrow at six in the evening. Find a way not to come in one of the household's carriages. Be prepared; it won't be easy. I shall arrange for your return to the house afterward." Lily wanted to rush back to Annushka and thank her, even throw herself at her feet and kiss her hands, but Annushka only said good night and looked away.

It was well after seven o'clock when Lily returned to the house. Masha opened the door and told her that Sergei was waiting for her in the hall, and that supper would be served as soon as they wished. Sergei stood in his shirtsleeves staring into the fireplace, an empty glass of vodka in one hand and a bottle in the other. He turned as she walked in, his face blazing with joy, and hurriedly set down the glass and bottle on the mantelpiece. *He knows,* she thought, *Maria Petrovna has told him.* This could have been easily anticipated, but now it further complicated things.

Slowly she strode toward him, heart racing, cheeks blushed; stiff with fear. He took her into his arms and kissed her hair. "I know you went to see Annushka," he said.

"I did," she said. They looked at each other, and she knew he was waiting for her to speak, but she held her silence.

"And how is Annushka?" he asked.

"She's well," she said.

She watched his face as he struggled with anticipation, while gauging how she would tackle him. She was afraid she might be dragged into his arresting smile and lose her presence of mind. It was going to require all her skill to get through this moment. And yet, skill was the last thing she felt in command of. A new set of baffling sensations and strange emotions were tearing her apart, lulling her capacity for thinking straight, for strategizing.

"That's all?" Sergei asked. "No impressions of her clinic? Of her work?"

For a moment, Lily wished she could just sit down and talk about Annushka's clinic as if her experience had been that of a casual, interested visitor, instead of a desperate round of beseeching, a merciless harping at Annushka's conscience to have her agree to her design. "I am very tired. I need to lie down," she said, and pulled away from him.

"Of course. I'll ask Maria Petrovna to prepare the bed. She can also bring supper to the bedroom," Sergei said, and helped her into a chair by the fire. He left the room while Lily sat petrified. When he returned he pulled a stool and sat across from her. He held her hands and kissed them. "If you knew how happy I am . . . I must be the happiest man in Petersburg. I might just burst any moment out of my own skin."

Lily looked away. "Seryozha, I cannot follow through with this."

"And why not? If you're worried about marriage, I will speed up procedures, I'll settle you financially in the meantime, and of course, I will adopt the child," he said.

"Seryozha, I don't want this child. And, I do not want to go to Vladivostok. I want to return home."

Sergei's face darkened. He sat back and thought for a while before saying, "I know you're still hurt about yesterday. I know it's hard for you to accept what I'm doing. I wish I had the words to explain why I need to pull through with this task." He took her face in his hands and forced her to lock eyes with him. "But now we're joined by this child and our life is about to change, and I need you to trust me more than ever."

Lily stood up. "I don't want my life to change. Not this way. That's why I went to see Annushka," she said.

"Annushka?" he echoed.

"Yes. She will help me," she said, and then seeing Sergei grow pale, she decided to lie. "She said she will help me if you agree."

"She said that? That's strange, she knows I would never agree."

"You would never agree? And all those high and lofty ideas about revolution and women's rights in the new society?"

"What would that have to do with a man loving a woman and wanting her child?"

Lily groaned. "No, it has to do with women not always having to do what men want, not having to withstand being humiliated and begrimed, or watch the world harrow their bastard children."

"I just said I would settle you and adopt the child."

"You cannot settle me. You know very well all your resources are requisitioned."

"Then my family will, until I clear my situation."

"Your family, settle me financially?" Lily sneered. A moment passed. Then she said in a softer tone, "Please, let's be reasonable. These are the facts: We cannot marry; you are bound to banishment in a few weeks; and, you're committed to a cause that excludes every other priority. Why would this be a moment for me to have your child?"

"How can you be so cold? You cannot measure life, or love, or the coming of a child by a listing of facts. Life brings things and we take them in, we cannot always plan every situation—"

"Seryozha, please," Lily interrupted, "admit that I'll be the main victim in all this, that you will just be the father of an adopted bastard child, while I . . ." She could not finish her sentence, just the thought of staking out her situation again dazed her. She added quietly, "I only ask that you side with me."

Sergei turned away from her and paced up and down the room; his hands made fists inside his trouser pockets, his jaw clenched.

"It's hard enough as it is, without having to beg everyone else to comply," Lily added through gritted teeth.

Sergei spun around, and she saw his face flushed with contained fury. "You want me to help you undo my child so you can walk away from me? Is that what you're asking me to do?"

"I'm asking you to consider my situation, instead of just thinking about your own grief," she replied, raising her voice above his.

But Sergei had already stormed out of the room. She heard him rush up the stairs and walk into the study, slamming the door.

She lay exhausted in the bed after devouring all the food that Masha brought her. She asked the girl to extinguish the lights but for the small lamp on her bedside table, and then leave the room. She thought she would plummet into sleep, but her mind wouldn't quiet down as she kept mulling over the events of the long day. In less than twelve hours her life had turned, like a beastly sea whipping up a sudden storm where the small vessel of her being was about to be gutted and drowned. Although, if she considered it carefully, it was easy to see how that very storm had been gathering for quite some time. This wild love with a man like Sergei, the engrossment with a remote, outlandish country like Russia, how had she allowed herself to become so entangled in it all?

No matter, the moment for turning around had come, and she had to keep her head together in order to take the necessary steps without slipping away from the main target. Tomorrow she would go to Annushka. Then she would rest for a few days before leaving for Paris. If Sergei became too strained, she would go to the Krügers and organize her departure from there.

Sergei. His overjoyed eyes came into her mind, and she watched them overturn and dissolve into misery. She had smashed up his heart. She felt his emptiness in the bed and thought of him locked up in the study. At first, she had followed him up the stairs and knocked on the door urging him to come out and finish their conversation, but he had not responded, and at length she had walked away. She had never seen him so upset. He might not come down to the bedroom at all tonight. She wondered if he might be reconsidering the possibility of going to Paris with her, if he would contemplate bending his rigid commitment in light of the new circumstances. But she knew he would not.

And would she? Would she accept to have his child if he changed his course?

Lily shifted uncomfortably in the bed. Her body felt bloated after all the food, but in a strange, pleasurable way. Like a tingling; an assortment of tiny, relishing sparks that flashed up and down as if little footsteps were dancing inside her. She rubbed her belly and thought about Annushka's room, the cold narrow table and the fearful instruments she had spied inside the metal cabinet, and shuddered. "It won't be easy," Annushka had said. Fear gripped her, and she was seized by a sudden yearning to be tightly wound inside Sergei's arms, to be comforted by his kisses and his voice.

She awoke the next morning feeling wretched. She sat up and barely had time to step out of bed before she was sick on the floor. Maria Petrovna and Masha rushed to comfort her, cleaned everything up, settled her back in the bed, and made her drink the same infusion they had given her the day before. When she was feeling a bit better, she asked them about Sergei, but Maria Petrovna only said, "Sergei Nikolayevich is still in his study."

After the two women finished dressing her and doing her toilette, she left the room and went to the study. The door was still closed. On the floor sat a tray with untouched food and drink that looked like it had been there for hours. Grisha came along bearing fresh vittles and kneeled as he replaced one tray with the other. "Has your master not left the room since last night?" she asked, and the boy shook his head, before giving her a small, grim smile and moving away. Lily approached the door and tried the knob, but it was still locked. Then she knocked gently. "Seryozha, please open the door." She waited, but no sound came from the room. She knocked again. "Can we talk about this? Can you bear to listen to what I have to say one more time? Just try to understand my position in all this." But she was met with dead silence.

She went to the drawing room and spent the morning first trying to read, and then attempting to write a letter to Harry. But she couldn't concentrate on anything. The anxiety about the upcoming appointment with Annushka mounted as the hours went by, and Sergei's silence gnawed at her as if she bore an army of fire ants inside her gut. Her initial dismay at his withdrawal was turning into annoyance and irritation. Even if he was disturbed, or repulsed, at what she planned to do, how could he forsake her so? To totally disengage like this was far crueler than if he had chosen to scream, reproach, or even humiliate and insult her. She felt small in the huge room, a foreign, isolated object in an unfamiliar, hostile space. She returned to her letter, and retraced once more the only words she had written down so far, *Dear Harry and Alice.*

What would Harry think of her situation? Would he support her? And Alice? She was so very innocent, and extremely religious. She would surely be shocked, horrified. Scenes of the three of them going to church together crossed her mind. Images of the Christmas services, sounds of sermons about the nativity of Christ, the faces of little children singing carols in the choir. What about her father and Betty? And her little sister Annie? They would all die of shame.

She stood up, crumpled up the letter, and hurled it away from her. She walked to the window and leaned her head on the cold glass. She couldn't afford these thoughts, they would just torture her, destroy her. She was in a desperate situation and the action she needed to undertake had become a matter of survival. This was not a time for remorse or regret. This was a time of extreme endurance.

She sat alone at the large table in the hall, and pushed away the plate of food. Even the smell of her favorite meals filled her with repugnance today. She got up, stomped out of the hall and up the stairs to the study. She rapped on the door with forceful knuckles. "I demand you open this door immediately and stop acting like a little boy," she said. "If you really love me, as you've pledged so many times, you need to think about me now," and she listed once more every fact that made her decision logical and desperately necessary.

Again she was met with silence.

For a moment she wondered if Sergei was still inside the study. But where else could he be? Grisha kept coming up at intervals with replacement food and drink, and took away the former trays untouched. She thought he might have drunk himself into a stupor, since there was always plenty of vodka lying around in the study. Although Sergei swilled down his vodka regularly, she had never seen him drunk. What could he be doing? She'd heard very few sounds in all the time she had spent knocking on the door.

She paced up and down feeling her desperation grow. *If he doesn't side with me,* she thought bitterly, *and Annushka finds out that he knows everything by now, she might go back on her decision.* It had been a mistake to be candid; she should have played them both. But it was too late now. Even if she had had enough money to rush to London or to Paris, how would she seek this sort of help in either of those cities? Who would help her? And the risks . . . She remembered Frances, the little seamstress at the Imperial Theatre who had bled to death in her bed one night after she visited a woman in Shoreditch. No, this was her only chance. And to take advantage of it, she depended on Sergei. She was in his hands. This reflection made her fly into a rage and she banged the door until her wrists and her arms hurt. "Open this door," Lily screamed, "or I shall leave this house instantly and you will never see me again." She followed with a long string of similar threats. Finally, she broke into uncontrollable sobbing. "Please, Seryozha, don't do this to me, you're killing me," she wept, sliding down to the floor.

Maria Petrovna and Grisha came to her, lifted her up, and walked her to the bedroom while she cried hysterically. After they laid her down on the bed, Masha brought in some sort of draught that they made her drink. She recognized the taste of chamomile infusion. It slowly calmed her down until she closed her eyes, exhausted, and fell into a blurred slumber. When she woke, she saw Maria Petrovna sitting by her side and watching her with concern. The light in the room was fast fading and she knew it must be after four o'clock. She sat up feeling agitation swelling inside her again, and asked Maria if Sergei had left the study, but she said no. The old matron took a tumbler from the bedside table and offered it to her, saying, "You must not fret, *matushka*, it is no good for the baby," at which Lily burst into tears again. Maria Petrovna comforted her by smoothing her hair and murmuring sweet words she didn't understand.

After a while, Lily sobered up, and making an effort to think straight, said to Maria Petrovna, "Please help me get ready to go out. I shall need the carriage to take me to Annushka's clinic."

But Maria stood up and replied, "Oh, no need. I already sent it out to fetch her. She will come here. It is too cold and wet for you to go out."

At that moment, Lily heard someone rushing up the stairs to the room, and in an instant Annushka appeared through the door. "Lily, what is the matter? I've been hurried here by Pavel with urgent reports. What's going on?" She sat on the bed while Lily told her in fragmented sentences all that had happened since she had been at the clinic the day before.

"You have worked up a fever," Annushka said with a frown, pressing her hands on Lily's brow. "This is not good. Stay here, and I will have Masha bring you a remedy. Meanwhile, I will talk to Sergei." She left the room in the company of Maria Petrovna.

Lily got up from the bed, wrapped herself in a long shawl, and followed them down the corridor. She found them standing outside the study door. Annushka was trying the doorknob and talking to Sergei in Russian. After a few moments of not getting any response, Annushka stopped, and Maria Petrovna bent toward her and started whispering in her ear. Lily watched them, feeling feverish and shivering, her unshod feet on the cold wooden floor. She took a step forward. "What is she saying?" she demanded. "I have a right to know what she is saying," she insisted.

Annushka turned to her with a grim face. "She is saying that he does this when he is extremely upset," she said. "The first time she remembers, he was four years old. Tatyana left Taganay and he hid in the garret of the old house. It took them three whole days to find him. He was half dead when they finally came upon him."

"Well, he's probably just dead drunk in there now," Lily sneered, "and anyway, what does all of that have to do with this?" But the women ignored her and, turning around, they recommenced talking to Sergei through the door.

She pulled the shawl tighter around her body and shuffled back to the bedroom. She crawled into the bed and curled up into a ball. She was shaking. Her whole body felt chilled, but for her smoldering face and forehead, and her belly, which tingled with a fuzzy feeling of warmth. She closed her eyes and pressed her head into her knees. She knew she had not just lost a battle, but the whole war.

A while later, Lily stirred as Annushka touched her forehead with cool fingers. Then she felt the small, cold diaphragm of the stethoscope pressing against her breast. "Your temperature has receded," Annushka said, "and you look much better. Nothing like a good little sleep. You should eat and drink now, I don't want you dehydrated," she added, looking at her with kind eyes. "But you must rest in the bed until tomorrow."

Lily seized her hand as she was getting up to leave. "Annushka, I still want to go to the clinic," she begged in a last desperate attempt. "Tell me that you will see me tomorrow, or even the day after tomorrow. Please."

Annushka sighed. She sat down again. "We cannot do this anymore, Lily," she said.

"Because Sergei has asked you not to?" Lily asked, ready to whip up a fury again.

"No. We haven't talked about this," Annushka said. "I know I agreed to it yesterday, and maybe I would have done it on the spot, as I have done it for other women. Or even if you had come today at six as we concurred. But now it's different. Because I've realized it's not my place. Not inside my own family. I am really sorry, Lily."

Lily let go of her hand and slumped back on the bed. A moment passed.

Then Annushka said, "Sergei is outside the door waiting to see you. He wants to apologize for his behavior, and how it might have hurt you. Shall I ask him in?"

Lily turned her back to her and burrowed her face into the pillows. "Ask him to go away. I don't want to talk to him. Ever again."

CHAPTER 21

The vast grasslands undulated in the breeze outside her window as the train crawled by. Random patches of flowers quivered over its rippling surface, and sprinkled among the endless bed of fluffy spikes, sprigs of hyacinth, iris and wild lilies. The grass was tall, as she had been told it always grew in the spring, so tall that sometimes a person could hide inside and not be seen at all. And all around, the eye was met with marshes and lakes, small and large, endless water configurations swamping the infinite fields.

It had been four days since she and Sergei had boarded the Trans-Siberian Express in Moscow, and, at the unnerving speed of fifteen miles an hour, they were finally approaching the city of Omsk. They had already left behind Kazan and Perm, crossed the Ural range, and now rolled through the open Siberian expanse.

It was by mere chance they had ended up in the *train de luxe* of the Wagons-Lits company, instead of following the originally prescribed official plan of riding the Russian *train d'état,* the plain post train that left for Irkutsk every day at three o'clock. They arrived well on time in Moscow on the St. Petersburg Night Express on a Saturday, but Sergei was detained by questioning officers and only released toward the evening when the post train was already gone. By luck, the luxury express was about to leave the station at that hour, and the difference in price not being an issue, the police authority had acquiesced to the change.

The first days on the wagon-lit, as they cut across the somber lands of eastern Russia with its big ragged cities of Syzran and Samara upon the banks of the Volga, Lily had been impressed by the hopeless aspect of the Russian villages with their miserable hovels of thatch surrounded by acres of overworked land. They spoke of centuries of toil, of millions of souls living and dying in monotonous obscurity, with relentless raking and reaping the same exhausted soils. Later, as they mounted the inclines of the Ural range, the great mountains that separate Europe from Asia, she was glad at their beautiful scenery of soft wooded outlines of taiga forest, and their fresh, invigorating air.

Now they were bound to Siberia, and once across the Urals, the wild mountains merged into the wide grassy plain of the steppe. Here, scattered along the open, endless fields one saw, instead of the cramped thatched hovels, rustic log cabins surrounded by rail fences, sometimes grouped around an ostentatious church, forming a village or a small town. Everything had the air of a new and crude world, an untamed, empty space, underpopulated, somehow free.

Lily sat in the dining car, the set of exquisite china with its silver teapot and samovar still clinking on the table, although breakfast had long been over and most of the other travelers had left for their compartments. Sergei sat opposite her, seemingly immersed in some sort of bulletin or newspaper. His two military custodians sat rigidly at the adjacent table, now that the car was mostly empty of customers, and had refused to take any tea when the waiter approached them at Sergei's request. They stared ahead with blank faces.

The chugging of the engine over the tracks lulled her into a dreamlike state as she looked out onto the unbroken miles of steppe. Many of her fellow passengers complained about the monotony of the landscape, but she loved these open stretches. They made her soul soar, the mere hint of their expanse got her flying into visions of the earth's beauty and its unlimited life forms. She caught herself smiling, and from the corner of her eye saw Sergei watching her. She straightened her face and, avoiding his glance, looked down at the little book she held over the table. It was a bilingual edition of *Eugene Onegin*, Pushkin's novel written in verse, that she had taken from the Petersburg house library with the intention of improving her Russian. She undid the tiny brass clasp that held the leather volume together, opened it randomly, and read:

Every moment of my days
to follow you, to catch your smile
and search your gaze with loving eyes,
to listen to your every word,
and in my soul explore
your perfect grace

She stopped short. This was not what she had intended for her morning literary perusal. She thought of closing the book and leaving instantly for her compartment. But she restrained herself, refusing to betray any emotion through abrupt behavior. Besides, Masha would still be ordering the cabin and would come to fetch her when it was ready. She turned back to the book.

But all this I'm denied; instead for you
I drag my footsteps all day long,
I count each hour the whole day through

She could feel Sergei's glance burning upon her. She lifted her eyes and stared at him in defiance, but Sergei was once more immersed in his paper. Every time he saw her with Russian books he asked her to let him read to her, but she always refused. This time he didn't ask; he just looked up and gave her the shadow of a polite smile.

His coolness incensed her. It filled her with ill temper. There he sat across from her, a model of restraint and exquisite civility, impeccable in the Imperial Army uniform in which General Rudakov had requested he travel, as part of the plan to restore him to his military grade. And he did look the part, this handsome, grave man, traveling with his English "wife," escorted by officers, aloof and dignified as if he'd never swatted a fly.

Fuming at these considerations, Lily stared down at the little book again, but wasn't able to read anymore. She pretended to be engaged with its pages while seething with mounting rage. It was intolerable that she had to withstand his proximity even for a few hours during mealtimes. It was still more ludicrous that she had acquiesced to pose as Madame Latvina within the small universe of this luxury train, when in truth she was only the loath prisoner of a prisoner, a woman dragged to the confines of the earth, shackled to her own subduer's chains.

Across the table she heard Sergei draw in a slight breath, like the utterance of a muzzled sigh. She knew that for him every moment of her presence was as equally excruciating as his was for her. She made sure that her indifference and her haughty insistence on silence kept him inside his own prison of suffering; that his every effort to reconcile fell on fallow ground. And the patience with which Sergei withstood her punishment filled her with even more disdain. These rich people, she thought sneeringly, who've been taught exquisite manners and elegant mores to the point where their breeding seeps into their emotions, into their very souls. Why, even if Sergei were being driven before a shooting squad, he would still smile around in good graces and treat his executioners with affability, too proud to even wince with fear or distress. All in the duplicitous style of that class of grandiose individuals who ruled the world and that, for the time being, had come to rule her.

She drew a long breath. It was becoming increasingly difficult to sustain high plateaus of indignation against him after all these weeks. Her initial fury had simmered down in great measure. In the beginning, after that doleful night with Annushka in Petersburg, she had shut herself up in the bedroom, refusing to see anyone but Masha. She had torn up every letter Sergei had sent her and dispatched them back, in pieces, unread, atop the same platter on which they were delivered. She spent her days alone, and after weeping out every tear she had in her body, had resorted to reciting each word of every play she had ever been in, over and over again, like a prisoner in solitary confinement avoiding going insane.

Finally, three days before Sergei's scheduled departure, Annushka walked into her room and sat across from her. "Lily, this is your last chance. Either we get you on your way to London or you travel to Vladivostok. I think this second choice might be your best. I'm sure you'll be able to come to some sort of personal or financial agreement with Seryozha in time."

Lily hung her head. Anything was preferable than returning now to London to bear a bastard child alone.

When they finally set out toward Vladivostok, she was glad to leave her self-imposed confinement and the city she had come to hate, and that would be by now swarming with scandalous gossip about her pregnancy. But she couldn't forgive Sergei. With him she remained implacable. She only condescended to monosyllabic responses, and short, icy notes if she or Masha needed something urgently. Sergei, on the other hand, had not lost his composure and remained watchful of her, thinking about her first in any matter, making sure she had the best of everything in her compartment. He also made constant attempts at conciliatory conversation. But Lily's heart had so hardened that she took everything for granted and snubbed him at any possible occasion.

Additionally, she flirted with every other man in the train who paid her attentions; in particular, with a young, attractive Dutch cartographer by the name of Hans Andriessen who had taken an interest in her and related to her all sorts of information about Siberia and the specifics of the journey. Every time Sergei was nearby, she made sure to smile sweetly at this cartographer and talk more animatedly than ever, ignoring Sergei's signs of distress. However, Lily soon had to put distance between her and Hans, as with all the rest, when her flirting started drawing them closer than she wanted. She wasn't interested in any of the men travelers. When she was feeling lonely, she shut herself up in her compartment and turned to thinking about Chut, fantasizing about their times together, idealizing their love story to a degree she knew was far beyond reality, but still holding him as the most kind, true man she had ever known.

As for the logistics of her situation, she tried hard not to brood over them. Here she was against her wishes, with child, following an outlaw across the vastest country in the world with no idea of what the future might hold for her. Pangs of bitterness and regret had assailed her when leaving Moscow, thinking that she would never now fulfill her dream of meeting Stanislavsky; and if she thought of Paris and Gerard's invitation to join him in his theater, she would plunge into dark hours of dejection. But she fought to rise above these thoughts. After all, what was the use of agonizing over all of that now?

Physically she felt more than fine. And if the mirrors in her compartment were at all truthful in their reflection, she was looking more beautiful than ever, as if the pregnancy were blasting her into bloom. Her face had opened up, her skin glowed in peachy complexion, the whites of her eyes sparkled around her amber irises. She ate well and slept well, and though she was hardly showing much at this stage, she was more than conscious of the changes going on inside her. No trace remained of her morning sickness, or of the sudden drops in vitality and mood. The swelling of her breasts and belly that had been so uncomfortable in the past had now turned to a strange feeling of fulfillment. She remembered having felt like this when, in just a few months, she had grown from child to woman, and had come into possession of a more powerful, mature body. She felt whole, self-contained and in love with all kinds of food. But food was not the only thing that triggered enhanced and delicious sensations. The smells of the Siberian spring, the beauty of the steppes unfolding through the window, and other simple things like these gave her deep, nuanced pleasure, as she had not known before. Her whole being was slipping into mellowness.

This might be in part the reason why it had become challenging to act harshly against Sergei. For increasing amounts of time, she found herself gliding into placid moments and forgetting her circumstances. But then there were other times when she would again be pierced by the consciousness of having lost the reins of her life, and this realization threw her into frenzy; fired up blind rebellion inside her heart like a sickness. And she pointed it back to Sergei.

Masha came along to announce that her compartment was ready, bearing a small envelope with a note. It was from Annette Maekin inviting her to join her in the library car. Annette was the most interesting person she had met in the train so far, an English writer who was working on a travel book about Russia, for which purpose she was riding the Trans-Siberian all the way to Vladivostok and then crossing over to Sapporo, in Japan. She traveled with her mother, an intrepid little old lady with an amusing sense of humor. Lily loved spending time with them, but unfortunately, they were about to leave the train today near the city of Omsk, where they planned to explore the territory of the Kirgiz, an ancient people known for archery and horse rearing. The day before Lily had seen some Kirgiz horsemen driving cattle on the steppe, a bunch of wild-looking boys riding fiercely among the grazing herds. Annette had a photographic camera with which she intended to take their pictures. How Lily wished she could step off the train with them and join her friends in their explorations.

Lily found Annette and Mrs. Maekin sitting in the library car. "Let's make plans to meet in Vladivostok," Annette said. "I think we will arrive in about four weeks."

"Or six," Mrs. Maekin added with a smirk. "We never know where we might be caught up. We shall be visiting one of their model convict settlements in Aleksandrovsk, you know."

"I hope you ladies are carrying a revolver with you," a lady who was sitting close by said in French. "Siberia is not a safe territory, particularly for women. I, personally, always carry two." This lady was known among the travelers as an eavesdropper and a chatterbox, a stout woman who rustled around in extravagant, convoluted dresses. She always talked about how much she hated Siberia, and how she was only traveling to Irkutsk to sell her deceased husband's lands. When she realized that Annette, Mrs. Maekin, and Lily were not in the mood for engaging with her, she got up with a huff and left the car.

"I wonder if she carries her guns inside her petticoats and crinolines," Mrs. Maekin said, following her with a twinkling eye, "not that she seems to have much space left in there." Annette and Lily smiled.

Annette and Mrs. Maekin soon left the train and Lily was sorry to have lost such good companions. Their case was not unusual, however; many travelers disembarked along the way, for some professional or leisurely reason or other, so making friends inside this chugging, lavish universe was an unstable, ephemeral affair. At times, though, the fleeting nature of these encounters was the essence of their intense enjoyment. They also warranted that there was not enough time for prying into Lily's personal affairs. She had already heard comments about the oddity of Sergei continually being escorted around, and the icy estrangement she and Sergei displayed. A snide woman from Petersburg, who had also boarded the train in Moscow, had spread a rumor after she overheard one of the conductors questioning Sergei on the contradiction of Madame Latvina having an English passport with a different name.

After her friends departed, Lily sat late that afternoon in the library car reading. But it soon filled up with chatter and cigar smoke. The library car and the dining compartment were some of the favorite spaces in the train, the former having been beautifully furnished with oak paneling, Moroccan leather chairs, and a bookcase with over a hundred books in four languages. There was no end to the marvels of this train. The bathroom compartment with its marble-trimmed bathtub and washbasin and her own lovely and comfortable coupé, as French travelers called their sleeping cabins, were stunning enough. She had been told there were even more luxurious cars, like carriage number 725, which was decorated in Louis XVI style and only rented to private parties. The express even had a wagon-chapelle, an Orthodox Church car staffed with Orthodox priests, mostly intended for railway staff, but also accessible to pious travelers.

But the library was definitively the most popular spot. Here, travelers met for conversation, and later in the evening gambling parties sat around the tables, drinking and playing into the night. There was no shortage of entertainment on the train, including piano concerts and singing in the dining car after supper, though Lily always retired early feeling tired and in need of sleep. But she knew Sergei joined the gambling groups at night. She had seen him one evening by chance, throwing winning cards onto a table, enclosed in a thick halo of cigar smoke amid excited faces. The next morning, a French diplomat who traveled with a little fluffy dog had told her that Sergei already had a fearsome reputation among fellow players for winning his rubles, as well as downing large shares of vodka. How he got his stiff custodians to stand by him in all of this until the wee hours was quite a mystery to Lily.

Indeed, this might be the only situation in which Sergei could bend his custodians' strict determination not just to watch him unflinchingly day and night, but also to make sure he made no contacts throughout the journey. They had always avoided having him in close groups of people. The exception around the gambling table possibly had to do with the fact that the older of the two custodians, Guguchov, had a soft spot for betting, as Masha had told her. Otherwise, they followed Sergei everywhere and never let him out of their sight. Even if Lily and Sergei had been in the throes of passion at this time, it would have been impossible for them to have any moments of intimacy away from their canine stares. "My human chains," Lily had heard Sergei call them in jest. But neither of them had reacted to the joke. They were gargoyle-faced, rigid, impassible, and had obviously been well and carefully selected for the task; trained to be implacable in the face of any temptation offered by Sergei's generous hand or even toward his irresistible personal charm.

Lily returned to her sleeping car and stood by the window on the corridor as the train approached a small station it would just pass through. A group of peasants stood by looking at the train, muzhiks with long beards and thoughtful faces, women with their kerchiefs and baskets in arm, and little children staring with awed eyes at the striking metal animal rolling away before them. It was not uncommon for local people to gather in the stations just to see the trains pass by. Those stations where the train did stop had their platforms quickly transformed into small markets, with a wide variety of vendors offering food on improvised wood stands. Sergei always sent Masha out to buy berries, sour cream, or entire trays of caviar and bring them to Lily's compartment; and these days she was so hungry, she found it impossible not to accept these irresistible offerings. She herself bought fresh milk from the little milkmaids who walked up and down along the train with their bottles. She loved these tiny vendors, dressed in colorful pinafores and head kerchiefs, so serious about their business, their chubby, girlish faces intent as they counted their change and placed their kopeks one by one into the client's open hand.

Sometimes the platforms were packed with people waiting for other trains, masses of peasants slumped in groups and surrounded by large bundles tied up in cloth or sacks. They were the quintessential passengers of the post train's fourth class. Hans Andriessen told Lily they were emigrants who had set out from Russia into Siberia, lured by government offerings of small plots of land in remote spaces. But sometimes they were not headed to Siberia, but back home, after having dragged the whole family out there and decided to return to the old misery, instead of risking the raw unknown. Their homecoming was hard, as they waited for reverse transportation, impoverished, hungry, and disillusioned. In the evening when it turned cold, they could be seen sleeping together on top of one another, in large mounds over the platform, as the only way to keep warm.

When the train did stop at a station, it was rare that it would leave without interviews with officials and customary guards. Police officers and occasionally soldiers would mount the train and ask everyone for their travel documents. At those moments Lily and Masha would have to sit patiently in Sergei's compartment, through convoluted explanations of why Sergei, a man banned to Vladivostok under military escort, had been granted permission to travel with two women who were not his kin. Although Sergei had all the paperwork in order, and what looked like a pile of recommendation letters from high officials, explaining the presence of a non-Russian woman with an English passport became an ordeal every time. Lily withstood these sessions with rancor, especially when she perceived sly, interested glances from the uniformed reviewers. However, it all came to winks among the men. The aristocracy was known to keep exotic mistresses, or even secret wives with hosts of children, as their role model the Czar Alexander II had done for years, until his official wife died and he could legitimize his second family. Sergei's frustrated look at the end of these parleys was her only consolation. If he still had any doubts about the root of her rage, he had been duly served with yet another pathetic reminder of her plight.

After the ninth day of travel, and within only a few hours of reaching the city of Irkutsk, the train ran along the borders of the Angara River. The Angara was wide, with pristine, rapid flowing eddies visible to the naked eye. Beyond its shores, blue-green hills almost the size of mountains rolled in the horizon, but against its tall banks stood a wall of logs, as she had never seen. It was as if all the forests of Siberia had been felled and lay here cast down, for miles on end. A swarm of activity milled around these mountain-stacks of horizontal timber, with hordes of muzhik log-men sawing and carrying the colossal trunks; sweaty, dirty, ragged men, weather-beaten and absorbed in grueling labor.

Lily stood at the window overlooking this scene alongside other fellow passengers, all too tired and edgy to sit in their compartments, anxious to arrive at the next destination. Suddenly, as the train took a bend, she caught sight of a rumbling commotion on the riverbank. A wall of logs falling, collapsing, and toppling toward the water. Cries and shouts of alert filled the air, and then a crash with shrieking and yelling. A group of workers was seen to scramble to the site where the logs had fallen over a group of men, crushing them. Frantic and backbreaking efforts to lift the wooden pillars ensued with frazzled back and forth running. A dark patch of red stained the taupe surface of the wood as they pulled out the first of the men.

"Good gracious, that poor soul," an old lady standing next to Lily said, "he's surely lost his legs, and probably with no doctor for miles around."

"Oh, this kind of thing happens all the time," a German merchant, who Lily knew to always make callous remarks, said. "These are backward, stubborn people. They won't learn to work in more efficient, orderly ways. They'll never change."

Then the old lady cried, "Look, they're pulling out another one. And he looks like he's only a boy."

Lily turned her eyes back to the scene and caught sight of a smaller body being moved. A smear of straw-colored hair flashed as the cap fell off the dangling head, and Sasha's fair face burst into her mind. She felt her lips quiver. Just then another lady fainted along the corridor, and the passengers' attention was pulled away from the accident toward the woman's body slumped on the floor.

Lily returned to her compartment, shaken. Masha got up when she saw her stagger in. "Mistress, what's the matter? Shall I call Sergei Nikolayevich?" she asked, but Lily just shook her head.

Masha helped her lie down. Then she went out and returned a few minutes later with Sergei.

He rushed to her side. "What happened? Are you all right?"

"I'm fine," she said, trying to sound cool, although her teeth were chattering. "I just need to rest a little, that's all. So please," she added, indicating for him to leave.

But Sergei didn't move. "You don't look fine," he said bitterly. He looked away, and then returned to her with anger flashing in his eyes. "This has to stop. We're traveling together. I don't ask that you be friendly, or even amiable, just cooperative and civil. I also have reasons to be dissatisfied. And it's all challenging enough without this constant stalemate." He spoke softly but with a cold severity that pierced her, and she was unable to come up with any remark on a similar tone. Instead, her eyes pooled with tears. Sergei paced around, impatient and annoyed. After a moment he sat down across from her. "I am going to bring in the doctor. I'm sure he will confirm that everything is all right. Meanwhile, Masha will order some tea and by the time we arrive, you will be recovered."

"I don't need a doctor, I just need to sleep a little," Lily said, still struggling to control her tears.

Sergei sighed. "We can't only think about you now," he said, softening his tone. "There's your condition that also needs to be taken into account." Lily saw him blushing, and looked away. Sergei left the compartment.

Once alone, she closed her eyes. Nausea lingered in the back of her throat, and she felt faint. Underneath the blanket that Masha had covered her with, her body felt suddenly in shambles. Falling apart, as if myriad grains of sand were sliding away from a growing mound that pushed up gratingly from the root of the ground. She thought of her hands and her feet, her shoulders and thighs, the parts of her that she used every day to tighten up the strings between her physical being and her will. But they seemed to lie prostrate, powerless and bland, unable to hold and to pull, and possibly ready to tumble away from it all, like the pile of logs she had just seen plummeting down the bank.

Sergei returned with the train doctor, who took her pulse and set a stethoscope to her breast and abdomen. She felt small as the men towered over her, a petty, trembling creature being handled with cold instruments for the purpose of scientific allocation. The doctor put away his stethoscope and smiled at her; he confirmed that it was all just a surge of fatigue and nothing was to come of it, if she rested for a while. He then held a whispered conversation with Sergei in Russian, which she couldn't understand.

Masha came in with tea, and the doctor left. Sergei accommodated himself in the seat across from her. "I hope you will have no objection to my staying here with you until we reach Irkutsk. Doctor's orders." She nodded and closed her eyes again, wishing she had the courage to break their standoff and tell him about the accident and her recollection of Sasha. But she was too weak to speak.

By the time they arrived at Irkutsk, Lily was fully recovered and happy to step off the train. Many passengers were staying in this town, where the Wagon-Lit Express ended its route. They had covered three thousand miles since they left Moscow, or 5,100 versts, as Russians would measure it. To reach Vladivostok, the last leg of the Trans-Siberian route, it was necessary to take the Trans-Manchurian railway through China, and that could only be done boarding the next post train after crossing Lake Baikal. A night stay in Irkutsk was mandatory then, and they left the train with their luggage and took a tarantass cab in search of a hotel.

As they rode in the mud-spattered carriage past handsome stone churches, public buildings, and even what looked like a large department store, Lily wondered about the fact that the streets were still unpaved. Hans, her cartographer friend who had left the train in Krasnoyarsk, had told her many things about this city, the so-called Paris of Siberia, with its gold-melting foundries and flourishing markets of animal fur and mineral ore, and yet still lacking in basic waterworks and electricity. Irkutsk, he had said, was also home to all manner of exiles, from Decembrist nobles and Polish nationals to avowed anarchists. Men of great value who had served severe prison sentences and later remained in Siberia, assembling in this city and turning it into an interesting, intriguing place. She wondered if Sergei was aware of all this, and if he had political connections here. But, of course, his custodians would be guarding him closely and preventing him from making any contacts. She watched

Sergei's pale face across from her inside the bumpy carriage, and the thin red scar that was still visible on his cheek. He gazed back at her, and for the first time in weeks they locked eyes and withstood each other's glance.

The tables had turned between them after the events on the train. She knew her days of rage and resentment had ended, and that Sergei's cooler power would be emerging strong from now on. She was somehow disappearing under the growing mass of the child, and all her energy had now to be devoted to keeping the loosening strands of her own being together. The impact of Sasha's recollection had blasted her like a gale blowing over unfastened haystacks in an open field, dazing her with a violence she hadn't anticipated, could not shield against or control. It was as if the buffer that stood between raw experience and perception had been dissolved, and she was left defenseless in the face of brutal gusts of feeling. Sergei had intervened efficiently to manage her chaos, but she had secretly ached for him to scoop her up into his arms and comfort her; reassure her that she wouldn't scatter into nonexistence under devastating experiences of this sort. In truth, he was all she had now. And yet, how difficult it felt to reach over and break the ice between them. She thought these things as they sat perfectly composed across from each other in the cab, breathing softly and holding back, as if trying to deny their yearning for each other and the wall of pride that stood between them like a forbidding fortress.

CHAPTER 22

At the Metropole Hotel, a scruffy concierge who only spoke Russian told them that he had one large room left, but furnished with only one bed. There was a fur-trading fair in Irkutsk during those days and every place was full. The concierge pledged to provide extra mattresses and screens to divide the room into three separate spaces. "The ladies can sleep on the bed," he said, "the gentleman in the middle chamber," he added with a smirk pointing to Sergei, "and his attendants behind the second screen."

Lily had heard from her fellow passengers how dirty and badly managed Siberian hotels were, and found the situation unbelievable. But she was glad to at least have a real bed, and to see Masha spread their own clean sheets and rugs over it, after having sprinkled a good deal of Keating's Powder over the mattress, a remedy Annette and her mother had brought from England and given her for the avoidance of fleas and bedbugs in such unclean places as these. Sergei, however, would not settle for these circumstances, and though he took the room and paid for it, he made incessant comments about the embarrassing arrangement and insisted on going around the town to find a more comfortable option. The two custodians finally agreed and the three of them set off.

Lily and Masha went down to the hotel dining room and ordered tea. Then Masha asked her permission to do some window-shopping in the nearby stores, and Lily agreed.

After the girl was gone, two ladies came and sat at the table next to Lily's, and she recognized the woman who claimed to carry two revolvers, and the matron from Petersburg who had spread the rumor about her and Sergei. The revolver lady seemed very disgruntled about something, and whispered with her companion in Russian. Then she turned to Lily. "Madame Latvin," she said, "I take it you will continue your journey toward Vladivostok?"

"Yes, madame," Lily answered.

"Well, be prepared for the worst. From now on, it all gets increasingly horrible. It will be mingling with fourth-class travelers, dirty immigrants who take up all space in compartments, and waiting for boats to carry you up and down the river, with very hot days and awful biting flies swarming everywhere. Not to mention the cold nights sleeping God knows where. Oh, how I shudder to remember my last trip to Amur."

"Was your late husband an officer, madame?" Lily asked, hoping to shift the conversation elsewhere.

"No, he was an engineer engaged to work at the gold mines in the region," the woman replied.

"And *your* husband, Madame Latvin," the woman who had spread the rumor asked, "is he in military custody for some specific reason?"

Lily stared into her small, malicious eyes and realized she had been burning to ask this question since she boarded the train in Moscow. "My husband, madame, is a political dissident," Lily said. "He has been banished for his political ideals."

The revolver lady gasped while her companion eyed Lily with renewed interest. "And you," she continued, intent on fishing for scurrilous material, "a foreign, elegant, and sophisticated woman, are following him into exile. With all the complications with your travel documents, and the rest . . ."

"Yes, madame, I am most definitively following him. Now, if you will excuse me," Lily said, getting up haughtily and walking out to the lobby toward the entrance door. There she stood looking out into the wilderness of mud on the street outside the hotel. It was the first time she had given any open explanation about Sergei's situation. All these past days she had dodged questions in every manner of clever ways. But now that she had spelled it out at last, the words lingered in her mouth, giving her a mixture of relief and deep angst.

"Forgive me, madame," a voice said behind her, and she turned to find a middle-aged man dressed in modest European garb, with gray hair and a longish beard staring at her with eager eyes. "I just wanted to express my admiration," he began in broken French, and Lily nodded at him coldly and sought at once to move away. "No, no," said the man, "I wanted to say you are very brave to undertake this journey. Again, forgive me. I couldn't help overhearing your conversation with those ladies. I am myself the grandson of a Decembrist who was exiled to Chità, and my grandmother followed him with the whole family. She was of noble birth and had much adapting to do. But she and other noblewomen bore it bravely and did much to improve the city. Now we have a street called The Street of the Ladies after them. If you care to stop at Chità, I would be honored to show you and your husband around."

"Thank you, monsieur," Lily said, "but as you may imagine, we cannot stop anywhere along the way."

"Of course. May God bless you and your husband," he said, but didn't leave. He stood looking around, nervously. The lobby was now filled with officers standing around in raucous groups, waiting to stream into the dining room. Two of them started an argument with the concierge, and others joined in to arbitrate. The man took a step closer to Lily. "Madam, I have a letter," he whispered, and she saw that he was shaking. "I was supposed to deliver it to your husband, but his custodians are ever watching. I was wondering if you . . ." Lily whipped around and glared at him. "It carries important information and he is expecting it," he added with downcast eyes. Now Lily understood Sergei's unreasonable insistence on going to look for another hotel after everyone had assured him it was useless. He was doubtless seeking an opportunity to make this contact. A strange thrill filled her as she considered her moment of power. She could either refuse to take the letter and thwart the operation, or she could take the missive and become part of the transgressive chain. She decided to take it.

She turned and saw that the concierge was finally leading the officers into the restaurant. "I shall quickly open my purse, monsieur, and you will place the letter inside." The man nodded and she opened her pocketbook and he hastily slipped in the envelope.

Sergei returned a few hours later having found no other available rooms. He looked restless and disgruntled. He sat down to supper and hardly touched the food. She tried to make eye contact with him, but he seemed too distracted, in one of his gloomy moods. The letter pulsed inside her purse as if waiting to scream out its contents. She had looked closely at the sealed envelope before when she was alone, wondering what it could contain. Instructions of some kind? A list of contacts and names? Would the information be encoded? The word *Odinnadtsat*, which meant the number eleven, was the only thing written on the front. Was that a code for Sergei, or a number pertaining to a consecutive series of missives? There had been a moment when she had regretted taking it. Helping link Sergei to the dangerous activities that had brought her so much dread in the past seemed like an act of folly. But now watching his distress across the table, all she wanted was to reach out and soothe him, tell him she had the letter, and see him relax and regain his self-possession.

After supper, Sergei tried to convince the officers to go for a walk around town, but they refused. He went up to the room and stood outside in the corridor looking dejected, while Lily and Masha settled in first and completed their bedtime routine. Later, Lily heard him coming in and slumping onto the cot just a few feet from her behind the screen. She woke up in the middle of the night. A ray of moonlight fell across the bed and reflected over the small mirror on the cheap console across the room, shimmering like a flash of silver light. Masha must have not closed the curtains properly, and the full moon she had seen rising earlier was stealing in through the open drapes.

She listened with a beating heart. All was still. Masha slept quietly by her side, and at the far end behind the last screen she could hear faint snoring, coming possibly from Guguchov, the older of the two officer custodians. Slowly she lifted the covers and slipped out of the bed. It was good she had kept on her woolen socks, for the floor was cold and she couldn't have worn shoes without making noise. Very softly she edged around the first screen, and stopped. A few feet ahead of her, Sergei lay in the shadows on one of the slim straw mattresses that had been carried earlier into the room by the concierge. He lay in his clothes, his shirt unbuttoned to mid-chest, with hands loosely placed over his breastbone. She glided toward him and kneeled at his side, wondering how she would deposit the envelope into his keeping without disturbing his sleep. Maybe inside his shirt? His military jacket and coat were hung on a rack by the door, too close to the sleeping guards. It would be best to slip it somewhere close to his body where he could find it quickly on waking. Carefully, she took the letter out of her bodice. Sergei opened his eyes and gasped, startled at her shadow. "Shhh," she said in a low whisper as she pressed the envelope into his hands.

"But . . ."

"Shhh," she repeated. A few feet beyond them, one of the officers turned on his mattress and mumbled as if in an anxious dream. Lily and Sergei stood breathless. Then the man drifted back into his former slumber. Lily lowered her lips to Sergei's ear and said, "I'll tell you tomorrow. . . ." and made to move away.

"Wait," Sergei said, pulling her back to him so close that she brushed his cheek. The officer shifted again, and then seemed to perk up as if alerted to something, and they both froze. Sergei tightened his grip on her wrist. She could feel his warm breath against her skin while her heart hammered inside her throat. But when the officer sighed and was heard to drop back onto his pallet again, Lily slid away from Sergei's hand and stole back to her bed. There she lay curled up, trying to quiet her agitation, not just about her dangerous little exploit, but about Sergei's pulsing proximity in the shadows.

Eventually, fatigue won her over and she drifted into sleep.

Early next morning they boarded the post train toward Lake Baikal, and rode another forty miles along the Angara River. Lily noticed that Sergei was being watched closer than usual by his custodians, and could not find any moment to talk to him away from their attention. The state trains they would be traveling in for the next ten days had very few compartments and, as the lady with the two revolvers had said, with hordes of emigrants constantly threatening to usurp any nook available for a seat or berth. There would be very little privacy from now on, and all members of Sergei's party would have to cramp together into a compartment or a given section of the train.

The air became colder and colder as they approached the great lake that had been described to Lily as the "Holy inland sea of Baikal," an ocean of freshwater over twelve thousand square miles in the middle of Siberia. When the train rounded the last curve and the landscape opened toward the lake, the first thing they saw was the famous icebreaker that would transport them across the vast waters; it stood tall above the pier, puffing dark smoke out of three stocky funnels. It was a huge ferryboat specially designed to cut across the lake's frozen surface in the winter, and Lily knew it had been built in England and transported in pieces all the way over here. She had also heard that in the dead of winter, when the surface ice thickened over four feet, the icebreaker could no longer cut through and the lake had still to be crossed the ancient way, by sleigh.

Once the train reached the station, there was a scramble of passengers rushing out to be the first to board the steamer, but as usual, Sergei was detained with his paperwork and she had to wait by him, thinking they would never get a decent cabin. However, the gigantic icebreaker proved to have ample space for everyone. Once inside, and after ascending the skeleton staircase to the upper level, Lily was surprised to find a luxurious saloon with a buffet and fitted with every comfort.

She walked about the deck after lunch, as the huge steamer scudded through the lake. All around, mountain chains rose with white ragged peaks and slopes covered in thick emerald forest. For endless miles ahead, the vast unwrinkled surface of clear water shone like a glass under the haze of the afternoon sun. It stirred old images of the Scottish Highlands she had visited one summer as a child with Harry and her father. How far away she was from home, she thought once more, and still pushing forward to the end of the earth.

Sergei walked up and leaned beside her on the rail. "I want to thank you," he whispered. "I wish I could tell you how important this letter is, and how complicated it would have been for me if I had missed it. . . ." Their elbows were touching, and she was aware of the officers standing right behind them. "I know how hard all this must be for you," Sergei added after a moment. "Let me be your friend again. Let me offer you every comfort I can to ease your journey." Lily nodded, but could not speak. A gust of emotion had filled her chest and was threatening to spill out of her eyes. They stood in silence looking out.

On the deck below, groups of people squatted around blankets as if they were having some sort of a picnic. Peering down, Lily recognized the rough, gray felt uniform of convicts on the men and saw that they were in the company of women, no doubt their wives, and numbers of children. They sat in circles eating, and the little ones held saucers of tea in one hand and pieces of bread in the other. Then one of the men got up to pour tea and Lily saw that there was a heavy chain fastened to each of his feet above the ankle and attached to his leather belt. She turned astonished eyes to Sergei, and he said, "Yes, Siberia is a land of convicts. Convicts of all sorts: murderers, petty thieves, conspirators, terrorists, idealists, dreamers; all nonconformists in one way or the other, and all mixed together in the hardship of a wild land."

She looked back down at the convicts and their families. She remembered having seen two prison vans attached to the end of the train at the Irkutsk station, with barred windows and sliding doors with heavy locks, which soldiers armed with bayonets guarded at all times. She had been surprised to catch glimpses of children's faces peering out through the window bars, instead of men. At one point, one of the soldiers had stooped down to pick some yellow flowers growing by the tracks, and handed them to the children through the bars. Little hands clasped around his as they received his gift with gasps of delight.

Lily thought she might have dreamed this last part, since she had dozed off a number of times in the train compartment while they waited to depart. But now, seeing these children eating contentedly amid the clangs of their father's chains, she realized she hadn't dreamed it at all. And it struck her that life was full of astonishing moments, and that unexpected splashes of color may always brighten the grimmest of paths.

CHAPTER 23

She would never forget her first impressions of Vladivostok. As soon as she caught sight of the waters of the Amur Gulf from the train and breathed in the delicious sea breeze that blew upon her face, she knew days of happiness awaited her in this place, so different and so far away from the oppressive cities from whence she came. The city, laid out like an amphitheater over the hills around the Bay of the Golden Horn, glittered in the sun. The stunning azure of the sea sent her heart racing as the bay unfolded before her eyes, curling around the undulating hills sprinkled with houses and rocking below with pretty boats along its dock-lined edge. Zolotoy Rog, it was called in Russian; and Vladivostok meant "Ruler of the East."

Neither would Lily forget her first drive along Vladivostok's streets, swarming with officers in full uniform and hordes of Chinese men dressed in blue cotton shirts. Boxes of fresh seafood, vegetables, and fruits carried over the shoulder on ends of poles threaded through the crowd like slithering collared ribbons before her eyes. Captain Meledin, an attendant of General Rudakov, was waiting for them at the station; a young officer with cropped black hair and a charming smile. He greeted them warmly and then drove them across the city in a series of ups and downs around the hills toward the house that the general had procured for them. Before leaving the station, they bid their farewells to the two officers who had never let Sergei out of their sight for almost four weeks. Though Lily knew they were not bad fellows, just seeing the back of them made her feel light and free.

She also liked the house right away; a double-story semi-European home with a cream façade of wood shingles, perched at the end of a steep road on a hill. It was a simple, medium-sized house, with six rooms aside from the kitchen and servant quarters. The rooms were painted in light colors and had large windows; they were furnished in sparse, but tasteful decorations. Captain Meledin showed them into the veranda that opened out of the drawing room. "The last tenant," he said, "was also an officer with his family. But he was reassigned and had to take off in a hurry, so he left everything behind." It was a sparkling morning. The veranda overlooked the bay and mirrored the brightness reflected from the harbor below. Everything was so different from the dark, old Petersburg mansion.

The servants who worked under the last tenant had also remained in the house. A Chinese manservant and cook called Ho Li was introduced to them, together with Kiku, a Japanese *amah*, or housekeeper, a middle-aged woman of slight build with a placid, watchful face. They only spoke Russian, besides their native tongues, but waited on Lily's directions from the first moment, following her around, opening pantries, cupboards, linen armoires, and the such, while explaining every intricacy of the house. Lily was very glad to have Masha with her, who, despite her youth, instantly emerged as a knowledgeable go-between, for Lily had never had servants of her own or overseen the running of a household.

As all of these things went through her mind, she also realized that she hadn't lived in a proper, normal house since she left her father's in Manchester. The overstated palaces and mansions of the Volkovs and Latvins in Petersburg were not, in her estimation, to be included in the idea of "normal" abodes. Here was the real thing, she thought as she walked through the largest bedroom into which Ho Li was lugging her travel trunk, a beautiful, simple space where one may not lose oneself among unnecessary luxuries, or the weight of family history and ghosts. Her room was airy and looked as though it had been just newly papered; it was furnished with a few stylish bamboo pieces and jute mattings covering the floor, things she wondered at because she had never seen before. There was a large window at the far end with a box seat in which to lounge or recline while overlooking the front garden and the water basin beyond.

They spent the rest of the first day settling into the house and resting, for they were all very tired. A delicious supper cooked by Ho Li was served in the small, beautiful dining room by Kiku; a feast of shrimp and crab salad, pheasant jelly with lemon slices, black bread and a platter of smoked salmon with hard-boiled eggs in the center cut in the shape of flowers; and to round it up, a boiled-fruit dessert of apricot and bilberry topped with cream. Lily couldn't take her eyes away from the veranda. "Last April," Captain Meledin had told her before leaving, "we had three whales blowing in the bay for three whole days."

The next day was a Saturday, and Sergei left early for the customhouse to report to Rudakov, but returned to the house after lunch and set about organizing the room that was going to be the study. Masha and Kiku were busy ordering the linen closets, and Lily could hear them chatting away in the corridor while she sat in her room, lazily looking out the window and musing about writing a letter to Harry. Then she heard a commotion on the road in front of the house. A carriage screeched to a stop, the whinny of the horse, a woman's cries. She saw Sergei rush out of the house followed by Ho Li. They ran up to a woman who had jumped down from the box and was kneeling by the side of the road. They engaged her in conversation, and Sergei appeared to be comforting her for she seemed in extreme distress. A few moments passed and the woman calmed down. Then she got back onto the carriage and drove on. Sergei returned to the house with something in his arms. There was a bit of a rustle as he came in and she heard him walk into the kitchen below.

She went downstairs, curious to find out what had happened. Sergei stood by the kitchen table, while Ho Li hastily spread a large piece of cloth over its surface. Then Lily saw Sergei lay down a dog. It was a small chocolate-colored dog, most likely a puppy; it panted and whined pitifully. "What happened?" she asked.

"He's been run over," Sergei said. "I think he's broken a leg." He then turned to Ho Li and asked him to hold the dog down. But the cook paled and shook his head; he was either horrified at his kitchen being improvised as an animal infirmary, or just afraid of dogs.

"I'll do it," Lily said.

"No, he might bite. He's very distressed," Sergei said. "Where's Masha?"

Masha was brought down in a hurry to hold the dog while Sergei muzzled him with a strip of cloth. With deft fingers, he felt around its mangled limb while talking softly to the mutt. Then he pulled slowly at the leg a few times while the dog struggled and whelped. "Hold him down well," he told Masha, and with a sharp, firm tug that sounded like a crunch, he straightened the dog's leg. The mutt squirmed and howled through his muzzle, but Masha held him tight. Sergei took over pinning him down while Masha fumbled in the jars of kitchen utensils and pulled out a bunch of chopsticks, which she handed to Sergei. Lily watched, fascinated, as he took the sticks and aligned them along the dog's leg, wrapping them around with multiple strips of cloth until the leg was fully immobilized.

Sergei removed the muzzle from the dog and looked up triumphantly. "There! Masha, give him some food, and find something to make him a bed with," he said. Then he turned to Lily and said, "Would you mind it very much if we kept him until his leg is well? It will only be for a couple of weeks at most. He doesn't need to leave the kitchen."

"No, not at all," she said. "Let's keep him. I like dogs. We'll call him Brownie." Then she asked, "And where on earth did you learn to fix a broken leg? Can you fix human legs with the same ease?"

Sergei shook his head and laughed. "Oh no, only animals. We did it all the time at the farm in Taganay, sometimes in the forest, too. There are very few veterinarians out there."

Lily hadn't seen him this happy since their first days together in Petersburg. She followed him with her gaze as he turned to the sink and washed his hands. A forelock of hair loosened over his downcast eyes as he dried his hands with a cloth. Then he rolled down his sleeves, took his jacket from the back of a chair, and put it on again. He made for the door, but first stopped in front of Lily and said, "I shall be in the study if you need me," and his face once more assumed the kind, formal look he wore around her of late.

"I was wondering if you could come with me for a moment," Lily said. "There's something I need to show you." She led him out of the kitchen up the stairs to her bedroom. Once there she shut the door, while Sergei looked around expecting to find something out of order. She walked up to him and reached for his hands; then placed them over her belly. That moment the baby kicked. She heard Sergei gasp, and hold his breath. They stood in silence for what seemed a long time. The baby kicked some more. She hadn't expected this to happen, although it wasn't the first time. It had started kicking after she ate Ho Li's food the day before, as if elated to receive its portion of delicious fare.

The baby quieted down after a while and they became conscious of their hands growing warm together over her belly. Looking up, she met the hunger in his eyes and reached for his mouth. They kissed with ferocity, as if they might be facing imminent death and it was the one last thing they could do; amidst desperate, clawing attempts at fitting together into some sort of an embrace. Then they stopped and held each other tight, breathing hard.

But Sergei broke off and stepped back. He took long breaths while staring at her with crushed eyes. "I'm a weak, despicable man," he said in a hoarse whisper. "I should have helped you; I should have let you go. That's what other people who are in this fight do. They cut off all their ties so they can plunge into it fully, without creating misery for those around them. But I couldn't do it. I couldn't bear to lose you. I'm a coward and an egoist. I understand your fury and your scorn."

Lily put her arms around him again. "Shhh," she said. "Please. Can't we just mince all of this into smaller portions? Otherwise, I'm afraid I'll be severely indigested." She meant it jokingly, in hopes of lightening the mood, but Sergei only stiffened. She clung to him for a moment more.

Then he pulled away again, took her by the hand, and led her to the little sofa by the empty fireplace. "No, we need to talk about this now." He sat thinking for a moment. "I'm finally in possession of sufficient means to settle you properly, anywhere you choose, and if you want to leave . . ."

Lily looked at him in disbelief. "And where would I go right now? This offer is coming a bit late, don't you think? I can't go anywhere until the child is born, and even then, I should have to wait a few months, most likely a year, before braving the sort of journey we just went through." A long moment passed. Then she added, "But if *you* want me to go, that would be a different matter."

"Of course I don't want you to go," he said. "But I couldn't stand it if you stayed with me only for the child. I don't want you to feel tied to me, trapped."

"But I *am* tied to you," she said with sudden fatigue, "at least for the time being. And there's not much we can do about it."

Sergei hung his head. Lily sighed. She didn't want to keep harping at the old bitterness between them, or agonize anymore over facts that couldn't be changed. She got up and walked toward the bed. She sat down. "Let's not talk about this anymore. I'm tired of going around in circles. I want us to live in peace, to love each other again." She fell back against the pillows. "Come over here and hold me," she said, and when he didn't move, she added, "That is, if you can bear my present monstrosity."

Sergei looked up, confused. Lily gestured around her body exaggerating her growing shape. "You don't look monstrous to me," Sergei said. "Anyway, there's nothing that would ever stop me from desiring you."

"Nothing? I'm afraid your imagination is quite lacking then. We'll see how you feel when I finally look like a whale."

Sergei grinned, amused. He got up and edged toward the bed. "In my opinion you'll never look like a whale. In any case, you'd look more like a seal. One of those nerpa seals from Lake Baikal; the only freshwater seals in the world, the most beautiful by far, with your small ears and round eyes, and your gluttony for little fish."

She laughed. "And how would you know they're the most beautiful seals in the world? Have you seen every seal there is to see?"

They lay on the bed kissing among the pillows with eyes riveted on each other, bodies quivering with suppressed emotion from their long estrangement. There was still distance between them—a feeling of having reached a spot after a long haul through arid lands, a place where precious water could be found, but the means of drinking it had still to be devised. She had buried her desire too deeply all this time and now she feared it would be difficult to open up to him. The rigid armor she had built to quell her clamoring for him was still firmly encased and refused to loosen up. She knew he would deliver pleasure to her, as he had done so many times before, but could she love him again? Could she trust him again? A part of her burned to return to their old togetherness, and yet she knew it was all a fantasy. The eyes that now watched over her infused with devotion still contained those misty landscapes down which dreamy journeys might be undertaken without her. The feature she had most loved in him had become the feature she most feared. But even within that fear there was an irresistible draw toward his power. His body pressed against hers felt warm and urgent; his musky scent filled her with voluptuous memories. Her reserve began to melt away. Her breath quickened as her flesh unfurled and gushed under his caresses, but she felt the baby kicking inside her and grew afraid that it might be rattled. Sergei eased up; a glint in his eyes illumined his face. He too understood there were three of them wrapped in the embrace. The baby ceased to move and tucked itself into a corner close to her heart, while she and Sergei broke into soft laughter. Then Sergei put a finger to Lily's lips as if to say, *Shush, the baby has finally fallen asleep.* She looked into his flushed, smiling face, and felt that they could come to a place of peace, after all.

Outside, the hooting of a ship mingled with the city churches' languishing bells, while the afternoon slipped into a palette of pearl with the harbor and town reflecting the milky sky. And when hours later, Masha knocked on the door to announce supper, Lily was stirred from the bottom of a glittering dream and had to force her mind to swim up in order to acknowledge the girl's call, strive to pull the bed linens over her torpid, naked skin, and over Sergei, who lay by her side, out cold, still plunged in the trance of sleep.

* * *

On Monday, she woke and found an envelope from Sergei on the breakfast table. He had left early for his first day of work at the customhouse, Masha informed her. Inside the envelope was a wad of money and a note asking her to make any purchases and arrangements for the house as she saw fit, and open up accounts in whatever stores or businesses she deemed appropriate. Then he added, "*Oh, and today I shall return to the house with Rudakov. I beg that you receive him as my wife and the lady of the house in the most amiable terms, for it will make a big difference for me, for us, during these first months in Vladivostok. . . .*"

So, today she was to meet Sergei's general in command. Lily had heard terrible things about Rudakov while in Petersburg, mainly from Annushka, who had described him as an unflinching authoritarian, and she awaited his visit with some trepidation. She organized Ho Li and Kiku to prepare tea and a light meal of sandwiches and hors d'oeuvres, and to buy flowers for the drawing room. She waited for the men on the veranda, sitting in the warm afternoon breeze, and surmising how an old, stiff Russian general would react to her, having been already informed about the situation between her and Sergei.

Rudakov, however, turned out to be very different than what she had expected. At first, Lily felt intimidated by his rigid stance and the abundant collection of medals on either side of his military jacket. His keen, wolfish eyes stared at her under black bushy eyebrows while his forbidding imperial moustache twitched a little. But Lily decided to ignore his martial prowess and stepped forward to meet him like a grand lady, self-possessed and natural. "General, how very kind of you to come," she said, extending her hand for him to kiss.

She saw his façade collapse and his face open into a wide smile as he gushed with all manner of gentlemanly adulation. "My dear, it is *my* blissful pleasure to meet you. And the privilege of Vladivostok to welcome such a lovely lady as you," and put down Sergei teasingly as "this dunce nephew of mine who does not deserve such a jewel by his side," and so on. As she led him on with smiles and animated talk, Lily realized that this elderly bachelor was one of those men who couldn't resist women, and that behind his portentous façade of military feats and command lay someone whose ultimate passion was surrendering flat out at the feet of the fairer sex, possibly to the point of making a fool of himself when in the hands of rapacious, meretricious girls. But this might not be so uncommon in such a town as this, a military garret swarming with officers who outnumbered women by ridiculous counts.

Meanwhile Sergei poured the general tea, and later, many glasses of port, while shooting approving, smiling glances at Lily. He looked very pleased indeed with her enchantment of "Uncle" Rudakov.

Before he left, the general turned to her and said, "My dear, how forgetful of me. I have received a letter for you in my care. From Petersburg," and he handed her a little envelope. Lily's heart thumped at seeing Ruby's handwriting. As soon as Rudakov left, she ran up to her room.

> *Oh darling, I am so, so worried about you and what you must be going through. I'm also upset that I never made it to see you before you left, but you know how things are with Lena and Kitty. I hear talk in the family about Sergei wanting to do right by you. I hope so, my dear. You deserve it. I must hurry now and seal this letter, for our old librarian, Herr Straff—who's as straffy as ever—will be sending it out with other documents in just a moment. Write to me to the Krüger house as soon as you can.*
>
> *Lots of love from your friend Ruby, who misses you always.*
>
> *PS And just to make you laugh, I'll add that I've recently found out that neither Freddy nor Chut married in the end—and how we both fretted about it, for nothing! What a silly affair life can be after all.*

Lily sat in the window seat holding the letter. Ruby's small handwriting scrawl clawed at her heart, making her ache with nostalgia. She read the note over and over again, the last sentence about

Freddy and Chut, and burst into tears. How absurd everything was. How illusions and misreports lead into strange paths that then become our destiny. Chut remained a free man, while she was entangled in a situation from which there was no return. She had been quick to believe he had resumed his life without her, committed himself to another woman impatient to run away from the mayhem of their breakup. Yet it all turned out to be a delusion. A bitter twist of fate. Shouldn't she have waited out the storm, fought harder to salvage what she knew to be a true bond between them? But it was too late now. That part of her life had bypassed her, and here she was about to bear another man's child.

Sergei knocked on the door, and she wiped the tears from her face before asking him to come in. He burst into the room beaming, but when he saw her, his face changed into inquiring concern. "Oh, it's just a short letter from Ruby," she said, feeling her eyes sting again. "It made me homesick for a moment."

He sat beside her and kissed her hands. "It made you homesick for England?" he asked, searching her eyes. "Would you rather be back there? I want you to tell me the truth."

He'd undone the buttons on his military jacket and his white shirt was showing underneath. He stared at her, his pale, handsome face innocent and raw like a boy's. *How young he looks sometimes,* she thought, *how tender.* And yet, she knew that behind that face lay the tight-jawed man who drafted revolutionary plans for reshaping the world; the man who could fix dogs' broken legs, speak four languages, and mingle with peasants and servants as if they were blood. The man who had seduced her and made love to her like a god. But also, the man who, for all his pledges of devotion, would always remain elusive, always walk ahead of her, distracted inside dreams of future worlds loosely written in faraway skies. The man she would never fully possess nor control. Or even understand. And how the hopelessness of that realization had made her writhe with fury all these past weeks. It had made her feel worthless, small, of no account. But now, considering him all over again, she saw that it was his baffling complexity that held her spellbound. That she herself was just as unique in her own recklessness and equally differently driven from most people she knew. It was undeniable that she hadn't been able to pull away from him. How could she? He was bound to her fate, and whatever was in store for them both, had to be ridden out to the end.

"No, this is my home now," she said. "And here's where I want to be. With you."

A great peace came with such surrender. As the summer weeks went by, Lily's life began to unfold in long, lazy, dreamlike days. The house on the hill with its lovely garden, her close relation with Masha, who was beginning to feel more like a little sister, their happy explorations of the town with shopping sprees. The only thing that was wanting was enough time to spend with Sergei, who worked long hours at the customhouse with Rudakov and then went to meetings and underground gatherings until late each day. But Lily had determined she would not interfere with him that way, for she knew that their truce was based on her acceptance of his political work. So at night she kept all lamps burning bright inside the house until he arrived, and waited for him, even if she was tired. She waited to run out to meet him, craving his embraces, his smiling eyes, everything she had lacked during the day.

Many Sundays when he was off work they would stay at the house, though there were plenty of tempting trips to take around the city and along the bay and neighboring islands. If it happened to be warm and sunny, Lily would ask Kiku and Masha to spread a blanket out on the lawn and serve a picnic lunch for the two of them. The back garden was large, shaded to one side by an old cork tree. Its walls were hedged by gleaming aralia bushes with large fanlike emerald leaves, and schisandra vines hung with long clusters of sparkling red berries, which Lily knew Ho Li used to make his medicinal wine. After lunch, Sergei would bring out his typewriter and place it on a table under the tree with the annoying intention of completing some report or other, while Lily lay down shading her eyes against the sun, basking in the beauty of the luscious garden and the lazy afternoon. She would then find all sorts of ways to tease Sergei and exasperate him enough to lure him into abandoning his typing and lie down beside her. "Tell me a story," she'd say. "But in Russian, I want to hear you speak your language."

And he would begin to whisper in those flexible, sibilant sounds that came in such singsong tones out of his throat, snug with condensed, sharp consonants, sweet with rounded notes. She'd close her eyes and feel the rushing breeze mingle with his voice. *So this is happiness*, she'd think. *This is peace.*

And how long it's been in coming.

CHAPTER 24

Lily had also made a friend. Eleanor Pray, the woman who had run the dog over, and who called at the house days later to inquire how he was. Kiku showed her into the drawing room. "Please forgive this unannounced visit," Eleanor said, "but I wanted to know if the dog is all right, and also thank your husband again for his kindness. You see, I was rushing to meet my sister-in-law who'd arrived from China in bad health. I couldn't stop, but the thought of leaving the poor injured animal behind was unbearable." She was about Lily's age, with a frank, open face and green candid eyes. She was an American from Maine, and her family ran the American store downtown. She was very chatty and lost no time in inviting Lily to her house on *jour fix*, or "call day." "A custom we have here, is that we open our house one day a week to anyone who wants to drop by, drink tea, and have a little talk. Mine is on Thursday afternoons, and I would love you to come." And she left, insisting on taking Brownie with her. "I owe the little fellow," she said, flashing a last charming smile.

Thus, the Vladivostok social scene opened up to Lily. Eleanor started by inviting her to garden tea parties with her friends. Her house was on Sodom Lane above the Post and Telegraph office in the center of Vladivostok, and it was called Dom Smith. There Lily was introduced to a Mrs. Anna Cornels, a Mrs. Sophie Wohlfahrt,

Elenora Hansen, Maria Dattan, Sarah Smith, and so on, a mixture of Belgian, American, German, and Russian women who met regularly at one another's houses and shared strong friendships. They accepted Lily readily, with few questions about her marriage or her past, save to admire the fact that she had been a seasoned actress working in London's West End. They all sat together in Eleanor's garden knitting and sewing, making small talk under the shade of trees swayed by delicious breezes coming from the bay. Through them, Lily found out many things about Vladivostok and its community, but soon became bored in their company. Eleanor's friends were mostly merchant wives who had no professional training of any kind and didn't work outside their families; as lovely and kind as they were with one another and to Lily, they spent hours talking about recipes, petty city news and gossip, the latest fashion from Paris, all the time with their needlework in hand and indulging in endless cups of coffee and pieces of cake. Serious politics and discussions about literature, art, or philosophy were not topics of their interest. They wondered why Lily didn't bring her own knitting or needlework to the meetings, and when she admitted to have never learned to do any of those things they were first shocked, and then offered to teach her. Lily thanked them, hoping they would forget and never insist again on such a project.

But she liked Eleanor. Eleanor was intelligent, enthusiastic, and very energetic. She was not just a garden-party sort of woman. She also played tennis, rode horseback, and hiked every week in the hills. When they met by themselves, they would walk down to the center of town, explore the Chinese shops with their exotic wares and beautiful printed silks, or sift through European imported goods at the German department store Kunst & Albers. Later, they would stroll along the docks admiring the ships, and end up drinking tea in some small parlor, sharing impressions about being foreign women in a remote land. "Do you know," Eleanor said to her once, "that there is not one day where I don't write a letter to my family back in Maine? Not one single day. They must have enough material to publish a whole book on life in Vladivostok," she added, laughing.

Lily wanted Eleanor to help her access books. She had already read the few books she had brought with her from Petersburg and was hungry for more. However, acquiring this sort of good was not easy in a military garret town like Vladivostok. There were no bookshops, and whatever meager libraries existed would be private or belonged to churches and similar institutions. But if anyone could access them it was Eleanor, with her wide network of acquaintances and her irresistible charm. Lily was also planning to study Russian seriously, and hoped Eleanor would set her up with exchange lessons. If after Sergei's banishment they returned to Petersburg or Moscow, she wanted to go back into acting and seek employment with Russian companies. Solid French would also strengthen her possibilities, even German. There was no time to lose.

In spite of her general state of happiness, Lily found herself beginning to feel restless. Boredom crept often into the long hours of her days, deprived of intellectual pursuits and away from Sergei's company. Eleanor invited her on boat trips and picnics in remote places along the coast, offering to introduce her to her larger group of friends, which included the husbands of the garden-party ladies and other professional men and officials working in the city. Though these outings promised to be much more interesting, she soon understood the need to decline them, since Sergei, careful to maintain a low profile around social circles, was not willing to accompany her. The presence of a pregnant, unescorted woman in such tight groups would have called unwanted attention, besides being in itself an act of social defiance. These were the disadvantages of a small city where everyone knew everyone else.

She turned her energies to the house, applying all her efforts to create the most beautiful, comfortable home possible. She bought elegant and exotic furnishings and decorated every corner; she made sure the place was always sparkling, stocked with flowers, ready to receive any of Sergei's guests and officer friends. She even delved into the kitchen and took charge of menus, went to market with Ho Li to buy the best foods, spent hours learning how to make jams, marmalades, pickled mushrooms, and tea cakes, all the womanly pursuits she knew were at the center of Russian family life and purportedly generated unending bliss in every husband.

But she soon had to admit to herself that she found all these tasks to be unbearably tedious. Once she overcame the initial thrill of redecorating an already pretty house and the attempts at adding to a perfect garden, these activities fell flat for her. Besides, even if she chose never to give household affairs another thought, the household would keep running impeccably thanks to Masha, Kiku, and Ho Li without requiring any of her intervention.

She ached to go back to the theater, to read and memorize scripts, work with directors and other actors, step onto the scaffold and act. But that was not possible. Vladivostok had no permanent theater, for the time being. Though certain productions, mainly operas, did come to town occasionally, they were performed in improvised places such as the public Reading-Hall, or even at one of the larger galleries of the Amurskiy Regional Museum. A group of Danes and Swedes engaged in concerts and theatricals at a German singing club called the Gesanverein, but that was hardly a theatrical venue in the real sense of the word. She became increasingly fidgety. She proposed to Sergei that they go back to writing articles together, but he declined, claiming he had no time. "But you should," he said. "Use my typewriter in the study."

As a matter of fact, Annette Maekin, who had hurried through Vladivostok and left Lily a letter in place of the promised visit, had asked her to write something about the city, and said that she would help her publish any article in British periodicals and magazines. But Lily decided she would be more interested in translating plays, the plays of the legendary Chekhov, a copy of which had recently landed in her possession.

Sitting at the desk in the study in front of the typewriter, she wondered if she would ever master the art of writing on such a bizarre, clunky piece of machinery. It would be best if she wrote by hand, and then find a way to get it typed. She started with a play called *Uncle Vanya.* By now, she could read Russian fairly well, but perhaps not to the level of producing a good translation into English. Her mind wandered uneasily, plagued by disquieting thoughts of inadequacy. Her ambitious endeavor was proving to be harder than she had expected.

She was about to quit for the morning when her eyes fell on a large metal box sitting on the floor by the bookcase. She had seen Sergei bring it in one night a few weeks ago, and lock it in one of the cupboards under the shelves, to which he had the only key. "What is this?" she had asked.

"Oh, just a box full of dreary documents," he said, but she'd instantly surmised that there was nothing trivial lying inside. The next day she tried the cupboard and found it unlocked and empty. Obviously, Sergei had moved it somewhere else now that she had been alerted to its existence. He was always impeccable in covering all tracks related to his activities. That was why Lily was so surprised to find the box once again in the study, sitting carelessly on the floor. And with the latch unlocked.

She got up and closed the door. Then she kneeled by the box and slowly lifted its lid. A collection of neatly organized vertical files stood stacked inside. She slipped her fingers into one of the files and pulled out an envelope. It was directed to Sergei at an address in Matrosskaya Sloboda, the sailors' quarter of Vladivostok, and the post stamp was from Paris. She extracted the letter, a small note joined by a metal clip to a faded carbon copy of a document. The note was written in French and read, "*I attach the latest and will follow up soon with news from the Paris office agent.*" She unfolded the carbon copy. It was written in Russian. Her heart was beating fast. The letterhead read, "*V. I. Lenin to the Combat Committee of the St. Petersburg Committee of the RSDLP.*" She scanned the document quickly, tripping over words she didn't recognize. Toward the end, she read, "*Form fighting squads at once, everywhere, among the students, and especially among workers, soldiers, sailors. Let groups be at once organized of three, ten, thirty, etc. persons. Let them arm themselves at once as best they can. . . . These druzhiny will be our combat detachments, and very useful when the time soon comes. . . .*"

Sergei's steps walking up to the house shook her out of her spell and she stuffed the document into the envelope and back inside the box. She closed the lid and rushed out of the room toward her bedroom as noiselessly as she could. Once in her room, she heard him walk in through the main door, then turn toward the study, enter it, and lock the door.

After a while he came upstairs. "I thought you had planned to write in the study today," he said, kissing her.

"I never made it to the study. I was feeling really lazy this morning," she replied, hating herself for the lie.

When he left again after lunch, the box had already disappeared from the study. In her bedroom she pulled out her dictionary and looked for the word *druzhiny: druzhina, drużyna* or *drużyna,* literally a "fellowship," she read, were retinues in service of a chieftain in the medieval history of Poland and Kievan Rus, also called *knyaz.* So Sergei was organizing combat detachments based on personal loyalty. Armed, secret groups, ready to spring when commanded. She shuddered. A part of her wished she hadn't looked in the box. It was as if she had opened a door into a dark, harsh reality that could never be sealed off again, and that would eventually find a way to seep into her hard-bought domestic peace, invade the broadening softness of her body until it reached her baby curled up inside. For the first time, she understood that in the event she were confronted with a dangerous situation, she would not just have to fend for herself, but before anything else, she would have to protect her child.

Summer drifted into autumn, and by the first days of September the light had already darkened. Thick wreaths of fog curled around the bay in the mornings, pierced only by the glint of mast lanterns and the hooting of foghorns. The air grew colder and preparations for the winter started in all households. Hours were spent putting on double windows and stuffing cotton in every crack before pasting them over with strips of paper, days spent bringing out blankets and bedcovers from wardrobes, washing or dusting them in the open. Ho Li was also hard at work hoarding wood and buying dry foods in the market that he stored scrupulously in pantry wares.

Lily's due date was now close and she was restless with the thought of her upcoming confinement. The baby would arrive in three weeks at most, as the old German obstetrician Eleanor had introduced her to, Dr. Herrick, had told her during his last visit. Her body felt hot and heavy; she could no longer sleep properly, for the volume and weight of her belly forced her to be in constant search of different lying positions. She had also stopped going into town because walking up the hill back to the house felt very wearisome, and riding carriages up and down made her queasy. She walked all day around the house until she tired, and then flopped onto a sofa or the bed for short naps. Eleanor had come with her tea-party lady friends one afternoon and brought her a baby basket lined in blue satin with all sorts of little blankets and sheets they had knitted and sewn for her. But no baby clothes, for gifting clothes to a child that was still unborn was considered unlucky. Masha and Kiku fluttered around her all day long, worried about any detail that might distress her, providing everything that could assuage her discomfort. And so long days of waiting went by, while Lily welcomed the cooler air and the autumn rain.

One morning Sergei turned to her before leaving the house. "I shall have to travel down to Port Arthur for a few days at the end of the week."

"But that's all the way out in Manchuria. It's quite a journey," Lily said.

"It is, but it'll be quick."

Lily paced around, uneasily. "Is it necessary? I mean, can't you remind Rudakov that I'm very close to the birth?"

"It doesn't have to do with Rudakov. I need to make an important contact there. This is my only chance."

"Can't it wait? I couldn't face any of this with you away," she started, but he took her in his arms and kissed her sweetly. "It will only be for three or four days, and there is still plenty of time," he said. And he left while Lily bit her lip. She was anxious to know more about the mission and how risky it was, but she knew it was useless to question him.

The night before leaving, Sergei came back to the house with three friends, all officers who worked at customs with him, but that Lily knew also collaborated in his other activities. Lily asked Ho Li and Kiku to improvise a supper for them, something she was in the habit of doing whenever he brought anyone home. Soon a lavish table was set before them and they stood around with glasses of vodka ready for a toast. Sergei raised his glass toward her. "To my lovely wife," he said, "without whom I'd be half the man I am."

One of the officers, named Duvov, who Lily knew to be a joker and a ladies' man, added, "Half the man, or even none," and they all laughed good-humoredly.

Then Sergei raised his glass again. "Or even none," he echoed, and drank without taking his eyes off her.

Lily exchanged a few pleasantries with the men, then excused herself and retired to her bedroom. There she paced up and down in the dark without switching on the lamps. She had hoped to spend the evening before his departure in his company, but that was not the source of her unrest. It had to do with the look she had seen in Sergei's eyes, that glimmer of excitement approaching frenzy she remembered him having in Petersburg when he slipped out of the mansion to accomplish dangerous tasks. Her old fears about his safety gripped her again, and she became so agitated that she had to call Masha in and ask her to lie by her side and talk to her of whatever nonsense she may. Hours later, when Sergei made it to the bed, exhausted and tanked, she was still awake and held him all night trying to quieten her dread.

The next day it rained heavily, and she sat in the kitchen with Masha and Kiku, listening to their chatter while drinking tea. The two women had taken to teasing Ho Li, and spent hours taunting him and chuckling at his impassible, dignified face. But today, Lily wasn't in the mood for their banter. She decided to return to the drawing room and take up her book again. She got up and the first stab of pain pieced her under the belly. She swayed and gasped, as the women ran to her. "It's starting!" Masha cried. "Ho Li, run for the midwife, and alert the doctor in Komarovskaya." They walked her to her bedroom, but Lily refused to lie down. She was convinced it was all a false start, as she had heard sometimes happened. *It's too early,* she thought, *and Seryozha needs to be back.* This was nothing. It would pass.

A short while later came another jab, and then another, and soon she had to face the fact that she was indeed in labor. When the midwife, Lizaveta Popova, arrived, Lily had just broken her water and Masha was changing her into a dry gown. Lizaveta examined Lily and determined that it was all going well. "Don't tire yourself, dear, we still have long hours to go." She was a short, stumpy woman of about forty, with a stern face, small eyes, and abundant dark down on her upper lip. But she was not unkind. She set about bossing Masha and Kiku for making the most intricate preparations. Her first command was for the women to bring into the room all the religious icons of the house. Lily, however, could no longer hold her attention on anything outside herself. The pain was coming now in close, intermittent waves. Every time it twisted, pulled, and squeezed her insides as if they would be torn out of her, holding her in frenzy until it slowly subsided. It was like getting caught in the undertow of a wave, breathlessly fighting against an invisible, all-encompassing enemy who would only release her when it may.

Hours went by and Lily lost the sense of time. She dragged herself from the bed to the chair to the window seat, as the whole space became a swirl where she lurched in agony and then collapsed, breathless and spent. At one point Dr. Herrick arrived in the house and came upstairs to examine her. He spoke afterward to Lizaveta, and Lily overheard him saying something about a big baby and a narrow-hipped mother, but when she asked him to repeat what he had said, he just patted her on the knee reassuringly and announced he would be waiting downstairs until it was time for him to intervene.

More hours went by. The afternoon turned into evening and then to night. The rain never stopped pelting the windowpanes. Lily was utterly exhausted by now, and in between the rippling lashes of unflagging pain, she tried to rest. But there was no peace even then. Images, distorted, fearfully deformed, appeared in her mind, her father displeased, shouting, the light in Harry's eyes, drowning in sadness; Wade towering over her amid stifling masses of smoke, cruel and full of glee. Other times she envisioned Sergei, smeared onto faded landscapes of war, trudging through endless fields of mud, gaunt and wrecked.

She opened her feverish eyes and saw Masha beside her, cooling her face with a damp cloth. "Masha, run to the customhouse," she panted. "Maybe he didn't leave, maybe he got caught up."

Masha smiled sadly. "Mistress, he's gone, he won't come just yet; but when he returns all will be over and well," she said, and then whispered a stream of soothing, sweet talk into her ear.

But Lily's brain couldn't focus anymore. She had stopped understanding Russian a long while ago, although she still babbled intermittently in different languages, asking everyone to search for Sergei. "Please, I'm sure he's back. He needs to be told." And then she would turn to Masha again. "Masha, if he dies, if he doesn't return, what shall I do? What shall I do?"

When the first bleak ray of dawn broke through the window, Lily's dank, sapped body was assailed by yet one more rush of pain. But this was different: a searing, burning pain tearing her apart. Lizaveta cried, "Push now, dear, with all your strength!" and she and Masha stood at her sides rubbing her belly and giving her little slaps on the cheeks and hands.

She remembered screaming, as if she was vomiting her life out with the cries, and something gushing out of her with unbearable tearing. She must have swooned then because she was suddenly aware of holding an image from above: Lizaveta, Masha, and Kiku crowded around something between her legs; the doctor's footsteps climbing up the stairs; and her body, like a discarded rag, poised lifelessly on the bed.

A while later she came back to herself and saw Masha approaching with a pink, wriggling mass inside a bundle of white cotton. "It's a beautiful girl, look, mistress," she said.

Lily saw the dreamy little face with marbled foggy eyes under delicate long brows, and the tiny, full lips that stretched out suddenly into a yawn. "Oh, you!" she gasped. "At last you're here, at last I get to see your face . . ." and holding her close to her bosom, she inhaled the sweet smell of the baby's little head. But Dry Herrick soon stepped in and ordered Masha to take the baby away.

He took Lily's pulse, turned to Lizaveta, and said, "She has a temperature and could be going into puerperal fever. She cannot feed the child. Hurry to bring in a wet nurse." Lizaveta didn't seem convinced and whispered to him, but the doctor was unmoved. "No, I don't deem it convenient at all. As I said—"

Lily then perked up. "I want to feed my child," she said.

"Dear madam, you are not well and would do better to rest," Dry Herrick said in broken English, looking at her with kind but condescending eyes.

"I said, I want to feed my child," she retorted in surprisingly clear and crisp German, looking him in the eye. "Masha, give her to me, please," and she took the bundle to her breast, ignoring the old physician's sullen stare, and wincing as the baby's little jaws clamped onto her nipple.

"Very well, madam, I shall return tomorrow to make sure everything is well," the doctor said, and left the room. Lily felt she had been rash and unfair. And yet, she couldn't have stood it if the baby would have been put to anyone else's breast.

When Sergei Nikolayevich returned four days later, Lily was still resting. She'd forgotten all about the long and difficult confinement and lay resplendent in the white bed holding the baby in her arms. Sergei dragged his feet into the room with Masha running up behind him to remove the long, mud-spattered coat off his shoulders. But before she could take it away, he turned to her and asked her to leave it over one of the chairs. His face was drawn with fatigue, eyes reddened as if he hadn't slept. Just by looking at him, Lily realized the trip had not gone well.

He knelt by the bed, his eyes tearing at the sight of the baby's face. "A daughter!" he said. "How could a man hope for a more beautiful homecoming gift?" Then, turning to Lily, he said with a sad smile, "And you, my love, you promised you would wait for me until I returned."

All the reproaches she had planned to bestow on him were instantly dissolved into the pang of joy she felt at having him back. "Wait for you!" she laughed, "as if life waited for anyone."

They kissed tenderly. "I want to call her Violet," Lily said.

"Oh, but she must follow family tradition and be called Olga, like my father's mother, and her husband's father's mother before that," he said, holding the baby's tiny hand in his fingers.

"Since when is a seasoned revolutionary like you so passionate about family tradition?" Lily asked.

"She's a Latvin," Sergei said. "She comes from a long, uninterrupted line of naming. Why would revolution need to disrupt innocent, beautiful traditions? Besides," he added with a grin, "Olga means 'holy,' and she is the holy miracle of our rocky love." Lily gave him an ironic look, while her mind flashed back to scenes in St. Petersburg, their quarrels about her pregnancy, the visit to Annushka's clinic, her hours of pleading, and her final fury at the changes that were being forced upon her life. And yet right now, there was nothing she wanted more in the world but to hold the warm bundle of her daughter's little body close to her breast.

Sergei reached for his coat and pulled out a small, flattened box. "This," he said, as he presented her with it, "is for you." Curled inside an aqua-blue velvet bed lay a silver pendant with a sparkling sapphire surrounded by diamonds, together with matching earrings and a ring. Lily gasped. "Where did you get this? Don't tell me you tramped all the way to Manchuria just to bejewel me!"

Sergei shook his head, smiling. "I should have. But no, I had them brought from Petersburg."

"I've never seen anything so beautiful in my life. They must have cost a fortune."

Sergei took out the ring and slid it onto her finger. "These are family jewels. They belonged to my grandmother Olga Alexandrovna Latvina. And now they're yours."

"Olga Alexandrovna Latvina," Lily echoed, and her eyes wandered from the jewels to the baby's delicate little face flush with sleep.

And so they named the baby Olga. Olga Sergeevna Latvina.

Vladivostok, January 6th, 1904

Dear Brother and Sister,

I'm finally able to send a picture of Olga. She's one year and three months old, and I can't believe how quickly time has passed. She is a very big little girl and she is already walking and even babbling a bit. How I wish you could see how beautiful she is! She looks just like Sergei and not at all like me. But everyone says that will change as she grows.

As for the rest, the whole of Vladivostok is swarming with talk of a possible war with the Japanese, a complicated matter for they're less than five hundred miles across the bay. The Russians think Japan is a backward country with a small, obsolete army that doesn't stand a chance. My merchant friends are not so sure about a quick Russian victory, and they worry about how a war would interrupt trade. Nobody is happy, and everyone hopes it will come to nothing.

I have started translating plays by a Russian playwright I love, a man called Anton Chekhov. I am thinking that when I next come back to England I shall try to find a publisher and a theater interested in staging them. My Russian is quite good by now, and I'm exchanging Russian-English lessons with a young officer who works with Sergei and who is very clever. Do you have any idea, Harry, of any publishing house in Manchester or London that might be interested in Russian stories and plays? Please do look it up for me.

Well, loves, how I wish I could visit you with Olga. Maybe in the spring I could make the journey over to England. Please, please, send me a picture of both of you and of Annie, so I can have you all with me; and give my love to Father, even if he doesn't take it. I keep dreaming that if he met Sergei and Olga, he would forgive me. But I know it's only a dream.

Sending thousands of kisses,
Lily

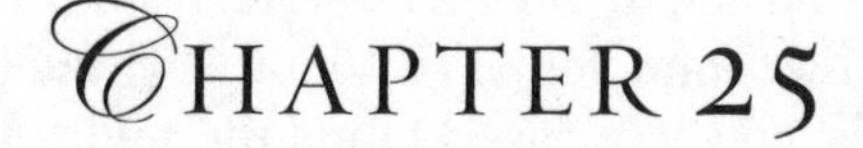

CHAPTER 25

Olga sat patiently as Lily and Kiku fitted her into the baby kimono. Masha held her while they pulled up the pantaloons and wrapped the red silk shirt scattered with pink flowers around her chubby little body. Then Kiku secured it at the waist with a maroon obi, and after putting tiny matching booties on both her feet, they stood her up. "Oh, if there was ever a beautiful baby girl in this world," Lily said, scooping her into her arms and covering her with kisses.

"Wait, mistress," Kiku said. "We still have to do the headdress." Lily reluctantly put the baby back into Masha's arms, while Kiku's small, delicate hands delved into the box in which the miniature costume had arrived.

Lily sat back and watched as the two women fussed about Olga's head. It was soon clear that the circlet of tiny fabric flowers could not be attached to the scanty, feathery hair, and Kiku hurried out to find a ribbon. Masha sat the baby on her lap while Lily gaped at the sight of her daughter in red and pink Japanese garb, and marveled at her pale, attentive eyes that were so much like Sergei's, so much like Tatyana's, definitively Volkov eyes, and yet had such a distinct light of their own. A light that made Lily quiver with happiness every time she encountered that little face; a light that dispelled every doubt, every pang that might exist outside the soul that shimmered through those eyes. She had never imagined she would be capable of loving so much. She had never known how violently she would leap with joy, or concern, or just mere yearning, at the small bundle of animated flesh that was her daughter. "How come nobody has ever told me about this before?" she mused. "Why, for all the reading I've done, for all the depths of Shakespearean texts I've had to study, nowhere have I found the slightest hint about this most amazing feeling." *I could die for her*, she thought looking at the baby's plump, peachy cheeks as she smiled back at her. In fact, she would happily die for her.

Kiku returned with a long pink ribbon and quickly sewed it onto the circlet. Then the two women tried to tie the ribbon around the child's pudgy chin, but it kept sliding off, and after a while Olga's round little face puckered, ready to burst into wails of protest. "No, don't cry now," Lily said, reaching for the baby's hand. "You've been so, so good, and when Papa comes you'll look so pretty. . . ." That very moment, she heard Ho Li walk to the front door. "Here he is," Lily said, and ignoring Kiku's sighs, took the girl up in her arms and rushed out of the drawing room to meet Sergei.

She caught him walking into the study. "Seryozha, look! Kiku had her family send a kimono for Olga," she said, but her face dropped at the sight of the shadowed figure who stood at Sergei's side, as she recognized his sinister collaborator, Kalinov. He nodded his head in her direction.

Sergei's face opened into a brief smile. "Yes, very pretty indeed," he said, looking shortly at the baby, before turning to Lily. "I need to step inside for a brief meeting. Please make sure we won't be interrupted." He walked into the study and closed the door behind them.

Lily swished around, back into the drawing room, and asked Kiku and Masha to change Olga into her party dress. It would not do in the present climate to have her dressed in a Japanese costume, though Lily had fantasized about inserting some beautiful exotic element into the conventional Christmas party she was throwing that day.

It was January seventh, the Russian Orthodox Christmas holiday, and the first time since they had arrived in Vladivostok that their house was being formally opened to friends and acquaintances for a celebration. In less than two hours, Eleanor would arrive with her daughter Dorothy, together with Sarah Smith, Maria Dattan, and three other friends who were bringing their own small children. Their husbands had also pledged to attend. Even Rudakov was coming over. Lily had made Sergei promise that even if the whole customhouse blew up in flames, he would be present at the party. Kiku and Masha had been busy for days decorating the drawing room, while Ho Li prepared the most exquisite, dainty foods. The house had never looked so beautiful. A tall Christmas tree glittering with glass figurines and feng-shui pendants amid candles burning inside tiny tin lanterns stood in the drawing room beside the bright fire burning in the hearth. Atop tables dressed in dazzling white starched linens sat plates of hors d'oeuvres arranged in lovely colorful patterns as only Ho Li could make.

But the resplendent universe she had worked so elaborately to create had just been penetrated by a dark, disquieting element that threatened to eclipse the day. She could not believe that Sergei had brought Vladimir Mikhailovich Kalinov to the house on a day like this. Kalinov was Sergei's inseparable companion of late, and after arguments where Lily had expressed her intense dislike of the man, Sergei had finally admitted that he was one of his main political collaborators and could not be dispensed with. But he would say no more, and Lily was left seething with her old discontent.

Kalinov was a sly, silent individual with an inscrutable, sallow face, who at first sight looked older than his years, although on closer inspection he was probably around thirty, Sergei's age. He was not part of Sergei's team at the customhouse, but worked in a small legal bureau next to the post office, where he posed as a commercial lawyer. His deep, languorous eyes surrounded by dark circles had a narcotizing effect on anyone on whom they rested long enough, but underneath they shone with contempt. A cynic, Lily had instantly discerned. But that feature was not the deepest reason for the repulsion she felt. It was something else that she couldn't quite put her finger on. A certain fluid, smoky presence, a shriveling influence; it was hard to define.

She had first seen him last January at the ceremony of the Blessing of the Waters, trailing Sergei, who, as one of the high officials of the port authority, walked behind the procession of Orthodox priests toward the harbor. When the three bishops leading the cortege reached the edge of the dock, they halted and stood looking out from under their tall felt hats, their long cassocks silhouetted against the pale gray sky, murmuring prayers and sprinkling holy water from their silver aspersoria toward the ships anchored in the bay. Then one of them lifted a tri-bar cross and threw it into the water. As soon as the cross fell under the freezing surface, three young shirtless sailors dove in to retrieve it. Seconds later, the champion emerged wielding it with both hands amid floating slabs of ice, gasping fiercely for breath, his face and torso blazing with chill, but grinning and triumphant, while the priests blessed him and the people surrounded him in acclamation. This Great Blessing of the seawater and the navy's ships was the city's most cherished religious ceremony, and when the crowd finally dispersed toward Svetlanskaya Street among the pealing of bells from the Blessed Nicholas Cathedral, everyone looked exhilarated, every face smiling, bursting with pride and euphoria after the event.

All but Kalinov's. Lily watched him standing behind Sergei like a shadow, looking around with reserve and disdain, as if he felt above everyone, a giant towering over an anthill ready to set it aflame. Later, when she was introduced to him by Sergei, Kalinov only nodded unsmilingly and said, "You speak Russian, madam," as if he hadn't expected her to be articulate at all. Lily was glad he didn't step forward and kiss her hand, which was the standard social grace toward a lady, for she couldn't have stood his touch. But Sergei only sang his praises that night. He was terribly intelligent, widely traveled and read, an amazing strategist, a great ideologue, and a most loyal and dedicated fellow. But Lily knew what she had seen. A hater of men.

She was presently shaken out of her thoughts when she heard quick, agile steps mounting toward the house, and saw Tarsky's face smiling through the glass as he approached the veranda. She turned to alert Masha, but saw that the girl had already jumped up and was rushing to the front door. Tarsky, Masha's sweetheart, was one of the young officers who worked at the customhouse with Sergei. From the drawing room's open door, Lily saw him and Masha exchange warm greetings. When Sergei and Kalinov stepped out of the study, a moment of startled confusion ensued as the four of them meshed in the hall. Lily saw Kalinov exchange somber glances with Sergei.

After Kalinov left and Masha and Tarsky went into the drawing room, Sergei closed the front door and turned toward Lily. "Can we have a word?" he said, and led her into the study. "What is Tarsky doing here?" he asked, and she felt agitation behind his words.

"I invited him to the Christmas party," Lily said. "He's very fond of Olga, but mainly of Masha."

"He's fond of Olga and Masha," Sergei echoed slowly, pacing. "Am I to take it he is a regular visitor to the house?"

"Well, yes, since last week. He's sweet on Masha, and I've given permission for him to call on her."

"And why haven't I been told this before?" Sergei said.

"Because you're never home, that's why," Lily said, beginning to feel annoyed at his questions. "Anyway, I did tell you days ago that Masha was in love. But I guess you took no notice." Sergei's face stiffened. He looked away. "Is it a problem? Are you going to make it part of your duty as absent householder to police Masha's affairs of the heart? After all, the girl is already nineteen and deserves an admirer."

Sergei didn't answer. Lily saw his jaw tighten as when he was upset. His silences in these types of conversations exasperated her. *You can't afford to have Tarsky coming to the house, but you can bring in a grim cad like Kalinov anytime you like,* she wanted to say, but bit her tongue. Starting an argument was not in the best interest of the upcoming reception; it wasn't even in the interest of their relationship, which felt more and more estranged every day. She sat down, defeated.

There was a moment of silence while Lily thought about Tarsky and why he might be eliciting banishment. She had first met Tarsky in the company of Rudakov. The old general loved to come in the afternoons for tea and have Lily tell him all about London. "Oh, how I loved that grand city when I was sent on a diplomatic mission in my youth," he'd say. These visits were very much approved by Sergei, who needed to sustain a family-man appearance with his superiors, and it couldn't be helped that the old fellow insisted on bringing with him young attendants. It was also difficult to restrain these young aides not to call later by themselves. Lily had heard Eleanor insisting about the need to host young single men in the city. "It has to be one of our missions," Eleanor used to say. "They have no home here, and if no one invites them in, they're almost sure to get into very bad company." Lily laughed at these words but decided to receive young officers on occasion. They were sweet; they brought little presents for Olga and amused her with anecdotes about Vladivostok's garret world.

That was how Tarsky ended up being a visiting guest. He was a short, muscular, good-looking man of about twenty-five, with cropped black hair and a wide smile that revealed a row of strong white teeth. He was self-made within the army, the son of a modest country doctor from the region of Kaluga, who had been private secretary to a number of officials, the last of whom was Rudakov. Tarsky amused Lily by telling funny stories about daily life at the customhouse. She soon sensed he might be participating in Sergei's political activities and she started asking him discreetly about Sergei's comings and goings. But Tarsky dodged her inquiries gracefully and started making inquiries himself. After a while, he declared to be smitten with Masha and requested Lily's permission to visit the house. And how could she not have given that permission? Masha's eyes had looked at her imploringly across the room.

There was nothing Lily would deny Masha at this point. She was like a family member to her, a loving companion; a basic pillar in the running of the household and in Olga's care. And how she had flourished in Vladivostok! In just one year, she had learned elemental reading and writing in Russian and become quite a marvel at arithmetic. She followed household expenses to the last kopek. Poor Ho Li every time he returned oblivious and happy with his wares from the market and had to account for his careless spending! But what would Sergei know of all this?

Sergei had become a stranger to them all. He looked stressed and gloomy most of the time, and sat alone in the study when he was at home. He spent increasingly less time with Lily and Olga, and arrived in the bedroom at night exhausted and unwilling to talk. There had been a time when Lily became obsessed with all sorts of efforts to anchor him back into the life at home. She made sure everything ran around his schedule, that his favorite foods were always on the table, that there was a constant inpouring of interesting and beautiful things into the house, such as new books or exotic artifacts she dug out of the town's obscure Chinese shops. But all these endeavors had yielded little results, so she reverted to her own routine, to writing and spending time with friends. She was beginning to enjoy the life of a singularly unique port city like Vladivostok.

But the gulf between Lily and Sergei kept widening, and at intervals she couldn't help being seized by the feeling that he was slipping away. She watched him across rooms as he sat lost in thought, his mind sailing into regions from which some day he might never return. At one point, she was stung with the suspicion that he had fallen for another woman. After two weeks of fruitless sleuthing, she decided to confront him about it. He denied it, looking genuinely hurt at the suggestion. Later that night he made love to her with such passionate tenderness that she put it out of her mind. "Why can't you be like this all the time, Seryozha?" she asked. "So I don't feel I'm losing your love."

"But I *am* like this all the time," he'd whispered in reply. "Only, I have to keep it locked deep inside. Otherwise, I wouldn't be able to do anything else." And for those hours, he lay in her arms as the old Sergei, the ardent, intoxicating lover of the past, instead of the sad, languid man she had endured of late. No, she was certain it was not about another woman. It was much darker than that.

Lily lifted her eyes and saw that Sergei was still brooding over Tarsky, leaning in the same posture against the desk, shoulders slumped and arms crossed over the chest. *How lonely he looks,* she thought. She got up, deciding for a truce. "Can we just enjoy our party and talk about this at another time?" She scanned his eyes. "Seryozha," she insisted, first pulling at his sleeve and then taking his hands, "what worries you? What's wrong?"

He shook his head as if dispelling remote, difficult thoughts, and said, "Nothing's wrong. I shall be in my room changing for the reception," and he let go of her. She followed him with her gaze as he left the room.

* * *

Lily's Christmas party turned out to be a splendid success. Not just every invited guest came, but some of them even brought a few extra friends, making the company merrier still. Olga and her little friends received countless presents, and all guests mingled spiritedly, immersed in ebullient conversations throughout the afternoon. The four-man military band from one of the city's ground battalions that Lily had hired to play traditional Russian Christmas carols started off by playing the "God Save the Czar" anthem, which many of the guests sang with tears in their eyes. Afterward, every bit of food was ravished, with wine and port running freely among adults, while the children stuffed themselves with sweet desserts that got smeared over their clothes and faces, as they ran or crawled around, fell down and cried, and ended up collapsed in various snug corners before their parents took them away. Even Sergei's face looked flushed with enjoyment as he moved among the guests, playing the elegant and graceful host he could be. After families with children were gone and the remaining guests sat contentedly around, the men with cigars, the women with tisanes, conversations inevitably turned to the war.

"I say we should go in and teach them a lesson," Grigoriev, a young naval captain from a Vladivostok squadron ship anchored in the bay, said. "They have no business interfering with the czar's plans in Port Arthur."

Rudakov eyed him jadedly across the room. "That's all very commendable from a patriotic perspective. But have you thought about the difficulties in transporting troops and supplies from European Russia to the East? I say we stay out of it, and find diplomatic solutions."

Grigoriev's face opened into a condescending smile. "But General, we have the Trans-Siberian line. We shouldn't worry about that."

"We have an unfinished line, Captain, with only one track," Rudakov countered. "Which means we can only transport in one direction."

"But sir, let's not forget we also have our fleet."

"Yes," Sergei said, stepping into the conversation. "In Petersburg. At least forty days away by sea." And so the conversation went on, while Lily left the room to attend to the guests who were departing and needed help gathering coats, muffs, hats, and overshoes to step out into the freezing night. After the last person left, Lily swept through a house strewn with empty plates, glasses, top-full ashtrays, ribbons and wrappings from presents. But mostly, a happy house throbbing with echoes of an evening very well spent.

"Please unbutton me," Lily said once in the bedroom. She turned her back to Sergei and started pulling the pins out of her hair to liberate her tresses from her too-tight, too-high chignon, the only regretful decision of the otherwise perfect occasion. She felt Sergei's fingers unfastening the back of her dress. "No, don't stop now. Undo the hooks underneath too." He unhooked her corset without a word.

When he was finished she leaned back against his chest. "Tell me you loved the party," she said. "Tell me it feels lovely to be a normal family and that we should do things like this more often." He held her for a moment in his arms, then gently disengaged and walked away. She stepped out of her dress, discarded her bodice and petticoat, and wrapped herself into her Chinese silk robe. When she turned around, she saw him sitting in the little sofa by the fireplace, his face sullen again, and she knew he was going to talk about Tarsky.

She went over to him. "Please, let's not spoil the evening. Let's not talk about anything, let's just be together."

Sergei fixed her with a dull stare. "No, it's important you know something," he said, and then added after a tense moment, "As from tomorrow, Tarsky will be removed from Vladivostok."

"Tarsky? Removed? Why? What has he done?"

"I can't discuss the why or the how. Orders have been given and they need to be obeyed."

"And who gives these orders?" Lily said, with fury beginning to choke her throat. "Kalinov?"

Sergei sighed as if exasperated by a rebellious child. "Lily, please. I'm only letting you know because it will affect our household, now that Masha is involved with him. And I shall need your help in making sure she makes no inquiries about him or his whereabouts."

"No inquiries! Why, what's going to happen to him?" Lily asked. When Sergei didn't respond immediately, she added with fury, "If anything happens to him, if anyone touches him, I swear as God is my witness that I shall pick up my daughter and leave. I can't live like this anymore. I can't stand all this secrecy, and now these threats."

He sat across from her. "Please don't raise your voice. Listen, Tarsky is thought to be a double agent; he is compromising the security of our whole network. He is not a safe person to have around, least of all in our house. We have no other alternative."

"But how can Tarsky be a double agent? He's so innocent and sweet. Are you sure about this? Couldn't it be someone else?" Lily's mind instantly conjured Kalinov.

"It's a long story. But there's evidence he's linked to the Paris Ochrana office. There have been leaks of information that have already affected the life and freedom of dozens. We can't afford anyone who arouses suspicion. They need to be cut off."

Lily knew the Ochrana was the czar's secret police; she also knew Tarsky had been stationed in Paris in the past, but still couldn't believe he was the culprit. "But you're admitting it's just a suspicion, and on a suspicion you are cutting off a man. This is just brutal. It's acting like the people who imprisoned you, beat you, cut your face, and banished you. Like those who . . ." She was going to say "killed Sasha," but she stopped when she saw Sergei's face grow livid. She got up with the intention of leaving the bedroom, but he said, "Sit down" with such quiet, chilling authority that she obeyed in spite of herself.

She steadied her breathing and Sergei paced with hands behind his back. "If you insist on knowing certain things, you need to be able to bear with the answers," he said. "This is how the party works. We do not take chances."

"How cold you sound, Seryozha," she said bitterly. "How you've changed and how quickly; I know you less and less every day. I shudder to think of what might come."

A moment of silence passed while Lily watched the glow of dying embers in the hearth. Then Sergei slumped beside her on the sofa. "I haven't changed in regard to you. You're still my wife, and I love you."

Lily threw back her head with a sneer. "I'm not your wife, Seryozha. I'm only your mistress."

"You're just saying this to hurt me."

"It's true. Your real wife is Mother Russia, and I'm just your mortal mistress."

From the nursery came the sound of Olga crying, but neither of them moved. A few minutes later they heard Masha rushing in to comfort her, after which the baby quieted down. Then Sergei spoke again. "I think you understand that the work I'm pledged to do needs to be accomplished through unconditional commitment, even if it requires sacrifices." His voice, dull and mechanical, as if he were reciting a script, reverberated with sadness underneath. "And that the fruits of that work are directed to you, to our daughter, to everyone who deserves a better world. The fact that I'm committed doesn't mean I don't love you, or that I don't care for our child. On the contrary—"

"But do you suppose," interrupted Lily, "you can get to a better world by trampling over everything along the way? Your loved ones' lives and feelings, suspicious little lieutenants and whoever, or whatever else gets in your way?"

"No, but in certain situations the end must justify the means."

"That sounds like a very dangerous principle," Lily said. She stood, scooped up her shawl, and walked out of the room without another word. In the nursery, she found Masha still sitting by the baby. "Go back to bed, Masha, I'll take over," she said, and when the girl was gone, she got inside the large cot and snuggled close to Olga, who was fast asleep. But Lily lay awake, until the first rays of dawn, smoldering with anguish.

The next morning she found Kiku crying at the kitchen table, and when she asked what was the matter, Ho Li told her that they had just seen on the street outside the market a group of Russian sailors slapping two Japanese manservants around and calling them "yellow monkeys." "She's very afraid of what might happen, mistress," Ho Li said gravely, "and so am I." When Kiku, despite Lily's reassurances that she would always be safe in the house, wouldn't stop sobbing, Lily realized that if the tension kept escalating she would have to put her beloved amah on a ship back home before the conflict broke out. The Japanese community was already holding meetings to discuss the situation and make collective decisions on what to do in the present circumstances. Many of Lily's merchant friends were thinking about leaving the city and resettling temporarily at a nearby Russian or Chinese port. Meanwhile, the Bay of the Golden Horn kept filling up with ships from the Vladivostok and Port Arthur squadrons; the *Russia*, the *Bogatyr*, the *Rurik* and the *Gromoboi* were some of the best-known ships anchored in the haven's waters fraught with winter ice. They were splendid in their lines and strong in their promise of protection, but mostly, undisguised harbingers of war.

Lily spent the rest of the day in total gloom. She couldn't write, she couldn't eat; she couldn't even enjoy her little girl. She couldn't face Masha, thinking of the pain that would soon explode inside her lovely eyes, and how she, Lily, would have to lie and pretend. She still ached with the altercation of the night before. The fury she felt, the despair at being unable to create a cordial, plausible life with Sergei. Her state of dejection was reminiscent of the times in Petersburg when she thought of returning to England and leaving him behind. Now that possibility was opening up again. Olga was older and could withstand a journey. Though winter was not a good time to travel through Siberia, it was possible to take a longer route by liner, via Ceylon and Suez, along the Mediterranean and all the way around Portugal to England. She had just read an article about American journalist Nellie Bly and her trip around the world by train and boat, and figured that a journey by sea from Vladivostok to England would take no more than fifty days. She would take Masha with her, and they would have a grand time. She would keep a travelogue and seek to publish it on arrival. Money was available too. A few months back, Sergei had opened an account in her name at the Russian bank of Pekinskaya Street with an initial deposit of thirty thousand rubles. That figure had seemed excessive at the time, but now it sounded just right.

On paper, it all looked perfect. Returning to England with money, ready to take on the stage again. Even ready to face up to Wade, who had actually written Lily a letter, telegram style, that had taken eight months to reach her: "*Dearest, unforgettable Mademoiselle Throop, Rumors reach London about your outrageous, outlandish Russo-Asian contingencies. Know that I still wait for you, and expect a double-fold honoring of your debt on your return. Your humble servant, HW.*" Oh, the rogue! What undying persistence! Lily found herself cringing at the whiff of entitlement that exhaled from the elegant handwriting of his note. But what a petty, small-time monster he seemed to her now in the light of her present troubles.

Nothing, she thought again, *lies in the way of my leaving for England immediately*. But that wasn't quite true. How could she leave Sergei in the grim anteroom of a war? How could she bear to deliver him entirely into the hands of Kalinov? The image of Sergei's light being sucked by Kalinov's darkness conjured up in her mind, giving her shivers. How many times had she had seen Sergei arrive pale and depleted, and take hours to replenish inside the warm, bright atmosphere of the house? And why had Sergei ended up deadlocked with a being of this sort? Couldn't he perceive his baseness, the depraved slime of his soul? Was this the standard type of individual with whom Sergei collaborated in his political work?

After finding the metal box hidden in a double-bottom cupboard in his room, Lily had done more probing into Sergei's files. She spent hours deciphering a ream of directives on the further development of more extensive and complex *druzhiny* combat groups. She had even found an instruction booklet on how to make bombs and explosives. Shuddering, she had locked it all back again. Stakes were getting higher and darker in Sergei's quarters, and now this business of the double agent. Of course, it could be Tarsky; no one was free of conjecture in this murky, deceptive world. But why couldn't it also be Kalinov?

Kalinov was the daily drop of poison administered to Sergei that back-ended into their private lives, contaminating everything it touched. The venom that leached into every doubt about the meaning of her life with Sergei; that fogged her eyes when she tried to envision the future.

"Let me have men about me that are fat; Sleek-headed men and such as sleep o' nights; Yond' Cassius has a lean and hungry look; He thinks too much: such men are dangerous." The image of Wade, clad in a Roman toga with a musty laurel wreath crowning his head, reciting *Julius Caesar* onstage regurgitated in her mind, making her laugh. Indeed it was as if her old enemy was pointing at her new foe, as if he had glimpsed Kalinov's spindly figure tucked away pensively in a dim corner of the room. He was admonishing her that Kalinov was to Sergei what Cassius had been to Julius Caesar, a treacherous conspirator, an embittered underling mortally jealous of a greater man's charisma, lurking in wait for an opportunity to bring him down.

"These judgments are unfair and arbitrary," Sergei had said many times. "You just don't know the man." But she was as certain of her instinct as she was dismayed by Sergei's guilelessness in the matter.

CHAPTER 26

One afternoon while Lily was having tea at Eleanor's house, Mr. Schwabe, the British Consular representative who was a friend of Eleanor's, told them that war would be declared that same night or the next day. The whole room froze. It was the seventh of February. Two of the visitors, Mrs. Hansen and Mrs. Ivy, became agitated and, gathering their things, left. Mr. Schwabe stayed a bit longer until he finished his glass of port, and then also took his leave.

"Well, we've been expecting it after all," Eleanor said with her usual practical attitude, when she and Lily were by themselves.

"What will you do?" Lily asked. "Will you stay in Vladivostok?"

"Where else will I go?" Eleanor said. "I'm not afraid. It's not like I'm a stranger in a strange place."

Back at the house, Lily assembled Ho Li, Kiku, and Masha and explained the situation. Kiku decided to start making immediate plans to leave, while Ho Li seemed undecided. When both of them left the drawing room, Lily turned to Masha. "Masha, what do you want to do?"

Masha only stared ahead listlessly. "I'll do whatever you do, mistress," she said flatly, without turning her head. Masha had languished with dejection after Tarsky's disappearance, which she had come to believe had been an act of desertion toward her. Lily had offered her a sum of money and suggested she return to her hometown near Taganay to start afresh, but Masha wouldn't hear of it.

The next morning, headlines on the front page of the *Far East* newspaper announced Japan's declaration of war. Sergei tuned the radio he had brought from the customhouse searching for more news, and soon hit a channel reporting that the night before, the Japanese had launched a surprise torpedo attack on the Russian squadron at Port Arthur. Sergei left immediately for the customhouse, while Lily prepared to go to market with Ho Li, since Kiku was too afraid to leave the house.

They drove along Svetlanskaya Street toward the wharves. Around them, the city felt uncannily calm, with everyone going about their business with an unusual measure of quiet and deliberate efficiency, as if to blot out the fact that anything out of the ordinary might be happening. The stalls at the market were half-empty. Many of them were just closed down, as vendors had begun leaving the city. Produce had been dwindling since the summer, but certain vegetables and dry goods were always available, and fish and seafood was never lacking. Today, everything was in short supply, and what was there had doubled in price since the day before.

In the early evening, Lily went to the customhouse and requested to see General Rudakov. She knew Sergei would have already left for some meeting or other and wouldn't be there. The customhouse was a large stone building facing the railway quay, and to get to Rudakov's office it was necessary to transverse endless corridors lined with metal shelves filled with stacks of files and ledger books, followed by a series of dim, dusty rooms scattered with desks submerged under piles of paperwork. The clerks, who were mostly young officers, aside from a few old, professional pencil-pushers, stood up instantly when she appeared, and a few of them hurried to accompany her to Rudakov's bureau like fluttering moths following the glow of a moving lantern.

The old general was elated to see her, as always. "What brings a beautiful young lady to the grimmest little spot in the whole of the Golden Horn?" He got up and greeted her gallantly, and led her to a leather chair facing his heavy, ornate desk. But before Lily could open her mouth, he said, "But I know exactly what brings you here.

And I've already anticipated your request, because I don't want you worrying about anything." He went on to tell her that he had secured a transfer for Sergei to be posted back to Moscow, where he would be involved in organizing the transportation of troops and supplies through the Trans-Siberian line. "He's very valuable, my dear. He could be a great asset for our government and our country," Rudakov said with emotion. Lily feared he was going to shed tears, but he sobered up and added with fatherly annoyance, "If only he weren't so stubborn."

Lily knew Sergei had excelled in his duties during his short time working under Rudakov; he had modernized a number of port procedures, reorganized the system of custom tariffs, and gained respect for these practices from every authority in the district.

Rudakov leaned forward and pressed her hand. "Furthermore," he said, looking her in the eye, "returning to civilization will give you a chance to expedite your legal matters." He spoke with the kindness of a concerned family elder. It was the first time he had hinted at anything related to her and Sergei's irregular status.

Lily rushed back home and spent the next few hours sizzling with excitement as she waited for Sergei. When she heard him come in, she dashed out to the hall and cornered him, putting her arms around him even before he had a chance to take off his coat. She then led him into the study where she had asked Ho Li to bring up a bottle of champagne with two glasses.

"What's to be celebrated?" Sergei asked with a grin, accepting his glass of champagne. "Not even our most barbarous, war-hungry generals are this gleeful today."

"Rudakov told me about your transfer to Moscow," Lily burst out. "I am so, so happy Seryozha! I think I shall die of happiness."

Sergei put down his champagne. "That will not happen immediately, though," he said, and then added cautiously, "I've accepted a commission to travel with the fleet to Port Arthur and report on the conflict."

Lily froze. "You've accepted a commission to travel to Port Arthur?" she repeated in disbelief.

"Yes, it's a unique opportunity to expose the government's irresponsibility and the czar's absurd imperial policy."

"I'm sure it's a good opportunity. But why does it have to be you? Can't someone else who doesn't have a family go?"

"Listen, this war won't last long," Sergei said. "It's a blunder on both sides, and it will be settled quickly, even if in an unsightly manner." Lily turned her face away as he continued, "I won't be away for more than three weeks. I'll be back before you realize it."

Lily slumped into a chair. "And in the meantime, you're planning to leave me alone with a baby in a situation like this?"

"The conflict will not affect Vladivostok," Sergei said. "Japan won't dare attack Russia on its national territory. All the action will happen in Port Arthur and Manchuria. The city will be the safest place in the whole region." This was not the first time Lily had heard this opinion. Ted Pray, Eleanor's husband, was of the same mind. But still.

She sat listlessly, feeling an increasing sluggishness, as if something or someone were draining all the blood from her body. The old helplessness seized her as she realized the futility of any convincing she might be tempted to undertake; she knew that no arguing, no bringing forth of rational contention, not even plain, doormat-style pleading would move him. It would be like wrestling with the wind.

"I finally need to admit that I've lost all hope," she said after a moment, in a slow, slurred voice as if talking to herself. "I've lost all hope in regard to any capacity we might have to ever agree, to work in unison, or make each other happy." She got up, and in her heedless stumble toward the door, her hand accidentally swept over the desk where her champagne glass stood. It chinked and clinked as it crashed against the floor, spilling its golden, bubbly contents over the hardwood. But Lily didn't even look down; she made for the door and quietly left the room, while Sergei sat back and sighed.

The next day she and Masha took Kiku down to the harbor where she was to board the ship that would take her to Nagasaki. The roads and streets were difficult to navigate, clumped as they were with mounds of ice and snow from recent storms. Although Chinese rough laborers, everyone called *coolies*, were all over, working hard at shoveling, it would still take days to clear these areas. The sky was low and heavy with a gray cottony fog, as when it was about to snow. Lily pushed through the multitude gathering on the dock, with Masha and Kiku following behind. Once they approached the ship's gangway, they turned to face one another and say their final farewells.

Beside them stood two men who shot leering glances at Kiku. "*Yaponskaya shlyukha,* Japanese whore," one of them said, and spat on the ground between his feet.

Lily was taken by such fury that she forgot her lady manners, and even her Russian, and screamed at him in English, "You vulgar, gnarled beast of a man, how dare you!" She put her arm around Kiku, who sobbed quietly. Later, she and Masha saw Kiku disappear among the passengers boarding the steamboat, but it was too cold to wait for the ship to sail away, so they turned and made for the house. The last time they looked around, Kiku still stared at them from the deck, huddled among a frightened, ashen-faced crowd encircled by flurries of snow.

The snowstorm did not abate until the evening of the next day and Lily found herself housebound, mulling over the circumstances that were wrapping around her life. Instead of fretting, though, she observed that a strange calm had overtaken her, like a numbness, against which the general tension and other people's moments of panic had very little impact. From her window, she watched battleships come and go across the bay with an impervious eye. The next day she attended a lecture by the Red Cross with Eleanor at the Amurskiy Museum and found herself becoming interested in the smallest, most trivial of details, such as what was the most appropriate width to consider while tearing fabric into strips meant for bandages, or how many teaspoons of boric acid one should dilute in a quarter of water to make a disinfecting solution, all the time forgetting that the whole thing was a preparation for the gruesome casualties that might come with the war.

She and Sergei related minimally to each other in the days that followed. They went about each other as if nothing special was happening, planning details of his departure in a matter-of-fact way. Sergei was putting two young soldiers at her disposal for helping with house chores, now that Kiku was gone, and Ho Li would also be leaving shortly. Port Arthur's telegram line had been cut on the day of the attack and there would be no possibility of communicating with her that way, so he would send letters through Rudakov whenever possible. She was to keep money hidden in the house, but no more than a few rubles at a time. At moments she felt his tension, his craving to reach out to her, but she shielded herself behind a façade of indifference with which she kept him at bay. They didn't make small talk during meals, if they ate together at all. And Lily closed her door at night, while Sergei sat up late in the study and later slept in his room.

The night before his departure, she retired to her bedroom early, after putting Olga to bed. She woke up hours later when she heard the door open and someone slip into the room. Through sleepy eyes she saw Sergei's shadow edging toward the bed, and then felt him slump down beside her like a dead weight. He was fully dressed and stank of vodka.

"You're drunk," Lily said.

"I am," Sergei slurred. "Forgive me."

She sighed. Sergei was not a man who got drunk easily. But recently, he had been drinking more and more, and tonight it must have gotten out of hand. "I'll wake Ho Li and ask him to take you to your room and help you undress," she said.

"No, I'll leave in a minute," Sergei said. "I'm all right." They lay in silence in the darkness, while Lily waited. "I came to tell you that something happened the day before I took the assignment," Sergei said in a slurred whisper. "I'd been aboard one of the battleships for an inspection, and as I walked along the formation of sailors, I suddenly realized that every face I was seeing had the same exact features." He faltered for a moment. "And that they were the features of Sasha. Every sailor had the face of Sasha! I thought at first I might be feverish, that I had eaten something wrong. But I felt otherwise fine; it was just that horrifying sense that I was facing an army of Sashas going to their deaths."

"You shouldn't be drinking every night after you work fourteen hours a day," Lily said wearily, but a pang took hold of her as she remembered her own incident with Sasha at the log-avalanche scene.

"True," Sergei said, "but I don't think it was about that. It was like being given a premonition, an omen of death, of massive defeat." He was silent for a while. "Then the next day our fleet was attacked, and the *Petropavlovsk* sunk, with its hundreds of casualties, men burning and drowning, drowning as they burned—"

"Seryozha," Lily interrupted, "do you really think that by your going down there you'll have any bearing on the course of events? These are huge circumstances, away from anyone's control."

"Maybe not, but how could I just stay here? No one will write the truth about how thousands of men die; all reports, all statistics will be censored. . . ."

Lily felt her stomach sink. Confronting Sergei's political zeal was difficult, but revisiting the wounded layers underneath was harder still. There was something both exasperating and heartbreaking about his sentimentality toward the suffering masses and the downtrodden victims of the world; about his impressionability with anything related to Sasha and what he represented. Sasha! What a strange little figure of destiny he had been for them both, a sort of child they'd lost together and could never cease to mourn. The boy's sweet smile glowed again in her mind, together with the words he had spoken to her at the lodge, "*Malen'kaya khozyajka,*" Little Mistress, "*prostite ego,*" forgive him; and then, the image of his small body lying asleep by the hearth.

She reached for Sergei's hands. "You're so cold, Seryozha, get into bed," she said, and shuddered at the thought of the horrific freezing conditions in which he would be traveling in just a few hours hence. But Sergei didn't move, and she realized he might be drunker than she'd assessed. She sat up and started unbuttoning his jacket and his shirt, and one by one she took off every piece of his clothing until he was down to his undergarments. Under her hands, Sergei's body felt listless, and yielded like a little boy as she moved and pulled, rolled him over or asked him to turn or sit up. When she was finished, she opened the blankets and made him lie inside the bed by her side. "You'll have quite a hangover tomorrow, is one thing I can predict," she said, wrapping her arms around him, warming his body with hers. They lay in silence, listening to the chilled wind blowing outside. "What will I do if something happens to you, Seryozha?" she whispered. "Do you ever think about that?" But Sergei had already closed his eyes and drifted into sleep.

The next day two officers came to pick him up in the early afternoon, and because it was far too cold to go down to the harbor with him, it had been decided that they would all bid him farewell at the house. From her bedroom window, Lily saw the sleigh carriage waiting at the end of the path, and beside the two horses snorting steam into the cold air, she spotted Kalinov standing to the side, a dark, elongated shape cut out against the snow. Why was Kalinov taking her place in going down to the quay to see Sergei off? Her heart sank. Instantly, she understood that Sergei's assignment had more to do with party policy than with anything related to any military or port authority. She went downstairs feeling unsettled and ready to say something to Sergei, but in the hall she was met with a sweet moment.

Masha, with Olga in her arms, and Ho Li stood in adoring silence, watching Sergei, who, impeccable in his full uniform, was putting on his cap and long coat by the door. He stepped toward Masha and took Olga into his arms. "They say that one good daughter is worth seven sons," he said, looking into her baby face. "But you, my little beauty, will be worth at least fourteen," he said, and kissed her.

A wave of savage grief washed over Lily and she could no longer bear the scene. She whipped around and dashed into the drawing room where she stumbled upon one of the sofa chairs and threw herself over its arm, choking with sobs. She heard Sergei walk in behind her and close the door. She jumped up from the chair and rushed to the window where she looked out through its thick, white-frosted glass wishing the frozen landscape outside would numb her again. He stood behind her. "Lily."

"Just leave, Sergei."

"Lily, look at me." When she wouldn't respond, he took her by the shoulders and turned her around. "I need you to be brave," he said.

"But I am not," she said, flashing at him in defiance, wiping the tears from her face. "And I don't want to be. I'm not a soldier's wife. I'm an actress and actresses act onstage, but in real life they stay in touch with their feelings. And if those aren't of courage and heroic fortitude, and are instead of plain gutlessness, cowardice, pusillanimity, or just those of an old, tremulous, fainthearted chicken, then so much the better." She stopped, breathless, and then added, "Oh, why am I rambling?"

"This won't last long, Lily. I'll be back soon. I promise," Sergei said, putting his arms around her, pulling her into his chest. But she resisted and held him at bay, while scanning the pale mirror of his reckless soul inside his eyes; a vast, watery landscape at once dreamy and unfathomable, a disturbing door into the unbound. She gritted her teeth. *I've loved you,* she thought, *but I've never really had you, and never will. When will I surrender to this and let you go?*

She pressed her lips to his, feeling his cheeks and nose against hers, his intermittent breath, the sweet taste of his mouth. When she looked up again, his eyes had narrowed into a smile and were pouring into hers with submissive tenderness, unguarded, with an affection that had no beginning and no end.

There was a shy knock at the door. "Mistress, they're asking if Sergei Nikolayevich is ready," Masha said in a small voice. Lily smoothed her face with her fingers, made toward the door and into the hall. There she let Sergei fold her into his arms again, and he promised once more to write and return very soon.

And so Sergei left, and Lily walked around the once happy, bright house that was now sad and empty, wondering what she would do for the next three weeks in a city poised for war at the far edge of the earth.

CHAPTER 27

The next day, Lily sat in the study working on her translation, when Ho Li knocked on the door and entered. "Mistress," he said, "there are two gentlemen to see you."

"Two gentlemen?"

"Yes, mistress, one of them is Vladimir Kalinov. They are waiting in the drawing room. Shall I bring them in here?"

"Oh, no," Lily said getting up. "Are you sure it's Kalinov?" she asked, though she was well aware that Ho Li knew Kalinov and also disliked him.

She walked into the drawing room and there was Kalinov standing by the fireplace, dressed in his habitual blackish, shabby town suit. Beside him was another individual she had only seen once, but knew his name was Shevchenko, a blond, beefy, ruddy-faced man, who now shot rapacious glances toward her. Kalinov lifted his sly, heavy eyes and curtly nodded his head. "Madam, forgive this unannounced visit," he said in French. "I would not inconvenience you if the matter at hand was not urgent."

"Of course, Vladimir Mikhailovich," Lily answered in Russian. "How may I be of service?" She strode into the middle of the room like a queen and stood there as if holding court with servants, not even deigning to ask them to sit down.

"Forgive me," Kalinov retorted in Russian with a tense smile.

"One forgets how accomplished you are in our language." She waited impatiently for him to continue. "You see, madam, it's a delicate request your husband Sergei Nikolayevich has asked me to convey to you." He stopped for a moment, carefully considering his words. "He asks that you make his files available to us, since he was being watched before his departure and could not transport them himself."

Watched! Lily thought in alarm, but she only said, "Do you have a letter for me, or a note, where he makes such a request?"

"No, madam, I don't. As you know, we try to avoid written evidence."

Lily eyed him with contempt, knowing that Sergei would have never requested such a thing without at least a small coded note, a silly poem, or something that contained clues related to the matter. "This is very strange, sir," she said, "because there are no files in the house belonging to Sergei Nikolayevich, not even paperwork from the customhouse."

Kalinov looked at her, trying to pin down her gaze with his lazy, languorous eyes, but Lily remained unaffected. "Madam," he spoke, lowering his voice, "we know for a fact that important operational files were kept here by him."

Lily made an impatient gesture. "Not to my knowledge, sir, and as you can imagine, I know the household inside out. I'm afraid they will have to be somewhere else."

There was a tense silence in which the men exchanged somber glances, and Lily glared at them with cold, disdainful eyes. *What did you do to Tarsky, you monster?* she wanted to scream. *And what will you do to anyone else whose names you find in those files?* Then Kalinov said, "If you would allow us to search, madame, we would be able to identify places that commonly go undetected. Of course, we would be respectful and very discreet—"

"Absolutely not!" Lily said with quiet ferocity. "You will have to go on my word that no such files exist in this house." Before he could say anything else, she added, "Now, gentlemen, if you will excuse me, I need to get back to my chores." She rang the bell for Ho Li to escort them to the door.

Kalinov and his accomplice slithered out of the room, shooting malevolent side-glances as they passed her by. Only when they were far away from the house did Lily collapse into one of the chairs, shivering with fear and disgust. How could Sergei put up with the presence of such a man? There was an unbearable viscous quality about him, something abominable at the bottom of his eyes. After a moment, she went to Sergei's room, locked the door, and looked into the cupboard's double-bottom space. The metal box was still there. Why hadn't she asked Sergei about what to do with it should a problem arise? She realized how valuable and dangerous this information could be in the wrong hands.

She went into the kitchen, where Ho Li was chopping a large piece of mackerel over a board with an enormous knife. He was supposed to leave in the next few days to join his mother in Mudanjiang, China, but he still had not given Lily a date. "Ho Li," she said, "before you go I need to ask you to do something for me."

The cook turned to her gravely. "Mistress, I changed my plans. I shall not leave until the master is back." Lily looked at him with surprise, and then with gratitude. He was a small, slim man with an impassible, solemn face. It was hard to read his features, but Lily understood he had become concerned after Kalinov's visit. He'd probably been eavesdropping behind the door, a fault of character of which Masha and Kiku used to accuse him jokingly, and that Lily had never paid much attention to since the man was impeccable in his loyalty to Sergei. In this precise situation, such a flaw could prove to be convenient. When she next asked him point-blank if he would help her bury Sergei's metal box underneath the cork tree, Ho Li didn't bat an eyelid. "Mistress, the ground is frozen. It would take three strong men to open it up and bury something deep inside." Lily agreed with an exasperated sigh, after which Ho Li gave a parsimonious nod of the head and went back to his chopping in silence.

Later that night, Ho Li came to the house with three Chinese laborers and said, "Mistress, we are ready for the digging." She watched the men through the window, shoveling at a secluded far-end corner of the garden behind the cork tree, while Ho Li held a lantern. She trudged after them as they carried the metal box outside and looked over their shoulders as they scooped frozen chunks of soil into the ditch, stamped over it and covered it with snow. Afterward, Ho Li led the men back into the kitchen and fed them. "They will not talk, mistress. They leave tomorrow for China." Lily gave them food and money for their journey.

Days passed and the city remained a swirl of comings and goings, between those who were leaving and those who were pouring in because of the war. The streets swarmed with soldiers and sailors marching in formation when on duty, and when not, ambling around in large, raucous groups, singing or speaking loudly, while the city's regular inhabitants shied away into their homes. There was a general sense of curious excitement in the air. Most conversations revolved around the war, news about Japanese attacks and details about battles and the destruction of either navy's squadrons. Eyes were set at all times on the harbor, watching for ships leaving the bay, or returning; and when they did return, many ran down to the docks to get news from the sailors. Had they sunk any boats? Did they take any prisoners? What was the news from Port Arthur? When had they last seen so-and-so? If the ships returned damaged in any way, banged or battered, raked by shot and shell, as they many times did, people flocked to the harbor sick with worry and grief, as if the vessels were loved ones returning bruised and injured from battles bravely fought. Sometimes, Japanese ships approached the bay to reconnoiter that the Vladivostok squadron was still in port, and everyone eyed them with hatred and dread.

The afternoon of March sixth, Lily was reading in the study when she heard the gunfire coming from the port and looked out through the window, thinking it might just be battery practice. When it persisted beyond the usual, she looked again and saw some of the Russian ships pulling up anchor in the bay, and noticed that many sailors were ashore.

Masha rushed into the room. "Mistress, someone has been killed at the end of town. Everyone is rushing up to the Eagle's Nest for cover."

Lily took Sergei's field glasses from the desk, went out into the hall where she and Masha put on coats and boots, and taking Olga inside a bundle of furs, left the house toward the hill called the Orlinnoye Gnezdo, or the Eagle's Nest, the highest promontory above the city. Masses of people were gathered there, viewing the drama unfold below. But the shelling was over when Lily and Masha reached the top. Seven Japanese cruisers were leaving the bay. Lily looked through the field glasses and identified the places that had been damaged in the attack, a few houses hit, a few dents in the roads.

They saw Ted Pray, Eleanor's husband, among the crowd and went up to him. "Damned devils!" he said. "This was just practice, a little bravado to keep us on our toes." When the general trepidation sizzled down, he asked Lily to come over to their house for supper, where Eleanor, who had sprained an ankle, was waiting to hear every bit of news.

It was dark when Lily and Masha returned home with Olga asleep in their arms. They were surprised to see the house totally unlit from afar. It was unusual that Ho Li, who had stayed behind, wouldn't have turned up the lights as he did every day at dark. Lily asked Masha to stay with Olga inside the carriage while she rushed up the path. She found the door ajar, and when she stepped in and switched on some lamps, she saw that most rooms were in disarray; furniture moved around, books and objects thrown about from shelves and cupboards, as if someone had raided every nook and corner of the place. There appeared to be no one around, and Lily grew more and more agitated when Ho Li was nowhere to be found. She thought of returning to Eleanor's house, but as she was heading to the door, she heard thumping noises coming from the kitchen. She ran down and determined the banging was coming from the cellar that had been latched from the outside. "Ho Li! Ho Li!" she cried, and thought she heard a muffled response from behind. On opening the cellar, she found Ho Li bound and gagged in the dark.

After they made tea, they sat around the kitchen table while Ho Li told Lily and Masha how four men had come to the house in their absence, and when he tried to stop them, they had seized him, tied him up, and locked him in the cellar. He had knocked his head against the wall as they shoved him down the stairs and now sported a purplish bump, which Masha had cleaned up and bandaged with gauze. At first, Ho Li had thought them common burglars, but then he'd remembered the metal box and Kalinov's visit, and knew why they had come. Lily rushed out to the yard, but saw that the ground where the box had been buried was untouched. "They won't come back again tonight, mistress," Ho Li said. "There'll be too many soldiers in the streets." But Lily made Masha and Olga sleep together in her room that night after bolting all doors, and the next day she sent word to Rudakov relating the incident and requesting bodyguards for the house.

Rudakov ordered the two soldiers that Sergei had allocated for helping with house chores to be stationed there permanently. Though this measure rendered the house officially secure, Lily still found herself looking out of windows at night in fear of seeing shadows lurking outside. When she went into town, she kept a tight watch behind her back. She was convinced that Kalinov and his henchmen would strike again, and soon, before Sergei returned. They obviously had a plan that was stipulated on Sergei's absence. It seemed quite plausible now that Kalinov was the double agent, and that he was seeking to destroy everything Sergei had worked to build these two years. In the light of these thoughts, Sergei's life seemed more fragile than ever, surrounded not just by active war, but also by undercover treachery. Furthermore, Olga and Lily herself might become additional grounds for extortion and revenge. All of these dark thoughts whirled in her mind as the days went by without any news of Sergei.

Rudakov came to see her at the house on the fifteenth of March. The stormy weather of the past weeks had cleared for once. A bright sun shone in the blue sky reflecting shafts of dazzling light off every iced surface. The azure line of the sea ran sharp against the horizon and the bay shimmered below, smooth and pristine. That morning, Masha had brought out a little wooden sled she had found in the scullery. They had taken it into the yard and sat Olga on top, and were pulling her over the crusted snow when Lily saw Rudakov mounting the path toward the house. She rushed to meet him indoors.

"Uncle!" she cried out from the hall as she took off her boots, but Rudakov seemed not to hear her. She had started calling him "uncle" recently, for their bond of affection had tightened since

Sergei left, and he kept close watch over her and the house, sparing no measures of comfort and protection. She watched him pacing in the drawing room immersed in thought, as she took off her coat and smoothed her hair. He looked serious and tired, but that was always the case when he first arrived, and then after the first glass of port he would be jolly and perky again. Of course, port was one of the first things that had been off every market shelf since the beginning of the war.

"Uncle!" she cried again, and he turned slowly as she entered the room with quick little steps. He seemed to have aged immensely in just days, she thought, but everyone was becoming jaded with the tension of the war. "I'm so glad to see you," she said, approaching him. "What news do you bring? Will you take tea?" She grew alarmed at his reluctant gaze. "What has happened? Please, tell me."

Rudakov took a letter from his pocket and put it in her hand. "A letter!" she cried. "Will you excuse me for a moment while I read it?" Rudakov nodded and took a few steps away, while Lily turned to the window with a beating heart.

My dearest love,

I have only a few moments to write before the next dispatch, so forgive the brevity of these lines. It has been a rough few weeks since I left you, and even worse lately as we've had clashes with Japanese ships and had to deal with the grim aftermath that these events always leave behind. But I don't want to write about this.

All I'll say is that being confronted daily with the possibility of death has made me learn a great deal about myself. I've also thought much about you; how I've hurt you with my rash decisions, and how you've always indulged me with your patience, with your acceptance, no matter how opposed or how furious you were from the start. Oh, how I miss those flashing eyes. How I miss those lovely, pouting lips threatening to bring down the house.

What don't I miss? To think of a life without you is unbearable to me. To think of everything precious we have together, of our beautiful child, of all the years we have ahead of us, and the way I've imperiled it all, fills me with grief and remorse. Will you forgive me, my love? Will you be willing to take in a repentant sinner and help reform him into a decent husband, a committed lover, into the man you deserve?

Because I already know I will love you until my death.

She wanted to read it over and over again, but instead went to Rudakov and took a seat by his side. "How can I thank you for bringing this to me? If you knew how happy . . ."

But Rudakov took her hand in his. "Of course, dearest, how wouldn't I rush to deliver something I know you've waited on for so long?" He searched her eyes. "But I'm also here to tell you that Sergei Nikolayevich was taken captive with a few others by the Japanese navy five days ago."

"Captive!"

"Yes, dear." He sighed. "And that in itself is not the worst thing. At least there are protocols for the treatment of prisoners of war that the Japanese will probably respect. But we think he was wounded at the time, and I haven't yet been able to ascertain the gravity of his state." He went on to relate how Sergei had been aboard the destroyer *Steregushchy*, which was sunk off Port Arthur at the end of a ferocious battle that lasted the night, and the resulting wounded had been taken aboard one of the enemy battleships before they finished shelling the Russian ship.

Lily listened as if she were living through a dream, where sound waves carrying strange, dissonant information bounced against her and about the room making no sense. She sat paralyzed, with ears and mouth as if stuffed with cotton, wondering when she would wake up and leave the nightmare behind. But soon the sound waves translated into images washing over her mind, harrowing snippets of vision quickening out of her numbed brain. Sergei's face, pale, with eyes closed, his hands blue with cold, blood congealed over his military jacket. Lying on the floor on a stretcher, like the one she'd seen as part of the demonstration at the Red Cross lecture. Waiting out the agony, with every breath, with every sigh. Waiting.

She got up and paced the room, wringing her hands. "Well, what can I do? Can I do something? Can I go somewhere?" she asked, holding back tears.

"No, we can only wait," Rudakov said. "But in the meantime, dear, we have to get you out of Vladivostok, and quickly."

Lily looked at him in disbelief. How could she leave before Sergei returned? That was impossible. She would need to nurse him when he came back, he would need care. No, it was out of the question. Rudakov sat with her hour after hour, with the patience of a true uncle, explaining that the war was getting out of hand, that he might be reassigned any day, that the city might be invaded by enemy troops, and what a horrific situation for civilians that would be. The more she waited, the harder it would be to find safe means of transportation. It would be better to wait for Sergei in Petersburg, where he'd be finally sent once repatriated or exchanged. "If not for yourself," Rudakov kept saying, "you need to do it for your child."

It was already evening when he left. Lily crept onto her bed, pressing Sergei's letter to her breast, and fell into a slumber. She didn't know how long she slept before Masha came in and shook her. "Mistress, he's back at the house."

"Who?"

"Kalinov," Masha said, and Lily felt her trembling.

"And where are the soldiers?" Lily asked.

"They left with the general to fetch us supplies from the customhouse, but they're still not returned," Masha said.

"Ask Kalinov to come back tomorrow morning."

"He won't leave, mistress, we tried everything."

"Is he alone?"

"I don't know, mistress. I'm very afraid," Masha said, bursting into tears.

Lily got up, took a few moments to calm Masha down and to smooth her own hair and dress, and went out into the hall. Ho Li stood there in his apron, with a rolling pin in his hand.

Kalinov took off his hat. "Madam, I'm so sorry for your loss."

"What loss, sir? My husband has only been taken prisoner."

"You haven't heard? No, of course you haven't, it's not official information yet, but word sometimes travels faster through our networks." He lowered his eyes as if in grief. "He died a few hours after he was captured. He had a bad shell wound in the stomach. I am sorry to be the one who bears such news."

Behind her Masha burst into sobs, but Lily stood speechless, stunned.

"I'm here to extend my sympathies, and also offer my services. As you know, Sergei Nikolayevich and I were close collaborators, and I would be honored to help you with anything—"

"Leave my house immediately, sir, and do not return. I shall go to the authorities if I need to," Lily said, pounding with sudden rage. But Kalinov only offered an awkward smile, and didn't move.

A second later, the door opened and Rudakov walked in with one of the soldiers. He took in the scene with an alarmed and somber look; then he turned to Kalinov. "What are you doing here, sir? You have no business coming here at this time."

Kalinov nodded curtly, first to him and then to Lily. "General. Madam, I'll be on my way," he said, and turned and left the house.

Rudakov walked up to Lily and embraced her. "Dearest, I'm so, so sorry. I just got the cable. I was hoping to be the one to reach you first."

Lily stood numbly in his arms for a while, then stepped back and dropped into the nearest chair. Wild despair pumped into her. She hadn't needed Rudakov's corroboration to believe Kalinov's words. The moment he'd mentioned Sergei's death, she knew it was true. She had felt it in every pulse of blood pummeling inside her veins. She had maybe felt it earlier through her own tremor as she read his letter. She had seen it in Sergei's eyes as she looked into them one last time, on his lips as he kissed Olga, in his smile as he ducked to step into the carriage and waved good-bye. Maybe she had known all along how short his life would be, how the gods had marked him as one who'd die young, a brash and beautiful creature to be squashed in the prime of manhood. And maybe her hatred of Kalinov was rooted in the fact that all along she had recognized him as the grim messenger who would one day bring news of death to her door.

She sat in the drawing room for an indistinct amount of time.

Rudakov sat across from her in silent sorrow. Masha sobbed by her side holding her hand, and Ho Li stood, with eyes lowered, leaning against the door. At one point, Olga began to cry in the nursery and Masha got up, wiped the tears from her face, and went to get her. As soon as she saw her mother, the baby girl cried out running toward her, and climbed onto her lap, yawning and rubbing her eyes. Lily wrapped her arms around her and pressed her against her bosom.

"Let's all go to bed," she said, looking at Masha and Ho Li. "Tomorrow we shall get up early and start packing. We are leaving Vladivostok."

CHAPTER 28

The storm that started the morning they left Vladivostok followed them for five days until they arrived at Chità. It raged outside, as the train wormed its way through a landscape enshrouded in frost, with gusts of wind swooping down, rattling couplers and links, whistling between the wheels of carriages and whipping windowpanes with sheets of snow. Most of the time, Lily lay against the pile of fur rugs on her bunk with eyes closed and mind plunged into a drab slumber. Sometimes the blizzard slowed to a lull and the chugging of the train pushing laboredly ahead would arouse her from her torpor. Then she would look around and take stock of her surroundings, the awkward compartment with boxes and wooden crates to the side, Masha and Olga playing quietly at one end, Ho Li by the stove, heating water for the samovar. She'd remember where she was, and why, and close her eyes again. Sometimes the train would stop at a small station, and she would peer out of the window at the frozen station building, icicles hanging from its eaves against the twilight, and glimpse figures, batteries of soldiers gliding over the platform in some coordinated activity, like schools of dark fish inside an opaque tank, drowned in sleet. Other times, the platforms would be empty and silent, with only the stationmaster or an engineer pacing about, wrapped in long, heavy coats half-covered in snow, with beards and whiskers frozen under clouds of steam billowing from their mouths.

It was boiling hot inside the compartment. The only way to procure a private carriage for her and her party had required she agree to occupy one of the luggage cars that Captain Davidov, into whose care she'd been entrusted to by Rudakov, had accommodated as best he could. A wood stove, too large for the space, had been installed at one end and needed to be fed timber constantly, and the heat it radiated was impossible to regulate. The beds had been improvised on large shelves originally suited for storage of large crates, scrubbed down and covered with straw mattresses and abundant blankets and rugs. A few chairs and a little table had also been brought in and set around the stove. It was all awfully uncomfortable, despite the good captain's industrious efforts. But Lily didn't care. She spent most of the time collapsed in her bunk. A monstrous fatigue had overtaken her and she could hardly shake herself out of her lethargy. Sometimes, Olga's cries would wake her and she would open her eyes and watch Masha's and Ho Li's excruciating efforts to keep the child distracted and away from her, so she could rest. Other times, the only way to keep the child from crying would be to take her to her mother, and then Lily would wrap her in her arms and hold her close until they both fell asleep. On the whole, though, Olga was quite accommodating. She spent hours playing, in content, bright moods, and enjoyed the visits of the soldiers who brought food, and timber for the stove.

The train carried soldiers and military supplies that were being sent down to Manchuria through Chità. It was the last train that would travel from Vladivostok toward the west for many weeks to come. There were only a handful of nonmilitary passengers cooped up in two compartments; no amount of ready money could buy a decent seat at this time. The Trans-Siberian line was now dedicated to supply the war and ran mainly eastward. "When you get to Irkutsk, dear," Rudakov had told her, "you'll need to find a hotel and wait for a train that travels in the direction of Moscow. They might still be running the express westward." Irkutsk was where her banker would also be placing additional money for her, since the Vladivostok branch had been emptied out of cash and very little had been available for withdrawal. The larger part of her funds would be waiting for her in St. Petersburg. Of course, traveling by liner, which would have been her first choice, was ruled out because of the war.

As the claustrophobic days inside the train compartment crawled by, Lily sometimes wondered if she shouldn't have stayed for a few more weeks in Vladivostok to grieve Sergei inside the house, close to the objects that had been his, his clothes, his books, the blotting paper on his desk. The textures he had been in contact with and that still retained imprints of his hands, even faint echoes of his voice. The spaces that elicited memories: little scenes; sweet, or even bitter, moments; things that had been said. Instead, she had gone out into the void like a madwoman, blown away by the blast of that brutal trumpet that had announced his death, scattered like a panicked flock of birds shocked by an explosion, crazed against the cruel culling of an absurd universe. Her flight had untethered her, had stretched her far out into space, anesthetizing her at first, but later deepening her pain. She had nothing to hold on to now. She throbbed with unbearable emptiness. She was unbound, free to dissolve into the night, or into the freezing day, with its thick, gray, deadened sky. But that wasn't quite so. She had Olga, and Masha, and their lives and well-being depended on how fast she could get back her grit. Every time she realized this, she just closed her eyes again and turned in her bunk.

One night she woke up as she felt the train come to a stop. She looked around and saw Masha asleep with Olga in her arms, and Ho Li lying on his top bunk facing the wall. She sat up, her lungs dry and taut from the suffocating heat. She reached for her coat and her mink hat, put on her boots, and bundled up. She walked out into the narrow corridor and opened the door. The driving snow and wind rushed to meet her and their chill pierced her like needles to the bone. She stepped down onto the platform and stood under the whirling snow, gulping in the freezing air as if she had never breathed before. Around her the snowdrift had piled up against the head house, its entrance door, over the sides and up to the roof. With every swooping gust, the top layers blew up into clouds of white dust that flurried around, frenzied, until they disappeared again into the icy night. She felt the frost biting at her cheeks, burning her nose and lips, stinging the rims of her eyes. But she couldn't stop watching the storm. It seemed magnificent now, a savage symphony; a great, orchestral painting of the world with rushing, shifting strokes of freezing white. It was as beautiful as it was merciless; as brutal as it was kind. Kind to the earth in the upcoming spring and kind to her, for there was nothing she wanted more than to be frozen and numb.

Ahead, the blurred figure of a man in a military overcoat stood under the flickering light of a lamppost, and for a moment Lily's heart stopped. The tall, slim body, the pale face looking askance, the way he held a gloved hand against the collar of his coat. She thought she would faint. He walked toward her and bowed slowly, lifting his hand to his cap. "Madam, is there anything you need? Can I be of service?" His countenance sharpened into focus and she recognized Captain Davidov's attendant, a young, handsome officer with cheeky, twinkling eyes and a silky moustache, who'd been many times in her compartment to deliver supplies. But she could say nothing, and just stood scrutinizing his features with unblinking eyes, as if they might be hiding those of another, those of the man she'd just seen behind the curtain of snow. The officer smiled. "I have hot tea and a little vodka in my compartment. Would you allow me to indulge you? It's so cold tonight." Still she said nothing, and he took her by the arm. She followed him in a trance, watching the steam streaming from his mouth as he whispered something reassuring she didn't fully understand. They walked down the line of cars while the train whistle went off and the engine puffed anew. He stepped up to one of the carriages, and as he turned to offer Lily a hand, she caught his gleeful, greedy glance.

What am I doing, she thought, and then said aloud, "My daughter needs me, I must go back," and she rushed down the platform to her compartment. As she stepped inside, the train lurched into motion and chugged away from the station, and she stood behind the door window looking toward the vanishing spot under the lamppost where she had seen Sergei. For the first time since the news of his death, she wept.

In Chità, Ho Li left the train to continue his journey south toward Mudanjiang, in China. Lily offered to pay his train ticket all the way there on the Trans-Manchurian line, but Ho Li declined, saying that it was safer on the roads for someone like him. Lily gave him the money anyway. "Remember, mistress, when one door closes, another opens," he said as they bid farewell. It was sad to see him leave the station, carrying the bundle holding his belongings tied to a long stick over his shoulder, and gazing back at them one last time with his serious eyes.

The storm dwindled and the train rolled through the white, silent plains of the Mongolian steppe, now glittering under the sun. For miles on end, they ran along the valley of the Selenge River, its bed a ribbon of ice reflecting the clear sky above. Now and then they passed a small village, a grove of pine trees, a lone log house, all topped with smooth, hanging canopies of snow, like toy figures breaking up the monotony of the immensity surrounding them. A landscape of wild solitude, Lily thought; so different from her recollections of endless, sweeping fields with tall grass under the warm spring winds. How could the world turn so quickly?

They arrived at Ulan-Ude in the late afternoon, and the platform outside her window filled with the bustle of soldiers and officers unloading the train. Captain Davidov came into their compartment. He looked flustered. "Madam, I have bad news. The train will only be able to carry you until Mysovaya, some hundred miles from here. All the cars have been reassigned to transport military cargo by orders from Moscow, and they will be turning back at that point. I myself have been ordered to travel back to Chità immediately. I'm so sorry, it's all beyond my control."

Lily sat up. "What should I do then?"

The captain dropped his eyes. "I think the best plan would be to stay on the train until the last possible stop, Mysovaya, by the lake. From there you could take a direct route by sleigh up to Irkutsk through Baikal."

"By sleigh!" Lily said in disbelief. "But Captain, with a child, with all our luggage? There must be some other way."

"No, madam, sleigh is the only way in the winter." He looked around uneasily. "I will assign two soldiers to travel with you all the way to Irkutsk, if you can pay for their transportation and other expenses privately. In the meantime, I will write to the stationmaster in Mysovaya, asking him to find you lodgings until you find transport," Davidov said. "It will all be very basic, madam. Mysovaya is a tiny post."

"As long as it's safe," Lily said.

When they reached Mysovaya, she was shocked to find it was only a short platform with no more than a log cabin for a station building. The two soldiers unloaded her luggage onto the platform and stood by, waiting for her orders. She walked into the log cabin and asked for Fyodor Chernikovich, the stationmaster. She was shown into a small room hectic with papers and volumes of registers, collections of lanterns and a row of filthy overgarments hanging from pegs on the wall. On a high stool behind a desk sat Fyodor Chernikovich, peering at her with small, piggish eyes over round spectacles. Lily introduced herself and explained the situation, while the stationmaster eyed her with suspicion. He asked for her papers and studied them. No, he hadn't received a cable from Captain Davidov. Yes, it would be impossible to obtain any transport to cross the lake. Every horse and carriage had been requisitioned for the war. Additionally, there was no place to stay in Mysovaya. Hotels didn't exist and everything else was taken up by troops. "There are less than twenty houses in this place, madam. I recommend you return to Ulan-Ude," he said and buried himself back into his papers.

Lily sighed with frustration. Through the window she saw that the train compartment she had occupied had already been emptied of the furnishings that had been provided for her journey, and was being loaded instead with heavy crates. She opened her purse and took out a wad of rubles. "I am prepared to pay handsomely for any room," she said, placing the money on the table.

Fyodor Chernikovich met her eyes. "I'll see what I can do," he said, grabbing the money and putting it in one of the desk drawers.

She waited with Masha and Olga for what seemed like hours in a small, bare room outside the stationmaster's office with two benches, and soldiers, officers, and station staff regularly walking past them. They sat by the small wood stove and ate the last of their food. Olga ran around until she finally collapsed on one of the benches and went to sleep. At one point, a Cossack officer wearing a tall black sheepskin hat and dressed in a long coat belted at the waist with a long saber hanging by his side came in and ordered the two soldiers who were standing by Lily to follow him. Lily tried to explain they were escorting her. "There's a war, in case you didn't know," he barked. "We need every single man." Without further ceremony, he marched them away.

Lily stormed into Chernikovich's office. "You promised me a room," she said, flashing with anger, while the stationmaster recoiled behind his desk.

Half an hour later a sleigh pulled by a horse stood on the road outside, while an old peasant with long, shaggy hair and a blighted eye loaded their bags onto the carriage.

They were taken to the house of Agafea Mikhailovna, the stationmaster's portly widowed sister, who had the same small, greedy eyes as he. They shined as they examined Lily and Masha, their handsome sable coats, their four pieces of luggage, and Olga's rosy face bundled up in Masha's arms. Agafea showed them into a grimy, rancid-smelling room with one bed, which shared a brick stove with the adjacent kitchen. Lily was exhausted and only wanted to lie down, but they had to sit in the kitchen while Agafea gave them soup and black bread, and talked endlessly about the calamities of a woman like her, who grew up surrounded by the conveniences of a large town, being stuck in a godforsaken place like this.

Later, as they rose to go to their room, Agafea put a hand on Lily's shoulder and said, "Madam, I would like it if you paid me for two weeks in advance."

"But I don't intend to spend two weeks here. I shall be leaving tomorrow, or the day after at the latest," Lily said.

"I'm most certain you won't," Agafea said. "It's very difficult to get out of this place as it is, and now, with the war, just inconceivable. And I will need to stock up on food and timber for the stove."

Lily eyed her wearily, but decided not to argue. "Let's settle for three days in advance, shall we?" But Agafea demanded five, and quoted an outrageous amount. "All right," Lily sighed, taking the money out of her purse and putting it into Agafea's plump, avaricious hand.

The next day Lily returned to the station, but Chernikovich was away from his desk. After coming back three more times and not finding him, she realized the old knave was avoiding her. Then she went out and scoured the town for transport, going from door to door, asking if anyone knew of someone who would help her cross the lake. But she was met with leery, reticent faces assuring her there was no possible way. She returned to Agafea's and found Masha in tears. "Mistress, someone has gone through our bags. There are clothes missing, the silver icon you gave me, your silk shawls."

Agafea denied that anyone had been inside the room. "When girl servants cry big fat tears," she whispered into Lily's ear, "they're already confessing to their crimes." But she said nothing about her own sinister servant.

Days passed and Lily grew desperate as she began to realize that securing transport was proving to be as difficult as everybody had said. She considered returning to Vladivostok, but boarding any train from this spot was impossible, for the very few that stopped were full to the brim with equipment and provisions for the army. Besides, why return to the theater of war? She had to push forward. Every morning she went out and walked along the narrow path on the other side of the railroad, overlooking the frozen expanse of the lake. She waited for a westward train to stop, and then sought out every officer in command and pleaded for two seats, or just standing space. But no trains would take passengers at this point.

Still, she returned to the station every day, and after hours of waiting, after all her hopes had been spent, she walked toward the lake. Most days, a small market was set up along the roadside, consisting of a few stalls laid out with smoked fish, heads of cabbage, and loaves of black bread wrapped in pieces of cloth. Lily bought items from the stalls while asking the vendors if they knew of someone who would take her across. But no one did, and some of the friendlier ones cautioned her against crossing. It was still too cold and the winds swept fiercely over the ice, they said, too many people had frozen to death. "Wait for the spring, *matushka,* until everything thaws," they advised, and she saw pity or contempt in their eyes. Everyone in the town knew her by now. She was becoming a sort of beggar, a woman alone, unescorted, unprotected by a man, dragging herself around daily, pleading for a way out.

Thus her determination to leave only intensified. She couldn't stand Agafea, who kept filching their things, and who demanded more and more money each day, to the point where Lily's reserves were running dangerously low. She couldn't stand the stuffy, dirty house, which was never ventilated and always kept unbearably hot. Lily woke up many nights feeling suffocated; sometimes she coughed for long bouts, even waking Masha and Olga with her hacking. She had caught cold the night she stepped out on the platform in the middle of the storm. Since then she had developed a cough that had escalated by the time they arrived in Mysovaya. Now she always felt a stifling sensation in the lungs, and sometimes broke inexplicably into a sweat. She was losing weight every day and felt restless, despite her fatigue. She was hungry for cold air, for breathing outside. When she looked into the mirror she saw her cheeks unnaturally flushed below her sunken eyes.

All of these things reminded her of the time three years ago when she had been sick in St. Petersburg. She knew her health was wearing thinner every day. What would happen to Olga and Masha if she broke down in a place like this? The thought of Agafea's greasy fingers going through Olga's golden curls made her shudder to no end. She had to get to Petersburg as soon as possible, by any means.

Though freezing, the days had been dry with sunny skies, and as they trickled by, she became mesmerized by the lake. How could such beauty lie side by side with the row of ugly, dreary little wooden houses that formed the front of town? She stood by its edge, watching its immense, slippery surface stretch away from her, shimmering in the sunlight, pure and transparent like a freshly polished window. Rows of snow-capped mountains surrounded her. Along the water's frozen edges lay large slabs of blue ice like rock crystals, in strange, beautiful formations, as if sculptures from fairy-tale frosted lands. *Sokui* they called them, and they formed caves and grottoes where, as legend had it, the lake's spirits might abide. It was difficult to describe the color of its frozen waters, she thought as she ventured a hundred yards or so from the shore. Beneath her feet, the ice was as translucent as cut glass, deep blue and interspersed with countless air bubbles, celeste in color, turquoise, sparkling blue, or blindingly white. It was all inexplicably beautiful. It dazzled her mind and filled it with light, dispelling the darkness of her grief. This would be a perfect stage on which to end her life, she thought, just keep walking ahead and then lie over the ice. In the spring everything would thaw, and the lake would take her deep into its gut and never bring her up again. But she soon shook her head. How could she even wish for anything like that? Her life and efforts now belonged to Olga and Masha, to their well-being and their safety. She just had to find a way to reach the opposite bank.

She watched the sun drop quickly, while out of nowhere the wind picked up, drifting rushes of snow along the ice. They streamed around her legs and feet, a torrent of sibilant, hissing, glacial breath, and she hurried back to shore and the house, as the world around her drained fast of color and joy, and evaporated into a fierce, cold night.

One day she went to the market with Agafea, resolved to pay for her own food instead of giving her hostess inordinate amounts of money that always remained unaccounted for. They walked along the stalls and she noticed a group of three men at the end of the row squatting around a small fire. They wore thick fur hats and were dressed in heavy skin jackets with boots tied with strings around their calves. Knives hung from their belts. Four huge, wolfish-looking dogs sat on the snow beside them, panting. Around them lay an assortment of large fishing hooks and bundles of animal furs. The men's faces were dark and striking, with large noses and slanted eyes, as those she had seen in Mongolian people, but weather-beaten and ruddier. She thought she might have seen them the day before at some distance on the lake, throwing hooks and lines through a hole cut in the ice.

"Those are Buryat trappers," Agafea said. "They are savages. They live in the wild like animals, and they're thieves and murderers. Don't go close to them, don't even look in their direction."

Lily ignored her and walked up to them. Over a bed of splintered ice at their feet lay four omul fishes, much larger than what she had seen sold anywhere else and apparently freshly caught. She pointed at the largest one. "Omul?" One of the men nodded. He looked like the youngest of the three, maybe the son of the man sitting next to him, carving a thick stick with a knife. They had the same eyes; dark and piercing, but honest, she thought, as she gazed at them. The third man was also young. Maybe a family of a father with two sons? All three were sinewy and robust, and didn't seem to mind the cold. They were worlds apart from the people in the village who were mostly Russians who had migrated only a few years ago, after the establishment of the railway stop. Lily bought the fish and was surprised at the small price they quoted, though she knew that fresh fish was always cheaper for it would later need to be salted or smoked.

Back at the house, Lily asked Agafea's servant to make a soup with the fish while she sat thinking about the Buryat men. She remembered Annette Maekin telling her about the Buryat indigenous populations around Baikal, cattle breeders and hunters descended from the ancient, nomadic Kurykans, who bred perfect horses that had become the most prized in the Chinese emperor's court. She had liked these men. Though they lived in the wild, as Agafea had said, they appeared clean and tidy in their animal furs, and their eyes had looked straight into hers, without guile.

That afternoon she went to the stationhouse. Chernikovich was not in the office, and in his place sat the railway point man polishing an old oil lantern. He was an older man with piercing blue eyes and cropped gray hair by the name of Zubrzycki. She had spoken to him twice before, and he had been kind, offering her a little tea when she had come in shaking with cold. She knew he was a Polish nationalist who had been arrested and sentenced to Siberia, and was kept working in railway stations around the lake. He was a cultured, intelligent man; his years of forced labor were inscribed in his tight lips and in his worn-down, hardened face.

"What do you think about the Buryat trappers that are camping by the railway?" she asked him. "Do you think they could take me across?"

His eyes flashed at her, and in them she saw alarm mixed with glints of hope, and she knew that this idea had occurred to him before. "I suppose they could," he said, dropping his eyes. "They're probably the only people who know the lake, who could navigate the cracks."

"The cracks?" she asked.

"You've heard the lake cracking, haven't you?" he said.

She had. In the mornings when she stood looking out at the immensity of its ice, she wondered at the lines and streaks that showed beneath the crystal surface of the frozen lake, like veins traced by huge pencils from down below. They changed every day; rather, they increased in numbers, depth, and width. Sometimes they creaked and groaned, or screeched as if they were being splintered from deep down. Other times they thundered with loud, sharp claps. She had been told that this always happened in winter. The lake was abysmal and had powerful undercurrents agitating it from beneath. The cracking increased as the ice became thinner toward springtime; then, larger crevices began to open up, preparing the frozen body of the lake for the great thaw.

"Would you trust these men?" Lily asked.

"I'm not a good reference point," he said. "I'd take any risk if it were at all possible for me to leave this place. Your situation is different, with a child, and two women alone. I recommend you stay nearby until early summer and then seek transport by boat."

Lily ignored this last remark. "How long does it take to cross the lake on sleigh?"

Zubrzycki sighed. "Around twelve hours, if there are no complications."

"How much money do you think they'd ask for a journey like that?" She was aware she had very few rubles left, and that even if she were to extract her jewels from the hems of her dresses, where Masha had sewn them in Vladivostok before they left, there would be no place here to sell them for a decent price.

"That's one of the problems," Zubrzycki said. "They wouldn't want money. When they come to town, they only sell their wares until they gather enough to buy some tools, and then they leave. Money is of no use to them. I know this time they want a hunting rifle, but they've already traded enough fur to acquire it."

"Do you think they're honorable?" she asked looking him straight in the eye.

He took a moment to consider her question. "It's difficult to know. They've always been honorable in their transactions. If anything, it's the villagers who swindle them. They are simple people. I know they take wives and stick to their families, but beyond that . . ."

She thanked him and prepared to leave. Zubrzycki got up, too, and walked her to the door. "I admire your courage, madam, but please be very careful."

Lily rushed back to the house where Masha and Olga were eating the fish soup in the kitchen with Agafea, who was bragging and telling all sorts of preposterous lies about her sophisticated past life in Novosibirsk. In the bedroom, Lily rummaged through the only bag still under lock and key, until she found the pouch that held the small collection of Sergei's belongings she had brought with her: his military medals from the academy, his gold cufflinks, the bowtie he had worn at their Christmas party, a ringlet of hair she had cut off one night. Oh, why hadn't she taken more of his things, she thought, as tears blinded her and she began to cough. These felt so small, so few. It took her a moment to steady herself, and then she went again into the bag and extracted the object she sought.

Sergei's compass.

She opened the latch to the small brass case and looked into its round face, engraved with the compass rose, over which the needle quivered pointing north. What an exquisite piece it was. The ornate symbols of the rose, the fine craftsmanship of the needle mounted on its ruby-jeweled bearing. This had been Sergei's most important treasure as a child, a unique heirloom, handed down to him by his father. It had his grandfather's name engraved on the lid, Aleksey Alexandrovich Latvin, the man who had purportedly carried it for years in his explorations of the north Urals and the Arctic Ocean coast. It had been the only personal item Sergei had brought with him to Vladivostok. How it hurt to let it go. What a betrayal it felt. And yet she knew that of all her possessions, this was the only one that might have any value in the eyes of the Buryat.

The next day she returned to the market, taking Olga with her and leaving Masha behind. The Buryat were still at their usual spot, but they seemed not be selling fish anymore. Instead, they had bundles of gear around them, as if preparing to leave. "No more omul?" Lily asked. The two younger men turned eyes to her, and then to the older man. He nodded and the youngest of them dug into one of their bags and brought out a fish. She paid for it, and then asked, "What is your name?"

He looked at her with some surprise, and then said, "Yuri."

"Is this your brother?" Lily asked, pointing at the other young man. When Yuri nodded, she asked for his name. "Borya," Yuri said.

"Yuri and Borya," Olga echoed. "Borya and Yuri," she repeated again, pointing at them with a sweet little laugh. Yuri smiled.

"And I take it this is your father?" Lily asked. Yuri nodded. "All right, Yuri. I have something to ask the three of you. I'm looking to cross the lake towards Listvyanka. Could you take me? I would pay you well."

Yuri looked at his brother, then at his father, and whispered some words in a language she had never heard. The older man shook his head. "We need to go back north. Listvyanka is not on our way," Yuri said.

"My husband died in the war," Lily said. "I'm alone with my daughter and my nurse. I need to get back to my family. I need to get to Irkutsk. Please."

Yuri translated again, but the older man remained unmoved.

Lily put Olga down, opened her purse, and pulled out a wad of rubles. "I can give you money now and I have more in Irkutsk. You could buy many tools there, rifles," she said, and her voice quivered, fearing they would never be convinced, while Olga clung to the skirts of her coat, her little body shaking with cold. But Borya perked up with interest at the idea of buying tools in Irkutsk.

Lily took the compass out of her bag and offered it to him. "This was my husband's. I can give it as part of the payment." The two young men took the compass and examined it admiringly. Then they showed it to their father, who for the first time looked up at her, and then down at the compass. The three of them conferred. Lily took Olga's hand and paced back and forth with her to dispel the cold. The sons seemed to be more positive about the project than their father, though the old man hadn't let the compass out of his hand.

"Mummy, lake," Olga said, pointing ahead. "Lake," she said, and pulled away from her and ran toward the edge. Lily caught up with her and took her up in her arms. *Please, please,* Lily screamed inside her mind, casting desperate glances at the lake. *Help me. Help me out of this place.*

Finally, Yuri walked up to her. "There will be a storm tonight. It will only clear the night after. We will come for you then. We will bring two sleighs and more dogs. It is a long ride," he said, returning the compass.

"How much should I pay you?" Lily asked.

"The price of two rifles and the compass," he said.

"Where shall I meet you?" Lily asked.

"We know where you stay. We shall come for you before the sun comes up."

Lily nearly burst into tears as she thanked him. "What is your father's name?" she asked.

"Dersu," he said, and Lily walked toward the older man and put the compass in his hand. "Thank you, Dersu."

That night the whole of Agafea's house was up in arms. "This is madness!" Agafea screamed. "How can you think you'll survive?" Masha sobbed sitting on the bed while Olga whimpered in sympathy by her side. Agafea's servant watched trembling from the door.

"But it's been done many times before, hasn't it?" Lily said. "Only a few years ago, before the railway, that's how people crossed. This is something that must have been done millions of times."

"I don't think so," Agafea said. "In any case, not in the company of savages—those men will rob you, abandon you, even kill you. They will, oh, I daren't even say the word!" She buried her face in her hands. Lily grew impatient while Agafea emitted fake little sobs. After wiping her eyes and nose with the back of her hand, she looked up. "As for exchanging my coat for yours, madam, no, I shall not. I won't do anything that helps you go to your death."

Lily had proposed to exchange her and Masha's beautiful, expensive sable coats for Agafea's fur cloaks, two awful, stinky pieces of thick hide lined with what looked like the back of an unshorn, matted sheep. But Lily knew the sheer weight of these pieces would do much better against the wind. She removed a small garnet ring from the middle finger of her left hand. "Agafea Mikhailovna," she said, sitting beside her, "I don't want us to part as enemies. You have taken me into your house, after all. I propose to give you this ring in addition to the coats. What do you say?" Agafea's mood changed instantly. She took the ring and tried to fit it over her fat little finger. After a few more hefty gifts, she agreed to help them with their departure.

When Lily and Masha were left alone, Lily put her arms around her. "Do you still trust me, Masha?" she asked. The girl nodded through her tears. "I promise you, we shall soon be safely back in Petersburg," Lily said, and kissed her on the cheek.

They settled down to sleep, though Lily lay awake for hours listening to the wolves howling outside.

At midnight on the second day, the snowstorm abated, and a few hours later, near four in the morning, the Buryat men came to fetch them. They heard the dogs barking outside and they knew the sleighs were ready.

Agafea saw them to the door with an oil lantern and bid them good-bye. "Madam, I so wanted you to stay, but now that you must leave, I wish you luck."

Yuri and Borya took their luggage and set it upon one of the sleighs with their own gear, tying it with ropes. Then they walked Lily and Masha to the second sleigh, a wider, canoe-shaped luge, where they had them sit side by side with Olga in their arms. They bundled them all together with large skins, and then with pieces of felt on top, until they were swaddled like multiple-fold babies on the sled.

The dogs whelped and barked anew as they pulled the sleighs over the snow. Yuri and Bora rode standing on the back of each sleigh, while Dersu ran along for a while, mushing the dogs with hoarse, guttural cries before jumping on beside the luggage. They rode through the snow between the dingy little houses, and when they reached the frozen expanse of the lake, the dogs broke into a full canter with the sleighs slithering behind.

Lily held her breath. The lake was like a silver cloth under the brilliant moon that still shone above. The silence, save for the muffled clatter of the dogs' feet and the swishing sound of the sleighs, was immense. As she looked up at the scintillating pattern of stars scattered across the night sky, she thought about Sergei's compass, about its round brass body now carefully tucked somewhere inside Dersu's hide coat; about how painful it had been to relinquish it. It had felt like a small act of amputation, as if she were shedding yet another piece of Sergei. But in the end, how much freedom it had bought her; it had been the sacrificial token required by the spirits of the lake to give passage through its gates.

A rim of flaming crimson appeared over the horizon and bled slowly into the sky, as the ice below became illumined with pink-orange light. Lily turned to Masha's round, wondrous eyes. "Oh, mistress, I never saw anything so beautiful in my life," she said. Lily smiled to see her contented at last. Everything would be all right now. They would survive the journey, they would make it across the lake to Irkutsk; from there they would find a direct way to Moscow and Petersburg; they would finally arrive at Tatyana's door, who, upon opening up, would recognize Sergei's eyes in Olga's, and would be filled with emotion. All of this she could feel in her bones.

Beyond that, she knew nothing else.

St. Petersburg, May 28th, 1904

My dearest Brother and Sister,

You will think I have just forgotten you, but you need to forgive me, for after the long journey from Vladivostok, I have been very ill in bed for two months. I don't know if you received any of my recent letters, but I will tell you, loves, that my husband died in the war. I am living quite alone now in Petersburg, save for my baby and a few servants. I feel very lonely without Sergei, and I am so sick I can't do anything.

Leaving Vladivostok in the middle of the war was dreadful. Firstly, I had to throw my house up in twenty-four hours. I left all my belongings back there as I could hardly bring a thing. Traveling twenty-seven days with a little baby—you may imagine what it must have been. I was so drained that as soon as I arrived in Petersburg, I fell sick. Indeed, up till today I feel very ill. I don't have any friends left here. My only English friend, Mr. Shuttleworth, has returned to England after his wife's death. Even Ruby is living in Moscow now. Of course, there's Sergei's family, and they are trying to be kind, although they never approved of my relation with him.

I am going to one of the best doctors here. He tells me I must be very quiet, that I must drink plenty of milk, but none of that helps me whatsoever. Yesterday, the doctor told me I must go to a sanatorium high up in the mountains in Switzerland or Germany. But I don't feel well enough to take the trip. Another doctor wants to admit me into a clinic close to St. Petersburg, but then I would not have Olga with me. Hopefully, it will not come to that.

As soon as I feel better, I shall travel back to Manchester to see you both. So much time has passed since we parted; the thought of it breaks my heart. Please write by return of post.

With fondest love and kisses from your little sister,
Lily

CHAPTER 29

The Zelenogorsk Sanatorium was situated in the outskirts of the town by the same name, on the shore of the Gulf of Finland some thirty miles northwest by rail from St. Petersburg. The town was a popular summer resort for the city's upper class; it was also home to a few rest homes for the rich, of which the sanatorium was the most renowned for the treatment of tuberculosis. It was most difficult to be admitted into its halls, requiring the highest influential contacts, and Tatyana had pulled such influences to have Lily checked in. Meanwhile, she took charge of baby Olga, a task she couldn't be happier to fulfill.

The sanatorium was an imposing gray limestone building, a central square structure surrounded by four tall octagonal turrets. These so-called wings served to compartmentalize the different types of patients by gender, degree of the advancement of their disease, and even by financial gradients within an already affluent social class. The halls and corridors inside were bare and impersonal, though the dining room sported beautiful arched windows overlooking a garden, and there was a small conservatory in the back filled with plants. There was also a library, though the books were mostly boring romance novels and cheap travel logs.

It was already the end of summer, and every morning Lily lay in the West Wing sun gallery with other female patients, all in a row of beds lined up toward the large open windows flanking the corridor-like room. The emphasis of the cure was rest in the open air for a large part of the day. Every patient reclined in her bed tucked under thick linen sheets and white cotton blankets; some read, some dozed, some stared around in gloomy dread. Today, a dazzling morning light streamed through the windows warming the foot of Lily's bed. She lay with closed eyes listening to the nurse's footsteps as she walked away.

"Have you ever seen those engravings of bee larvae lying side by side in their little cells?" she heard a heavily accented voice whisper beside her in French. "That's exactly what we look like in this silly row of beds." She opened her eyes and saw her right-hand neighbor stretching her neck in her direction, mouth twisted into a little grin. She recognized Theresa de Guimaraes, the Portuguese lady married to a German Russian tea merchant of Petersburg, who had recently been admitted to the sanatorium and placed in the room next to hers.

A nurse shot them a look from the opposite side of the gallery, putting a stern finger to her lips. Theresa lifted an eyebrow and lowered her head back onto her pillow. Lily knew she would wait for the nurse to turn away before trying to strike a conversation again. She was a strongly opinionated woman, a rebel, who disapproved of the sanatorium and its mores, and was always in search of an ear for her trenchant remarks. Lily admired her antagonistic zeal, for she had long ago ceased to censure or even resist.

There were many rules in the Zelenogorsk Sanatorium, and many had to do with silence and secrecy. Talking was not allowed during cures, and animated discussions were discouraged during meals; conversations that dealt with information about one's symptoms or anyone else's state of health were proscribed, and any signs of grieving for other patients' decline or eventual death severely frowned upon. "None of that sort of thing is conducive to recovery," the head matron kept reminding them at any possible occasion. "Dwelling needlessly in grief negatively affects the lungs."

Under such a restrictive atmosphere communication between "guests," as they were called, was conducted in subtler ways. Whole sign languages were encrypted in pining, languid glances, in long, charged silences, or on torpid, lethargic body gestures. If one took the time to observe, there were constant messages of gloom emitted by the figures spiritlessly recumbent over garden rattan chairs, by cadaverous-looking ladies drooping on sofas in the conservatory, or by the irrepressible, quiet sobs of pale young girls during the occasional evening piano concertos. There was also the battery of plethoric, breathless, red-faced men, always intent on recounting fantastic plans for their future lives, smoke-screen chatter to hide their anguish at lost years in sanatoriums and rest houses. Variations of the same silent themes lay behind every poised expression: desperation, hopelessness, and terror of impending death.

"The fact that after accepting the intake application, the nurse asks for advance payment not just to cover your time in the sanatorium, but also for a return ticket home. Doesn't that tell you what they expect of us all?" Theresa de Guimaraes whispered again. "They want to have the ticket to send us home when there's no more hope. Or realistically, to use it to transport our corpse."

This time Lily couldn't suppress a little laugh. "It's true," Theresa said. "Only yesterday, I saw them carry out two gurneys in the middle of the night. But no one ever says anything. Everyone is crazy here. You are the only person who's still sound in the head and not already dead," she added, looking scornfully around while knitting her dark, bushy brow.

Oh, Lily thought, *if you only knew*.

Theresa cocked her head and pulled a smirk, waiting for the tall, lanky nurse to disappear behind the door. "I'm so glad to have you as a friend," she said, giving her puppy eyes and wrinkling her long Roman nose. "I'd be desperate in a place like this if you weren't around."

Lily gave her one of her sweet, calculated smiles. She wasn't in the mood for camaraderie, but she knew Theresa was scheduled to undergo a surgical pneumothorax the day after next, a procedure where they would puncture and collapse her right lung, to allow it to rest while it healed. "Collapse a lung?" Theresa had sneered at first. "Do they suppose lungs are obedient little children who go to sleep when they are told, and then wake up refreshed?" But behind her sarcasm, Lily felt her terrible dread. Fear was what everyone shared in this place. Fear and despair.

Lily had been at the sanatorium for nearly a year and was considered, if not a veteran, a seasoned guest within its ranks. It had taken all this time to stabilize her condition, which didn't mean she was cured; just temporarily recovered from the dire state in which she had arrived. She had landed in Petersburg quite ill. The first night at Tatyana's house, she awoke coughing up blood. From there on she had only declined. Doctors had come and gone, diagnosing bronchitis, bronchial influenza, pneumonia, and finally tuberculosis.

Upon admittance into the Zelenogorsk Sanatorium, she had spent the first two months in the Gedroitz Pavillion of the East Wing, where a number of single rooms close to the infirmary were kept for critical cases. She had vague remembrances of those weeks. The room was covered in tiles and slabs of drab-looking marble for easier disinfection. Doctors and sanatorium personnel attending her always wore masks. She remembered drifting in and out of feverish states of consciousness; she recalled the exhausting bouts of sweating, endless coughing, and the porcelain bowls for sputum kept by the bed. She remembered a distinct sound threading through her febrile reveries, a drop of water falling on a metal surface from high above: *plip, plip, plop, plip, plip, plop, plop.* It was incomprehensible, since she had never been able to find a leak or a faulty faucet in the room, but every time her temperature went up and she drifted into a dream state, the phantom sound returned.

Scenes of her recent life tossed and churned inside her mind during those long, delirious episodes. Dark, sleepless nights gliding around the Vladivostok house waiting for Sergei, spades thudding and clumping into the frozen ground while she waited by the secrets-filled metal box, Sergei's farewell love letter covered in soot and dried blood. Images of flight from the war, protracted train rides in stuffy carriages, imploring negotiations for transport, and then sliding through the iced Baikal, numbing, silent, gifted moments of suspended beauty before resuming the grueling, breathless race toward Petersburg, toward the final moment where she pounded on Tatyana's door with her fists in the middle of the night.

Images encoded with her grief had played themselves over and over behind closed eyes, as if they were being rung out of her inflamed mind by every flurry of assailing fever, by each episode of coughing that shredded her lungs in the night. Slowly, the images had faded, one by one, taking away with them a part of her spirit, of her zest for life.

She finally recovered enough strength to be moved to the West Wing, where the patients who didn't require round-the-clock care were housed and supervised in daily cures of rest and the overeating of rich foods. Her health further improved since the arrival of Dr. Schiller, a young German physician who used a medicine called homeopathy, of which she had never heard before. He treated her with little white pills in vials labeled FERRUM METALLICUM, STANNUM, PULSATILLA PRAETENSIS, TUBERCULINUM, and so on. And now, a few months later, she found herself past the infectious stage of the disease.

"I'm certain you'll recover, Madam Throop," Dr. Schiller had said, "but you have a family tubercular constitution and your lungs are already scarred. You will need to take extreme care of your health if you don't want to relapse." He was a thin young man with woolly red hair and a reddish beard and moustache. He wore gold-rimmed spectacles and looked at her with small, pointed blue eyes from behind the desk. She knew he was partial to her, for he spent much more time in her consultations than the stipulated fifteen minutes he gave to everyone else.

"Tuberculosis," he liked to say, "is an interesting disease. It's our mal du siècle, the evil of our times, agitated times of great change. It's also the disease of the romantic, of the highly sensitive—and you being an actress—"

"It's also the disease of the poor and the underfed, Doctor," Lily interrupted.

"That's true. It's rampant all around," he said with a sigh. "But you, madam, should stay away from excessive emotion, of any excitement of the senses, and just make sure you rest."

He was a bit annoying with his flights of fancy on romanticism and consumption, but he was an aspiring poet after all, and Lily was grateful to him for having allowed her to visit with Olga more frequently, and let her spend time with her child in the garden without a mask. The first few times she had seen Olga she had been obliged to wear a mask, and it was requested she avoid embracing or kissing the child, or even standing too near. Both she and Olga had cried as the little girl pulled at the piece of cloth, saying, "Mummy, take this off, I want to kiss you, I want to see your lips. Mummy!" She had made such a scene that it had been necessary to pull her away and the visit came to an abrupt end. Now, Lily was free to visit with her even at Tatyana's house, for everyone agreed that the sanatorium was not a commendable atmosphere for a little girl.

But with Lily's recovery had come another blow. She had been reported to the city's sanitary authorities as a foreigner infected with tuberculosis, and a decision to deport her back to England had been made. It was a standard rule for any non-Russian diagnosed with an infectious disease. In vain, Tatyana and the rest of the Volkovs appealed to everyone they knew in positions of authority. The law was implacable. It had only been possible to obtain an extension of her departure date. Meanwhile, Lily would have to stay at the sanatorium accruing strength for the journey back home.

Herr Straff, the Volkov palace librarian she remembered from the past, had been commissioned by the family to act as a go-between with lawyers and immigration officials. He visited her in the sanatorium to inform her about the progress of the case. At first, she had been happy to see a familiar face, and he had greeted her warmly, but then he cleared his throat and adopted an aloof, professional stance. "I am very sorry to have to inform you that it will not be possible for you to travel with Olga Sergeevna," he said.

"But that is ridiculous. She's my daughter. Who's to say I may not travel with her?" Lily had said, flustered and on the verge of coughing again.

"Madam, she is your daughter indeed. But she is also a Russian citizen legally adopted by her deceased father, and in these situations the state takes over custody of the minor," Straff said.

"What does that mean?" Lily said with a gasp. "That she will be taken to an orphanage?"

"Thankfully, it will not come to that. Tatyana Mikhailovna is willing to adopt her as Sergei Nikolayevich's next of kin. As you know, she dearly loves the child and will provide for her generously."

"But isn't it true that if Tatyana doesn't adopt her, it will be easier for me to recover guardianship in the future?" Lily asked.

"That is correct," Straff said. "But in the meantime she would have to go to a state institution, and you would have to prove four years of uninterrupted, noncontagious health before initiating the process of recovering guardianship. It would never take less than five or six years in all. I believe the solution of having her adopted by her grandmother is best. But for Tatyana Mikhailovna to be able to take charge, you must agree. You must sign these preliminary forms so we can draw the final legal documents and avoid tutelage by the state," he explained, reaching into his leather case.

Lily sat back, feeling faint. "Not now, Herr Straff," she said. "I need to think this over. Please."

"Of course, madam, I understand," Straff said, dropping his eyes. "Shall I return tomorrow?" Lily didn't answer. They sat looking away from each other for a long moment. Then Straff reached again into his case and brought out a pile of books. "I thought you would like to read these, now that your Russian is so proficient and you have time on your hands." He spread them over the table and Lily's eye caught some of the names engraved on their covers: Chekhov, Nicolai Gogol, Alexander Ostrovsky, Alexander Sumarokov, and realized he had brought her a fine collection of Russian plays.

Tears rushed to her eyes. "Thank you, Herr Straff."

After this, Lily had lost all desire to get back her health. What was the point if she was going to be deported anyway and torn away from her child? She slumped into one of her numb, deadened states of mind. She wasn't interested in anyone or anything anymore. She just yearned to be back in her room, to abandon herself to her grief. To be forced out of the country, to be made to leave her child back, how monstrous could that be? Should she sign the papers allowing Tatyana to adopt Olga? Did she have any other choice? She couldn't allow her baby to be placed in a state institution, in a building even stricter, grayer, and grimmer than this. But to sign her over to someone else, even her father's next of kin? On the other hand, if she wasn't going to survive this illness, wouldn't Olga be better off with her Russian family, in a wealthy, doting atmosphere where she would be educated properly, where she would inherit her father's fortune and titles? Even in the unlikely event that she'd be allowed to take Olga with her to England, what would happen to the child if she died? To be left an orphan in a place like London, with no family, no one to take care of her interests. Lily still had the large sum of money that Sergei had put under her name, but money without a worthy guardian could not protect a child. Even if Harry and Alice adopted her in Manchester, how would she grow up in the midst of a hostile family who had shunned and felt ashamed of her mother; and how much would Harry, also quite sick most of the time, be able to safeguard her? Was it then fair to tear Olga away from her homeland?

The last time she had seen Olga had been at a gathering in the Volkov palace in St. Petersburg, where Olga's great-grandmother, Princess Anna Alexandrovna, had organized a tea party. A large part of the family was assembled there, and Olga was the sensational center of it all. Dressed in an exquisite sky-blue silk dress with a red sash and matching ribbons threaded through her long blond curls, she went around the room from lap to lap holding everyone enthralled. Even Kitty and Lena had traveled from Moscow for the event, without Ruby of course, and appeared to be totally charmed by her. The Volkov was an aging family with very few young children among its ranks, and Olga had been received as a sort of miracle. Every bit of adoration that had been dispensed to Sergei was now being lavished on Olga. Tatyana herself had been transformed by the child; she had shed her former scowl and replaced it with a beaming shine.

"I'm sorry for all your losses, Lily," Kitty had said quietly, as she sat next to her holding an exquisitely cut glass filled with port wine. "I don't blame you, like others in the family, for going along with Sergei's schemes instead of trying to put some sense into his head. But you cannot say I didn't try to warn you."

"I don't regret anything," Lily said, looking her in the eye. "I'd do it all over again, if you want to know. At the very least, it brought Olga into my life," she added, feeling with satisfaction how her proud words staved Kitty's heart. But she stopped short. She had meant every syllable, but was there any use in hurting Kitty now? All the woman had ever wanted was to be loved by Sergei; and if anyone understood that, it was Lily.

"*Maman, Maman*," Olga cried in French, running up and taking Lily's hand, "come see my nursery room." She had forgotten all her English and now spoke mostly French since Masha had been relegated to the kitchen in Tatyana's house and Olga had been placed in the hands of a proper French nanny. The princess had reopened the old nursery for her so that each time she came to visit she would have a place to play. It was a lovely, large blue room on the second floor, scattered with all sorts of toys, dollhouses, musical boxes, trains, a rocking horse, a little table set with a miniature tea service around which sat an assortment of teddies and dolls; an endless collection of trinkets and playthings as Lily had never seen. Olga opened an ornate toy chest and pulled out a fairy costume, a pirate's hat, a glittering tiara, and a wand, and laughing, started trying them all by turns. Lily stepped back and watched her. To think that Sergei had played with these things at one point, and all the happy days he must have spent with his cousins in this very spot. And now his daughter looked so joyful here, a little princess stepping into a little kingdom of her own.

That night, when Lily returned to the sanatorium, she was sadder than ever. Although the Volkovs had been civil to her, gracious even, she had felt a total stranger among them. Even if she recovered her health and was allowed to stay in Russia, she would never belong in their ranks. Everyone was waiting for her to disappear, so they could fully appropriate Olga and return to their placid, hollow lives. She turned in her bed and wept.

Days passed with these thoughts swirling around in Lily's mind, until her health began to decline, and doctors again became concerned. But they had no cure for her anguish, no means of slowing her descent into despair. She lay in her bed with eyes closed. Why had she rushed back to St. Petersburg just to end captive in a sanatorium that was no better than a plush prison, with a life-long death sentence hanging over her head? Why not have tarried along the way?

Memories of crossing Lake Baikal with the Buryat returned to her mind, visions of dazzling ice and the silence of immense landscapes that had filled her soul with awe. A part of her dreamed she could have stayed with the Buryat, lived with them in their yurts in the wilderness, cooked for them, helped them skin their catch; away from civilization, far from prejudices and twisted judgments, from the corruption of the white man. Olga could have run around in the snow with the dogs and the sleighs, happy and free. But why would the Buryats have accepted her and her child? What value could there be in taking in a "civilized" woman into the wild? Unskilled, delicate, unequipped for life without comforts, resistant to adapt. Not that the two brothers hadn't liked her and Masha. They had, and had been attentive around them, courteous and sweet. *Razbitym glaza*, broken eyes, sad eyes, they had called her, and respected her grief.

How clean and beautifully simple their life had felt to her. To live in harmony with nature, adapted to cold or to heat, enmeshed with plants and animals, following up on each day as if it were their last. How different and complicated was this so-called civilization by contrast; the laws, the lies, the politics, the greed, the deceit. What a waste everything seemed to her, and how she yearned to leave it all behind. Yet the mere thought of Olga still pulled at her with irresistible urgency, like a tenacious rope tethered to a kite refusing to let it sail away, an obstinate tugboat determined to take her to shore. How could she leave Russia without her, relinquish her lovely, smiling face, and her beautiful pale gray eyes that were so much like Sergei's? It would be easier to walk out of the sanatorium one day and find a secluded spot along the coast in which to die. At least her bones would rest close to the little one she loved.

CHAPTER 30

There was a knock at the door. "Madam, there's a gentleman to see you. He's waiting in the visitors' lounge."

Lily perked up. A gentleman? Straff again? Someone from the British Embassy? One of the sinister clerks from the Ministry of Health? She dragged herself to the door, opened it, and said to the young nursing assistant standing there, "Please, ask them to leave a card. I am too fatigued to receive anyone now."

"Madam, the gentleman doesn't speak Russian," the girl said, avoiding her eyes. Well, that eliminated Straff, ghastly clerks, and embassy minions; in fact, every other man she knew in Petersburg. Who could it be? But then, this poor, sweet girl was so simple she surely must have missed something.

"I shall be down in a few minutes," Lily said, closing the door. She sat down to comb her hair in front of the boudoir's small looking glass. Gaunt eyes stared back at her, glistening with a melancholy, feverish glow; her face looked thin, her cheeks hollowed and unnaturally blushed, a mirror of her drawn-out exhaustion, of her defeat. She got up and changed into her best dress. She had a hunch that this encounter might have the weight of a twist of fate, and she was going to face it at her finest, like a queen sentenced to death.

In the visitors' lounge, a man stood looking out the window with his back to her. She froze at the door, studying the trim figure and determined stance with legs slightly apart, the black hair combed back. He turned around.

"Chut!" she said, her heart pounding against her ribs. "I don't believe this! What on earth are you doing here?" She rushed to him, scanning him with greedy eyes, as if to make sure he was not a phantom but a true person of flesh and blood.

"I—" Chut began, and broke into a smile. He wore a short, dark beard that made him look much older than she remembered, and sterner. He was dressed in a town suit with wide lapels in Continental fashion and carried a long coat draped over his arm.

"Oh, Chut, you look so English," Lily said, tears welling in her eyes.

"Is that a bad thing?" he asked, and smiled again, though with unease this time.

"Oh, not at all," Lily said. "It's just that I've been away for so long and missed everything so much. Anything English now seems like a marvel to me. But come, do you have time to take tea? I would so love for us to sit down and catch up." Without waiting for his answer, she rushed out of the room, found the young nurse outside the door, asked her to order tea for two and have it served in the conservatory.

Lily walked back to Chut and threaded her arm through his. "Oh, Chut, if you knew how glad I am to see you. You're the last person I expected," she said, sweeping him down the corridor toward the conservatory. They sat at one of the elegant little tables and a maid soon brought them tea. Lily thanked and dismissed her.

She poured tea for them both while Chut observed her in silence. "You're fluent in Russian, I see," he said after a moment.

"Well, how else could I have survived here all this time?" she said, smiling at him. Chut didn't respond, and Lily saw a shadow cross his face.

They sipped tea while he explained his presence in Petersburg. He was working as one of the managers for the famous Adelphi Theatre back in London, and had travelled to Russia with Gerard to make contact with the Bolshoi Theatre in Moscow and the Mariinsky in Petersburg in order to organize exchange engagements for the coming summer season. It had been Gerard who brought him up-to-date on Lily's situation and whereabouts.

She sat back. "So you already know I have a daughter."

"I do," Chut said, unease creeping into his eyes again. "I also know that the father died and that you fled the war."

She nodded, feeling a wave of sadness wash over her. "How many more days will you be in Petersburg? At what hotel are you staying?" she asked, trying to steer the conversation elsewhere.

"I took a room here in Zeleno—zelgo—I can't even pronounce the name," Chut said.

"Here, in town? Why so far from the city center, where all the theaters are, all the museums and restaurants?" Lily asked, trying to sound cheery. But her mood had been spoiled and she felt faint, yearning to end the interview and get back to her room. They talked for a while more about Petersburg and Gerard's projected plans with the Mariinsky and the Bolshoi, and then Chut left.

Lily returned to her room. She locked the door and collapsed onto the bed. She felt a strange agitation. She had first been overjoyed to see Chut, but as the moments trickled by, she had felt not exactly judged, more like observed, calibrated for how much her life might have changed her, measured against the younger, more innocent woman she had been in the past. Might this be a forerunner of what she could encounter back in England, where she would be examined and criticized, have blown-up tales about her choices dangled before her by mischievous tongues and spiteful eyes? All this reminded her that London and Manchester wouldn't be easy havens in which to set anchor. But surely Chut hadn't meant it that way. He had been gentle and respectful; he had been shy about questioning below what was proper. And his eyes had watched her with tenderness.

She didn't go to supper that evening, despite the nurses' repeated insistence, but stayed in her room, alone.

Chut returned the next day and she went down to see him after the morning rest cure. They sat together in the dining room eating lunch while other residents shot them gleeful, interested looks, anticipating the juicy whisperings the scene would provide them with for the coming days. Oblivious of their surroundings, Lily and Chut talked about the people they knew from the past, including Freddy, Maisie, Ruby, and everyone else who had worked at the

Imperial; even Lizzie Matchet, who had married someone else and died birthing her first child. Harrison had also died, affected by a sudden stroke, and Wade had gone into a crazed state after his uncle's demise, abusing alcohol and opium, plunging into endless, dissipating nights, and he had fast become a shadow of himself, both as actor and man and even as the legendary ruffian he'd once been.

"I guess our faults catch up with us all in the end," Lily said.

Chut's eyes flashed. "Some ought to catch up faster and harder," he said, and Lily was surprised to feel his hatred for Wade still fresh, while she felt only indifference mixed with a mild sense of grief. Chut seemed less composed today than the day before, when he had acted as a reserved, formal gentleman, paying a social visit to an old friend. Today he looked restless, somehow anxious, his gaze shot around, troubled and dark.

Lily stood up. "Let's take a walk. I want to show you the gardens before you go," she said. They strolled the grounds, but Chut didn't leave afterward. He lingered until Lily took him into the conservatory again where they sat at one of the tables. Nurses trickled in a few times to remind her that she was expected at her afternoon rest cure, but after she firmly declined, they left them alone.

Lily and Chut sat looking at each other. He had changed quite a bit in these three years. He had become more refined, his dress and demeanor quite elegant, his speech polished. But his eyes were still inky and deep, as quick to reflect emotions as she remembered them from the past. They locked into hers, and for the sliver of a moment she was back with him in Putney, inside the room overlooking the river, rustling sounds of summer breeze over the water mingling with their caresses and gentle sighs. Blood rushed to her face and she averted her eyes. She called for the attendant and ordered tea, and then sat in silence looking down at her hands.

"Lily," Chut said, "I want you to return to England with me."

She looked up, surprised, and said quickly, "But I couldn't, Chut, I need to stay as long as I can to make sure I exhaust every possibility concerning my daughter."

"I thought all decisions had been made and the situation is now irrevocable."

"Oh, I don't know, there's always some hope," she said, tears streaming down her face. She checked herself while Chut offered her a handkerchief and she dabbed it daintily over her cheeks and eyes. "Chut, I am very happy to have had you visit me, and I appreciate what you just offered, but I don't want you to worry or to feel responsible for me. I don't want sympathy, or pity, or anything like that. I'm quite all right, I assure you. I've fended for myself for a while now, and . . ." She trailed off, not sure where she was taking her speech.

Without taking his eyes off her, Chut pulled a stack of letters out of his pocket and set them on the table. "Good heavens, what's all this?" Lily said, recognizing the collection of notes and envelopes she had sent him back in London when they were separated after his arrest.

"These are all your letters that my sister Emily intercepted and hid from me all this time. I only found them six months ago," Chut said.

"But I left this particular one with Genevieve," Lily said, taking up a small blue envelope that had been folded up and torn, "and made her swear on her death that she would deliver it into your hands alone."

"Well, it ended up at Emily's. I was very upset to realize what she'd done. I've broken all relations with her."

Lily fingered the envelopes one by one over the table. "And all the time I thought you had torn them into pieces and didn't want anything with me anymore," she said with a forced little laugh. "How young we were then, Chut, how innocent and raw."

"I'm glad you can laugh about it," Chut said darkly. "I don't find it funny in the least."

"Of course it isn't funny," Lily said, frowning. "I only laugh because I have no more tears to shed. What else can I say? That we were fortune's fools? Indeed, we were. Life is not at all funny, I've learned. Look at me now, confined in a Russian sanatorium with an incurable disease, about to be deported and torn away from my daughter, from my own love child," and she stopped herself, realizing her rambling might end up making her weep again.

Chut rose abruptly and walked toward the windows. He stood there for a moment looking out, and then turned to her with stormy eyes. "Do you still love him?" he asked in a flat voice.

Lily was taken off guard. "I'm still grieving him, yes," she said, slumping back in her chair, "and if I'm honest, I'm not sure it'll ever end." She saw Chut frown, and added, "Why, you seem surprised."

Chut shrugged. "Surprised? No. It's just that from what I know, I don't think the said gentleman ever understood or respected your true worth—"

"You didn't know him, Chut," Lily snapped, "you cannot judge."

"No, I didn't. And it's just as well." Chut walked back to his chair, took up his coat and, without another word, left the room.

Lily followed him with her eyes, confused, feeling a sudden rush of fatigue. What was it with Chut? Why was he acting like this? He had always been moody and impetuous, but this was plain rude. How dare he even comment on Sergei? She would certainly refuse to see him if he returned the next day. She fumed for a moment. But her mood soon cooled down. Chut had touched a forbidden chord. His words had stung her with a truth she still worked hard to encapsulate. As much as she romanticized Sergei, there was no denying he had hurt her with his recklessness, that his folly had bent her fate. Chut had not meant to offend her, only to align himself with her. A strange relief pumped into her at this reckoning.

Back in her room, she lay on her bed reading the letters Chut had left behind, marveling at the way they transpired a long-forgotten version of her younger self. How she had loved Chut, how hurt she had been at their breakup. How simple that love appeared now in contrast with the feelings she'd had for Sergei, and yet, how painful it had been in its own way. Loving Sergei had always felt like a losing race, a wild chase after a rush of wind that would sometimes turn, take a moment to twirl and flutter and caress, but quickly dash ahead again. Loving Chut had been more like stepping into a river, a flow of smoothing and satiating emotions while it meandered placidly, but abrupt and dangerous when unexpectedly becoming the rapids where she had once nearly drowned.

And yet, there was more to hold on to in a river than in a wild rush of wind.

That night, an envelope was brought to her door by the young nurse's assistant. She tore it open and found a short note:

> *Please forgive my boorishness of this afternoon. I have no right to judge anyone you've loved. I only came to St. Petersburg to ask you this: Marry me, and return to England with me. I shall come back tomorrow for your answer. CB*

She waited for him the next day in the conservatory, trying to quiet her agitation while rehearsing the words she would say. He came in and sat beside her in silence. The weather had turned and flurries of snow were falling behind the large windows, covering the garden in a coat of white.

"You don't know half the story, Chut. I cannot marry, it wouldn't be fair to you," she said, and enunciated once again the long list of grim facts in a hushed, curt voice. Her ongoing illness, the limitations of married life with a consumptive spouse, her broken state after Sergei's death, and now the certainty of Olga's loss. He listened, looking out into the snowfall. "It doesn't mean I don't have affection for you," Lily added, "or that I don't appreciate this proposal, it's just that—"

"We were counting on all of these points already," Chut interrupted. "What else?"

"Too much has happened, Chut, I'm not the same woman you knew."

"Oh, yes, you are," Chut said, looking into her eyes. "Still the same stubborn, willful woman determined to remain free. It's all about your freedom, isn't it, and your refusal to commit. Why is your freedom so important, Lily? I'll never understand." There was a sort of wary musing to his tone, devoid of any anger or guile.

Lily laughed. "I suppose it's because my freedom is all I've ever had; all anyone ever has, really." Her mood had so brightened since last night, but now she found herself creasing her brow into a frown. "And yet, it will always be a double-edged sword. I've always wanted to be as free as a bird, but look where pursuing my freedom has landed me."

"Promise me you will think about it," Chut said, and she nodded.

She took his hands. "It stopped snowing. Let's go for a walk."

They walked along the path flanked by tall poplar trees to the sanatorium's entrance gate, leaving behind the somber building and turning right, toward the grove of birch and aspen trees that lay along the road. They followed a narrow path through the sylvan clusters of woodland, toward an open glade from which a pale-gray, docile sea could be seen bordering the coastline. The snowfall had been light and its thin mantle lay melting on the silvery bark of the trees, over the carpet of early autumn leaves at their feet, a flare of auburn, maroon, and ocher glistening in the opaque morning light. A thin mist rose up from the warm ground underneath, muffling the world around.

"I can't believe it's only September and it's already snowing," Chut said. "What will the winter be like then?"

"Oh, you have no idea," Lily said, smiling.

Chut put his arms around her and held her tight. She felt his warm body against hers, his silky beard against her cheek. "I can't lose you again, Lily, I'd never forgive myself. I need to bring you back with me. I need to know that you're close, that you're safe."

"Shhh," she lulled. "It's already a miracle that you're here with me."

A moment passed. "Let's get back, love," Chut said. "It looks like it'll snow again."

"No, let's stay for a little while," she said. "I want you to see how beautiful a Russian snowfall can be."

CHAPTER 31

The day of her departure, Lily followed the two sanatorium porters down the stairs carrying her luggage to the entrance hall, where Chut awaited her. Before she stepped into the long, bare room toward him, she caught sight of a nurse pushing a wheelchair down the corridor. She recognized Theresa de Guimaraes in the emaciated, lifeless figure that lay collapsed in the chair.

Lily rushed to her and took her hand. "Theresa, I haven't seen you since the operation. How are you?" she asked.

Theresa looked at her through droopy eyes enclosed in dark rings, as her sallow face broke into a faint smile. "I'm told I'm in God's hands, but don't worry about me. I heard you were leaving and wanted to say good-bye," she said in a wheezy voice, and then, grasping Lily's hand with surprising strength and pulling her nearer, she whispered, "Farewell, my beautiful friend, I wish you the best of luck. And whatever happens, make sure you never come back." She gave Lily a last, wistful look, and asked the nurse to wheel her back to her room.

At the Moscovsky station, Tatyana was waiting with Olga by the platform, alongside two of her personal valets and the French nanny. One of the valets held a bouquet of yellow roses and, kneeling beside Olga at Tatyana's indication, put the bouquet in her little hands. "These are for you, Mamman," Olga said, in a rehearsed script taught to her, no doubt, by her mademoiselle, "so you will get better soon and come back to visit me."

Lily scooped her into her arms. "Yes, my sweet, I shall get better, and I shall return for you," she said, struggling to control the rush of emotions flooding her voice. She embraced and cuddled her child until the train whistle went off for the second time, then put her down and kissed her beautiful, pale-gray Volkov eyes one last time.

Chut helped Lily into the compartment and sat by her side, clutching her hand in his, while she looked out the window with a heavy, pounding heart. Images of her child standing in her little white coat and waving to her flickered in her field of vision, and then faded, as the train chugged out of the station, advancing over intercrossing rail lines, past arched, gray sheds, along façades of buildings she knew well: the Komedianty Theatre, the bell tower of the Cossack Church of the Exaltation of the Cross, over the Obvodny Canal, through bridges flanked by stone cemeteries, along rows of taupe buildings, painted wooden houses, sights of distant mansions with gardens fenced in by iron gates, until it reached open landscapes of farmland, patchworks of green, viridian, and sienna fields, as they finally left behind the great city of St. Petersburg.

Whitechapel, London, January 5th, 1906

Dearest Harry and sweetest, darling Alice,

How long has it been since we've seen each other? My urgent task is to get well, stand up from my "reclining convalescence," as I call it, for the doctor still has me on bed rest, and take the first train to Manchester to see you both, spend a whole afternoon drinking tea and catching up on news and stories. Oh, how lovely that would be. But for now I shall have to be contented with writing the long letter I've so many times promised you. . . .

As you know, we arrived in London mid-November after a long journey by train and boat; a journey in which some of the advances I had gained on my health were overturned because of the freezing weather having set in so early this year. Chilled rain followed us along the way; the passage from Calais to Dover was not just again tempest-tossed, but also howling with the highest winds recorded in years.

I was very anguished about leaving Olga in St. Petersburg and not knowing when I will be able to go back for her. Being in such low spirits also affected my health. Worrying is something I need to push to the back of my mind if I want to regain my strength, because I know that the process of recovering my child will be a very difficult one. All I could make her grandmother Tatyana promise me in our last meeting was that I would receive news from Olga once a month and that her picture would be sent to me yearly. I guess it's a fair effort on their part, but hardly enough for a mother who yearns to see every minute of her baby's changing face. As for my chances of reentry into Russia even just as a visitor, I'm afraid they're now very restricted. My passport was stamped "deported" in large red letters; only when I obtain a set of perfect health certificates running for three consecutive years will I have a chance to get a new visa. As you may imagine, all these things have kept me sleepless at night and heartbroken all day long. I had come to think that Mother Russia had gifted me with a precious child, but it turns out it is I who's lavished a beautiful daughter upon her.

How hard it is to accept loss. How hard to learn that while we think we're flying in one direction, the wind is already deflecting us in another. Life brings strange surprises. Though sometimes, among the sea of difficulties and disappointments, we might be blessed with instances of good fortune. My recent reunion with Chut is one of those instances. What were the chances that a person I so loved from the past would appear in a lost sanatorium outside St. Petersburg and pull me out of my miserable situation? Harry, I swear, I would have perished in that awful place. It was a limbo for the half-dead, a place from which no one ever emerges again. How lucky was it for someone as lucked-out and forgotten as I came to be after a year in that graveyard to have a true friend come fetch me?

Of course, I shouldn't ascribe it all to happenstance, since I know very well that Chut made the trip to Russia just to bring me back. But so many things could have happened, he might not have found me, or arrived too late. . . . There was certainly some luck involved—or maybe it was fate. But above and beyond, there was Chut's unbending heart. Oh, darlings, how fortunate am I to be loved by someone like him? It's as if my life has finally atoned me for all my misfortunes, for all my silly mistakes, for the hard luck that has followed in my footsteps ever since I was a girl. Every time I turn now and see Chut, with his quiet, thoughtful stance, his limpid, soulful eyes, the ways in which he tames the world with utmost patience and single-minded determination, I marvel . . . He is the reason I still have hope for the future, even on those days when I'm overcome with sorrow and dreadful fatigue. My heart is so full of him that sometimes I think it might burst.

And how bizarre that life has taken me around the loop before it would allow me to return to someone who was always there, committed and loving from the start. I guess I had to run my course, get a mouthful of hard knowledge, humble myself in the face of my delusional ambition. I thought I had set out to conquer the world's treasures, but my riches already lay around me—I just had to open my eyes to see them. But I'm not one to regret my ventures. Whatever path I had to tread to come to my present happiness also gave me my time with Sergei, and all the things I saw and learned in that most peculiar and extravagant land of Russia; above all, it brought me Olga. So you see, I'm in possession of many more jewels for it.

And on the note of riches, I will also tell you that the Volkov family has been very gracious about helping wire the money Sergei left me into my London bank. So Chut and I are in the throes of negotiating the lease of a small venue here in Whitechapel, a theater called The Grove. It was originally an old tavern turned into a music hall that was later taken over by a group of Russian Jews who staged plays in their Yiddish language. It has now been closed for over a year. It's small—I don't think it even sits three hundred, but can you imagine, Harry, a theater of our own? It's our dream come true, and I want you to feel it's also yours and Alice's, and that the two of you must get ready to come to London as soon as the doctor allows you to leave the house. Oh, will we finally end up together in this amazing city as we always imagined we would?

I already know the first play that will go up on the bill. It will be Chekhov's Uncle Vanya, *my very own translation of it that has taken me so long to finish. But now it's done, and I'm confident it will be a huge success. I love the idea of bringing a modern, foreign play to London, a breath of fresh air into our very traditional theater scene. I can't wait to step on the stage as Yelena, twirling my parasol as I chide Voitsky, "Why can't you look calmly at a woman unless she is yours? The doctor was right, you are all possessed by a devil of destruction; you have no mercy on the woods, or the birds, or on women, or even on one another."*

But as usual, I'm already flying ahead of myself.

Yours, always loving,
Lily

A READING GROUP GUIDE

WE SHALL SEE THE SKY SPARKLING

Susana Aikin

About This Guide

The suggested questions are included
to enhance your group's reading of
Susan Aikin's *We Shall See the Sky Sparkling*!

DISCUSSION QUESTIONS

1. At the beginning of the book, we learn that after Lily's death her family buried her story and created a "bad girl" legend about her that got handed down the generations as a cautionary tale. Does this happen frequently in families? Is there a bad girl or boy in your family who brought shame and whose memory was suppressed? Is hiding family secrets useful?

2. Lily leaves her family at seventeen against her father's will to become the actress she's always dreamed of being. Little does she know at that time the price she will have to pay to become an independent, free woman able to fulfill her dream. Do you think this sort of thing only happened back in the nineteenth century, or is it still true today? How have things changed? Is there still a price for women to pay when they reject the rules of the establishment in order to become independent and free?

3. Lily gets raped by Wade, but doesn't report it, or tell anyone with the exception of her friend Ruby. She has the hardest time of all telling her sweetheart Chut about it. Is this something women did only in the past or is it still prevalent today? Discuss how this situation is changing today, and why modern women may be bolder reporting harassment and sexual violence.

4. Wade is a villain in the story because of the way he hurts Lily with his violence and high-handed behavior. But he also trains her to become a great actress. Discuss the nature of abusive relationships between teachers / mentors and pupils / students. Do the abusers only have the upper hand because they tend to be in a position of authority, or also because they can manipulate the victim by withdrawing the teachings that he / she craves?

5. Wade is the obvious villain, but is Sergei also a villain? Doesn't he also put Lily in difficult and excruciating situations because of his political affiliations, even though he's convinced he loves her, and furnishes her with the money she will later use to start her own theater? Are both Wade and Sergei antagonists to Lily's interests? Are antagonists in novels all negative, or can they also have positive traits? Who are your favorite antagonists in fiction works?

6. That artists' lives tend to be difficult is a well-known trope of all times. Are the lives of women artists more difficult than their male counterparts'? Was that just true of past times or do women still have a harder time today making it as artists?

7. Consider the letters from Lily to her brother, Harry, and his wife, Alice, and how much narrative information they convey in the novel. Before modern communications, letters were a major means of expression, in which stories, travel experiences, and whole philosophical discussions were exchanged between people. How has that changed after telephones and the Internet? How does modern e-mailing and texting differ from classical letter writing? What about social media like tweeting or using Instagram—how differently do they contribute to interpersonal communication?

8. Consider now the love letters in the novel, Lily's to Chut when she's leaving London thinking she will never see him again, and the letter Sergei writes Lily from the war. What is the value of written communication in love relationships? How has that changed? Are modern chatting and texting equivalent to love letters?

9. After reading about the prevalence of a disease like tuberculosis in the nineteenth century and the beginning of the twentieth, and about the hardship and risks of childbearing for women in that time, reflect how health conditions and

maternal mortality rates might have changed in the twenty-first century. Were things really much more difficult health-wise for women back then? Consider what other health risks we have developed in modern times instead.

10. Are you interested in visiting Russia after reading this book? Where would you go? Would you consider taking the Trans-Siberian train all the way to Vladivostok?

11. Does the initial depiction of Sergei and his friends change your perception of the Russian Revolution, as a process that might have started out as an idealistic movement, even if it ended up becoming a communist dictatorship? Are you interested in reading further about the history of Russia?

Connect with Us
Visit us online at
KensingtonBooks.com
to read more from your favorite authors, see books
by series, view reading group guides, and more.
Join us on social media
for sneak peeks, chances to win books and prize packs,
and to share your thoughts with other readers.
facebook.com/kensingtonpublishing
twitter.com/kensingtonbooks
Tell us what you think!
To share your thoughts, submit a review,
or sign up for our eNewsletters, please visit:
KensingtonBooks.com/TellUs.